Denis F. MacCarthy

Shelley's Early Life from Original Sources

With curious incidents, letters, and writings, now first published or collected

Denis F. MacCarthy

Shelley's Early Life from Original Sources
With curious incidents, letters, and writings, now first published or collected

ISBN/EAN: 9783337388164

Printed in Europe, USA, Canada, Australia, Japan

Cover: Foto ©Andreas Hilbeck / pixelio.de

More available books at **www.hansebooks.com**

SHELLEY'S
EARLY LIFE

FROM ORIGINAL SOURCES.

WITH CURIOUS INCIDENTS, LETTERS, AND WRITINGS,
NOW FIRST PUBLISHED OR COLLECTED.

*No. 7. Lower Sackville Street, Dublin, from the balcony of which
Shelley and his wife threw the first Irish pamphlet.*

BY DENIS FLORENCE MAC-CARTHY, M.R.I.A.
AUTHOR OF "DRAMAS AND AUTOS FROM THE SPANISH OF CALDERON," ETC.

LONDON: JOHN CAMDEN HOTTEN, PICCADILLY.

SHELLEY'S
E A R L Y L I F E

FROM ORIGINAL SOURCES.

WITH

CURIOUS INCIDENTS, LETTERS, AND WRITINGS,

NOW FIRST PUBLISHED OR COLLECTED.

BY

DENIS FLORENCE MAC-CARTHY, M.R.I.A.
AUTHOR OF "DRAMAS AND AUTOS FROM THE SPANISH OF CALDERON,"
ETC.

LONDON:
JOHN CAMDEN HOTTEN, 74 & 75, PICCADILLY.
1872.

PREFACE.

THE present work, within the limits prescribed to itself, is founded almost entirely on original research among sources of information not previously known or examined. How it grew up the following narrative will explain.

Keats, in the well-known passage of the noble sonnet which records his astonishment " on first looking into Chapman's Homer," compares his wonder to that of an astronomer who in searching the depths of space has suddenly discovered a new star :—

> " Then felt I like some watcher of the skies,
>   When a new planet swims into his ken."

Something of the same delight and the same surprise was awakened in my mind, when in making researches into a particular period of Shelley's life which had not received the attention that I conceived it merited, I came upon the extraordinary fact that he had published a volume of verse just on the eve of his expulsion from Oxford, which was unknown to his companion in that misfortune, which his friends, his family, and his biographers have been ignorant of, and which now, at the expiration of sixty years, is first identified with his name.

This poem, for the volume contained but one, it may be as well to state here is not to be confounded

with the *Posthumous Fragments of Margaret Nicholson,*
or the *Original Poetry by Victor and Cazire,* of which
more or less satisfactory accounts have already been
published. In the order of publication the poem
referred to came third, but of the two preceding works
I shall have something additional to say in the following pages.

The discovery I speak of is that of the fact of
publication, for of the poem itself, notwithstanding
all the exertions I. have made, extending over a considerable period, and in every possible direction, I
have not yet been successful in finding a copy.* To
continue or rather to vary the illustration from Keats,
I may say that I have discovered the surrounding
light that indicates the presence of the star, but have
not yet detected its nucleus; or rather, that I have
demonstrated its existence without having seen it,
and at a time too when I did not know even its name.

A distinguished mathematician has referred in
eloquent language, and with justifiable pride, to what
he calls "the great effort of scientific genius which
our time has witnessed—the discovery of Neptune."
"Need I remind you," continues the same learned
person, "that it was no astronomical observer—no
practical skill—which gave to us that great discovery?

---

* It is needless to say that this interesting volume is not to be
found in any of our public libraries. To the courteous librarians
of the Bodleian at Oxford, and of University College at Cam-
bridge, I have specially to return my thanks for the search they
had kindly made for it. A printed circular sent by myself to
almost every second-hand bookseller in the three kingdoms was
equally unsuccessful. To advertisements in the public journals,
and special inquiries instituted by Mr. Quaritch, Piccadilly; Mr.
Stibbs, Museum Street; Messrs. Longmans, Paternoster Row, and
others, no reply has ever been received.

We owe it not to the telescope of the astronomer, but to the pen of the mathematician. And surely it would be hard to find in the history of the human intellect anything more irresistibly attractive to the imagination—more poetic (if I may use the word)—than the thought that on the scribbled page, in these grotesque symbols, lay a power which enabled the mathematician to look up from his table in the solitude of his own study—to point to the heavens with the unerring finger of science, and to say—I cannot see it, but it is there."*

Though the discovery of a poem even by such a poet as Shelley is a matter of trifling importance compared to that of a planet, yet there is a slight resemblance perhaps in the mode, as will be described in the following pages, by which the lesser fact was ascertained.

This curious story must doubtless be one of the most interesting portions of the present volume, but the other subjects discussed will be found to contain much new and valuable information connected both with the life and works of Shelley. The republication of the Irish pamphlets is alone a matter of considerable importance. They had become so scarce that no biographer of Shelley but one has stated that he had even seen them.† It seems paradoxical to say so, but it is quite true, that no portion of the

---

* *Address delivered before the Royal Irish Academy at the Stated Meeting, on Wednesday, Nov. 30th,* 1870. By John H. Jellett, B.D., President, p. 14. Dublin. 1870.

† The two English pamphlets published by Shelley in 1817, under the name of *The Hermit of Marlow,* which are nearly as difficult to be met with as those he printed in Dublin, are also given as a supplement to the present volume.

early life of Shelley is so little known and so much misrepresented as that which includes his first visit to Dublin in 1812. The cynical Mr. Hogg, in his incomplete Life of the poet, surpasses himself when referring to this event and the subsequent visit of 1813. Of the former he knew nothing at the time, as Shelley was then totally estranged from his college friend by a well-founded mistrust in the sublime virtue of that stoical gentleman, which rendered it advisable that the unsuspicious philanthropist and the innocent *Harriet* should terminate, for a while at least, all communication with the immaculate Mr. Hogg. Nearly thirty years ago the writer of these lines was the first to allude with any precision to the interesting episode of Shelley's visit to Dublin in 1812.* Three years later, a more elaborate paper was published by the same writer on the general character of Shelley's poetical genius.† The portions of this essay referring to the literary and political labours of Shelley during his visit to Dublin in 1812, have been incorporated by Mr. Middleton in his *Shelley and his Writings,* and are to be found verbatim in vol. i. of that work from p. 211 to p. 229. This account as originally given in the articles just

---

* In letters, under the signature of "An Admirer of Shelley," to the editor of *The Dublin Evening Post,* Nov. 24th and Dec. 6th, 1842. Seven years earlier, in *The Dublin Weekly Satirist* of October 10th, 1835, a juvenile poem "To the Memory of Percy Bysshe Shelley," was published by the same writer. The motto shows the extent of his Shelley enthusiasm at that period. It is from *Prometheus Unbound.*

> "My soul is an enchanted boat,
> . Which like a sleeping swan doth float
> Upon the silver waves of thy sweet singing."

† In *The Nation,* Dec. 20th and Dec. 27th, 1845.

mentioned, notwithstanding its meagreness of detail, is the only one hitherto published that can be relied on for accuracy and truth. Since then, however, the whole matter has been re-investigated by me with almost unhoped-for success. The earliest public allusions to Shelley that ever appeared have been found in occasional numbers of rare old Irish newspapers, and are now published for the first time in connexion with his biography. A copy of *The Dublin Weekly Messenger* of the 7th of March, 1812, the paper sent by Shelley to Godwin on the day following, has been recovered. It is in this paper, thus authenticated by himself, that I found the allusion to a poem published by Shelley which has so strangely escaped the knowledge of all his biographers The other local and contemporary allusions to Shelley are very valuable. These will be found in the letters of "An Englishman" and "A Dissenter" in *Faulkner's Dublin Journal*, a paper first established by Swift's publisher, but long since extinct. This was the organ of the Irish Government and the Protestant Ascendency party, and the only hostility experienced by the young philanthropist when in Dublin came from it. The letter of "An Englishman" is particularly interesting. It describes Shelley's appearance and manner at the celebrated meeting in Fishamble Street Theatre, at which he spoke. The writer calls him "a stripling," denounces him as a "degenerate Englishman," studiously avoids mentioning his name, but bears the most unequivocal testimony to the eloquence of the young speaker, and to the enthusiastic reception which he met with from the assembly. This letter is decisive as to the probabilities of Shelley's success as an orator had he devoted himself to a political career,

b

The late Chief Baron Woulfe, after the lapse of many years, endeavoured to recall the manner of the youthful poet on this occasion when making his maiden speech, but the contemporary description here for the first time produced, written not in admiration but in anger, proves that the recollection of the learned judge on this subject was erroneous. The conduct of the audience towards Shelley at this memorable meeting, which has been so recklessly misrepresented by Mr. Hogg, and so carelessly adopted without inquiry by his followers, is here for the first time described with truth.

More valuable, however, than these public allusions, are some private memoranda still existing in the handwriting of Shelley himself on this and other important events in his life during these eventful years. These, with some remarks in the autograph of Harriet, then his happy and kind-hearted young bride, I have been permitted to see and transcribe. From these truthful and precious memorials I have extracted many passages which will put the whole motives and preparation of Shelley for his Irish Avatar in a clear and intelligible point of view. Some biographical particulars relative to the two remarkable men with whom Shelley became acquainted in 1811, 1812, and 1813 are given. Independently they would merit and repay a separate inquiry, but their connexion with Shelley, one by the poem of 1811, which was published for his benefit, and the other by the *History of Ireland*, projected and partly printed in 1812, will be at the present day, at least in England, their chief source of interest.*

---

* I wish to modify a statement at p. 4 of the present volume, in which the first of the gentlemen above alluded to, is said to

Of these two historical characters and of Shelley's political projects at the time, some curious particulars will be found in the present volume, partly derived from the State Papers in the Record Office. Those that relate to the seizure of the Irish pamphlets at Holyhead and the attempt to circulate the *Declaration of Rights* at Barnstaple are in themselves important and interesting documents. For the very curious letter of the Earl of Chichester, and the correspondence between Mr.—afterwards Sir—Francis Freeling and the Post Office agents at Holyhead, I have to return my very grateful thanks to the Right Hon. Chichester Fortescue, M.P., President of the Board of Trade, who has obligingly placed them at my disposal. A separate correspondence, referring to the same seizure, between the officers of the Board of Customs at Holyhead and the Home Secretary, the Right Hon. R. Ryder, is also preserved among the State Papers. It has hitherto escaped notice, and is here published for the first time. The simple but affecting letter of the kind and gentle Harriet, a copy of which is preserved among the State Papers, will be read with much interest.

To my friend Dr. R. R. Madden, M.R.I.A., I have

---

have " succeeded Leigh Hunt as editor of *The Statesman*," after that paper was given up for *The Examiner*, by Hunt and his brother. He was probably only a contributor. Who the editor of *The Statesman* may have been in 1808–9 is uncertain. In the latter year the proprietor was Daniel Lovell. An autograph letter of his, which I have recently seen, shows that in March, 1809, he had been long enough connected with the journal to authorize in some way his making a claim on a distinguished nobleman, a member of the Ministry, for the sum of 1300*l*., " agreeable to the account delivered," as he says, " for balance due to the Statesman Paper." This claim throws some light on a passage in the letter of Leigh Hunt, which will be found at p. 74 of the present volume.

to return my best thanks for the copy of *The Dublin Weekly Messenger* of March 7th, 1812, which first drew my attention to the singular fact in Shelley's literary life, of which so much is said in the following pages. I have since procured a second and a more perfect copy of the same number. It would be difficult to find a third. All the old newspapers once preserved in the Irish Stamp Office, previous to the abolition of stamp duty, were removed some years ago to London, as I am informed by the Solicitor of the Irish Stamp Office, by direction of the Government. What has become of them I am unable to discover. Nothing is known about them, as I have learned on inquiry, at the British Museum.

To another of my kind friends in Dublin, John David O'Hanlon, Esq., Barrister-at-Law, Under Treasurer to the Honourable Society of King's Inns, I am indebted for Shelley's second pamphlet, *Proposals for an Association*, &c., and I take this opportunity of tendering him my best thanks. The first pamphlet, *An Address to the Irish People*, has been in my own possession for forty years.

These introductory remarks have exceeded the ordinary limits of a preface, so that I am unable in this place to return my thanks individually to other friends who have kindly borne with my troublesome inquiries during this investigation, or who, like Philip H. Howard, Esq., of Corby Castle, and W. J. FitzPatrick, Esq., of Kilmacud Manor, have presented me with original documents of considerable value. Collectively, however, I wish to do so, trusting that I have not omitted, as opportunity arose, to draw attention to each particular act of courtesy with which I have been favoured.

In conclusion I may say with perfect truth that no published or unpublished source of information to which I could gain access has been neglected in my preparation for this volume, which though containing only a portion of the matter collected and dealing with a brief period of the poet's history, I think I may venture to offer to the public as an honest contribution to those authentic materials out of which sooner or later a thoroughly trustworthy Life may be written of Percy Bysshe Shelley.

POSTSCRIPT.

At the moment that this, the concluding sheet of the present volume, is going to press, an elaborate article on Shelley has appeared in the current number of *Blackwood's Magazine.* It is a careful *résumé* of the supposed facts of Shelley's life, as given in former biographies, and will probably be the last in which much reliance will be placed upon them. On the most momentous circumstances of the poet's personal history, I am glad to find that the opinions expressed in the following pages are confirmed by the just and well-founded conclusions contained in this able paper. It must be said, however, that on less important matters the writer, in following the usual authorities, falls into the usual mistakes. Two of these may be noticed. A point is made of Shelley's supposed brief stay in Dublin. But Shelley left Dublin at the time he had from the first arranged to leave it, and the duration of his visit is erroneously abridged by about three weeks. The allusion to O'Connell is also unfounded. He had no recollection of Shelley, and appears never to have seen him. He probably left the meeting at Fishamble Street Theatre after the delivery of his own speech, and before the young poet had addressed the assembly. I had twice the opportunity of speaking to O'Connell on the subject of Shelley, once in the autumn of 1844, at Darrynane Abbey, after "the unjust captivity," as he calls it in an autograph paper presented to myself. This visit to Darrynane I paid with two distinguished friends—one the present Prime Minister of Victoria, and the other a leading member of the Irish bar, a gentleman equally loved and admired for his many virtues and his various gifts. On a later occasion O'Connell himself introduced the name of Shelley. It was in the study of his town house in Merrion Square, Dublin. He alluded to an article on Shelley which had just appeared in *The Nation* of Dec. 20th, 1845. It attracted his notice, probably from some allusions to himself. He paid it the undeserved compliment of attributing it to the powerful pen of Mr. John Mitchell, and was surprised to find it was written by me. On both the occasions I refer to he only spoke of Shelley, to use his own words, as "the man who wrote *Queen Mab*." The writer in *Blackwood* says, " Perhaps that astute demagogue was not sorry to have the name of the son of an English Member of Parliament in the list of his supporters at that early period." At the meeting in question there were several Protestant gentlemen, one a noble lord, of higher social position than Shelley ; but whatever his rank, I believe that O'Connell would have repudiated his political support until he had withdrawn the atrocious calumnies on the religion of the people of Ireland, which Shelley had so innocently put forward in both of his Irish pamphlets.

Another matter, of interest perhaps to some of my readers, may here be mentioned.

The exact locality of Mrs. Fenning's school, where Shelley first saw Harriet Westbrook, having been disputed, I have made some inquiries in this neighbourhood, and find the conclusions I had already arrived at, given at p. 114 of the present volume, quite correct. The school stood on the north side of Clapham Common, near the "Old Town," directly facing Trinity Church, a position from which it probably derived its name, the mansion having been called "Church House." The site is now occupied by a range of about six houses, known as "Nelson Terrace." Old inhabitants of Clapham recollect "Church House" very distinctly. It was approached by an elaborate antique gateway and neat grass lawn. For some of these particulars I am indebted to the kindness of a lady, the granddaughter of Mrs. Fenning, residing in Kent, to whom I beg to return my best thanks.

2, CAVENDISH TERRACE, CLAPHAM COMMON,
London, S. W.

CONTENTS.

CHAPTER V.

CHAPTER VI.

CHAPTER VII.

CHAPTER VIII.

CHAPTER IX.

CHAPTER X.

CHAPTER XI.

CHAPTER XII.

CHAPTER XIII.

SUPPLEMENT.

APPENDIX.

PERCY BYSSHE SHELLEY,

ETC.

CHAPTER I.

ON the 12th of February, 1812, a young Englishman, with his wife and sister-in-law, arrived in
the capital of Ireland, and took up his residence in
the principal street of that city. The gentleman had
completed his nineteenth year a few months before,
but still preserved the appearance of a boy. His wife,
remarkable for her fair and girlish beauty, was still
younger than her husband, and her sister, the eldest
of the party, was but little in advance of her companions as to age. This not very formidable-looking
trio had come to Ireland on a business of no small
importance, for which they had been long preparing.
Their object was, " as far as in them lay"—to use the
language of the chief organizer—to effect a fundamental change in the constitution of the British
Empire, to restore to Ireland its native Parliament,
to carry the great measure of justice called Catholic
Emancipation, and to establish a philanthropic association for the amelioration of human society all over the
world. The young man was perfectly unknown in
Ireland, or even in England outside the circle of his

B

own family and a few friends. He had published anonymously two or three little books, both in prose and verse, which perhaps may be considered the least promising first attempts ever made public by a man of genius. One poem, indeed, is said to have been " very beautiful," but as yet we are not in a position to judge if the laudatory epithet was well deserved. Of that poem and its history we shall have much to say.

Undeterred by these literary failures, and with a consciousness of possessing intellectual powers which had not yet found their proper mode of expression, he determined to devote himself to the work that lay nearest to his hand in the great and universal scheme of philanthropy which he had projected. The condition of Ireland particularly attracted him. His sense of justice revolted at the oppression which that country had long endured, and his benevolence was enkindled by the miseries from which it still suffered. He determined to devote himself to its cause. He resolved to become a true Knight of St. Patrick, and to extirpate from its soil those serpent forms of bigotry, prejudice, and misrule which had unfortunately replaced the less venomous reptiles that had fled before the staff of the Apostle. How he prospered in that generous undertaking is partly the object of the following pages to relate, for the first time, truthfully and in detail.

Bearing in one hand, as Cæsar did his Commentaries, his unpublished *Address to the Irish People*, and in the other a letter of introduction from a celebrated though rather ineffective philosopher to an illustrious Irish orator and wit, he crossed the stormy Channel and boldly raised at once the standard of Philanthropy.

On the 12th of February, 1812, he arrived an unknown stranger; by the 27th of the same month he had already become famous. To use his own language in an unpublished letter, he had within that short time "excited a sensation of wonder in Dublin," and "expectation was on the tiptoe." The day following the date of this letter he made his first public appearance in a great assembly, which he roused to enthusiasm by his fervid eloquence, and a week later appeared the first of the innumerable papers which year after year, and perhaps century after century, were destined to be written upon the genius and the story of that then unknown young man, under the now familiar headline of *Percy Bysshe Shelley*.

This article, which was the first to foreshadow the proud anticipations of Shelley himself, that his fame would one day become

"A star among the stars of mortal night,"

and which was the earliest to recognise the benevolence at least of his intentions, would for these reasons alone be worth preserving. It will therefore be given entire in its proper place, but its concluding paragraph may be here extracted for the exceedingly interesting fact in his literary history which it records, and which by this casual allusion alone has been rescued from complete oblivion. To the accidental preservation of an Irish newspaper published sixty years ago, we are indebted for the following singular and most unexpected piece of information.

"We have but one word more to add," says *The Dublin Weekly Messenger* of March 7, 1812: "Mr. Shelley, commiserating the sufferings of our distinguished countryman Mr. Finerty, whose exertions in

the cause of political freedom he much admired, wrote
a very beautiful poem, the profits of the sale of which,
we understand from *undoubted* authority, Mr. Shelley
remitted to Mr. Finerty. We have heard they amounted
to nearly an hundred pounds. This fact speaks a
volume in favour of our new friend."

What was this " very beautiful poem ?" and who was
" Mr. Finerty ?"

Such are two of the questions I propose to myself
to answer in the course of this inquiry.

Since the 7th of March, 1812, until the publication
of the present work, except in the private researches
set on foot by the author for its recovery, it may
safely be asserted that no other allusion can be found
to the existence of the poem referred to in the
paragraph just quoted. As to Mr. Finerty, the case
is somewhat different. The *State Trials* by Cobbett,
the eloquence of Curran, and the history of the United
Irishmen, preserve the earlier incidents of his story ;
while the annals of English journalism, the disastrous
Walcheren expedition, and the debates in Parliament,
supply ample materials for his later career. But the
connexion of Shelley with him, and the ignorance of
Shelley's friends as to that connexion, are alike extraordinary.

Mr. Finnerty, as he subsequently wrote his name,
must have been personally well known to Leigh Hunt.
He succeeded Hunt as editor of *The Statesman* newspaper, when that journal was given up by the future
friend of Shelley for the more successful *Examiner*.
It was an article written by Leigh Hunt in the latter
paper that drew the attention of Shelley to the case
of Mr. Finnerty, and led in a very short time to the
remarkable fact of his publishing a poem for his

benefit. Shelley, it is true, was not personally known
to Leigh Hunt until two years after the publication of
this poem; but Mr. Finnerty lived until 1822, the
year of Shelley's death, and Leigh Hunt long survived
both. It is strange that in all this time Leigh Hunt
should have been silent as to a fact which it is difficult
to conceive he could have been entirely ignorant of.
It is just possible that he heard of it at a time when he
had no conception of the astonishing dimensions to
which Shelley's fame would eventually grow. That
he preserved no accurate recollection of his own first
acquaintance with Shelley himself is certain. It will
be shown hereafter that what he has written on this
subject is full of errors. Another friend of Shelley,
and an earlier one—his biographer, Mr. Hogg—in a
letter of remonstrance to John Joseph Stockdale, the
publisher, alludes with approval to the conduct of a
gentleman who it will be proved was Mr. Finnerty.
This letter is published in *Stockdale's Budget.* But
neither in the Autobiography of Leigh Hunt, nor in
the so-called Life of Shelley by Mr. Hogg, is there
any mention of the journalist to whom the poet paid
this singular mark of respect, or of the poem itself. It
is scarcely necessary to say that later biographers do
not supply the omission. The time when this poem
was published, and the place where it was written,
render Mr. Hogg's ignorance of its existence most
remarkable. The redeeming feature of Mr. Hogg's
egotistical and eccentric book is generally considered
to be that portion of it which, written many years
before under the title of *Shelley at Oxford,* is incorporated with the later work. What authority can be
placed even on this division of Mr. Hogg's book will
be seen further on. At present it need only be said

that while he loads his page with trivial details and apocryphal conversations, he forgets, or was never told, that his incomparable friend, " the Divine poet," as he sometimes almost derisively calls him, with whom he represents himself as living in daily and almost nightly intercourse, had published a poem when at Oxford which, in a pecuniary point of view, was the most successful he had ever written.

There is another place where the absence of any allusion to this poem is also remarkable. Mr. Finnerty, as will subsequently be more fully stated, had been prosecuted by the Attorney-General for an alleged libel on Lord Castlereagh. Being prevented by Lord Ellenborough from proving that the statements com-plained of were true, he declined to enter into his defence, and allowed judgment to go by default. He was sentenced to a long imprisonment in Lincoln gaol. The liberty of the Press being considered to be involved in the persecution of Mr. Finnerty, an important meeting was called at the Crown and Anchor Tavern, at which Sir Francis Burdett presided. A vote of sympathy and approval of Mr. Finnerty's conduct was passed, and a subscription to sustain him in prison at once set on foot. I have taken the trouble of ex-aminirg all the lists in reference to this fund which I could find in *The Morning Chronicle* and other papers of the period. In the course of the year the amount exceeded the sum of one thousand pounds. I have, however, been unable to meet with any acknowledg-ment of so handsome a contribution as one hundred pounds—the profits, as we are told, of the poem which, as will be shown, Shelley published for the benefit of Mr. Finnerty. I was, however, rewarded by finding the personal subscription of " Mr. P. B. Shelley," not

in a London paper indeed, but in a very unexpected
quarter, as will subsequently be given in detail.

It is perhaps equally singular that no recollection
or tradition of this circumstance, and no copy of the
poem, or even of the fact of it ever having been
published, have been preserved by the collateral descen-
dants of Mr. Finnerty who are still living. Two
gentlemen have kindly responded to my inquiries, but
have not been able to give me any information. And yet
there can be no doubt that the statement in *The Dublin
Weekly Messenger* of March 7th, 1812, is true. At the
time this statement was publicly made, Mr. Finnerty
was still in prison. He was not released until the expiration of his sentence in the following August. *The
Weekly Messenger* frequently alluded to his martyrdom
for what was considered to be the liberty of the Press.
He on more than one occasion wrote from his prison
to the editor of that journal. A famous speech
delivered by him before his incarceration, which was
made the excuse in Parliament for the revival of the
Convention Act, will be found fully reported in the
volume of the paper for 1810. Nothing published in
The Weekly Messenger could possibly have escaped his
notice. It is incredible that he would not have contradicted this statement of the presentation to him of
the profits of a poem if it were not true. This statement, too, it should be remembered, is authenticated
by Shelley himself, for he sends the paper containing
it to Godwin, and pointedly refers to the article in
which it is given. In his first pamphlet, printed in
Dublin, Shelley expressly alludes to Mr. Finnerty by
name. The subject, in whatever point of view we
regard it, is full of difficulties, but as much light as
can possibly be now thrown upon it is endeavoured to

be supplied in the following pages.   It is here alluded
to in order to direct the attention of the reader to
what will perhaps be found to be one of the most
interesting incidents recorded in this narrative.

To tell the story satisfactorily, it will be necessary
to give, in the first place, the only authentic allusion
hitherto published, which Shelley himself has made to
the extraordinary episode in his life comprised in his
first visit to Dublin in 1812, and the pamphlets which
he printed and circulated there in furtherance of the
great objects which led him to undertake so singular
an expedition.   We shall then review his career as a
student both at Eton and Oxford; his early publications, including the missing poem of 1811; some
singularly interesting particulars of his married life,
particularly at York; his residence at Keswick; until
at length we find him at the age of nineteen years and
five months in Dublin, a political agitator and emancipator, an advocate for " Home Rule," a repealer of
the Union, and a universal philanthropist.

Percy Bysshe Shelley, in a letter to a literary
friend in London, thus writes from Lymouth, Barnstaple, on the 18th of August, 1812 :—

" In the first place, I send you fifty copies of the
letter [to Lord Ellenborough].   I send you a copy of
a work which I have procured from America, and
which I am exceedingly anxious should be published.
It develops, as you will perceive by the most superficial reading, the actual state of republicanized Ireland, and appears to me above all things calculated
to remove the prejudices which have too long been
cherished of that oppressed country.   I enclose the
two pamphlets which I printed and distributed whilst

in Ireland some months ago (no bookseller daring to publish them). They were on that account attended with only partial success, and I request your opinion as to the probable result of publishing them with the annexed suggestions in one pamphlet, with an explanatory preface, in *London.* They would find their way to Dublin."*

Without referring at present to the letter addressed to Lord Ellenborough, about which I shall have to mention subsequently some interesting facts not previously given in any biography of the poet, we have here the important statement by Shelley himself, that so far from being ashamed of his Irish crusade, in the early part of the same year, as insinuated by Mr. Hogg, he had the deliberate ·intention of publishing in London the pamphlets which he had printed and distributed in Dublin a few months before.

For the republication of these pamphlets, even after the lapse of sixty years, it may be said that we have in this letter Shelley's own express sanction. It is true that his object in republishing them at the time would have been a political one. But in a literary point of view, I think he must have regarded them with some complacency. The second pamphlet, at least, he considered to be written in his " own natural style." In this respect, however, it differs very slightly, if at all, from the first, and both pamphlets may be favourably compared with the letter to Lord Ellenborough, which has been reprinted, though incompletely, by the poet's family.

---

* Letter of Shelley to Mr. Thomas Hookham, of Old Bond Street, "a valued friend of Shelley."—See *Shelley Memorials,* pp. 38, 39.

It is not, however, for their literary value or their political significance that the pamphlets are now republished : it is for their biographical, perhaps I should say their autobiographical, interest. The political importance of these eloquent protests against intolerance, injustice, and misrule has passed away ; but as historical memorials both of the writer and of the time and place in which they were published, they will always be read with interest. Many of the evils against which these fervid appeals were directed have been, at least in recent years, honestly attempted to be remedied. One of the two great measures which Shelley so ardently supported, not only by his pen but by his voice, was passed within seventeen years of the time when it received the enthusiastic advocacy of the young poet. What is more to the purpose, the great victory of Catholic Emancipation was won by the very means and in the very way which Shelley himself had projected. That way and those means, it is scarcely necessary to say, were not suggested by Shelley to the powerful mind that organized and made them effective. They were in existence before the youthful philanthropist visited Ireland, and they were practically worked out after he left. With him, however, they were original, and their success in other hands only proves the sagacity with which he suggested their use. To whomsoever the merit is due, the fact remains that an association, the mere probability of which Godwin looked upon with terror as inevitably leading to bloodshed, anarchy, and defeat, carried its point successfully, without violence and without even a word of insulting exultation over those who opposed it. In this way the youthful poet proved himself a wiser teacher and a truer prophet than the mature philosopher.

Before proceeding to describe the actual facts of Shelley's first visit to Dublin, hitherto so briefly alluded to or so strangely misrepresented, I have thought it right to trace, if possible, the source of that interest in the cause of Ireland which he retained all his life, and which led him to begin his public career as a reformer and a philanthropist by becoming its avowed champion. This investigation will have a value outside the particular subject here alluded to, as an opportunity will be thereby afforded for the correction of several important errors connected both with the life and works of Shelley, which, having been once stated with an air of confidence in some biographical account of the poet, have been adopted without examination by succeeding writers.

The first published work of Shelley was the little prose romance called *Zastrozzi.* It appeared in June, 1810, and advertisements of it will be found in *The Times* of the 5th and the 12th of that month. According to the recollections of a schoolfellow, Shelley gave a farewell banquet to some of his companions at Eton out of a sum of 40*l.* which he is said to have received from Messrs. Wilkie and Robinson, of Paternoster Row, for the privilege of publishing this puerile extravaganza. Lady Shelley, who gives this recollection of Mr. Packe, apparently contradicts it in subsequent pages of her *Memorials.* She states that "in 1809, Shelley left Eton and returned home" (p. 12), and "when still at home, he had written a great many romances in prose, some of which have been printed" (p. 20). This, however, is a mere inadvertence on the part of Lady Shelley. It was probably *St. Irvyne* alone that was written in the interval between the time of Shelley's leaving Eton and his entrance at Oxford. The other "wild romances," including *Zastrozzi*, were probably composed when Shelley was "at home" before he went to Eton.

Whatever may have been the arrangement between Shelley and Messrs. Wilkie and Robinson, *Zastrozzi* was published by them on the 5th of June, 1810. Its success does not appear to have encouraged the generous publishers to renew their somewhat dubious liberality, as we find Shelley arranging with a different but more celebrated publisher in reference to another matter of very singular interest.

This was the transfer on the 17th of September, 1810, to John Joseph Stockdale, 41, Pall Mall, of the entire impression of a volume as yet undiscovered, entitled *Original Poetry by Victor and Cazire*.

It is rarely that a publisher becomes the biographer of one of his authors ; seldom is it that the fable is reversed, and the lion depicts the man. Mr. Stockdale did not become the biographer of Shelley in any very extended sense ; he only gave an episode in the poet's life which it is evident he considered by no means an unimportant one—as being connected with himself. In fact, at the conclusion of the series of papers which he devotes to Shelley in that curious *mélange* of vanity and vindictiveness called *Stockdale's Budget*, he declares that but for this accidental though fortunate intercourse between himself and the poet, the family of the latter would have been deprived of "the only ray of respect and hope which may illumine their recollections of a father when they have attained an age for reflection, and shed a gleam of ghastly light athwart the palpable obscurity of his tomb."*

---

* *Stockdale's Budget*, No. 9, Wednesday, February 7, 1827.

The principal facts connected with Shelley's brief intercourse with Mr. John Joseph Stockdale have been given by Mr. Richard Garnett in his well-known paper entitled *Shelley in Pall Mall.** A few interesting particulars, however, are omitted. One of these is important as giving additional grounds for hoping that a copy of *Victor and Cazire* may yet be found. Another refers to Mr. Hogg. In reprinting Shelley's letters as given in *Stockdale's Budget,* Mr. Garnett says, " We have not scrupled to occasionally correct an obvious clerical error, generally the result of haste, sometimes of a misprint." Considering that we have not the originals of these letters, but only a transcript of them by Stockdale, these corrections, though extending sometimes to the substitution of a more appropriate for a less appropriate word, may be justified. In such extracts, however, as I shall give, I think it will be more satisfactory to print them exactly as they are given in the original publication.

As *Stockdale's Budget* is now difficult to be met with, and as the passage has not been extracted by Mr. Garnett, it may be interesting to quote in his own words the account which the publisher gives of his first interview with Shelley. This is found in the first number of the publication, dated Wednesday, Dec. 13th, 1826. It commences thus :—

" Percy Bysshe Shelley.

" The unfortunate subject of these very slight recollections introduced himself to me in the autumn of 1810. He was extremely young. I should think he did not look more than eighteen. With anxiety

---

* *Macmillan's Magazine,* June, 1860.

in his countenance, he requested me to extricate him
from a pecuniary difficulty in which he was involved
with a printer whose name I cannot call to mind,
but who resided at Horsham, near to which Timothy
Shelley, Esquire, afterwards I believe made a Baronet,
the father of our poet, had a seat called Field Place.
I am not quite certain how the difference between the
poet and the printer was arranged; but after I had
looked over the account I know that it was paid,
though whether I assisted in the payment by money
or acceptance I cannot remember.   The letters show
that it was accomplished just before my too conscientious friendship caused our separation.   Be that as it
may, on the 17th September, 1810, I received fourteen
hundred and eighty copies of a thin royal 8vo volume
entitled *Original Poetry by Alonzo and Cazire*, or
two names something like them.   The author told
me that the poems were the joint production of himself and a friend, whose name was forgotten by me
as soon as I heard it.   I advertised the work, which
was to be retailed at 3*s*. 6*d*., in nearly all the papers;
but I was told that, though paid for, it did not appear
in *The Times*, and from my frequent experience I
consider that such omission was far from improbable,
and I fear *The Times* was not singular in the omission.
In many papers, however, I saw it.   I am only particular on this point because few if any were sold—a
consequence which, as I intimated, was not unlikely
to be the case; though even from these boyish trifles,
assisted by my personal intercourse with the author, I
at once formed an opinion that he was not an every-
day character."

Passing over the mistake of Mr. Timothy Shelley,

the poet's father, having been "made" a baronet, we
come to the curious statement that the advertisement of
Victor and Cazire, though paid for, was not inserted
in *The Times*. This omission, of which Stockdale
had no doubt, was, he considers, done designedly. In
this supposition the publisher must have had a consciousness that at some period of his career a certain
watchfulness and caution were occasionally exercised
in the offices of respectable journals before advertisements from the house of "Stockdale Junior" were
given to the public. This, however, refers to a later
stage of his business. In 1810 he had not commenced
that downward course that ended in his ruin. For
more than half a century the house of Stockdale had
been an eminent one. The elder Stockdale and his
sons had carried on a respectable and extensive business in Piccadilly before and after John Joseph had
set up for himself in Pall Mall. Theology, history,
and fiction issued continually under their name. They
were in great request among amateur poets and
poetesses, who, if they could "write," could also pay
"with ease." The lady song-birds flocked to them by
hundreds. I have seen a large collection of poetical
works written exclusively by women, the greater part
of which was published by the Stockdales. Among
these was Mary Stockdale's *Effusions of the Heart*, a
volume published in 1790 by her father, John Stockdale.

The house being thus established for the production
of this not very dangerous class of literature, the
statement that an advertisement of a harmless book of
juvenile poetry like *Victor and Cazire* was deliberately
suppressed by *The Times* seemed very improbable. An
examination of the file of *The Times* for 1810 removed

all doubt upon the point.   Mr. Garnett had found in *The Morning Chronicle* of September 18th an advertise-ment of the volume, but twenty-four days later—that is, on Friday, October 12th—*The Times* contains the following :—

"In royal 8vo, price 4*s*. boards, ORIGINAL POETRY.   By VICTOR and CAZIRE.   Sold by Stockdale Jun., 41, Pall Mall."

This is important as showing that the volume was on sale for more than a fortnight longer than Stock-dale remembered it to have been.   In that time some additional copies were doubtless sent out for review, or presented by the author and publisher to their friends, thus increasing the probabilities that this very interesting volume may yet be found.

The cause of the suppression and destruction of the volume was as follows : A short time after its appear-ance, Mr. Stockdale tells us that, on examining his new venture with more care than he had previously bestowed upon it, he discovered that one or other of the bards who concealed their names under the romantic pseudonyms of Victor and Cazire had contributed anything but " Original Poetry " to the volume thus infelicitously entitled.   " Thin" as the royal 8vo was, Mr. Stockdale found it was thick enough to contain at least one poem by the well-known Matthew Gregory· Lewis.   The name of this poem is not given ; but as we have seen that Stockdale, in first mentioning the volume, gives the title as " Original Poetry by *Alonzo* and Cazire," instead of *Victor*, it is not improbable that the appropriated poem may have been that of " Alonzo the Brave and Fair Imogene," which appeared in the *Tales of Wonder* of " Monk" Lewis in 1801. Shelley was indignant at the imposition which had been practised upon him, and ordered the whole impression to be destroyed. Stockdale, however, considers that before the sentence was carried out nearly a hundred copies had been put into circulation.

Mr. Garnett has some ingenious conjectures as to Shelley's probable coadjutor in this curious volume. He considers that *Cazire* represents a female name, which is very likely. But he has not noticed, neither has the coincidence been remarked by any other writer, that the *Posthumous Fragments of Margaret Nicholson*—Shelley's next publication—are alleged to be edited by " Fitz-Victor"—that is, as I understand it, by the *son*, or literary executor, of the " Victor" of the suppressed volume. It would be curious to find, should a copy of " Victor and Cazire" ever be met with, that the " Posthumous Fragments" were to some extent but a re-issue of Shelley's original contributions to the preceding work.

I now come to a very important event in Shelley's life—his matriculation at the University of Oxford. One would think that the exact day on which his name was entered on the books of University College could easily be ascertained, but it has never been given. Lady Shelley says that Shelley went to Oxford in 1810, " *in which year* he became an undergraduate of University College." This is rather vague. Mr. Hogg gets over the difficulty very adroitly. Describing the first evening which he spent with the young poet, he says, " I inquired of the vivacious stranger, as we sat over our wine and dessert, *how long he had been at Oxford, and how he liked it ?* He answered my questions with a certain impatience, and, resuming the subject of our discussion, he remarked that," &c.— This is in Mr. Hogg's best style. He always found it easier to invent or embellish a conversation than to

C

state a fact. He tells us when he first met Shelley, but that does not fix with any certainty the period of the poet's entrance at the University; otherwise, what was the meaning of the question? The passage of Mr. Hogg's book is well known, but it is always a pleasure to read it and to quote it.

" At the commencement of Michaelmas Term—that is, at the end of October, in the year 1810—I happened one day to sit next to a freshman at dinner: it was his first appearance in hall. His figure was slight, and his aspect remarkably youthful, even at our table where all were very young. He seemed thoughtful and absent. He ate little, and had no acquaintance with any one. I know not how it was we fell into conversation,"* &c.

At first sight, the palpable inaccuracies of Mr. Hogg's book seem to arise from defective memory— though it seems strange that a gentleman who could so minutely remember the very words of lengthy conversations after an interval of twenty-two years should have fallen into the grave mistakes as to matters of fact which will presently be pointed out. A more careful study of the book, however, and a fuller knowledge of Mr. Hogg's character, create a strong presumption that a good deal of deliberate mystification as to dates, conversations, and letters, has been practised by that gentleman.

Captain Medwin was a careless writer, and the mistakes in his *Life of Shelley* are so numerous as totally to destroy its authority. Mr. Hogg, on the contrary, perhaps from the fact of his having been a

---

* *Life of Shelley*, vol. i. p. 51. The passage quoted was originally published in the *New Monthly Magazine*, 1832.

successful conveyancer, is generally supposed to be accurate, except in those instances where his personal prejudices lead him astray. Thus it is that most of his statements pass unquestioned, and are repeated over and over again without examination by those compilers who find in his two bulky volumes an inexhaustible storehouse of supposed facts. But even on questions which apparently he could have no motive in misrepresenting, he is just as inexact as Captain Medwin. The following is an instance of this, although the later biographer supplements the error of his predecessor by a greater one of his own :—

" *During the whole period of our residence there"*— that is, at Oxford, says Mr. Hogg, in one of those unguarded moments when he enables us to test his statements by a reference to a fixed date—" the University was cruelly disfigured by bitter feuds arising out of the *late* election of its Chancellor : in an especial manner was our own most venerable college deformed by them, and by angry and senseless disappointment. *Lord Grenville had just been chosen."* (i. p. 254).

Captain Medwin, who, it must be admitted, generally throws the whole responsibility of all statements relative to Shelley's life at Oxford on Mr. Hogg, adopts of course the foregoing narrative, and thus supplements it with the following marvellous details :—

" It might be supposed that it was not without some reluctance that the master and fellows of University College passed against Shelley this stern decree" [his expulsion on Lady-day, 1811], " not only on account of his youth and distinguished talents promising to reflect credit on the college, but because his father had been a member of it, his ancestors its benefactors.

I know not if these considerations had any weight with the conclave, but it appears that Shelley was by no means in good odour with the authorities of the college, *from the side he took in the election of Lord Grenville,* against his competitor, a member of University. Shelley, by his family and connexions, as well as disposition, was attached to the successful party, in common with the whole body of under-graduates, one and all, in behalf of the scholar and liberal statesman. Plain and loud was the avowal of his statements, nor were they confined to words, *for he published, I think, in The Morning Chronicle,* under the signature of " A Master of Arts of Oxford," a letter advocating *the claims* of Lord Grenville, which, perhaps, might have been detected as his by the heads of the college. *It was a well-written paper,* and calculated to produce some effect ; and as he expressed himself eminently delighted at the issue of the contest, ' as that wherewith his superiors were offended, he was regarded from the beginning with a jealous eye.' Such at least was the impression of his friend."

This story thus *ben trovato* was too good to be lost, and thus we have so painstaking and generally so accurate a writer as Mr. Rossetti adopting it without the least misgiving.

Under the title of " Minor Writings of Shelley," Mr. Rossetti assigns to the year 1811—that is, two years after Lord Grenville was elected Chancellor—the composition of this apocryphal letter.

" He published, under the signature of ' A Master of Arts of Oxford,' probably in *The Morning Chronicle,* a letter *upholding the candidateship* of Lord Grenville as Chancellor of the University."—Rossetti's *Memoir of Shelley,* p. clxxiv.

A few words will show how utterly irreconcilable these statements are with the date of Shelley's entrance at University College.

The Duke of Portland, who preceded Lord Grenville as Chancellor of the University of Oxford, died on Wednesday, the 30th of October, 1809. The election of Lord Grenville as his successor took place two months later—on the 13th and 14th of December in the same year. The following is the result of the contest as given in *The Oxford University and City Herald* of Saturday, December 16, 1809 :—" The committee for the election of a Chancellor of the University, in the room of the late Duke of Portland, met between nine and ten o'clock on Wednesday morning, and continued sitting day and night, without any adjournment, till ten o'clock on Thursday night, when the numbers were declared as follow :—

" For Lord Grenville. . . . 406
  „ Lord Eldon 393
  „ Duke of Beaufort . . . 222
  Majority for Lord Grenville . 13 "

The candidateship of Lord Grenville, therefore, extended from the 30th of October to the 14th of December, 1809. But in 1809, as we have seen, Shelley was at Eton and Field Place, and did not go to Oxford until the end of October, 1810—that is, exactly a year after the candidateship of Lord Grenville commenced, and ten months after he had been elected. Even the installation of Lord Grenville as Chancellor preceded the entrance of Shelley into the University by four months. That event took place on June 30, 1810. It was attended with great rejoicings, the recitation of many odes, amongst which was one by the

Rev. W. Lisle Bowles; the striking of a medal in
honour of the event, and though last, not least, the
ascent of Mr. Sadler in a balloon. The poem of
Bowles appeared simultaneously in *The Morning Chronicle* and *The Oxford Herald* on Saturday, July 21st, 1810.
A poet was found also to describe, perhaps satirically,
the great event of Oxford life in the midsummer of
1810. The following advertisement appears in *The
Oxford Herald*, Saturday, June 30th, 1810, the day of
the installation, so that not only the bard, but the
printer, must have had the power of improvisation :—

"This day is published, price 3*s.* 6*d.*, *A Poetical Account of the
Installation of a Chancellor of the University of Oxford.* Oxford : Printed by and for J. Munday, and sold by Longman, Hurst,
and Orme, London."

As Shelley did not enter the University of Oxford
until the end of October, 1810, it is therefore simply
impossible that he could have taken any part, as a
member of the University, in the election of Lord
Grenville. That nobleman had not " just been chosen,"
as Mr. Hogg writes; he had been elected ten months
before. It is equally untrue that during " the whole,"
or any part of Shelley's residence there, " the University was cruelly disfigured by bitter feuds arising out
of the late election of its Chancellor." All outward
animosity or dissatisfaction had long since ceased.
Even in July, 1810, three months before Shelley
entered, *The Oxford Herald* declined to publish a letter
on the subject through fear of *reviving* any unpleasant-
ness that may have arisen out of that event. In the
number for Saturday, July 21st, 1810, the following
notice was given :—

" *To Correspondents.*—We acknowledge the receipt of
a letter on the election of Lord Grenville, and, although

we cordially agree with the sentiments of our correspondent, we are unwilling to *revive* any question which
may create party animosity, and therefore decline its
insertion."

These explanations conclusively dispose of Mr.
Hogg's careless and erroneous statements. The express
declaration, however, of Captain Medwin, that he had
read an effective letter which Shelley published on the
subject of Lord Grenville's candidateship, requires some
further notice. We have seen that during the whole
period that Lord Grenville's name was before the con-
stituency of Oxford, Shelley, who had left Eton, was
residing with his father at Field Place. Mr. Timothy
Shelley had been a student of University College, and
had graduated there.* It is admitted on all hands that
he took a warm interest in the affairs of that college,
and was a staunch adherent of the Liberal party both
in and out of Parliament. The contest for the
Chancellorship must have roused all his energies. He
had a vote, and possessed, doubtless, considerable influence, which we infer from his character he was not
slow to use for the benefit of the cause. It was *his*
exertions, and not those of his son, who had not then
entered, that may have provoked that hostility and
unfriendliness which the poet experienced later, and
at a critical moment. From the specimens of his
letters which have been published, the epistolary powers
of the future Sir Timothy were certainly not considerable. What more likely thing than to employ the
ready pen and the sympathetic liberalism of his talented

---

* He received the Degree of B.A. Jan. 16th, 1778, and of
M.A. Feb. 16th, 1781.—*Catalogue of Oxford Students*, 1841,
p. 598.

young son, who was then preparing for his entrance
into the great University? How better account for
Shelley assuming the title of a Master of Arts of
Oxford when he had not even entered the University,
in which he never took a degree? I had previously
searched *The Morning Chronicle* and *The Oxford Herald*
during " the whole period of his residence there," as
Mr. Hogg says, for a letter on the election of Lord
Grenville, answering the description of Captain Medwin,
but in vain. As Longfellow sings, it was like looking
for the birds in last year's nest. Not so, however,
when I came to the right period, and when this
thought occurred to me, that Shelley might possibly
have written a letter on the impending election in his
father's name. In *The Morning Chronicle* of November
15th, 1809, there is a long letter on the subject, signed
" A. M. Oxon," substantially the signature remembered
by Captain Medwin. The commencement of the letter
seems to have been "inspired" from a different source
than that which dictated the conclusion. The former
is more personal, and reflects on the nepotism or family
partiality attributed to Lord Chancellor Eldon. It
attacks the Duke of Beaufort also, but more lightly.
The letter rises in dignity as it advances, and appeals
to larger and more general principles. This portion
may be quoted. It is not unworthy of Shelley, even
at a more advanced period of his life than he had then
attained.

" Lord Grenville," says the writer, " between his
pigmy rivals, rises with a colossal grandeur of character,
with all the private worth that belongs to both of his
competitors, and without the infirmities that are imputed to one of them. He unites the accomplished

scholar with the eminent statesman. As a parliamentary orator, hé is considered by a celebrated author whose works now lie before me, since the extinction of the great luminary, Mr. Fox, without an equal. But Lord Grenville not only promises appropriate excellence for the Chair of the University, but is also particularly recommended to the admiration of the country by his manly political career. Twice has he given up place and power, and lately refused them, solely upon *public principle*. These are facts which confer real dignity, and constitute a great man. In these times, when independence is so rare, and when place is generally sought alone for the *profit* it produces, it is the duty of those with whom the expression of any part of the national voice is entrusted, to honour, with all the distinction they can bestow, him who is almost a solitary exception to the opprobrium cast upon public men. A contrary course of conduct must induce suspicion, especially if it be seen on the present occasion, that if public virtue be seldom found in the statesmen of the present day, it is because the public itself is degraded.

    " I am, Sir, your obedient servant,

                        " A.M. Oxon."

" Oxford, Nov. 13th, 1808 " [a misprint for 1809].

CHAPTER II.

THERE is another and a curious reason for supposing that Oxford affairs occupied a large share of the attention of the good people at Field Place in those stirring months of September and October, 1809. *The Oxford University and City Herald,* of which I have spoken so frequently, and about which I shall have much more to say, circulated largely in the southern counties. We may be sure that Timothy Shelley, Esq., M.P. for Shoreham, was one of its subscribers. It is extremely likely from the following circumstance that the paper was not unfrequently in the hands of his son. Captain Medwin (vol. i. p. 48), referring to the facility with which Shelley wrote Latin verse, has the following passage :—" That he had certainly arrived at great skill in the art of versification, I think I shall be able to prove by the following specimens I kept among my treasures, which he gave me in 1808 or 9." The first is the epitaph in " Gray's Elegy in a Country Churchyard," " probably a school task."

" The second specimen of his versification," says Captain Medwin, " is of a totally different character, and shows a considerable precocity :"—

" IN HOROLOGIUM.

" Inter marmoreas Leonoræ pendula colles
Fortunata nimis machina dicit horas.
Quas manibus premit illa duas insensa papillas
Cur mihi sit digito tangere, amata, nefas ?"

These lines, which Mr. Rossetti prints in his edition (vol. ii. p. 501), more correctly than Captain Medwin had given them in his *Life of Shelley*, he assigns, with doubtful accuracy, to the year 1808. It is evident that Captain Medwin considered the thought to be not only precocious, but original, with Shelley. In this opinion probably Mr. Rossetti agreed. Something of the precocity is explained, however, and all of the originality removed, by a reference to *The Oxford Herald* of Saturday, September 16th, 1809, where the following English epigram appears :—

> " *On seeing a* FRENCH *Watch round the Neck of*
> *a Beautiful Young Woman.*
>
> " Mark what we gain from foreign lands,
>   *Time* cannot now be said to linger,—
> Allow'd to lay his two rude hands
>   Where others *dare* not lay a finger."

It is plain that Shelley's Latin lines are simply a translation of this epigram, which he most probably saw in *The Oxford Herald,* but may have read in some other paper of the time, as I distinctly recollect having met with it elsewhere when making my researches among the journals of the period.

In giving an account of the next poetical venture of Shelley while at Oxford, it will be necessary to draw particular attention to the manner in which this story is told by Mr. Hogg, and the place in his narrative assigned to it. The evidence already existing establishes a case at least of grave suspicion against him, and proves that, for some reasons best known to himself, he has not told certain events and circumstances of his hero's life in the actual order of their succession. This mode of dealing with his materials

is very remarkable in the way that he introduces to
our notice the *Posthumous Fragments of Margaret
Nicholson.* Every one interested in Shelley has read
the lively papers which Mr. Hogg contributed to the
New Monthly Magazine in 1832, under the title of
" Shelley at Oxford." To these we have previously
alluded. They form a considerable part of the first
volume of his incomplete life of the poet, and are
certainly the most interesting portion of it. If they
cannot be taken as a perfectly faithful account of
what actually took place between the young men
during their intercourse at Oxford, they have been
generally received as a clever elaboration of what by
possibility may have occurred. The conversations
are too minutely remembered and too elaborately reported to be taken for more than an attempt on the
part of the writer to fill up an outline that must
have well-nigh faded from his mind after an interval
of twenty-two years. Such descriptions as the following betray rather the trick and artifice of a novelist
endeavouring to produce an effective picture than the
serious aim of a historian able and willing to tell the
truth. It will be remembered that this is the account
which Mr. Hogg gives of his first visit to the rooms
of a young student whose acquaintance he had made
the day before, and with whom he had no grounds
for supposing he would ever be much connected in
after life.

" Books, boots, papers, shoes, philosophical instruments, clothes, pistols, linen, crockery, ammunition,
and phials innumerable, with money, stockings, prints,
crucibles, bags and boxes, were scattered on the floor
and in every place ; as if the young chemist, in order
to analyse the mystery of creation, had endeavoured

first to reconstruct the primeval chaos. The tables, and especially the carpet, were already stained with large spots of various hues, which frequently proclaimed the agency of fire. An electrical machine, an air-pump, the galvanic trough, a solar microscope, and large glass jars and receivers, were conspicuous amidst the mass of matter. Upon the table by his side were some books lying open, several letters, *a bundle of newspapers* (!), and a bottle of *japan* ink (!), that served as an inkstand; a piece of deal, lately part of the lid of a box, with many chips; and a handsome razor that had been used as a knife. There were bottles of soda-water, sugar, pieces of lemon, and the *traces* of an effervescent beverage (!). Two piles of books supported the tongs, and these upheld a small glass retort above an argand lamp. I had not been seated many minutes before the liquor in the vessel boiled over, adding fresh stains to the table, and rising in fumes with a most disagreeable odour. Shelley snatched the glass quickly, and dashing it in pieces among the ashes under the grate, increased the unpleasant and penetrating effluvium."*

In this story there may be one or two of the circumstances which we can rely upon as having actually occurred; as to the rest of the description, it is evidently as complete a *study* as a chapter in *The Old Curiosity Shop*. Mr. Hogg had forgotten that he told us a few pages before that Shelley had but just entered the University, that he had dined the preceding evening for the first time in hall, and that, as far as Mr. Hogg's information goes, this might have been only the third day of Shelley's residence at Oxford, and

---

* *The Life of Percy Bysshe Shelley*, vol. i. pp. 69, 70.

yet there was time in this short interval to burn the carpets and the tables, and create the chaos which Mr. Hogg depicts with the hand of a master. The " bundle of newspapers,"* the " bottle of japan ink," and the " traces of an effervescing mixture," recorded after twenty-two years, are wonderful results of the imagination if not of the memory of the writer.

It is, however, with these graphic but perhaps not very faithful details that more than 300 pages of Mr. Hogg's book are taken up. The " Imaginary Conversations," as they would have been called had they been written by Savage Landor, we may be sure, are quite as good as the real ones, and they may be taken at any rate as evidence of the subjects that occupied the attention of the friends during the period of their residence at the University. It seems strange, however, that so little transpires in these interminable discussions about the literary occupations of Shelley at the time. He either did not confide in Mr. Hogg at all, or Mr. Hogg considered a report of his own clever mode of arguing with Shelley would be more interesting to the reader than a detail of those poetical pieces which Shelley not only wrote but published when at Oxford. He makes an exception to this reticence, indeed, in his account of the *Posthumous Fragments of Margaret Nicholson,* but it will be noticed that he does not do so until nearly the end of his paper called " Shelley at Oxford "—after 210 pages have been filled with those apocryphal walks and talks to which I have been alluding. It is quite evident that Mr. Hogg wished

---

* " *A newspaper never found its way to his rooms the whole period of his residence at Oxford,*" says Mr. Hogg in another mood, and totally forgetful of what he had previously written.— *Life of Shelley,* vol. i. p. 257.

it to be understood that the events and conversations
recorded in those 210 pages preceded the publication
of *Margaret Nicholson,* and that it was not until after
an acquaintance of some duration, and a close intimacy,
that Shelley showed him the proof-sheets of this
work, and announced to him his intention of publishing it. So far from this being the fact, it will be
seen from the evidence here given for the first time,
that it must have been at the very beginning of their
intercourse—probably on the very first visit ever
paid by Hogg at Shelley's rooms—that the mention of
the poems published *seventeen days after* was made.

The whole of this story is very curious, and must
be told somewhat in detail. Mr. Hogg represents
Shelley's first attempt at authorship while at Oxford
as the result of that personal and private application
to study which was stimulated and aroused by
the public neglect of his college. " The University
at large was not less remiss than each college in particular. . . . The languid course of chartered laziness
was ill-suited to the ardent activity and glowing zeal
of Shelley."—*Life,* i. p. 259.

" Since those persons who were hired at an enormous charge by his own family and by the state to
find due and beneficial employment for him, thought
fit to neglect this their most sacred duty, he began
forthwith to set himself to work. He read diligently
—I should rather say he devoured greedily, with the
voracious appetite of a famished man—the authors
that roused his curiosity ; he discoursed and discussed
with energy; he wrote—he began to print—and he
designed soon to publish various works " (vol. i. p. 260).

" Shelley," says Mr. Hogg, on the same page as
that from which I have just quoted, " was quick to
conceive, and not less quick to execute." He must

certainly have been " quick to conceive " in one day's
experience of the University the extent of the tutorial
and maternal want of care that was in store for him—
quick, too, to devour all the authors that roused his
curiosity, and quick to execute those overt acts of
authorship that were the result of all this individual
industry and collegiate neglect.   But Mr. Hogg must
be allowed to tell his tale out fully in his own way.

" When I called one morning at one, I found him
busily occupied with some proofs, which he continued
to correct and re-correct with anxious care.   As he was
wholly absorbed in this occupation, I selected a book
from the floor, where there was always a good store,
and read in silence for at least an hour.

" My thoughts being as completely abstracted as
those of my companion, he startled me by suddenly
throwing a paper with some force on the middle of the
table, and saying in a penetrating whisper, as he sprung
eagerly from his chair, ' I am going to publish some
poems.'

" In answer to my inquiries, he put the proofs into
my hands.   I read them twice attentively, for the
poems were very short, and I told him there were
some good lines, some bright thoughts ; but there were
likewise many irregularities and incongruities.   I
added that correctness was important in all compositions, but it constituted the essence of short ones ;
and that it surely would be imprudent to bring his
little book out so hastily ; and I then pointed out the
errors and defects.

" He listened in silence with much attention, and
did not dispute what I said, except that he remarked
faintly that it would not be known that he was the
author, and therefore the publication could not do him
any harm.

" I answered, that although it might not be disadvantageous to be the unknown author of an unread work, it certainly could not be beneficial.

" He made no reply; and we immediately went out and strolled about the public walks.

" We dined, and returned to his rooms, where we conversed on indifferent subjects. He did not mention his poems, but they occupied his thoughts; for he did not fall asleep, as usual. Whilst we were at tea, he said abruptly, ' I think you disparage my poems. Tell me what you dislike in them, for I have forgotten.'

" I took the proofs from the place where I had left them, and looking over them, repeated the former objections and suggested others. He acquiesced, and after a pause asked might they be altered? I assented.

" ' I will alter them.'

" ' It will be better to re-write them; a short poem should be the first impression.'

" Some time afterwards he anxiously inquired, ' But in their present form you do not think they ought to be published?'

" I had been looking over the proofs again, and I answered, ' Only as burlesque poetry;' and I read a part, changing it a little here and there.

" He laughed at the parody, and begged I would repeat it.

" I took a pen and altered it, and he then read it aloud several times in a ridiculous tone, and was amused by it. His mirth consoled him for the condemnation of his verses, and the intention of publishing them *was abandoned*.

" The proofs lay in his room *for some days*, and we occasionally amused ourselves during idle moments by making them more and more ridiculous—by striking

D

out the more sober passages, by inserting whimsical
conceits, and especially by giving them what we called
a dithyrambic character, which was effected by cutting
some lines in two, and joining the different parts
together that would agree in construction, but were
the most discordant in sense."—*Life of Shelley*, vol. i.
pp. 261, 2, 3.

It is necessary here to interrupt Mr. Hogg for a
moment. The *Posthumous Fragments of Margaret
Nicholson*, though a rare volume, is not inaccessible.
A copy of the original edition is in the British Museum,
and a *fac simile* reprint, of which a limited number of
copies were issued some time ago, may be seen without
much difficulty. The poems, with the exception of the
first,* which extends to eighty-eight lines in couplets,
are also given in Mr. Rossetti's edition (vol. ii. p. 511).
They are thus within the reach of all, and it will be
found that in no single respect do they bear out the
description of Mr. Hogg.

There is no intentional burlesque traceable in them.
There is no example of this process of cutting lines
in two and then joining them, so as to agree in construction but to differ in sense. Indeed, Mr. Hogg
seems to have had a misgiving, after all this display of
his own drollery and cleverness, that some day or the
other his statements would be examined and his description put to the test. This difficulty did not put
him to much inconvenience. Three pages later he in-

---

* It is to be regretted that Mr. Rossetti omitted this poem from
his edition, on the mere statement of Mr. Hogg that "the MS. had
been confided to Shelley by some rhymster of the day." It is the
only poem Shelley refers to in his "advertisement" to the volume,
and its omission renders that "advertisement" unintelligible.

troduces this saving clause, which is highly creditable to his professional skill :—" The work, however, was *altered a little,* I believe, *before the final impression ;* but *I never read it afterwards* " (vol. i. p. 267)—a statement that may well be believed after his utterly erroneous description of its character and contents.

It was to Mr. Hogg, however, as it appears, that we owe its name.

" I hit upon a title at last, and we inscribed it on the cover.

" A mad washerwoman named Peg Nicholson had attempted to stab the King, George the Third, with a carving-knife ; the story had long been forgotten, but it was then fresh in the recollection of every one. It was proposed that we should ascribe the poems to her. The poor woman was still living and in green vigour within the walls of Bedlam ; but since her existence must be uncomfortable, there could be no harm in putting her to death, and in creating a nephew and administrator to be the editor of his aunt's poetical works.

" The idea gave an object and purpose to our burlesque—to ridicule the strange mixture of sentimentality with the murderous fury of revolutionists that was so prevalent in the compositions of the day ; and the proofs were altered again to adapt them to this new scheme, but still without any notion of publication. When the bookseller called to ask for the proofs, Shelley told him that he had changed his mind, and showed them to him.

" The man was so much pleased with the whimsical conceit, that he asked to be permitted to publish the book on his own account, promising inviolable secrecy, and as many copies *gratis* as might be required. After some hesitation permission was granted upon the plighted honour of the trade.

"In a few days, or rather in a few hours, a noble quarto appeared; it consisted of a small number of pages, it is true, but they were of the largest size, of the thickest, the whitest, and the smoothest draw-ing paper; a large, clear, and handsome type had im-pressed a few lines with ink of a rich glossy black amidst ample margins. The poor maniac laundress was gravely styled 'the late Mrs. Margaret Nicholson, widow;' and the sonorous name of Fitz Victor had been culled for her inconsolable nephew and ad-ministrator. To add to his dignity, the waggish printer had picked up some huge text types of so unusual a form that even an antiquary could not spell the words at the first glance. Shelley had torn open the large square bundle before the printer's boy quitted the room, and holding out a copy with both his hands, he ran about in an ecstasy of delight, gazing at the superb title-page" (vol. i. pp. 265, 6).

Without noticing the remarkable good fortune of Mr. Hogg in being always on the spot at a critical moment of the conception, gestation, and safe delivery of this poetical bantling, it may be stated that, with the exception of Shelley's probable delight at the appearance of the volume, all the other circumstances may be attributed to the fertile imagination of Mr. Hogg.

The poor maniac laundress is *not* gravely styled "the late Mrs. Margaret Nicholson, widow," nor is her name mentioned in the whole volume except on the title-page. The printer was "waggish" only to the extent of using the type that he had in most abundance. The paper to which I have already re-ferred, *The Oxford University and City Herald*, and of which I shall have much to say further on, was the property of the same printer, and in it there is not a column of advertisements that does not contain frequent examples of this type. It is used in the advertisement of the book itself, as will presently be seen.

The name of the printer Mr. Hogg does not condescend to give us, although it will be found that Shelley had other transactions with him besides the publication of the *Posthumous Fragments*. Captain Medwin, to whom it appears a copy of the volume was sent, though he takes his whole description of it from Mr. Hogg, states that it was "published at Parker's." This of course is a mistake. It was printed and published by John Munday, a name long and honourably known in connexion with the city of Oxford. Of him and of his family I have been favoured, by the present representative of the firm of Munday and Slatter, Mr. Rose, with some interesting particulars, in a letter which will be found below.*

It will be seen from Mr. Hogg's own acknowledgment that a considerable interval elapsed between his first seeing the proofs and the final appearance of the volume under the title of *Posthumous Fragments of*

---

* " Oxford, High Street, Dec. 3rd, 1870.

" Sir,—Your letter asking for information about a *Poetical Essay*, 1811, came duly to hand. I have made what inquiries were possible, but without any success. There does not appear to be any trace of the tract in the old books, so far as they are in my possession. The family of Munday have disappeared from Oxford long since, with the exception of a daughter of Joseph Munday, living in the neighbourhood; but the son, who succeeded to the printing business, left Oxford many years since for Bristol, and is since dead, so that all chance of discovery from that source is hopeless. " I am, sir, your obedt. servt.

" JOHN ROSE."

Margaret Nicholson. They were condemned, altered, recast, retouched, rejected, and finally adopted after much cogitation, and after intervals of " several days." To produce a volume of the elegance described would in itself require a good deal of mechanical skill and considerable time. It should also be remembered that the book was produced in a printing office busily occupied in bringing out a large weekly journal. Altogether, the most impatient author could scarcely expect under these circumstances that his productions should be offered to the public in less than three weeks. These reasonable conditions, if they are admitted, establish beyond doubt that these poems were first shown to Mr. Hogg, not as he insinuates after his intimacy with Shelley had been matured, and as a natural result of their long acquaintance, but most probably, as I have stated, on the first occasion he ever paid the young poet a visit.

Mr. Hogg has told us that it was " one day at the end of October, 1810," on which he first saw Shelley. The end of October must, of course, mean about the 30th or 31st of that month. The two young men thus for the first time brought together spent the evening at Hogg's rooms. The host obligingly tells us that he slept very soundly after the departure of " the vivacious stranger"—so soundly indeed that next day he forgot, not only the stranger himself, but the promise he had made to visit him at his rooms. The long conversation to which several of the preceding pages had been devoted, thus congealed by the frost of forgetfulness in one night, came out like the tunes in the horn of Baron Munchausen's courier twenty-two years afterwards. An hour, however, after the time Mr. Hogg had promised to meet his young friend, he remembered his engagement and repaired to Shelley's rooms. I have given the description of those rooms, but we have now to do with the date. It was probably the 1st of November. At the utmost stretch it could only be a day or two earlier. On Saturday, the 17th November, 1810, that is sixteen or eighteen days after Hogg by his own showing first saw Shelley, the following advertisement appears in *The Oxford University and City Herald* :—

"Just Published, price 2s., Posthumous Fragments of MAR-GARET NICHOLSON ; being Poems found amongst the Papers of that noted female, who attempted the life of the King in 1786. Edited by 𝕵𝖔𝖍𝖓 𝕱𝖎𝖙𝖟 𝖁𝖎𝖈𝖙𝖔𝖗. Oxford : Printed and sold by J. Munday."

In this advertisement, which is almost identical with the title-page, the name JOHN FITZ VICTOR is printed in the large black-letter type used in the volume itself. The advertisement is repeated a week later in the next number of *The Oxford Herald*, the price in the interval having risen to 2s. 6d.

The extent of the very slight acquaintance that could have existed between Shelley and Mr. Hogg whilst the *Posthumous Fragments* were passing through the press being thus established, we may, without much injury to Shelley, give Mr. Hogg the whole credit of assigning them to Margaret Nicholson. That was a stroke of humour quite worthy of some others complacently recorded of himself by the biographer. Shelley had written a wild rhapsody entitled *Frag-ment — Supposed to be an Epithalamium of Francis Ravaillac and Charlotte Cordé*. This is described by Mr. Hogg, in his most characteristic manner, as " a poem concerning a young woman, one Charlotte Some-body, who attempted to assassinate Robespierre or some

such person." Poor Margaret Nicholson's happily
unsuccessful attempt on the life of the King preceded
by seven years the famous act of tyrannicide perpe-
trated by Charlotte Corday in 1793, not on Robespierre,
but on Marat. Careless of the anachronism, Mr.
Hogg boldly assigned the poem to the " mad washerwoman" as a happy stroke of humour. The supposed
authoress speaks in the first poem of " wife and
children ;" this, too, must be taken as a delicious bit
of burlesque, in making Mrs. Nicholson imagine herself
to have been a man and a father.* On the whole, we
cannot but think that the poems would have fared all
the better had they been published by Shelley, as they
evidently were written by him, as serious compositions.
One of them, " The Spectral Horseman," is interesting
as showing that at this early period Shelley had begun
to take that interest in the history and legends of
Ireland which led to such extraordinary results two
years later. We have here " The Banshee's moan on
the storm ;" " A white courser," like that of
O'Donoghue, " bears the shadowy sprite ;" " The
whirlwinds howl in the caves of Innisfallen."

> " Then does the dragon, who, chained in the caverns
> To eternity, curses the champion of Erin,
> Moan and yell loud at the lone hour of midnight."
>
> *Fragments,* p. 25.

Extravagant as all these passages are, they show that
Shelley's sympathies for Ireland had already been
awakened, and that his practical efforts for her benefit
at a later period were not the result of any sudden or
passing caprice.

---

* This poem which, as previously noticed, Mr. Rossetti omitted
from his *Annotated Edition,* is given in the faithful reprint of the
original editions of Shelley's early poems recently issued by Mr.
Hotten—a volume remarkable for its accuracy and cheapness.

CHAPTER III.

WHILST the *Posthumous Fragments of Margaret Nicholson* were thus passing through the press at Oxford, Shelley was in communication with Stockdale about the publication in London of a more important work. This was the prose romance of *St. Irvyne; or, The Rosicrucian.* Only three days before *The Oxford University and City Herald* had announced the publication of *Margaret Nicholson*—that is, on the 14th of November, 1810—Shelley returned to Stockdale the manuscript of *St. Irvyne,* thanking him at the same time for the trouble he had taken " to fit it for the press." The work thus " fitted for the press " by Mr. Stockdale was placed at once in the hands of " S. Gosnell, Little Queen Street, London," by whom it was printed. By the 17th of December, exactly one month after the publication of *Margaret Nicholson, St. Irvyne* was so far advanced that Stockdale announced its immediate appearance. The announcement was forwarded to Shelley, then at Field Place, who wrote to the publisher in the following terms :—

" Field Place, December 18th, 1810.

" My dear Sir,—
" I saw your advertisement of *The Rosicrucian,* and approve of it highly : it is likely to excite curiosity. . . . . Mr. Munday, of Oxford, will take some romances ; I do not know whether he sends directly

to you, or through the medium of a bookseller. I will enclose the printer's account for your inspection in another letter.

"Dear Sir, yours sincerely,

"P. B. SHELLEY."

From the last passage in this letter it would appear that Shelley had undertaken the risk of printing *St. Irvyne* himself. Mr. Stockdale, it is evident, had the pleasure not only of inspecting the printer's account, but of paying it also. This probably formed the foundation of the debt due to him by Shelley, which, "interest included," he calculated in 1826 amounted to 300*l.* The rate of interest must have been high indeed if it be true, as stated in a MS. journal of Dr. Polidori, that the principal sum due on the 1st of August, 1811, was about 100*l.* Whatever the amount was, Shelley, writing to Stockdale on that day, declared his inability to pay it. He admits "the imprudence of publishing a book so ill-digested as *St. Irvyne*," but still asks with a faint glimmer of hope, "Are there no expectations on the profits of its sale?" This gleam, however, is but momentary; for in the next sentence he offers a new solution of the difficulty— "My studies have, since my writing it, been of a more serious nature. I am at present engaged in completing a series of moral and metaphysical essays— perhaps their copyright would be accepted in lieu of part of my debt."

It is needless to say that this offer did not tempt Mr. Stockdale to indulge a second time in the luxury of inspecting and paying a printer's account, even with the hope of adding the ideal interest thereon which had so mysteriously expanded the first.

Whether these moral and metaphysical essays were substantially the same work to which Shelley alludes in his letter to Stockdale of the 18th December, 1810, from which I have already quoted, it is now impossible to say. In that letter he writes : " I have in preparation a novel; it is principally constructed to convey metaphysical and political opinions *by way of conversation.* It shall be sent to you as soon as completed, but it shall receive more correction than I trouble myself to give to wild romance and poetry." Mr. Garnett, referring to this subject, says : " Speedy extinction, too, was the fate of the MS. novel, of which the above is the first and last mention." As to the *novel,* this remark is doubtless true; but we certainly do hear again of a work conveying "metaphysical and moral opinions by way of conversation." The idea or plan of a fiction may have been abandoned, and the substance and conversational form of the essays preserved in a book of which Mr. Hogg gives us the following curious account :—

"The year 1814 had come upon us. In that year —and at the beginning of the year, I think—Shelley published a work entitled *A Refutation of Deism : in a Dialogue.* It is handsomely, expensively, and very incorrectly printed in octavo. It was published in a legal sense, unquestionably; whether it was also published in a publisher's sense and offered for sale I know not, but I rather think that it was—the preface informs us that it was intended it should be. I never heard that anybody bought a copy; the only copy I ever saw is that which my friend kindly sent to me; it is inscribed by his own hand, on the title-page, ' To his friend T. Jefferson Hogg, from P. B. S.' I never heard it mentioned any further than this, that

two or three of the author's friends told me that it
had been sent as a present.   It is a short dialogue,
comprised in 101 pages of large print.   Euscbes and
Theosophus discourse together and dispute with each
other, much as the author loved to dispute when he
could find an opponent—whenever Eusebes could find
a Theosophus, and get up an antagonistic dialogue.
It is written in his powerful, energetic, contentious
style, but it contains nothing new or important, and
was composed and printed also in a hurry.   He never
spoke of it to me, or in my presence.   It attracted
no attention, and doubtless Shelley himself soon discovered that it did not merit it."—*Life of Shelley*, vol.
ii. pp. 484, 485.

How Mr. Hogg could have known that this work
was "composed and printed also in a hurry," when
Shelley never spoke of it to him or in his presence,
is one of those mysteries of intuition so frequently
propounded for our belief throughout his book.   It
is apparently the same work which Shelley had planned
in December, 1810, and which he determined should
receive "more correction than he troubled himself to
give to wild romance and poetry."   The description
Mr. Hogg gives of this book is fuller than usual, and
may lead to its recovery.   There is always, however,
something incomplete and unsatisfactory even in his
most minute analysis when dealing with facts.   He
tells us that "a long quotation is given in a note from
Plutarch's treatise on eating flesh.   It is in the
original Greek, without any translation either in
English or in Latin—a convincing proof that the
dialogue was not addressed to unlearned readers" (*Life*,
vol. ii. p. 486).   This Mr. Hogg gives without the

slightest reference to what he had printed but a few pages before, in a letter of Shelley's dated Edinburgh, Nov. 26th, 1813.

" I have *translated* the two Essays of Plutarch, περὶ σαρκοφαγίας, which we read together. They are very excellent. I intend to comment upon them, and to reason *in my preface* concerning the Orphic and Pythagoric system of diet."—*Life,* vol. ii. p. 482.

It will be amusing, as another example of Mr. Hogg's sublime indifference to facts, to find, whenever a copy of *A Refutation of Deism* is discovered, that the "long quotation from Plutarch's treatise on eating flesh," left in the original Greek for learned readers as a note, is translated into English for "unlearned readers" in the "Preface."*

But we must now return to *St. Irvyne,* which we have abandoned rather unceremoniously on the first day of its existence.

An announcement of the birth was published, as we have seen, a day or two before the 18th of December, 1810; but the new arrival showed little signs of life, if we may judge by the silence of the papers, until towards the end of January, 1811. The advertisement,

---

* A long quotation from the same treatise of Plutarch, both in Greek and English, concludes the notes to *Queen Mab,* in Clark's edition of 1821. It would appear from a notice signed " W. Clark," on p. 92 of this edition, that the notes of the original *Queen Mab* of 1813, " in French, Latin, and Greek," were not translated. In the editions of *Queen Mab* by John Brooks (1829), Mrs. Shelley and Mr. Rossetti, the passage from Plutarch is not translated. In those of Clark, 1821 ; Carlile, 1822 (the same book with Carlile's imprint) and Carlile 1823, with the titlepage of the original edition of 1813, the passage is given in Greek and English. In the edition said to be printed at " New York, by William Baldwin," 1821, the translation alone is given.

which Shelley thought was "likely to excite curiosity," began to appear more frequently. Except the heading, "The University Romance," there is nothing in it different from ordinary advertisements. I transcribe it from *The Times* of Saturday, January 26th, 1811, and Saturday, February 2nd, 1811 :—

"THE UNIVERSITY ROMANCE.—This day is published, price only 5s., *St. Irvyne; or, The Rosicrucian :* A Romance. By a Gentleman of Oxford University. Printed for Stockdale Junior, 41, Pall-Mall."

St. Irvyne has one advantage, and one only, over *Zastrozzi*—it is considerably shorter : in every other respect it is as unreal, imperfect, and puerile as his first attempt. Shelley believed that at least it would have made a bigger book than *Zastrozzi*, but in this he was mistaken, as though printed in a somewhat larger type it fills exactly sixteen pages less. *St. Irvyne*, though not published until the end of 1810, was probably written while *Zastrozzi* was passing through the press in the earlier part of the same year. He tells us himself that the second title of the story, *The Rosicrucian*, is derived from *St. Leon :* " What I mean as ' Rosicrucian' is, the elixir of eternal life. Mr. Godwin's romance of ' St. Leon' turns upon that superstition " It has not, however, been noticed that its first title, *St. Irvyne*, may have been suggested to him by a locality in which he had spent some of the happiest hours of his life in the company of his first love, Harriet Grove. Lady Shelley calls this place *St. Leonard's*,* but Mr. C. Grove, who formed one of the party described in the following interesting passage of a letter addressed by him to Miss Hellen Shelley,

---

* Meaning probably *St. Leonard's Forest*, in a part of which lay the seat of the Duke of Norfolk.

the poet's sister, in 1857, speaks of it as *St. Irving's,* a name singularly like that of Shelley's romance :—

" I did not meet Bysshe again," says Mr. Grove, " till I was fifteen, the year I left the navy, and then I went to Field Place with Harriet [Grove]. Bysshe was there, having just left Eton, and his sister Elizabeth. Bysshe was at that time more attached to my sister Harriet than I can express, and I recollect well the moonlight walks* we four had at Strode, and also at *St. Irving's;* that, I think, was the name of the place, then the Duke of Norfolk's, at Horsham."† After this, in a parenthesis, is the following fuller description : " St. Irving's Hills, a beautiful place on the right-hand side as you go from Horsham to Field Place, laid out by the famous Capability Brown, and full of magnificent forest-trees, waterfalls, and rustic seats. The seat was Elizabethan. All has been destroyed." Mr. Grove adds " that was in 1810"— evidently a mistake for the summer of 1809, as correctly given by Lady Shelley.—Hogg's *Life of Shelley,* vol. ii. pp. 550, 551 ; *Shelley Memorials,* p. 13.

* The moon, as might be expected, figures conspicuously in *St. Irvyne.* One or two passages may be given:—" The moon became as bright as polished silver, and each star sparkled with scintillations of inexpressible whiteness" (p. 194). And again, " I gazed in eager anticipation of curiosity on the scene before me ; for a mist of silver radiance rendered every object but myself imperceptible ; yet was it brilliant as the noonday sun" (*St. Irvyne,* p. 194).

† " Hill Place" is the name given to it in *Beauties of England and Wales.* London, 1813. " In the same direction, on the right of the road, is an old seat called *Hill Place,* formerly the property of the late Viscountess Irwin, but now belonging to the Duke of Norfolk" (*Sussex,* p. 97).

Mr. Howard, of Corby Castle, tells me it was sold after the death of Duke Charles in 1815. The " Viscountess *Irwin*" may perhaps have suggested the name " Irving" to Mr. Grove.

As the place was called *St. Irving's* by Mr. Grove, it may so have been remembered by Shelley; and even apart from the associations connected with the presence of Harriet Grove and Elizabeth Shelley, it was a locality that may well be supposed to have lingered in the memory of the poet.

It is stated that *St. Irvyne* as well as. *Zastrozzi* received a good deal of notice from the press. This statement, which seems rather improbable, I have not been able to confirm after a diligent search. In examining the reviews and periodicals of the period for some trace or record of the missing poem published by Shelley in 1811, which will presently be more fully described, the names of these romances would have arrested my attention, but I do not recollect having met a single allusion to them. The second romance, however, had an admirer, and a warm one, in a very unexpected quarter. " Fortunately for himself," says Mr. Rossetti, in his *Memoir of Shelley* (p. lxi.), " Hogg had probably not read *St. Irvyne*, or he would have found that that name designates a locality, and not a man." It might be urged that perhaps it designated neither. The interest of more than half the story, and that its concluding portion, entirely rests upon Eloise de St. Irvyne, a sort of newer *Nouvelle Heloise*, who may be considered its heroine, after the astounding Megalena de Metastasio is disposed of, and from whom it may have derived its name. But whether Mr. Hogg read the romance or not, he praised it; so much so, indeed, that the modest and perhaps conscientious author had to deprecate the infrequent, perhaps the unique, adulation of his friend. " Why will you compliment *St. Irvyne?* " says Shelley in a letter to Mr. Hogg, dated Sunday, May 17th, 1811—

a question which that gentleman doubtless would have found it very difficult to answer.

As in the case of Margaret Nicholson's *Posthumous Fragments, St. Irvyne* supplies additional proof of the interest which Ireland was then beginning to awaken in the mind of Shelley. The witchery of the *Irish Melodies* had already enthralled him. He even goes the length of making the exceptional moral person in his book an Irishman. Compared with " the unhappy Wolfstein" and the " awe-inspiring Ginotti," the Englishman, Mountfort, may be regarded with some favour, but he is not immaculate. He has, however, a more perfect companion.

" What companion ?" Eloise interrupted him, inquiringly. " Why," replied he, " a friend of mine, who lives at my cottage ; he is an Irishman, and so *very* moral, and so averse to every species of *gaïeté de cœur,* that you need be under no apprehensions." " He wanders about, writes poetry, and, in short "—appears to be a very harmless sort of person. He eventually becomes the husband of Eloise, who having " stout notions on the marrying score," would have willingly dispensed with what she considered a superfluous ceremony. " Nay, do not start," says the gentle Fitzeustace, when he proposes to the fair Eloise the hard condition of submitting to the " harmless " formality of being legally married. He probably composed her by the charm which he had found so potent in an earlier scene.

" Recline on this sofa, then," said Fitzeustace, " and I will play some of those Irish tunes you admire so much."

" Eloise reclined on the sofa, and Fitzeustace, seated on the floor, began to play. The melancholy plaintive-

E

ness of his music touched Eloise—she sighed, and concealed her tears in her handkerchief. At length she sank into a profound sleep : still Fitzeustace continued playing, noticing not that she slumbered. He now perceived that she spoke, but in so low a tone that he knew she slept " (*St. Irvyne,** pp. 209, 216, 217, 280).

The way in which Shelley disposes of all his characters—not in the book itself, but in a private letter to his publisher—is amusing. Stockdale, after " fitting the work for the press," rubbed his eyes when all was over, to perceive if possible what had become of the various personages. Like the ferryman in the ballad of Kopisch,† he stood bewildered ; the elfin people had all vanished, and he held in his hand nothing but crumpled leaves. Shelley came to his relief.

" Ginotti, as you will perceive, did *not* die by Wolfstein's hand, but by the influence of that natural magic which, when the secret was imparted to the latter, destroyed him. Mountfort being a character of inferior import, I did not think it necessary to state the catastrophe of *him,* as it could at best be but uninteresting. Eloise and Fitzeustace are married and happy, I suppose, and Megalena dies by the same means as Wolfstein. I do not myself see any other explanation that is required."—Letter dated " University Coll., Nov. 14th, 1810," in *Stockdale's Budget.*

As my readers will probably be not more exacting

---

* In 1822, after the death of Shelley, Stockdale reproduced the old sheets of *St. Irvyne,* with a title page dated that year. It is from a copy of this reissue in my own possession that the above extracts are given.

† *The Fairies' Passage.* The translation of James Clarence Mangan.

than Mr. Stockdale, with this epilogue of the author we shall take our leave of *St. Irvyne.*

In the second letter which Shelley addressed to Godwin, then personally unknown to him, dated " KESWICK, January 10th, 1812," he thus epitomizes in one sentence the results of his academic career :—

" Classical reading and poetical writing employed me during my residence at Oxford " (*Hogg*, vol. ii. p. 56).

As far as we have yet gone in this investigation, the only evidence of poetical writing that has been presented to us is the collection of poems, serious or burlesque, whichever they may be considered to be, that he published under the name of *Margaret Nicholson.* Indeed Mr. Hogg leaves it to be inferred that with that sublime effort of genius the poetical aspirations of his young friend were satisfied, and that he printed nothing subsequently, either in prose or verse, while at the University, but the unfortunate syllabus entitled *The Necessity of Atheism.* How completely this is the reverse of the fact will presently be shown. It will be proved that he not only indulged in " poetical writing " to a much greater extent than might be supposed from the silence of his biographer on that point, but that he published a distinct volume of verse—the earliest that came entirely from his own hand—a fact which, after the lapse of sixty years, it has been the good fortune of the present writer to have discovered.

Among the many loose though dogmatic assertions of Mr. Hogg, for which there is not a tittle of evidence, and that are absolutely contradicted by the facts, is one to the effect that Shelley not only had a dislike to newspapers, but that they never reached him while at the University. " A newspaper never found

its way to his rooms the whole period of his residence
at Oxford " (*Life,* vol. i. p. 257).   How Shelley could
have written and published a volume of verse without
his friend knowing anything about it, and yet be unable
to receive a single newspaper unseen by that keen-eyed
Argus, is a difficulty not easily got over.   And yet this
reckless assertion is adopted by later writers without the
slightest investigation.   So far from Shelley being indifferent to newspapers and to writers in newspapers,
we find him at Oxford alive to the passing political
events of the day—writing to the editors of newspapers, identifying himself with their opinions, congratulating them on their triumphs, indignant at their
persecution, and, stranger than all, publishing a poem
for the sustainment in prison of one of them who was
considered by the leading Liberals of the day, as well
as by Shelley, a martyr for the liberty of the Press.

Captain Medwin was determined not to be outdone
by his rival biographer Mr. Hogg, in affecting an
intimate acquaintauce with the private habits of their
illustrious friend.   The infallible Mr. Hogg had
declared *ex cathedrâ* that " a newspaper *never* found
its way to his rooms *the whole period* of his residence
at Oxford."   At a time when Shelley was engaged
in writing to the editors of three newspapers, and
publishing a poem for the sustainment of one of them
who had been imprisoned, Mr. Hogg puts into the
mouth of his friend the following marvellous statement :
" With how unconquerable an aversion do I shrink
from political articles and reviews !" Sometimes, alas !
he had to endure the affliction.   " When waiting in
a bookseller's shop or at an inn," says Mr. Hogg,
relaxing a little from the severity of his first assertion,
" he would sometimes, although rarely, permit his eye

to be attracted by a *murder or a storm !"* What a careful watch had Mr. Hogg at this time over his young friend, when he stole behind his chair and looked over his shoulder to know the precise article that engaged the attention of the poet! What a high idea he gives of the subjects most interesting to the youthful philanthropist!

Captain Medwin, as we have said, affects to be equally well informed as to Shelley's habits in this respect at a later period of his life. Speaking of his visit to the poet, at Pisa, in 1821, he says :—" Never have I seen him read a newspaper." This, no doubt, may be perfectly true when taken as a personal recollection of the writer. It is, however, relied upon by those who, having adopted the earlier assertion of Mr. Hogg as to Shelley's dislike to newspapers, see in Captain Medwin's statement a complete confirmation of it. We have already disposed of Mr. Hogg's delusion—the imparting to his friend sentiments and prejudices that were clearly his own. If additional arguments are necessary, they will be found in the single fact that within twelve months of the time at which this aversion to newspapers is said to have existed in the mind of Shelley, he was endeavouring to establish one himself, of which he would have the entire control. This occurred in Dublin, as will be fully detailed in our subsequent account of Shelley's visit to that city.

The fact is immaterial whether Captain Medwin ever saw Shelley read a newspaper or not, when we have it under his own hand, in letters written from Italy, that he not only received newspapers, but subscribed for them. The following extracts are taken from Mr. Peacock's papers in *Fraser's Magazine,* where the letters are published. Writing from Leghorn, June, 1819, Shelley says—" Cobbett still more and more delights me, with all my horror of the sanguinary commonplaces of his creed" (*Fraser,* March, 1860, p. 308). Later in the same year he says—" The *Examiners* I receive. Hunt, as a *political* writer, pleases me more and more" (August, 1819). "Many thanks for your attention in sending *the papers* which contain the terrible and important news of Manchester. . . . . Pray let me have the earliest *political* news which you consider important at this crisis" (September, 1819). "I have received all the papers you sent me, and the *Examiners* regularly" (September, 1819). "*I take in* Galignani's paper, which is filled with extracts from *The Courier*" (Pisa, May, 1820). "The Paris paper *which I take in* copied some excellent remarks from *The Examiner*" (Leghorn, July, 1820). Finally, at the end of the same letter, he begs of his friend Peacock to send him, with a number of books which he mentions, "*Papers,* 'Indicators,' and whatever else *you may think interesting.*" So much for the accuracy of Shelley's biographers, from Mr. Hogg to Captain Medwin, and the followers of both.

Putting aside this newspaper controversy, at least for a while, we may return to the account which Shelley himself gives of his occupations during the brief term of his University career. "Classical reading and poetical writing employed me during my residence at Oxford" (Letter to Godwin, Keswick, January 10th, 1812). The only evidence of "poetical writing" that has yet been adduced is the curious volume entitled *Posthumous Fragments of Margaret Nicholson.* That work, slight and trifling as it is, was published, as we have shown, within three weeks after Shelley's entrance at the University. If the time of his going to Oxford is correctly given by Mr. Hogg and by Lady Shelley, these poems must have been written by Shelley in the interval between his leaving Eton and his entrance at University College. One would expect more results from this systematic prosecution of " classical reading and poetical writing" than the *Fragments,* which are plainly the product of earlier studies and earlier inspirations. Whenever the missing poem—the fact of the publication of which we have discovered—is found, it will probably justify the assertion of Shelley, that when at Oxford he occupied himself in "poetical writing" as well as "classical reading." While waiting for the appearance of that poem, which will be most interesting as the first poetical work published by Shelley without the assistance or co-operation of an ally, any poems published at this period which with reasonable probability may be attributed to him must awaken a certain amount of curiosity.

We have spoken of *The Oxford University and City Herald,* of which John Munday, the publisher of *Margaret Nicholson,* was printer. We shall shortly find Shelley's name avowedly in that paper, and in that paper is the earliest advertisement of the missing poem to which we have so often referred. The English epigram on a watch, which Shelley translated into Latin, appeared, as we have pointed out, in *The Oxford Herald* so early as September 16th, 1809. We have suggested that the member for Shoreham (Mr. Timothy Shelley) could scarcely have done less than support by his subscription a Liberal journal which probably circulated largely in Sussex and the adjacent

counties. Should this surmise be correct, the paper
was, of course, week after week forwarded to Field
Place, and thus, even before he went to Oxford, may
have been frequently in the hands of the young poet.

It seems strange that no one has hitherto examined
the Oxford journals of 1810 and 1811 for some traces
of Shelley while at the University. The details given
by Mr. Hogg are so copious, and appear to be so
authentic, that curiosity was satisfied, and subsequent
writers were content with reproducing in one form or
another the elaborate narrative of that gentleman. It
was difficult, it is true, to see those papers even at
Oxford, as I am informed by the courteous librarian
of the Bodleian that no Oxford journals of those years
are preserved in that library. The British Museum
is more fortunate, as it possesses in a tolerably complete state a copy of *The Oxford University and City
Herald* for the years in which, on Shelley's account,
we are most interested. This copy was " purchased·
at the sale of Mr. Heber's books, June, 1834," as
mentioned on the fly-leaf of the volume, which contains,
with some exceptions, the numbers from December,
1806, to the 28th February, 1815. The numbers for
1810 seem to be quite perfect, as are those of 1811 to
the 29th of September.

Through all these years *The Oxford Herald* seems
to have preserved a uniform character. Its politics
were ultra-Liberal, especially on all questions connected
with the liberty of the Press. It appeared once a
week, on Saturday, and was " printed and published
by John Munday, at *The Herald* Office, High Street,
Oxford." The name of J. Munday as printer is
changed in the number for January 12th, 1811, to those
of "Munday and Slatter," by whom it was subse-

quently carried on. In the same number there is an advertisement of " Munday and Slatter, Printers and Booksellers, *Herald* Office, High Street, Oxford." A son of John Munday succeeded him in the business, but on his leaving Oxford, as mentioned in the interesting letter by the present representative of the firm, Mr. John Rose, which has already been given, the establishment was carried on under the names of Slatter and Rose.

The Oxford Herald appears to have been conducted with a good deal of literary ability and taste. A column was usually devoted to a prose essay on some of the older English poets. Crashaw and other writers of the same period and school—such as Cowley, traces of whose influence may perhaps be found in the lyrical poetry of Shelley—are frequently mentioned. One of these essays, signed " P. S.," appeared during the period of Shelley's residence, and may possibly have been written by him. There is a marked absence, however, of original poetry in *The Oxford Herald,* or of verse written expressly for publication in that journal. Political squibs and lengthy odes are in abundance, but they are generally taken at second-hand from *The Morning Chronicle.* Sometimes a poem appeared on the same day in the two journals. With the approach of Shelley a change appears in this respect in the pages of the paper; original verse begins to appear, is continued during his residence at the University, and ceases when he leaves it. By original verse I mean, as I have said, verse published originally in *The Oxford Herald.* Most of these are signed with the letter " S." They are chiefly translations from the Greek *Anthology* (of which in his collected works we have undoubted specimens) and from the Latin poems of Vincent Bourne. Here is curiously combined in the same pieces some evidence of the " classical reading " and " poetical writing " of which he himself has spoken. These translations do not possess any remarkable merit, nor have they that peculiar Shelleyan flavour by which we can so easily recognise his later poems. They are, however, not inferior to most that he had written up to this period. The signature attached to them, the time at which they appeared, the journal in which they were published, and the course of his studies at the time, all create an amount of presumptive evidence that justify me in offering them here as having in all probability been written by Shelley.

Before the ordinarily received time of his arrival at Oxford, however, and as an *avant-courier* of the coming poet, there appeared in *The Oxford Herald* a short poem which, as I conceive, possesses to a remarkable degree that peculiar Shelleyan flavour of which I have spoken. This little poem cannot, of course, be put in comparison with some of those exquisite lyrics written by Shelley in his later years—lyrics with which, in fact, nothing in the language *can* be compared. But there is something essentially Shelleyesque both in the language and the ideas. If the lines were not written by Shelley, they were the composition of some young poet who anticipated Shelley himself in what was peculiarly characteristic of Shelley. As Pope said of Chapman's translation of the *Iliad*, that it was " something like what one would imagine Homer himself would have writ before he arrived at years of discretion ;" so this little poem may be offered as something like what Shelley would have sung before he attained the full faculty of lyrical expression :—

˙ ODE

TO THE DEATH OF SUMMER.

Zephyr, whither art thou straying,
   Tell me where :
With prankish girls in gardens playing,
   False and fair ;
A butterfly's light back bestriding ;
Queen bees to honeysuckles guiding,
Or in a swinging harebell riding,
   Free from care ?

Before Aurora's car you amble
   High in air ;
At noon, when Neptune's sea-nymphs gambol,
   Braid their hair ;
When on the trembling billows rolling,
Or on the smooth sands idly strolling,
Or in cool grottoes they lie lolling,
   You sport there.

To chase the moonbeams up the mountains,
   You prepare :
Or dance with elves on brinks of fountains,
   Mirth to share ;
Now seen with love-lorn lilies weeping,
Now with a blushing rosebud sleeping ;
Whilst fays from forth their chambers peeping,
   Cry, Oh rare !

The braiding the hair of the sea-nymphs by the breeze—the personification of the "love-lorn lilies"—the intense enjoyment of Nature throughout, and the abrupt exclamation at the end, all raise a strong probability that this lyric was written by Shelley. It appeared in *The Oxford Herald* of Saturday, September 22nd, 1810. Shelley was then at Field Place, as we have letters in the Stockdale correspondence dated there, both before and immediately after. As Shelley had sent so far as Edinburgh to the Messrs. Ballantyne the MS. of his long poem *The Wandering*

Jew, written in conjunction with Captain Medwin, to which they refer in their curious letter of the 24th of September, 1810, there is no improbability in his having sent a short lyric to Oxford for publication in a local paper. It should be noticed that the poem is printed very conspicuously in *The Oxford Herald*, at the top of a column not usually devoted to literature, whether in justice to the merits of the composition itself, or in deference to the social position of the supposed writer, cannot now be ascertained.

The evidence of authorship in the " Ode to the Death of Summer" is altogether, or nearly so, internal. In the translations from the Greek *Anthologia* it is perhaps exclusively external, arising from the signature and the classical character of the poems themselves. The first of these versions from the Greek is given in *The Oxford University and City Herald* of Saturday, January 5th, 1811:—

THE GRAPE.

From the Greek Anthologia.

This grape, of future wine the store,
Who from the tree unripen'd bore ?
And, loathing its yet acid taste,
Thus on the ground half-eaten cast ?
To every footstep passing by
The spurn'd remains obnoxious lie ;—
To him, the foe of mirth and love,
May Bacchus ever hostile prove,
As to the barb'rous prince of yore
Who Thracia's blooming vines uptore :—
This grape, thus wantonly abus'd,
When in the sparkling glass infus'd,
This might have warm'd some poet's lay,
Or chased corroding care away !　　　S.

In the next number, for January 12th, 1811, is the following :—

EPIGRAM.

From the Greek Anthologia.

Supposed to be spoken by some Roses on the Birth-day of a Beautiful Girl who was on the Point of Marriage.

We that were wont in Spring's soft lap to bloom,
Now early blush, 'mid Winter's dreary gloom,
And on this day we smiling hail thy charms,
That soon, sweet maid, shall bless a husband's arms;
More pleased thy lovely temples to adorn,
Than wait the rising of the vernal morn. S.

The series of epigrams from the Greek is here interrupted by one from the Latin. The signature " S. " is changed also for " VERSIFICATOR," but the writer is evidently the same person, as the translations from the *Anthologia* are resumed under the latter signature on March 9th, 1811, sixteen days before Shelley's expulsion, after which they no longer appear.

In *The Oxford Herald* of Saturday, February 23rd, 1811, is the following :—

TRANSLATION OF AN EPIGRAM OF VINCENT BOURNE.

Down the river's gentle tide,
As to London Bridge we glide,
Hark ! the bells of Mary's tower
Sweetly warbled music pour !
With what harmony and grace
Each preserves its stated place !
While the air, above, around,
Trembles with the varied sound.

Merry changes ceaseless glide
To old Thames's willow'd side :
Still recede, and sweeter still
Through the raptur'd breast they thrill,
Such the pleasure to our hearts
Distant melody imparts—
Enter once within the tow'r,
All the harmony is o'er.—VERSIFICATOR.*

---

* Since this page was in type I have found in *The Oxford*

The Oxford Herald of Saturday, March 9th, 1811, contains two epigrams from the Greek, with which, as I have stated, the series closes :—

ON OLD AGE.
From the Greek Anthologia.

Mortals for áge, when distant, pray;
Age, when at hand, they wish away;
The thing of which we're not possest,
We constantly esteem the best.—VERSIFICATOR.

VENUS AND THE MUSES.
From the same.

The Queen of Love once threat'ning vow'd,
Unless the Nine her sway allow'd,
That Cupid's never-erring dart
Should quickly pierce them to the heart.
Then they : "On Mars your menace try,
The little urchin we defy."—VERSIFICATOR.

There is one thing very remarkable about these last two epigrams in connexion with the suggestion I have ventured to make as to their authorship, and it is this, that they appear in the same number of *The Oxford Herald* which contains the earliest advertisement of the poem unknown to all Shelley's biographers, to his widow and to his family, which he published on that day.

Before entering on this curious and most interesting subject, we have to retrace our steps a little, and resume the inquiry as to Shelley's connexion with the editors of newspapers, and the interest which he took in the political questions of the day.

Herald another translation from Vincent Bourne, signed " S. S——Edmonton." Whatever effect this may have on the suggestion thrown out above, it is only right that it should be mentioned.

CHAPTER IV.

IT is not the least of the peculiarities connected with Shelley's singular story, that while so much that was not only written but published by him remains, and will probably always remain, undiscovered, so many attempts have been made to pass off forged and supposititious documents as his. The most celebrated example of this ingenious mode of trading on the growing celebrity of the poet is the well-known collection of so-called *Letters of Percy Bysshe Shelley*, published in 1852, and edited, it is to be presumed much to his own subsequent chagrin, by Mr. Robert Browning. This publication, it is scarcely necessary to say, was immediately withdrawn from circulation, and has now become scarce. That some of the letters are forgeries there can be no question, but others, it is almost certain, are genuine. Indeed, it is not easy to see how the counterfeits could have been manufactured without the forgers having some authentic originals to imitate. All the circumstances of the case point to the first letter of the collection as being a genuine document. If so, it is the earliest piece of political writing which we have from the pen of Shelley.

Shelley, into whose rooms, if we are to believe Mr. Hogg, "a newspaper never found its way the whole period of his residence at Oxford," thus addresses the editor of a London newspaper from Oxford :—

" To the Editor of The Statesman, *London.*

" University College, Oxford, Feb. 22, 1811.

" Sir,—The present age has been distinguished from every former period of English history by the number of those writers who have suffered the penalties of the law for the freedom and the spirit with which they descanted on the morals of the age, and chastised the vices or ridiculed the follies of individuals of every rank of life, and among every description of society. In former periods of British civilization, as during the flourishing ages of Greece and Rome, the oratorical censor and the satirical poet were regarded as exercising only that just pre-eminence to which superior genius and an intimate knowledge of life and human nature were conceived to entitle them. The *Mac Flecknoe* of Dryden, the *Dunciad* and the satirical imitations of Pope, remained secure from molestation by the Attorney-General; the literary castigators of a Bolingbroke and a Wharton enjoyed the triumph of truth and justice unawed by *ex-officios ;* and Addison could describe a coward and a liar without being called to account for his inuendos by the interference of the judicial servants of the King.

" But times are altered, and ·a man may now be sent to prison for a couple of years, and ruined perhaps for life, because he ' calls a spade a spade,' and tells a public individual the very truths that are obvious to the most partial of his friends.*

---

* This passage proves almost conclusively that the person addressed as " Editor of *The Statesman"* must have been Mr. Finnerty. The " public individual" of whom he published those " obvious truths" that were pronounced a libel by Lord Ellenborough was Lord Castlereagh. The former editor of *The Statesman,* Mr. Lovell, was suffering imprisonment for a different offence.

" As I am not in the number of those determined censors to whom Newgate is an elysium, and whom the very idea of being persecuted by the Attorney-General exhilarates more effectually than all the treasures of the Castalian fountain; yet as I love to speculate on the virtues and the vices of the world, it has been the object of my anxious study to discover some honest and easy means of speaking the whole truth, without incurring the vengeance of Government. *The ultimate intention of my aim is to induce a meeting of such enlightened, unprejudiced members of the community, whose independent principles expose them to evils which might thus become alleviated; and to form a methodical society which should be organized so as to resist the coalition of the enemies of liberty, which at present renders any expression of opinion on matters of policy dangerous to individuals.*

" *Although perfectly unacquainted with you privately, I address you as a common friend to liberty, thinking that, in cases of this urgency and importance, etiquette ought not to stand in the way of usefulness.* With the hope of securing your co-operation,

" I remain, Sir,

" Your most obedient servant,

" PERCY BYSSHE SHELLEY."

This letter, whatever its claim to authenticity may be, is dated February 22nd, 1811. Six days later— that is, on the 2nd of March in the same year— Shelley addressed, for the first time, another news-paper editor then personally unknown to him, but who became a few years later one of his most valued and intimate friends—Leigh Hunt.

Whatever question may be raised as to the

F

genuineness of the letter " to the Editor of *The Statesman,*" there can be none as to that which Shelley addressed " to the Editor of *The Examiner.*" The original autograph is still probably in existence, having been in the possession of Mr. George Henry Lewes in 1841, who published it for the first time in his article on Percy Bysshe Shelley in the *North British Review* of that year. There is, however, some difficulty about it. In the first place, the super-scription of the letter is not given, and we are therefore in doubt whether it was addressed "to the Editor of *The Examiner*" or "to Leigh Hunt "by name. In the copy of this letter which Mr. Hogg very re-luctantly published in the second volume of his *Life of Shelley,* and which he was not aware had been already in print for seventeen years, the words " to Leigh Hunt " are no doubt added ; but this was merely done for his information by Mrs. Shelley, as will be plain from his own account of the matter :—

"A strange epistle," says Mr. Hogg, " of which a copy in Mrs. Shelley's writing has lately been placed in my hands, may be conveniently introduced and noticed in this place as being connected with the subject, *although it was written two years before,* during our residence at Oxford."—*Life,* vol. ii. pp. 187, 188.

This is truly a wonderful specimen of Mr. Hogg's " convenient " mode of manipulating materials en-trusted to him when he finds they are directly contra-dictory to some passionate or petulant dictum pro-pounded by himself in some other portion of his confused and chaotic biography. One would think that a letter written by Shelley when at Oxford might be more " conveniently introduced and noticed" when describing his residence there in 1811, than forcibly

wrenched out of its proper place and given in his correspondence from Tanyralt in 1812. But this would not
suit the plan of Mr. Hogg. Having committed himself
in his original essays published in the *New Monthly
Magazine* to the absurd declaration that " a newspaper
never found its way to his rooms the whole period of his
residence at Oxford," it would not do in the reprinting of those papers to put side by side with that statement a document which completely established its
inaccuracy, if not its absolute untruth. He therefore
relegates the tell-tale letter of March 2nd, 1811, to the
safe limbo of his second volume, by which time ordinary
readers had quite forgotten the fable of the first.

The disconcerted biographer had, however, to publish
the letter somewhere, and he does so at length, but
with a very bad grace. A better biographer than Mr.
Hogg, but one who has unfortunately adopted too
many of the loose and unfounded statements of that
gentleman, speaks of the two volumes of the *Life of
Shelley* as " Mr. Hogg's irresistibly amusing book."
If it be amusing, it is certainly at the expense of Mr.
Hogg himself, and not at that of some of his characters
(including his hero), whom he attempts to hold up to
ridicule. Thus it is, that when he discovers Shelley
had done certain acts and written certain letters about
which he had not thought it necessary to consult his
" guide, philosopher, and friend," Mr. Thomas Jefferson Hogg, those acts and those letters are at once
condemned as the *ne plus ultra* of folly, of which in
his after-life Shelley was heartily ashamed. Had Mr.
Hogg lived to find out that the divine poet, his incomparable friend, not only ventured to send letters without his knowledge, but absolutely had the audacity to
write and publish poems and pamphlets without the

" imprimatur " of Mr. J. F. H., what would have
been his surprise ! how " amusing " the description of
Shelley's subsequent shame !   Unhappily, however,
we have not the third and fourth volumes of the
" irresistibly amusing book," and must be content
with the first and second.   The present sample could
scarcely be exceeded.   " The truth is," says Mr. Hogg,
making a clean breast of it, " my poor friend knew
well that it was quite wrong " (that is, to have written
a generous letter to Leigh Hunt), " *because he never
communicated his intentions to myself*, or to any of his
friends ; *he never told me* what he had done, being unquestionably ashamed of his precipitancy ; he never
showed me the letter or the answer to it, if he ever
received one."—*Life*, vol. ii. p. 190.

Before giving this letter, which it is necessary to print
for the illustration of this part of my subject, one or
two other instances of these overt acts of high treason
against the sovereign rights of Mr. Jefferson Hogg
may be mentioned.   In 1812, as will fully be detailed
hereafter, Shelley visited Dublin on a political crusade,
without the necessary forms of obtaining permission
from his despotic master.   This was evidently a pira-
tical proceeding, which, though unintelligible, could
not be silently passed over.   With a sort of mild
severity, but still using the stereotyped phrases, he
says :—" He did not communicate his intentions to
me at the time.   I never heard of his exploits in
Dublin until after their termination, and but little did
I learn at any period from himself.   He seldom spoke
of them.   If he ever referred to the subject at all, it
was briefly : and in truth he appeared to be heartily
ashamed of the whole proceeding " (ii. p. 75).   When
we come to treat of this period, the last statement

will be found to be contradicted by Shelley's own reflections on the subject, as given in an unpublished letter. But when at Dublin Shelley published two elaborate pamphlets in furtherance of his political scheme. On this additional proof of the young reformer's want of confidence in his constitutional adviser, the elderly Tory gentleman of 1858 thus descants :—

" Bysshe invariably sent me a copy of all his other works, whether long or short, in verse or in prose, as soon as they were published, or, more commonly, as soon as they were printed; but he never gave me, either at the time of their appearance or subsequently, his two Irish pamphlets. He never named them to me, and I saw them for the first time a few months ago " (ii. p. 76).

It will be found, quite apart from the private grounds of complete separation between Shelley and his college acquaintance about this period, that there were other publications of the poet besides the Irish pamphlets which were not sent to Mr. Hogg, probably because the writer knew they could meet with little sympathy from one the depth and shallowness of whose prejudices, both personal and political, the young enthusiast had by that time pretty well gauged.

Shelley's first letter to Leigh Hunt, as Editor of *The Examiner*, is as follows :—

" University College, Oxford, March 2nd, 1811.

" Sir,—Permit me, although a stranger, to offer my sincerest congratulations on the occasion of that triumph so highly to be prized by men of liberality ; permit me also to submit to your consideration, as one of the most fearless enlighteners of the public mind at the present time, a scheme of mutual safety and mutual indemnification for men of public spirit and principle, which, if carried into effect, would evidently be productive of incalculable advantages. Of the scheme, the following is an address to the public, the proposal for a meeting, and it shall be modified according to your judgment, if you will do me the honour to consider the point.

" *The ultimate intention of my aims is to induce a meeting of such enlightened and unprejudiced members of the community, whose independent principles expose them to evils which might thus become alleviated ; and to form a methodical society which should be organized so as to resist the coalition of the enemies of liberty, which at present renders any expression of opinion on matters of policy dangerous to individuals.* It has been for want of societies of this nature that corruption has attained the height at which we now behold it ; nor can any of us bear in mind the very great influence which, some years since, was gained by ' Illuminism,' without considering that a society of equal extent might establish national liberty on as firm a basis as that which would have supported the visionary schemes of a completely equalized community.

" *Although perfectly unacquainted with you privately, 1 address you as a common friend to liberty, thinking that, in cases of this urgency and importance, etiquette ought not to stand in the way of usefulness.*

" My father is in Parliament, and on attaining twenty-one I shall, in all probability, fill his vacant seat. On account of the responsibility to which my residence in this University subjects me, I, of course, dare not publicly avow all I think ; but the time will come when I hope that my every endeavour, insufficient as this may be, will be directed to the advancement of liberty.

> " I remain, Sir,
> " Your most obedient servant,

" To Leigh Hunt."   " P. B. Shelley.

The general resemblance of these two letters—one to the Editor of *The Statesman*, and the other to the Editor of *The Examiner*—is at once apparent, but it has not previously been pointed out that two important passages in each are identical. These, for the sake of comparison, I have printed in italics. It will be remembered that the circumstance which first created a suspicion of the genuineness of the letters published in 1852 under the superintendence of Mr. Browning, was the introduction into a letter purporting to have been written to Godwin in 1819 of a passage published long subsequently in *The Quarterly Review* by Sir Francis Palgrave. The passage in *The Quarterly* lingered in the memory of Mr. Palgrave, the son of the writer, but escaped the notice of Mr. Browning, although the subject of the paper in which it is found, " The Fine Arts in Florence," might reasonably have attracted the attention of Mr. Browning, who resided so long in that city. The forgetfulness of one so deeply read in Shelleyan literature is more surprising, as he must have been long familiar with the letter to Leigh Hunt, originally published by Mr. Lewes in 1841. This identity should, of course, have been pointed out, but in the opinion of the present writer it by no means establishes the fact that the letter to the Editor of *The Statesman* is a forgery. The object which Shelley had in view was the same, but the position of the two editors at the time was different. The

Government had succeeded in its prosecution of *The
Statesman*, but was defeated in that of *The Examiner*.
While condoling with the Editor of the former on his
imprisonment, and congratulating the latter on his
triumph, Shelley proposes to each the formation of
an Association which, among other things, would place
in greater security the freedom of the press. We have
here the outline of those " Proposals," which he published a year later at Dublin in the second of his
Irish pamphlets.   It is not at all improbable that on
the general subject of his letters, which were intended
rather as a circular to the Liberal papers than a special
communication to any, he would have repeated the
exact phrases which seemed best to express his ideas.
It does not appear that he received any reply to either
of the letters.   I shall have presently to inquire who
in all probability was the person whom Shelley may
have addressed as Editor of *The Statesman*.   The
account which Leigh Hunt gives of the letter addressed
to himself is so confused as to raise the presumption
that he did not receive it until some years later, when
Shelley personally sought his acquaintance, if indeed it
ever reached his hands at all.   He never published the
letter himself.   In 1841 it is found in the possession
of a stranger, who first prints it.   Mr. Hogg, in 1858,
not knowing that it had been published before, prints
it from a MS. copy in the handwriting of Mrs. Shelley,
who probably took it from the printed version of Mr.
Lewes, and finally it is given—most likely from the
same source—by Mr. Thornton Hunt, in the correspondence of his father, with no further explanation
than this, that " among the letters of this period I
find the first from Shelley."   Leigh Hunt, in his
Autobiography, thus describes his earliest recollections

of Shelley :—" He was then a youth not come to his full growth, very gentlemanly, earnestly gazing at every object that interested him, and quoting the Greek dramatists. Not long afterwards he married his first wife, and he subsequently wrote to me while I was in prison, as I have before mentioned."—Leigh Hunt's *Autobiography*, edited by his eldest son. London, 1860, p. 255.

This is, of course, entirely wrong. The letter " before mentioned" was written in 1811, two years before Leigh Hunt was in prison. There is no evidence to show that Shelley was personally known to Leigh Hunt until long after his marriage with his first wife ; and Thornton Hunt expressly mentions that among the literary and political visitors to his father when imprisoned in 1813 and 1814, he has no recollection of Shelley. Mr. Thornton Hunt supplies the omission of his father, and tells us how, but not *when*, Leigh Hunt and Percy Bysshe Shelley became acquainted. Speaking of Mr. Hunter, the bookseller in St. Paul's Churchyard—who it would seem was the second husband of Mrs. Kent, the mother of Marian Kent, Hunt's wife—he says : " It was indeed Mr. Rowland Hunter who first brought Leigh Hunt and his most valued friend personally together. Shelley had brought a manuscript poem which proved by no means suited to the publishing house in St. Paul's Churchyard ; but Mr. Hunter sent the young reformer to seek the counsel of Leigh Hunt" (p. 255). The poem here referred to may have been *Queen Mab*, which Shelley privately printed in 1813 (though Hunt could scarcely have forgotten a circumstance connecting that famous poem with his first personal acquaintance with its author) ; but the anecdote cannot by any possibility refer to 1811.

We return now to the question, who was the Editor of *The Statesman* newspaper, to whom Shelley is alleged to have written on the 22nd of February, 1811 ; and what were the circumstances that provoked the letter we have transcribed ?

The Statesman newspaper was the first political speculation of Leigh Hunt and his elder brother John.' In a letter to his future wife, Marian Kent, dated Gainsborough, Sunday, February 23rd, 1806, Leigh Hunt says : " My brother John sent me a letter last night, begging that I would come to town as soon as possible, as the first number of *The Statesman* will be published on the 26th." .... " The Earl of Moira has taken the paper under his immediate patronage, and it will no doubt have a large circulation in the Ministerial circles" (*Correspondence*, vol. i. p. 17). " His brother John," says Thornton Hunt, " with whom he resided for a time, was a printer, and they had already endeavoured to unite their forces. John had sought to establish the paper already mentioned, *The Statesman*" .... " but it was relinquished apparently through some want of perseverance in the capitalists. Early in 1808 the brothers set up *The Examiner*" (*Ibid.* vol. i. p. 42).

In the British Museum there is, unfortunately, no copy of *The Statesman*. That noble library, which with all its shortcomings is one of the finest in the world, contains but a *single number* of a paper which, if for nothing else, would be interesting from having been established by Leigh Hunt, and contributed to by Shelley. It is also memorable from the sufferings of at least one of its proprietors. Shelley's letter to the Editor, as given in Mr. Browning's suppressed volume, naturally awakened in me the desire to know

if in the paper itself there was any acknowledgment
of its receipt. Unfortunately, but *one number*, as I
have said, of *The Statesman*, and that of a date subsequent to the period we are investigating, is preserved
in the British Museum. A few facts connected with
it may, however, be given from other sources.

The Statesman was established, as we have seen, in
1806, by Leigh Hunt and his brother John. It remained in their hands until 1808, when *The Examiner*
was started. In September, 1810, it was found, to his
cost, to be the property of one Daniel Lovell. The
character of the paper and the cause of its misfortunes were very succinctly stated by Lord Folkestone
in a speech delivered by him in the House of Commons on the 28th of March, 1811. "*The Statesman*,"
said he, "is a paper which has attracted notice by its
opposition to Ministers" (Cobbett's *Political Register*, April 3rd, 1811, p. 818). An excuse was easily
found to set the machinery of the law against it, the
Editor having copied into his own journal two articles
which had appeared in contemporary newspapers.
One of these was from *The Day*,* which severely com-
mented on the conduct of the military in Piccadilly
on the 7th of April, 1810, at the arrest of Sir Francis
Burdett. No prosecution was instituted against the

---

* *The Day*, according to the late Master of the Rolls in
Ireland, Mr. Walsh, was established by James Farrell (the associate of Robert Emmett, but subsequently an eminent merchant in
London), Irish Johnson, Quin, and *Peter Finnerty*. "Among
other literary speculations," says the late Judge, "they established
a newspaper called *The Day*, which did not succeed. It was
proposed to improve its appearance by a new and expensive arrangement and an improved title, which Farrell suggested should
be, 'Sufficient for *The Day* is the evil thereof.' The evil day was
then given up."—*Ireland Sixty Years Ago*, p. 185.

papers in which these articles originally appeared, the whole vengeance of the Government being concentrated on the head of Mr. Lovell. Making no defence except that the articles complained of were copied in the usual way of selection, the Editor allowed judgment to go by default. The excuse assisted him little in a Court presided over by Lord Ellenborough. Mr. Lovell was sentenced to an imprisonment which extended to the incredible length of nearly five years, in consequence of his being unable to procure the necessary bail. In the session of 1815 attention was drawn to his case in Parliament, and he was at length released from his imprisonment, which he had endured from the 29th of November, 1810.

This was a case that even in its inception might surely have aroused all the generous indignation of Shelley, but it will be remembered that on February 22nd, 1811, when the letter to the Editor of *The Statesman* was written, Mr. Lovell had been already three months in prison. It is difficult to understand the sudden interest taken by Shelley in Mr. Lovell, supposing him to be the person addressed as the Editor of *The Statesman*. It is possible, however, that the individual addressed was not Mr. Lovell at all, but a totally different person, who either had been acting as editor since the incarceration of Lovell in the previous November, or who, from having published in *The Statesman*, as well as in *The Morning Chronicle*, the so-called libel on Lord Castlereagh, for which he too suffered a long imprisonment, might have been considered by Shelley as the editor of the former paper. This individual, whose name the present work has been the first to mention in connexion with that of Shelley, as we have briefly stated in our opening chapter, and in a preceding note, was Mr. Peter Finnerty.

The eloquence of Curran, as we have said, has preserved the name of Peter Finnerty from oblivion; but few could imagine that perhaps a more enduring fame has been reserved for it in the poetry of Shelley. Such, however, is the fact, and such is the singular story I have to relate.

The story of Mr. Peter Finnerty has been told and the principles involved in his prosecution discussed by no less skilful a hand than that of Leigh Hunt. The future author of *Rimini* had not yet made the acquaintance of Shelley, but as Editor of *The Examiner* he courageously defended in the person of Mr. Finnerty the conduct of a brother journalist, and upheld a cause then very much imperilled, the liberty of the press. Expecting to be an immediate sharer in Mr. Finnerty's imprisonment, he was not deterred from avowing a complete participation in the opinions for the publication of which that gentleman was then enduring punishment. This thorough knowledge of the case of Peter Finnerty renders it peculiarly strange that Leigh Hunt, of all people, should have been ignorant that his illustrious friend Shelley had sustained as a poet the same man whom he himself had defended as a journalist.

In *The Examiner* for February 17th, 1811, and February 24th, 1811, are two elaborate articles on the prosecution of Peter Finnerty. Both have the usual signature used by Leigh Hunt in his political writings. The first article deals with the principles involved in the case; the second, with the facts. The reader will scarcely consider the latter tedious, giving as it does the history of a man for whose benefit Percy

Bysshe Shelley wrote and published a volume of
verse :—

From *The Examiner*, February 24th, 1811.

" The immediate cause of Mr. Finnerty's present
misfortune is well known to the public. · He had
accompanied the expedition to Walcheren* at the
request of Sir Home Popham, in order to write an
account of it for publication, but was forced to return
home by an order to that effect by Lord Castlereagh,
the then Secretary of the War Department. Finding
himself deeply injured in profit, reputation, and health,
by a proceeding so directly calculated to put him to
loss and expense, to degrade his character, and to prey
upon his mind, he thought on his return of bringing
an action against his lordship, but was dissuaded from
it as of no use ; and therefore he vented his feelings
in a letter to Lord Castlereagh, which was published in
The Morning Chronicle [and *The Statesman*], and in
which he plainly accused the Viscount of an intention
to harass and destroy him,—reminding his lordship at
the same time of the tyrannous and horrible cruelties
practised upon the people of Ireland during the noble
lord's administration in that country. In consequence
of this letter, the ATTORNEY-GENERAL was directed to

---

* The Walcheren Expedition is best remembered at the present
day by the celebrated epigram, which has been published in a
variety of forms. The following is the original version, which I take
from *The Morning Chronicle* of Monday, Feb. 26th, 1810 :—

*Abstract and Brief Chronicle of the Documents and Evidence
concerning the Expedition to the Scheldt.*

LORD CHATHAM, *with his sword undrawn,*
Kept waiting for SIR RICHARD STRACHAN ;
Sir Richard, eager to be at 'em,
Kept waiting too—for whom ?—LORD CHATHAM

file an information for libel against Mr. FINNERTY, and
the result, as everybody knows, has been the imprisonment of that gentleman—a heavy expense in addition
to his past losses, and a prospect of total ruin in his
removal to a distant gaol, far from the scenes and
occupations in which his pen had hitherto enabled him
to procure a subsistence.

" But these later facts disclose little. It is naturally
asked why the Secretary of State, who suffered and
even encouraged other persons to accompany the
expedition, should demand back Mr. FINNERTY alone?
The Ministerialists easily satisfy themselves on the
occasion by saying ' his lordship must have had
excellent reasons ;' and *The Morning Post*, that epitome
of all that is accomplished and interesting, in order
to settle the matter for ever, informed the public that
Mr. FINNERTY was a suspicious person, with a very
treasonable cast of mind. As the Ministers and their
friends, however, have been long discovered not to
abound in ' excellent reasons ' for anything, and as
decent people, who look to facts and events, are
accustomed to believe the reverse of what the said
Post advances, the public waited to hear what Mr.
FINNERTY himself should produce on his trial in explanation ; and they were not surprised at discovering
that a long antipathy, common between my Lord
Castlereagh and his countrymen, had subsisted ever
since 1798 [1797] between his lordship and Mr.
FINNERTY, in consequence of the view which each took
of the other's character—the former regarding his
opponent as a bad subject, the latter considering his
lordship as an execrable Minister. Here then the
parties are at issue : the dispute resolves itself into a
question of political character, and by looking a little

at their past actions—by observing which of the two
has most offended honest people, and, consequently,
which of the two is most desirous of concealing the
wrong he has done—we shall quickly see to which of
the two the general support belongs, and to which the
universal contempt.

"To begin with Mr. FINNERTY, who is the person
first accused.   This gentleman, it must be confessed in
the outset, has one deadly sin in the eye of a number
of persons—he is an Irishman, a native of that country
where to feel for the people about you is to be
accused of bloodthirstiness, and to differ with the
propriety of cheating them is to show that you are
not fit to be trusted.   What will at once determine
the persons aforesaid to conclude him guilty beyond
question is, that he long ago expressed those feelings
warmly, and has been in the habit of so doing whenever an opportunity offered.   It was in this way, like
the rest of his countrymen, that he acquired the particular notice of LORD CASTLEREAGH. In 1798 [1797],
Mr. FINNERTY, at that time twenty years of age, was
following his business as a printer in Dublin, where he
was concerned in a paper called *The Press*.   This
and another print called *The Northern Star* were the
only newspapers, it seems, which ventured to notice
the house-burnings, the scourgings, the pickettings,
the half-hangings, and other dreadful inflictions
then practised against suspected people—atrocities
which, in proportion to their iniquity, it was the
natural wish of the perpetrators to keep from the
knowledge of the people of England.   The destruction
of the latter paper was effected, and *The Press* alone
remained to repeat the groans of the country, and to
waft them over to the ear of this nation; but not

long. If to speak the truth is accounted a punishable offence even in England, where it may be spoken without shaking everybody's conscience, what must it be accounted in Ireland, where every scourge was reeking, and every dungeon echoed, with the crimes of the rulers? Mr. FINNERTY was soon convicted of libel, and the customary miscreants were not wanting to bring forward an accusation of treasonable connexion. Another informer, whom the fellow known by the appellation of Major Sirr (Town Major) had been encouraging to make the same charge, congratulated himself, as he afterwards declared in print, on being 'relieved from the necessity of adding another to the list of innocent men imprisoned through his means.'

" Mr. FINNERTY, after suffering a public punishment which is inflicted on the lowest and vilest of our species—the pillory—was committed to gaol, where he had been but a short time when the superintendent magistrate of Dublin, with a summary mode of proceeding perfectly astounding to all of us who are accustomed to regard our property as secure, took a party of soldiers to *The Press* office, and 'destroyed,' says the affidavit, 'not only the papers ready for publication, but the types and other printing materials, amounting in value to about 500*l.*' This man was a creature of Lord Castlereagh, who had been understood for some time to hold the Secretaryship under the Lord Lieutenant as *locum tenens* for Mr. Pelham, from which circumstance and his predominant influence in affairs the ostensible Administration was usually called Lord Castlereagh's Government. Be that as it may, his lordship openly succeeded to office during Mr. Finnerty's imprisonment; and the latter, who was

G

confined in a gaol-room sixteen feet by nine, with fourteen other persons, some of them convicted of capital
offences, and who was otherwise subjected to those
attendant circumstances of degradation and disgust
which render imprisonment trebly painful to decent
minds, wrote twice to his lordship on the subject,
stating the sickness and pain of mind which he suffered
in consequence of such treatment; but no notice was
taken of the applications.   Upon his liberation, finding
that he was in no way of procuring a subsistence, Mr.
FINNERTY waited upon the noble lord to request a
passport for leaving the country, but this too he was
refused, not without harshness and insult; and at last
he found himself under the necessity of escaping to
England in the disguise of a sailor.   Here, where
printing-presses are not to be cut up by a magistrate,
and where fifteen people are not confined at a time
in a room sixteen feet by nine, Mr. FINNERTY concluded
himself safe from persecution; and for a time past his
pen had enabled him to live comfortably in the metropolis; but he formed a strange estimate of the mag-
nanimity or conscious virtue of his enemies, if he
thought that the decided part which he continued to
manifest against their proceedings would induce them
to be regardless of his.   To write warmly in newspapers, to speak warmly at public meetings, and to
prepare the statements of aggrieved officers* for the
public eye. were so many stimulants that kept alive
their memory and their dislike; and the first time Mr.
FINNERTY subjected himself to the arm of power, he
felt it in all its weight.   In addition to the vexation

---

* The "aggrieved officer" here alluded to by Leigh Hunt, was
the gallant Sir Home Popham, afterwards Admiral.   The " state-

of being obliged to return from Walcheren, he had the
mortification of seeing his character become an object
of the lowest suspicion, in consequence of the suddenness and apparent alarm of the order for that purpose ;
and people whose subserviency or whose temper inclines
them to believe anything on these occasions, were not
slow, as usual, to give the worst colour to what they
thought.   Some of them, however, went beyond their
policy in so doing.   A certain nobleman connected with
Lord Castlereagh was heard to say at a tavern in Middle-
hurst, in the presence of several officers, ' I wish some
one would shoot that fellow out of the way at once.'
Without pushing this speech to its extremity, and in-
sisting, as an Attorney-General might insist, that the
said nobleman being a malicious and murderous person, and manifestly intending, conspiring, and devising
the death of the said PETER FINNERTY, did hope to
stir up some person or persons to take a loaded musket and discharge said musket in the face of said
Peter—it may be fairly asserted that such an ebullition
of impatience argued a malicious feeling against him,
and showed that the person who uttered it was prepared
to chagrin and annoy him in order to gratify those
who wished his injury.   And what could have dictated
the order for his return but his personal obnoxious-
ness to men in office ?   So confident were those who
invited him to Walcheren of the harmlessness of their
object in so doing, that they even proposed to him to

---

ment" of his case prepared by Mr. Finnerty will probably be found
in the " Full and Correct Report of the Trial of Sir Home Popham,"
&c. London: 1807. "And may be had of the different booksellers in the seaport towns."   It is likely that Mr. Finnerty was
also the Editor of this volume, which contains an elaborate preface
extending to xxxii pages.

inform the commander of the expedition, beforehand, of his intention to write a mere military account of it for the public—a proposition which he very properly rejected as humiliating and servile. What then could it be? His friend Sir Home Popham was in the confidence of the Ministers ;* they would not willingly let us suppose that they were conscious of defects in the military system not altogether fitted for the inspection of a shrewd observer; and if the expedition terminated in deadly disgrace, it is hardly to be supposed that they anticipated such determination. It is,

---

* The preceding note has shown the connexion between Mr. Finnerty and Sir Home Popham. The treatment the former received is the more remarkable from the high estimation in which the gallant Admiral was held by many members of the government. It is singular that the letter, about to be quoted, was written by Sir R. Strachan, the most intimate friend of Sir Home Popham and the godfather of one of his sons. Even in the second generation a grandson of Sir Home Popham has " Strachan" prefixed to a name of great historic interest, connected both with Ireland and England in the reign of Elizabeth. The following is the letter :—

" His Majesty's Ship *Venerable*, Downs, July 26, 1809.

" MEM.—It is my directions that the captains and commanders of his Majesty's ships and vessels under my command do report whether there is a person or gentleman of the name of Peter Finnerty on board any of his Majesty's ships, and in what capacity, and if he is, to send him here. It is my directions that the agents of transports make inquiry, and report the same.

" (Signed)   R. STRACHAN.
" To the respective captains, &c. &c."

Case of Peter Finnerty.   London : 1811, p. 7.

If a letter of this description had been addressed during the Crimean war " to the respective captains" before Sebastopol, referring to a " person or gentleman" named William Russell, we know what would have been the result. The injury to Mr.

on the contrary, certain that they anticipated a signal triumph; that they expected the Dutch, on being put to fire and sword, to fall affectionately into their arms, and that my LORD CHATHAM intended to cover himself with glory with as much ease and leisurely gaping as he would put on his night-cap. But, says *The Post*, Mr. FINNERTY had been suspected in Ireland of treasonable connexion. Then, says common sense, why was not the business investigated, when he himself repeatedly requested an investigation of this very LORD CASTLEREAGH in consequence of the language held by his lordship against him? But no; the truth is that he had annoyed the Irish Government; in other words, he had been a libeller—a character which, when regarded with reference to the definition lately given of libel, and to the times and the *country* in which he wrote, the first impulse of honest men is, I verily believe, to look upon with respect. Had he written in liquor of a different colour from ink—had he practised the scourge against which he exclaimed— his usage might have been very different; for the public will not easily forget that the same Govern ment which recalled from an expedition a man who had proved himself the foe of cruelty and oppression

---

Finnerty was really too serious to admit of jocularity, yet the following squib or travesty of the letter which I have seen somewhere was absolutely written :—

"SIR HOME POPHAM AND MR. FINNERTY.

Sir R. Strachan to the Respective Captains.

Should Peter Finnerty be found
On board the Fleet to Walcheren bound,
   You're ordered, sir, to stop him—
Too dangerous to be let to roam;
Arrest the rogue, and *pop him home*,
   In spite of Sir Home Popham !"

sent out with an expedition, in a situation of emolu-
ment and honour, a man who had been convicted upon
trial of *both;* no less a man—no less a *man,* did I
say ? no less a monster—than Governor Picton. The
reader ought to remember that in consequence of the
anxieties which Mr. FINNERTY underwent on this
occasion, he was seized with a severe illness which
affected his mind ; he ought to be told, also, that when
the defendant applied to the prosecutor's attorney to
be allowed a postponement of the trial on account of
the absence and distance of several persons whose
evidence he thought necessary on the occasion, he received a peremptory refusal ; and, in fine, that no
littleness and pertinacity of annoyance might be wanting to the last stage of the business, he ought to be
informed that when another dangerous illness seized
Mr. FINNERTY, and the trial was compelled to be postponed, a person who is understood to be a confidential
friend of Lord Castlereagh called upon the defendant's
attorney, and impatient, it should seem, at the delay,
loaded the sick man with opprobrium.

" Of the noble lord, who has the honour of being
better known than his antagonist, the reader may not
desire to hear much further. But it is right that he
should call to mind what Mr. FINNERTY wished to
produce against his lordship in evidence *of the truth ;*
for let some judges contradict *others* as much as they
please in defining libel, no generous and just people
will ever endure to confound truth with falsehood
in any way, much less in determining between the
merits of two parties, one of whom is anxious to *prove,*
and the other to punish only. With his lordship's
private character, as far as it is distinguished, or can
be, from his public one, we have nothing to do. I

know that people differ with respect to the indissolubility
of the two ; and whatever I may think myself on the
matter, as far at least as regards principle, I cannot
but remember that Sir Robert Walpole was an affectionate husband, and that King Charles I. was as good
a master to his household as he was a bad one to his
country. Considering, therefore, the character of his
lordship in a light altogether public, it is impossible
to help a feeling of the ludicrous in hearing him complain of an intention to bring it into contempt—
' public hatred and contempt' is the phrase ; probably
the indictment would have been more correct had it
said ' hatred in Ireland,' and ' contempt in England.'*
What makes the thing still more singular is, that he
should think such prosecutions as these a likely mode
of diminishing either. To look at England alone—
has his lordship forgotten two simple facts that are
quite sufficient for all reasonable detestation of his public
conduct :—1st, his attempt to barter and trick away
a seat in the House of Commons, in flagrant violation

---

* In *The Morning Chronicle*, February 11th, 1811, is the following epigram :—

TO LORD CASTLEREAGH.

*On some expressions respecting him in Mr. Whitbread's Speech,
as reported in* The Chronicle *of 26th ult.*

" Quid immoventes hospites vexas, canis,
  Ignarus adversum lupus ?"—HORACE.

Wherefore, dread peer, thy heaviest vengeance shed
On luckless FINNERTY's offending head ?
Or at St. Stephen's, in sarcastic tone,
Why vent thy anger on Burdett alone ?—
A nobler, worthier foe is now in view,
For WHITBREAD e'en proclaims thee *cruel* too ;
He calls in doubtful phrase, yet half unwilling,
Thy candour *merciless*, thy very kindness *killing*.

of his oaths and public faith ; and 2nd, his concern
in planning and prosecuting the infamous expedition
above mentioned—an expedition which wanted no extreme of negligence, folly, and misfortune to render it
useless to our friends, ridiculous to our enemies, and
agonizing to ourselves ?   Yet these are nothing to the
offences of which he is accused in Ireland.   Mr.
FINNERTY would have produced in court, had he been
suffered, above fifty affidavits charging his lordship
with the knowledge and sanction of the tortures
notoriously inflicted upon Irishmen.   One of them,
as the public have seen, stated that in the year 1798,
floggings, half-hangings, &c., were practised in Dublin,
close to the Castle gate, where the Secretary of State's
office was, and that Lord Castlereagh must have heard
the cries ; another, that in the same year a Mr.
Dixon saw three persons whipped and tortured without
a trial ; a third, from a Mr. Hughes, that he was seen
by Lord Castlereagh after suffering the torture which
had rendered his back raw and his shirt a mass of
gore ; and a fourth, that under his lordship's government a father and son had been tortured side by side.
Had these four affidavits been allowed a hearing, there
would still have remained above six-and-forty ; so that
we have no alternative but to believe either that LORD
CASTLEREAGH was the wicked Minister he is described
to have been, or that upwards of fifty persons have
voluntarily come forward to perjure themselves in a
court of justice, and subject themselves to the most
degrading penalties for the mere sake of obliging Mr.
FINNERTY.   It is true, we are ignorant of the character
of these persons, but then we are not ignorant of my
Lord Castlereagh's.   If he could prove them guilty of
perjury, why, as Mr. FINNERTY asked, did he not come

forward and do so, instead of choosing a mode of trial which stopped the mouth of proof? ' If he had proceeded against me by information,' said Mr. FINNERTY, ' he might have shown my statement was false; if he had proceeded by action, I might have sworn it was true; but no: he chooses to proceed criminally, where neither can take place, and this he calls a vindication of his character.' In fact, setting aside Mr. FINNERTY's case altogether, and all the affidavits that might rise up against his lordship from Londonderry to Cork, it is quite manifest that till LORD CASTLEREAGH can disprove the fact of his having undertaken to market for a seat in Parliament, he has no particular character to lose, and it is as ridiculous for him to bluster on the subject as it would be for a wooden leg to complain of a pain. He may have something he chooses to call a character, and may truly be afraid of having it touched; in like manner, a person with a false nose may affect to sneeze at taking snuff, and will be equally alarmed at the approach of a fist—not for fear that the thing itself should be hurt, but that the disguise should be pulled off.

" Convinced, however, as any humane and independent mind must be of the ill-treatment Mr. FINNERTY has undergone, and of the brightness of contrast with which he comes from the side of LORD CASTLEREAGH, it does not appear that in his latter appearance in court he had to complain of the interruption from the Bench. There seemed to be two distinct features in his case—the one general, arising from the ground upon which his letter was declared libel; the other relative, arising from contingencies which, in fact, he created against himself. The former, which declares that truth

is libel, and even aggravated libel, meets with the
unqualified and hearty indignation of all Englishmen
who value freedom of speech and of person; the latter,
while it excites their regret, does not allow them
wholly to exculpate Mr. FINNERTY when *rigidly* judged.
I allude to the hope under which he was induced, in
the first instance, to let judgment go by default,
thereby acknowledging in word, if not in deed, that he
had committed an offence worthy of punishment.   I
know, as he afterwards declared, that such was not his
real opinion ; and I believe that he thought he was justified in availing himself of what he imagined would diminish the punishment, but on both these very accounts
the proceeding was unworthy of him.   He felt that he
had spoken the truth, and he should have felt also
that it could do no honour and no *good* to that truth
to submit even to the smallest approaches towards a
double dealing, fit only for his and truth's opposers.
There are times, places, and classes of people in which
those approaches are considered as nothing, particularly
if the end of them, as they say, is good and patriotic ;
but there are other persons equally patriotic on this
subject who consider them as worse than useless, and are
inclined on that account, and on no other, either of
pride or affectation, to hold themselves aloof from those
who practise them.   Mr. FINNERTY has tried both ;
and his spirit, in rising above the little clogs and
puddles of expediency, and proving itself equal to the
most elevated sentiments, has gratified beyond measure
the truest friend to reform.

> ' Scarce vanish'd out of sight,
> He buoys up instant and returns to light.'

The original cause for which this gentleman has exposed himself to imprisonment and poverty must ever

awaken but one feeling in the minds of freemen ; and
it rejoices us to see that the spirit he has evinced has
awakened as much sympathy in Englishmen as his
long suffering has endeared him to the Irish, and his
display of talent has raised him in the estimation of
everybody."

On Thursday, February 7th, 1811, Mr. Finnerty was
brought up for judgment. He was sentenced to be
imprisoned in the gaol of Lincoln for eighteen months,
and at the expiration of that period to give security
for his good behaviour for five years, himself in 500*l.*,
and two sureties in 250*l.* each.

To conclude this portion of Mr. Finnerty's history,
the following additional facts, partly derived from
State Papers in the Record Office, may be given. The
arrival of Mr. Finnerty at Lincoln Gaol to commence
the long period of his imprisonment, is described at
considerable length in *The Examiner* of March 3rd,
1811, the article being taken from the *Stamford News*.
One passage may be quoted.

" We are happy to say that Mr. Finnerty has met
with good friends here ; some of the most wealthy and
most respectable gentry have intimated that he may command any alleviation of his troubles they can furnish."

There is a curious letter in the State Paper Office
which has not been printed, confirmatory of the foregoing allusion to the sympathy felt for Mr. Finnerty
by respectable inhabitants of Lincoln. The letter has
no address, but as the writer signs himself "D. P. M."
which may mean Deputy Post Master, it may have been
forwarded to Mr. Francis Freeling, afterwards Sir
Francis, the Secretary of the Post Office, of whom and to
whom there are numerous letters in the Record Office.

"Domestic, Geo. III., 1812.   No. 239.

"Lincoln, August 19th, 1812.

"Sir,—I am much obliged to you for the Gazettes, and many loyal inhabitants of this place were gratified with a perusal of them; but I am sorry to confess that the disloyal party have very much increased here : Mr. Drakard and Mr. Finnerty are the cause.   The latter I consider to be a dangerous character, and yet, strange to tell, his conduct is admired by many respectable people.

"I am, sir, your obliged servant,

"JOHN DRURY, D.P.M."

If the signature "D. P. M." means Divisional Police Magistrate, the letter must have been addressed to one of the Under-Secretaries of State, Mr. Ryder or Mr. Becket.

Before Mr. Finnerty's removal from King's Bench Prison, London, he had been visited by the Hon. Leicester Stanhope.   This act of courtesy brought down upon that gentleman the abuse of a scurrilous magazine called *The Satirist, or Monthly Meteor*, of which thirteen volumes were published—1808 to 1813. Mr. Stanhope condescended to notice this attack, in which the editor, a person of the name of G. Manners, affected to be indignant that "a son of that universally respected nobleman, Lord Harrington, should become the bearer of a message from Mr. Finnerty." In his letter, the Hon. Leicester Stanhope calls Mr. Finnerty "a high-minded and honourable man."— *Satirist*, vol. ii. pp. 408, 504.

In Lincoln, as we have seen, the same feeling was shown to Mr. Finnerty by persons of position outside the prison; but inside the case was very different.   He

was treated with considerable harshness, put into an
unhealthy room, and deprived of the privilege of
taking exercise in the place usually assigned for
prisoners not convicted of felony. Charges of mis-
conduct were brought against him by the officials of
the gaol, and a very curious investigation took place
before the visiting magistrates, the whole of which is
given in a folio MS. in the Record Office, of considerable length : " Domestic, Geo. III., No. 226."
The matter was also brought before Parliament several
times. Mr. Finnerty succeeded in obtaining a less
rigorous treatment, and the remainder of his imprisonment passed quietly. In the same collection of State
Papers is the original petition to the Prince Regent,
presented by Mr. Finnerty through the hands and by
the advice of Mr.
Whitbread. It
contains the re-
markable signa-
ture of Mr. Fin-
nerty, May 23rd,
1811, of which the above is a tracing. The
petition is substantially the same presented to Parliament about the same period.

Mr. Finnerty's sentence expired on the 7th of
August, 1812, as mentioned in the following extract
from *The Dublin Weekly Messenger*, August 22nd, 1812,
the same journal, it will be recollected, which contains
the singular allusion to Shelley's poem :—

" Our countrymen will hear with pleasure that Mr.
Finnerty has been liberated from confinement, from
the incarceration which for eighteen months he had
suffered in the cause of truth, justice, and his country.
On Friday the 7th instant, a public dinner to celebrate

his liberation was given at Lincoln, to which Mr.
Finnerty was invited.   George Langton, Esq., a patriot
and a magistrate, took the chair."

In *The Morning Chronicle*, August 18th, 1812, there
is a fuller account of this dinner, which took place at
the Reindeer Inn, Lincoln.   " Mr. Finnerty addressed
the meeting at considerable length, and expressed his
gratitude for the kindness and attention with which
he had been favoured."

The Mr. Drakard referred to in the letter of Mr.
Drury in the Record Office, was the proprietor and
editor of *The Stamford News.*   In 1822 he published
a very excellent History of Stamford.   He was
prosecuted in 1811 for printing in *The Stamford News*
an article on military punishment.   Though ably
defended by Brougham, he was sentenced on March
13th, 1811, to precisely the same punishment as Mr.
Finnerty, whose imprisonment he shared.   The trial
is reported in the following rare 4to tract.   " Report
of the Proceedings on an Information filed by His
Majesty's Attorney-General against John Drakard,
Proprietor of *The Stamford News,* for publishing in
that Paper an Article on Military Punishment.   STAM-
FORD: printed and sold by J. Drakard; and sold by
Crosby and Co., Stationers' Court, London."   It may
be interesting to note here that " Crosby and Co.,
Stationers' Court, London," were the publishers of
Shelley's poem which will presently be described, and
which appeared two days before the conviction of Mr.
Drakard.*

---

* In January, 1813, Mr. Drakard started in London *Drakard's Paper. A Weekly Political and Literary Journal.*
In January, 1814, it changed its name to *The Champion,* and
became eventually the property of John Thelwall.

CHAPTER V.

THE sympathy awakened by Mr. Finnerty's spirit and ability, as shown by the article from *The Examiner* quoted in our last chapter, was not confined to Englishmen. It was felt throughout the three kingdoms, and various local bodies were formed in the chief towns of England, Scotland, and Ireland to support the movement commenced by Sir Francis Burdett* at the Crown and Anchor Tavern, London, on the 20th of February, 1811, for the purpose of sustaining Mr. Finnerty in prison.

These manifestations of public feeling do not appear very remarkable in the larger towns, where there is always a considerable amount of political excitement ready at any moment to be aroused. But one would scarcely expect to find that the earliest voice of sympathy and co-operation the London movement to

---

* Sir Francis Burdett came in, of course, for a good deal of abuse in Tory journals for the part he took in this movement. Alluding to this, and to his duel with Mr. Paull, arising out of the Westminster election, the following epigram is to be found in one of the publications of the day :—

EPIGRAM

ON PETER FINNERTY'S SUBSCRIPTION.

Knights of the Post, of old, strove all
By robbing *Peter* to pay *Paul ;*
Sir Francis Burdett nicks it neater—
He pistols *Paul* and pensions *Peter !*
The Satirist, or Monthly Meteor, vol. viii. p. 335.

sustain Mr. Finnerty received, should come from the tranquil city of Oxford and its learned University. The meeting at the Crown and Anchor Tavern, in the Strand, took place on Wednesday, February 20th, 1811. In the next ensuing publication of *The Oxford University and City Herald*, on Saturday, February 23rd, only three days after, appears the following article, to which we would draw the reader's special attention, in connexion with the alleged letter of Shelley to the Editor of *The Statesman*, dated the 22nd of February—*the day preceding.* The tone, and occasionally the language, of these two documents are so similar, particularly when read in the light of a fact that will subsequently be mentioned, that I have no difficulty in believing that Shelley either wrote the article in *The Oxford Herald* himself, or saw it in *proof*, the day before the paper was published—the same day on which he addressed the "Editor of *The Statesman,*" whom he must have believed to be Mr. Finnerty. Here is the article which appeared in *The Oxford University and City Herald*, February 23rd, 1811 :—

" We are happy to find that the case of Mr. Finnerty has made a strong impression on the public mind, and that, in consequence, the frequent informations which have been lately filed by the Attorney-General will become the subject of parliamentary inquiry. Of Mr. Finnerty in his private capacity we know nothing ;* but as Englishmen, and living under what has always been esteemed and what we hope

---

* The language of Shelley's letters "to the Editor of *The Statesman*" and "The Editor of *The Examiner*" is almost the same :—" Although perfectly unacquainted with you privately, I address you as a common friend to *liberty*," &c.

will always remain a free constitution, we are bound
to respect the LIBERTY OF THE PRESS, as far as it involves a free discussion on the merits of public men,
and the probable consequence of public measures; for
these are a public concern, are supported and carried
on by the public purse, and become the fair objects
of public praise or censure; and our readers need not
be informed that a peculiar hardship attends the case
of informations filed *ex-officio*, as a heavy punishment
necessarily precedes the verdict; for the individual
against whom the information is filed may be perfectly
innocent, and, though acquitted, may be previously
ruined by the expenses of a trial to which he is brought
by the will of the Attorney-General, and without the
case being submitted to a grand jury. For these
reasons we have just opened a subscription at THE
HERALD OFFICE in favour of Mr. Finnerty—a measure
which will, without doubt, subject us to the invectives
of sycophants and flatterers, pensioners and expectants;
a tribe of gentry, however, whom we heartily despise,
and will always endeavour to expose."

The Oxford Herald was not slow in making its
arrangements for the collection of the subscription
thus so warmly encouraged. In the same number the
following announcement is conspicuously given :—

" LIBERTY OF THE PRESS.—The friends to the
Liberty of the Press are informed, that a subscription
in behalf of Mr. Finnerty is opened at the office of
The Oxford Herald.

" Subscriptions already received : Proprietors of *The
Oxford Herald, 5l. 5s.;* Mr. Bird, *1l. 1s.;* Mr. Hobbs,
1l. 1s."

In the next number of *The Oxford Herald*, Saturday,

March 2nd, 1811, the same announcement appears, and is followed by the same list of subscribers, with the addition of one name indeed—a name that will, we think, be of some interest to our readers—namely, that of

"MR. P. B. SHELLEY, 1*l.* 1*s.* 0*d.*"

The circumstance that Shelley's name is not given in the first list strengthens the alternative which I have suggested above, that he was not himself the writer of the article on Finnerty's case published on the 23rd of February, but that he saw it in proof when the rest of the paper was set up, and when it was too late to have his name inserted as a subscriber in that week's impression.

There are abundant reasons for believing that Shelley must have been a constant visitor at this time to the printing-office of John Munday, who was, we have little doubt, the proprietor as well as the printer of *The Oxford Herald.* Without attaching too much importance to the fact that one of the poems which I have ventured to suggest as having probably been written by Shelley, appeared in the same paper with the article on Finnerty, there is conclusive proof that between February the 9th and March the 9th, 1811, Shelley, being then at Oxford, was engaged in printing *two* works—one of them of fatal omen to him, the tract entitled *The Necessity of Atheism*; and the other the missing and hitherto unknown poem, the title and story of which I have been the first to discover and to trace.

A strong corroboration of the view I am maintaining, that Shelley had a very early acquaintance with the articles, particularly on this subject of the Liberty of the Press, as they appeared in *The Oxford Herald,* is found in the fact that in the number for March 2nd, 1811, which contains his own name as a subscriber to the Finnerty Fund, there is a leading article on the triumph of *The Examiner* in the special prosecution directed against it. Our readers will remember that it was on this very day, March 2nd, 1811, Shelley wrote his first letter to Leigh Hunt, inspired probably by the following remarks, as he had been the week before by those on Finnerty :—

" The acquittal of the proprietors of *The Examiner,*" says *The Oxford Herald,* " for a libel, on a criminal information filed *ex-officio* by the Attorney-General, gives us extreme pleasure, as we conceive it will prove a salutary check to the mode of proceeding which of late has been so frequently adopted, and which, if persevered in, will reduce the press to a state of tameness and servility, and prevent that open and free discussion which leads to the repeal of obnoxious laws, and the general advantage and comfort of society."

The article does not end here, but the passage quoted is sufficient for our purpose. It will remind the reader as much of the letter to the supposed or real " Editor of *The Statesman,*" of the 22nd of February, 1811, as of that to Leigh Hunt on the 2nd of March.

The story of the publication, or at least the intended publication, of the unfortunate tract, *The Necessity of Atheism*, though perhaps in chronological order it should now be given, may be more conveniently deferred until we treat of the termination of Shelley's academical career at Oxford—a termination rather violently produced by the tract itself.

The name of Peter Finnerty, sentenced on the 7th

of February, 1811, first appears in *The Oxford Herald*
of the 23rd of February. Shelley's subscription to the
fund for his benefit is acknowledged in the number for
March 2nd, 1811; and in the next number, for March 9th,
1811, we find the following remarkable advertisement,
filling a space of about three inches, and printed in
the most conspicuous part of the paper, at the head of
the first column :—

𝔏iterature.

Just published, Price Two Shillings,

A POETICAL ESSAY

ON THE

Existing State of Things.

AND FAMINE AT HER BIDDING WASTED WIDE
THE WRETCHED LAND, TILL IN THE PUBLIC WAY,
PROMISCUOUS WHERE THE DEAD AND DYING LAY,
DOGS FED ON HUMAN BONES IN THE OPEN LIGHT OF DAY.

Curse of Kehama.

BY A

GENTLEMAN of the University of Oxford.

For assisting to maintain in Prison

MR. PETER FINNERTY,

IMPRISONED FOR A LIBEL.

LONDON : SOLD BY B. CROSBY AND CO.,
AND ALL OTHER BOOKSELLERS.
1811.

This poem was written and published by Percy
Bysshe Shelley. In the absence of direct proof, it is
impossible to say with absolute certainty what the
precise character of the poem was. A pretty exact

inference, however, may be drawn from its title, and from an allusion here and there in Shelley's letters which may possibly refer to it. There can be very little doubt that the *Poetical Essay on the Existing State of Things* was a satire dealing with the condition of Ireland, particularly in reference to the miseries of the late rebellion, and the persistent misgovernment of that country. The quotation from Southey points to this. The powerful picture of famine there drawn, and the phrase " the wretched land," were in those days unhappily too applicable to Ireland. The lines are from the sixth part of *The Curse of Kehama*, entitled " The Enchantress," and will be found at page 588, second column of the one-volume edition of Southey's Poems. This quotation puts an end to one of Mr. Hogg's most apocryphal stories. He tells us that nearly a year after this period, when Shelley was living at Keswick, during one of his visits to Greta Hall, the residence of Southey, the elder poet, taking an unfair advantage of his opportunity, locked the door of his study on his young visitor, and mercilessly read him to sleep from the MS. pages of *The Curse oj Kehama*—a poem from which, in its published form, Shelley had printed a quotation twelve months before. The egotistical buffoonery which Mr. Hogg mistook for humour, almost more than its want of reliability, has been the ruin of his book. This farcical tendency of Mr. Hogg's mind seems to have shown itself at a very early period, and, if we may judge by the following character of him, was as little relished by his friends then as by his readers now. Mr. Thornton Hunt, in an article on Shelley in the *Atlantic Monthly* (February, 1863), thus describes the future unsuccessful biographer of the poet :—

" His school-friend Hogg was a gentleman of independent property. Shelley detected the sensitiveness of his nature, and I know that the man has been capable of truly generous conduct. How is it then that he has written such utterly unintelligible stuff, and has descended to such evasions as to insert [qy. invert ?*] initials, lest people should detect amongst Shelley's correspondents a most admirable friend, who happened, it is supposed, to be of plebeian origin ? Mr. Thomas Jefferson Hogg, I surmise, was conscious somewhat early in life that his better qualities were not fully appreciated ; and his love of ease, his wit, his perception of the ludicrous made him take refuge in cynicism until he learned almost to forget the origin of the real meaning of the things he talked about. His account of Shelley is like a figure seen through fantastically distorting panes of glass."

Shelley was at home during the Christmas vacation of 1810. His first letter to Hogg was written there, and is dated " Field Place, December 20th, 1810." He mentions that his father had called upon " S."—that is, Stockdale—in London, and we are prepared for the quarrel that soon after took place between Shelley and the publisher of *St. Irvyne.* Towards the end of the letter is the following curious passage :—" I am composing a *satirical* poem. I shall print it at Oxford, unless I find, on visiting him, that R. [qy.

---

* This must refer to the letters addressed to Mr. Thomas Hookham, of New Bond Street, both by Shelley and Harriet, as given in Hogg's *Life,* vol. ii. pp. 206–211. The initials are not "inserted," but *inverted,* " H. T." being invariably used for " T. H."' But might not this have been done to prevent careless readers from confounding letters to " Thomas Hookham " with those addressed to " Thomas Hogg ?"

Robinson ?] is ripe for printing whatever will sell. In case of that, he is my man."—*Hogg,* vol. i. p. 143.

We have heard, and indeed we know, that " Shelley was quick to conceive, and not less quick to execute ;" but with all this rapidity of conception and facility of · execution it would almost have been impossible for him to have written, printed, and published a poem which from its price must have been at least as large as *Margaret Nicholson,* in *one fortnight.* As I have already pointed out, that was exactly the time that elapsed from the first mention of Mr. Peter Finnerty's name in *The Oxford Herald,* until a poem for his benefit was announced in that paper as "just published." It is plain that Shelley must have had some poem ready, the title of which he had not decided on, when his attention was drawn to this case of injustice, as he conceived it to be, when it occurred to him to connect his work with the charitable movement to sustain Finnerty thus set on foot. The *Poetical Essay on the Existing State of Things* I believe to be the " satirical poem " above referred to. Whether it was submitted to " Mr. R.," of Paternoster Row, or not is uncertain ; but there is no improbability in supposing that it was. The second letter in Mr. Browning's suppressed volume is addressed to " J. H. Graham, Esq.,"* at whose house, 18, Sackville Street, Piccadilly, as we know from Hogg's book (vol. i. pp. 388, 389, 417), Shelley occasionally stopped, and where he directs his friend's letters to himself should be addressed. This letter to Graham, if it be genuine, shows that

---

* Mr. Graham is represented in Mr. Hogg's book as being the "factotum " of Mr. Shelley senior, the poet's father.—*Life,* vol. i. p. 307.

Shelley was in the habit of sending him from Oxford (for the letter is dated there—" University College, February 26th, 1811 ") his poetical pieces according as they were written, perhaps to have them offered for publication to some bookseller. The date admits the possibility that the allusion may have referred to the *Poetical Essay.* Mr. Graham may have suggested that it was too slight for separate publication, to which Shelley replies : " What I sent you last is not enough for a pamphlet, I grant you, but I cannot help it. A subject soon exhausts itself with me. You must get some of your *volume* friends to spin the text for· you."*

Should the " satirical poem " referred to by Shelley in his letter of the 10th December, 1810, have been the *Poetical Essay,* he was right for once in his estimate of what was likely to " sell." In a document authenticated by himself, as we have seen, it is said to have produced the sum of 100*l.* for the object it was published to sustain. This alone is such a phenomenon in the pecuniary results of Shelley's writings during his lifetime, that it intensifies our desire to recover a copy. No doubt it was bought, not for the sake of the verse, but for the sake of the cause. Yet when we are told that the *Epipsychidion* " fell dead from the press—not a copy of it was sold—not a single review noticed it " (*Medwin,* vol. ii. p. 76), and that the *Poetical Essay on the Existing State of Things* produced a profit of 100*l.*, we have only an additional

---

* It is curious that Mr. Hogg makes no allusion to these poems sent up to London for the approval of Mr. Graham. This is an additional corroboration of the fact that Mr. Hogg did not possess the entire confidence of Shelley.

proof of the seemingly capricious fate that so often
befalls poems as well as individuals.

The advertisement of the *Poetical Essay* in *The Oxford Herald* of March 2nd, 1811,though the earliest and
the most important, was not the only one which announced the publication of a work that would now be
read with an amount of interest and curiosity little
anticipated by the author or the public whom he addressed. In point of fact, it happens to have been the
last which I discovered in my researches into this most
curious subject. Before it occurred to me to inquire for
some Oxford paper of the period, and of course before
I had seen *The Oxford Herald*, I had worked my way
into a knowledge of the title of the poem. The
evidence of the fact that Shelley had published
some poem, the name of which is not given, in connexion with the case of Mr. Finnerty, is contained, as
we have seen, in a newspaper, a copy of which Shelley
sent to Godwin from Dublin, the receipt of which is
acknowledged by Godwin in his letter to Shelley,
March 14th, 1812 (*Hogg*, vol. ii. p. 96). Shelley
himself makes no allusion to the *Poetical Essay* in his
letters to Godwin, unless indeed he may have referred
to it in the list of the "*publications* of my early
youth" under the altered title of the "*Essay* on Love,"
"a little poem," which he gave to him in his letter from
"Keswick, January 16th, 1812" (*Hogg*, vol. ii. p. 62).
The word "Essay" gives great probability to this
supposition; but whether this be true or not, I found
the *Poetical Essay on the Existing State of Things*
advertised in *The Morning Chronicle* of March 15th and
March 21st, and in *The Times* of April 10th and
April 11th, 1811. It was thus more than a month
before the world, by which time, it may be presumed,

the whole impression was bought up, as we hear no more about it except the allusion in *The Dublin Weekly Messenger* of Saturday, March 7th, 1812, which states that a poem for the benefit of Mr. Finnerty had been published by Percy Bysshe Shelley, and that the sum of nearly 100*l.* produced by the sale of that poem had been presented to Mr. Finnerty by the author. This article, authenticated by Shelley himself as having been forwarded by him to Godwin, will be given in due course. We wish again to impress the fact on the attention of our readers that Mr. Finnerty was still in prison when this act of liberality on the part of the young poet was publicly announced; that he was in communication with the paper in which it appeared; and that it is utterly impossible such a statement could have passed uncontradicted if it were not true.

Reserving a further consideration of the *Poetical Essay on the Existing State of Things* until we have to speak of Shelley's first visit to Dublin in 1812, we resume our account of his remaining literary efforts while at Oxford.*

---

* The earliest London advertisement of the poem that I have found is in *The Courier*, March 11th, 1811, two days after it was announced in *The Oxford Herald*. The advertisement is repeated in *The Courier*, March 15th, 1811.

CHAPTER VI.

L ITTLE dreaming that Shelley had printed and published a poem after the appearance of the *Posthumous Fragments of Margaret Nicholson*, and before the printing of *The Necessity of Atheism*, Mr. Hogg thus proceeds in his history of the intellectual progress of his friend :—

"The operation of Peg Nicholson was bland and innoxious : the next work that Shelley printed was highly deleterious, and was destined to shed a baneful influence over his future progress" (vol. i. p. 269).

This work was the little tract entitled *The Necessity of Atheism*, for which Shelley was expelled.

Mr. Hogg, whose statement has been adopted by every succeeding writer, has said that this little pamphlet " was never offered for sale," and that " it was not addressed to an ordinary reader, but to the metaphysician alone." That it was " never offered for sale" was certainly not the fault or the intention of the author, as proved by the following advertisement, which is now for the first time given in connexion with Shelley's life. It was this bold and open announcement on the part of the author that the work would be published and sold in the ordinary way, that probably compelled the authorities of Oxford to take notice of a tract, the existence of which they might otherwise not have known. Had it been announced in the London papers that a work entitled *The Necessity of Atheism* was about to be published, even "by a gentleman of the University," it would have provoked little attention at Oxford, whither the waifs and strays of blasphemy, ever floating in the metropolis, seldom found their way. Far different was it when in a journal circulating largely in the University, and calling itself "The Oxford *University* and City Herald," the following portentous announcement appeared :—

Speedily will be published,

To be had of the Booksellers of London and Oxford,

THE

NECESSITY OF ATHEISM.

"Quod clara et perspicua demonstratione caveat pro vero habere, mens omnino nequit humanæ."—*Bacon de Augment. Scient.*

This advertisement appears in *The Oxford University and City Herald* of Saturday, Feb. 9th, 1811. It has hitherto been unknown. Should the authorities of Oxford University require any defence for the manner in which they acted towards the author, this advertisement will, I think, show that it was scarcely possible for them to overlook the carrying out of an intention so audaciously announced.

In January, 1811, this tract had been offered to Mr. John Joseph Stockdale for publication. *St. Irvyne,* Shelley's second prose romance, had just been published by him. Mr. Hogg, as Shelley's friend, had called on Stockdale, and appears to have impressed the publisher very unfavourably. "I really did not credit," writes Mr. Stockdale, "that with, as I thought, a mind so infinitely beneath that of his friend, he could be the master spirit to lead him astray." Some inquiries instituted by Mr. Stockdale, and the fact that Mr.

Hogg was made the medium of submitting to him for publication the manuscript of *The Necessity of Atheism,* removed all doubt from the conscientious mind of the worthy publisher. The author of *Shelley in Pall Mall* tells the story of the quarrel between the young author and Mr. Stockdale, but Mr. Garnett does not give the letter of Mr. Hogg to the latter, which has a double interest : first, in evidently referring to the manuscript of *The Necessity of Atheism ;* and secondly, in alluding to Mr. Peter Finnerty, whose conduct, it would seem, had met with the approval even of the fastidious Mr. Hogg.

Writing from Oxford, Jan. 21st, 1811, he says :—

" The bare mention of the MS. which I entrusted to you was an unparalleled breach of confidence. There have been instances of booksellers who have honourably refused to betray the authors whose works they have published, although actions were brought against them. I believe that one gentleman had honour enough to submit to the pillory rather than disgrace himself by giving up the name of one who had confided in him, however unworthy he might be of such generous treatment."— *Stockdale's Budget,* p. 34.

The gentleman who had honour enough to submit to the pillory, there can be no doubt, was Mr. Finnerty. The circumstance is alluded to in the article already quoted from *The Examiner,* but which was known to Mr. Hogg earlier, probably from the letter of Finnerty himself—the so-called libel—which had been published in *The Statesman* and *The Morning Chronicle* of January 28th, 1810.

The story of the expulsion of Shelley, and also of Mr. Hogg, from Oxford, is too well known to be re-

peated here; but one or two circumstances hitherto
unnoticed may be mentioned in connexion with his
residence at the University, which, though of no great
importance in themselves, may be useful to the future
biographer of Shelley.

In Mr. Hogg's book (vol. i. p. 396) there is a letter
of Shelley's to that gentleman, undated as usual, but
written probably about the end of April, 1811.   In
this letter, referring to his sister Elizabeth, he says:—
" Elizabeth is indeed an unworthy· companion of the
Muses.   I do not rest much on her poetry now.
Miss Philipps betrayed twice the genius; greater
amiability, if to affect the feelings is a proof of the
excess of the latter."   In another letter printed a few
pages earlier (p. 386), though written certainly after
the preceding, as it is dated from Rhayader, Shelley
again mentions the name of Philipps.

" I have at this moment no money, as *Philipps's* and
the other debt have drained me."   The " other debt"
may have been, perhaps, some part payment to Stockdale, as we have a letter of Shelley's from the same
place on August 1st, 1811, promising to settle the
publisher's account as soon as possible.   Mr. Hogg
gives us no information as to who the lady was in
whose poetry Shelley felt so interested, neither does
he explain what " Philipps's debt " could mean.   The
accident of my finding on a book-stall a little volume
entitled " *Poems by Janetta Phillips.* Oxford: Printed
by Collingwood and Co., 1811," may perhaps clear up
the mystery, and will exhibit Shelley in the amiable
light of being an active encourager of a youthful muse.
The little volume possesses a greater interest than this.
It is probably the only· place where the names of
Percy Bysshe Shelley and Harriet Westbrook ever

appeared together in public before their marriage.
The poems are preceded by a long list of subscribers,
chiefly belonging to the various colleges of Oxford.
The particular copy which I picked up belonged to
one of these, " Mr. Coffin, University College," whose
name is written on the cover.   The list is an alphabe-
tical one. Under the letter " S." I had the pleasure of
finding the following entries :—

> " Mr. P. B. Shelley—six copies.
> " Miss Shelley, Field Place, Sussex.
> " Miss Hellen Shelley."

In letter " M." we have " Thomas Medwin, Esq.,
Horsham," and " Mr. Munday, bookseller, Oxford."
Elsewhere we find the names of " Mrs. Grove, Lincoln's Inn Fields—three copies," " C. Grove, Esq.,"
" Mr. Graham, 29, Vine Street, Piccadilly."   But
perhaps the most interesting name in the entire list is
that of " Miss H. Westbrook."   It should be noticed
that to Shelley's name the address " University
College " is not added.   This is usually the case with
those subscribers who were members of the University.
Of this class there are upwards of eighty in the list.
This would imply that the printing of this part of the
volume at least was not completed until after Shelley
had left Oxford.   The obtaining such a numerous list
of subscribers, among whom is the present venerable
Duke of Leinster, who left Oxford in 1811, must have
taken a considerable time.   With the exception of a
" Mr. Philipps," probably a relative of Janetta Philipps,
the author of the poems, who took six copies, no one
subscribed for so many as Shelley.   This circumstance,
taken in connexion with the fact of so many of his
relatives and friends uniting to sustain the work,

raises a strong presumption in my mind that Shelley
had undertaken the responsibility of bringing out the
volume, and that to this the phrase " Philipps's debt"
refers. The Oxford subscribers were probably secured
while Shelley was at the University, and those of his
sisters and Harriet Westbrook during the Christmas
vacation of 1810-11, when he was at home. It is not
at all improbable that Harriet Westbrook's name was
first obtained by Hellen Shelley, who was at school
with her at Clapham, and to this circumstance may be
attributed the first acquaintance of the poet with his
future wife. It may have been in return for this subscription that Shelley, on January 11th, 1811, requested
Stockdale to " send a copy of *St. Irvyne* to Miss
Harriet Westbrook, 10, Chapel Street, Grosvenor
Square," where she was at home with her father for
the Christmas holidays.

Shelley and his friend Mr. Hogg, as is well known,
were expelled on Lady-day, 1811, and left Oxford for
London on the following morning. They took lodgings
at 15, Poland Street, Oxford Street, and remained
together for about three weeks, when Mr. Hogg went
to York, where he entered the chambers of a conveyancer. It is very curious that during the three weeks
they lived together in Poland Street, the *Poetical Essay
on the Existing State of Things* was advertised several
times in the London papers without Mr. Hogg being
let into the secret of the composition and publication
of this poem. Advertisements will be found in *The
Times*, April 10th and April 11th—that is, about the
middle of that period of unrestricted confidence, as
Mr. Hogg would have us believe, in which the friends
lived together in London after their expulsion from
Oxford.

Mr. Timothy Shelley, the father of the poet, had, during the Stockdale affair, expressed an opinion that Mr. Jefferson Hogg was "the original corruptor" of his son's principles; so at least Shelley had informed his friend.   Up to this time there was nothing but eulogy and admiration expressed by Mr. Hogg in his book towards "the divine poet," but now he had a duty to discharge from which he did not shrink.   " I do not believe," says Mr. Hogg, " that Mr. T. Shelley ever let fall the expressions which were imputed to him"—thus charging Shelley with having written a deliberate falsehood.   " It is my duty to speak the truth, the whole truth," says this veracious biographer, " and therefore I cannot but confess that the poor fellow [Shelley! his "incomparable friend," the "divine poet"] had *many underhand ways; these* I found out, sometimes long subsequent to the event" (vol. i. p. 329).

The " underhand ways " here referred to may, per- haps, mean those opinions on the character and conduct of Mr. Hogg himself which, though unpublished, still exist in the handwriting of Shelley.   There was nothing " underhand " whatever in those communications.   In less direct language, Shelley had written to Mr. Hogg himself on the same circumstance.   And there cer- tainly was nothing " underhand " in his breaking off for twelve months all communication with his college friend on account of the same transaction.   The ex- istence of these letters Mr. Hogg probably " found out," and he thus attempts to prejudice the judgment of the public when they shall have been given to the world.   But one notable instance at least of Shelley's " underhand ways" he did not find out—namely, that while to his guileless friend the romantic young poet

I

appeared to be only thinking of Thaddeus of Warsaw in their trellised chamber in Poland Street, he was engaged in constant intercourse with Messrs. Crosby and Co., of Stationers' Court, Ludgate Hill, and advertising through them in the public papers a poem which he had written and published without the knowledge of Mr. Hogg.

Harriet Westbrook was the schoolfellow of Shelley's sisters at a boarding-school kept by a lady of the name of Fenning. I have already suggested that the acquaintance between Shelley and Harriet arose out of her subscription to the poems of Janetta Philipps. With the usual carelessness attending every statement made about Shelley, four different localities are assigned to the school at which Shelley's sisters and Harriet Westbrook were fellow-pupils. Miss Hellen Shelley, who was at the school, says " Clapham ;" Lady Shelley, by a slip of the pen, writes " Brompton ;" Mr. Hogg calls the place " Wandsworth ;" and Mr. Middleton, " Balham Hill." The following extracts from unpublished letters of Harriet herself will show that the school was situated at Clapham. The following was written a few months after her marriage, to a lady of whom we shall hear a good deal more in the following pages :—

(*From an unpublished letter of Harriet Shelley.*)

" But I know you now, and this blessing I should not have had if I had never been to Clapham. So I must be content and think myself very happy that I did go, though I was not aware of the happiness that would result."

In another unpublished letter to the same person poor Harriet again fixes the locality of the school, and refers to the horror with which she had heard while there of Shelley's peculiar opinions.

(*From an unpublished letter of Harriet Shelley.*)

" Being brought up in the Christian religion, you may conceive with what horror I first heard that Percy was an Atheist—at least so it was given out at *Clapham*. At first I did not comprehend the meaning of the word, therefore when it was explained I was truly petrified. I wondered how he could live a moment professing such principles, and solemnly declared that he should never change mine."

Alas for human resolutions ! the sequel proves, unfortunately, how easily and how fatally they were changed.

If we fix the first week in January, 1811, as the date at which Shelley became acquainted with Harriet Westbrook, we find that either by letter or personal observation he had eight months to form an opinion of her disposition and character before she became his wife. The circumstances of the marriage are well known. In the first week of September, 1811, Shelley and Harriet proceeded to Edinburgh and were married according to the Scottish law. How Shelley then regarded her, and still regarded her a year later, we shall have the opportunity of showing a little further on from an unpublished letter of Shelley himself. In 1813, two years after the marriage, he dedicated to her *Queen Mab*.

" Whose eyes have I gazed fondly on,
    And loved mankind the more ?"

Shelley asks in the dedication of this poem, and answers his own question thus—" Harriet, on thine ;" and yet the reality, or at least the intensity of

I 2

his love for Harriet at any time has been questioned.
On the 24th of March, 1814, he re-married her at the
Church of St. George, Hanover Square, " in order,"
as the certificate states, " to obviate all doubts that
have arisen or shall or may arise touching or concerning
the validity of the aforesaid marriage " in Scotland.
On the 28th of July in the same year—that is, in less
than four months after having thus made assurance
doubly sure—Shelley went off to the Continent with
Miss Mary Wollstonecraft Godwin, accompanied by
Miss Clairmont, the daughter of Mr. Godwin's second
wife by a former marriage.

Mr. Garnett, in his interesting little volume, *Relics
of Shelley*, published in 1862, refers to certain unpublished letters of Shelley and Harriet which he
believes will place this painful matter in a more
favourable light than the circumstances of the case
itself unfortunately present it. If any documents
exist showing that Harriet was a party to the separation, they certainly should be published. It is
expressly denied on her own authority that she was
so, by Mr. Peacock, who saw her several times after
the occurrence. Should any such letters be forthcoming they will put an end to the charge of
desertion as it is usually understood, but they scarcely
can excuse Shelley for a worse kind of abandonment—
the leaving a young girl, whose moral and religious
principles he had overthrown, to the guidance of those
fine-sounding philosophical axioms she had learned
from him, which *he* did not follow in the hour of trial,
and which brought *her* to destruction.

After a few weeks' residence in Edinburgh the young
married couple were joined by Mr. Hogg. Towards the
end of October the whole party proceeded to York, where

Mr. Hogg was to resume his attendance at Chambers. On the morning after their arrival there Shelley was compelled to go up to London to consult his father's solicitor about some arrangements that were then pending. According to Mr. Hogg, Harriet was left in York under his own immediate protection. Other evidence would show that she accompanied her husband on this occasion, and that Mr. Hogg in this part of his book mixes up and confuses two distinct transactions. Something, however, unquestionably did occur at York in the absence of Shelley, that necessitated the arrival there of Eliza Westbrook, the elder sister of Harriet, in the position, as Mr. Hogg sneeringly admits, " of a guardian angel." Shelley himself returned from London or perhaps from Keswick, on the following day, when the whole party got immediate notice from their landlady to leave their lodgings. A few days later Shelley, Harriet, and Eliza Westbrook, without telling Mr. Hogg of their intention, or bidding him good-bye, abruptly left York and proceeded to Keswick. I have collected a good deal of curious matter on this subject, which though most important in a complete survey of Shelley's life, would occupy too large a space in this investigation. It is enough to say that those who feel an interest in the subject can get a tolerably clear idea of the circumstances which put an end to all intercourse between Shelley and his friend Mr. Hogg for more than a year, if they turn to the second volume, p. 490, of that gentleman's so-called Life of the poet, and read there what is very questionably called a " Fragment of a Novel." The substitution of two real names for those of " Charlotte" and " Albert," will greatly assist them in understanding the true meaning of this singular

" Fragment," which there can be little doubt is a
portion, however altered, of a genuine letter.

Mr. Hogg doubtless had very good reason for repre-
senting this affair as a fiction, but in mere matters of
fact he is equally untrustworthy. On the 28th of
October, 1811, the day before he left York for
Keswick, without taking leave of Mr. Hogg, Shelley
wrote to the Duke of Norfolk the letter which has
been published by Mr. Philip H. Howard of Corby
Castle in *Notes and Queries*, Nov. 20th, 1858. Mr.
Hogg, owing to the estrangement which had taken
place, was not informed of this letter. Wishing it to
be supposed that a friendly intercourse still continued
between himself and the poet after the abrupt departure of the latter for Keswick, he says, " My instructions with regard to Shelley's correspondence, were to
open all letters that should come to York for him,
and to despatch such only as appeared to me worth
the postage. Many letters arrived daily, but few of
them merited to be sent farther. One of the few was
an *invitation*, kindly and cordially worded from the
Duke of Norfolk, to visit him at Graystoke. It was
franked by his grace and dated November 7th, 1811.
The letter was transmitted to Keswick, and the visit
was paid."—vol. ii. p. 23.

This is really too good a specimen of Mr. Hogg's
power of invention to be passed over. The reason
alleged for not sending all Shelley's letters forward
was to save postage on those that were not worth it.
Now as the letter of the Duke of Norfolk was not
only " franked by his grace," but probably sealed with
his arms, one might expect that Mr. Hogg could have
let that important document pass without examination. But no. Mr. Hogg's instructions were too

precise, and he accordingly opened the ducal letter and read in it "an invitation" *which it did not contain.* The substance of that letter is given in the private Diary of Charles, Duke of Norfolk, still preserved at Corby Castle, some interesting extracts from which have been kindly transcribed for me by Mr. Philip H. Howard, whose father was the executor of his grace. So far from inviting Shelley to Greystoke, in the letter so curiously misdescribed by Mr. Hogg, the Duke of Norfolk seems to have thought that the poet's father was not without justification in the way he was acting towards his son. There is a little of sternness in the reply of his grace to the young poet's appeal, but he nevertheless proposes to call on Shelley in York to speak to him more fully on the subject of his letter. The invitation which formed the subject of a second letter was not written until the 23rd of November, and could never have passed through the hands of Mr. Hogg. He knew, however, that Shelley, his wife, and Eliza Westbrook spent some days at Greystoke, and he not unnaturally considered that the letter of the 7th of November to York, " franked by his grace," contained the " invitation." But he should not have said he " opened " and read the letter, which from his misdescription of its contents he certainly could not have done.

The following are the extracts kindly furnished me by Philip H. Howard, Esq., of Corby Castle :—

" *Diary of Charles, Duke of Norfolk.*

" 1811, *Nov.* 7.—Wrote to T. Shelly that I would come to Field Place on the 10th, to confer with him on the unhappy difference with his son, from whom I have a letter before me.

" To Mr. B. Shelly in answer that I
should be glad to interfere, but fear with little
hope of success; fearing that his father, and
not he alone, will see his late conduct in a different point of view from what he sees it.

" That I propose going into the North next
week, and will come to York to see him, provided he will inform me when I may find him
there.

" *Nov.* 10.—Wrote to Mr. Shelly, dined at Horsham.

" *Nov.* 23. — Wrote to Mr. B. Shelly to invite
him,* his wife, and her sister to meet me at
Greystoke. Came to Parlington, dined and
slept.

[Reaches Appleby it appears on the 25th.]

" *Nov.* 26.—Greystoke—Wrote to Mr. and Mrs.
Howard of Levens, inviting them to Greystoke,
to Mr. and Mrs. H. de C." (Howard of Corby,
the father and mother of Mr. Philip Henry
Howard), " to Mr. and Mrs. B. Shelly do.

" *Dec.* 1.—Mr. and Mrs. B. Shelly, his wife, and
her sister came. Wrote to his father thereon.

" *Dec.* 6.--Wrote in answer to Mayor of Thet-
ford, &c.

" In this week, Lady Musgrave, Mr. and
Mrs. H. de C., Messrs. Calvert, and James
Brougham at the castle.

" *Dec.* 9.— Came with Mr. Wybergh to Greta
Bridge.

---

* The date of this entry, "November 23rd," conclusively disposes of Mr. Hogg's assertion that the invitation to Greystoke was
given in the letter of November 7th, 1811.

" *Dec.* 10.—To Parlington.

" *Dec.* 11.—To Doncaster.

" *Dec.* 12.—To Worksop [whence he writes many letters, and one] " to T. Shelly, on subject of his son, from whom I expected a letter, when he should again hear from me."

Mr. Philip H. Howard not only favoured me with this very interesting extract from the Diary of the Duke of Norfolk, but kindly explained some of the allusions. Thus, in reference to Parlington, he says :— " Parlington named several times was the seat in Yorkshire of Sir Thomas Gascoyne, the last Bart. and male representative of that ancient family." With regard to Lady Musgrave, he says—" The Lady Musgrave named would be the widow of Sir John Charden Musgrave, of Edenhall, a daughter of Sir Edmund Filmer, Bart., of Kent, a near neighbour." He further adds, " Lady Musgrave, of Edenhall, Cumberland, and Hartley Castle, Cumberland, was a good Italian scholar, and a person of considerable attain‑ments, the mother of the present and two preceding Baronets. You will remember that an ancestor, Sir Philip Musgrave, was the celebrated cavalier leader (*temp.* Car. I.) The Shelleys seem to have left 8th December, or perhaps the 9th. The Duke in his Diary generally names my father and mother Mr. and Mrs. H. de C., that is, Howard of Corby."

Mr. Calvert and Mr. James Brougham are also described by Mr. Howard in his valuable letter, but these I defer until the equally interesting extract from his mother's Journal, describing the party at Greystoke, is given.

There is a published letter from Shelley to Mr.

Medwin senior, referring to this intended visit to
Greystoke. It is well known, and has some distressing
passages in it. Two referring to his actual circumstances may be given. The letter is dated
" Keswick, Cumberland, November 30th, 1811, My Dear
Sir . . . . " We are now so poor as to be actually in
danger of every day being deprived of the necessaries
of life," . . . . " and it is nearly with our very last
guinea that we visit the Duke of Norfolk, at Greystoke, to-morrow. We return to Keswick on Wednesday. I have very few hopes from this visit."—
Medwin's *Life of Shelley*, i. p. 376.

The 30th of November, 1811, fell upon a Saturday,
so that the visit was intended to last until Wednesday, the 4th of December. Mr. Howard considers that the Shelleys remained at Greystoke until
the 8th, or perhaps the 9th. The following is the
extract from Mrs. Howard's Journal, sent by her son :—

" *Extract from my Mother's Journal.*

" Corby Castle, 1811; December 1st, 2nd, 3rd.

" I had a terrible journey [to Greystoke], with
hail, snow, and sleet, and only arrived at half-past
six.

" I had the pleasure of finding the Duke of Norfolk
very well, and in good spirits. Lady [Musgrave ?*]
with Mr. and Mrs. Shelley, and Miss Westbrook, her
sister ; Mr. James Brougham, and Mr. Calvert, were
the party."

---

* The name is inadvertently omitted by Mrs. Howard in her
journal, but there can be no doubt from the entry in the Duke of
Norfolk's Diary, December 6th, that it must have been Lady
Musgrave who, with Mr. and Mrs. Howard, Mr. James Brougham,
and Mr. Calvert, met the Shelleys at Greystoke.

Mrs. Howard's journal being intended only for her own use, she doubtless thought it superfluous to mention her husband. Her son says: " My father, Henry Howard, will have been there all the time." Of Mr. Brougham and Mr. Calvert mentioned in the journal, Mr. Philip H. Howard says in his letter to me :—" James Brougham, named as having met the Shelleys at Greystoke, was second brother of the late Lord Brougham. He represented Kendal in the first reformed Parliament, having sat previously for Tregony and Winchelsea. Mr. Calvert, of Greta Bank, was a Cumberland Squire, very popular in his day." The Calverts were neighbours of Southey, and became Shelley's greatest friends at Keswick. We shall see subsequently in what terms he spoke of Mrs. Calvert in particular, in some of his unpublished letters. As neither Mr. James Brougham nor Mr. Henry Howard could have been correctly described as " elderly " in 1811, the allusion in the following most interesting extract from an unpublished letter of Shelley to a friend, refers in all probability to Mr. Calvert :*—

(From an unpublished letter of Shelley.)

. . . . " We met several people at the Duke's. One in particular struck me. He was an elderly man, who seemed to know all my concerns, and the expression of his face, whenever I held the argument, which I do

---

* Mr. Howard, who met Shelley at Greystoke in 1811, was then fifty-four years of age. I am indebted for this information to his son, Philip H. Howard, Esq., of Corby Castle, who tells me that his father was born on July 2nd, 1757, in the reign of George the Second. Mr. James Brougham, the eldest brother of the first Lord Brougham, was born January 16th, 1780, and was therefore in his thirty-second year when he met Shelley at the Duke of Norfolk's.

everywhere, was such as I shall not readily forget. I shall have more to tell of him, for we have met him before in these mountains, and his peculiar look struck [me?] [and] Harriet."

The manuscript is a little illegible in the place I have marked, but the two words do not affect the sense. The latter part of the passage, referring to Harriet and himself having met the "elderly man" among the mountains, corroborates an impression which I had previously entertained that Shelley had removed to Keswick earlier than Mr. Hogg would have us to believe. As already mentioned, another passage, which will subsequently be given in full, shows that Shelley had made the acquaintance of Southey before the 20th of October, the day it will be remembered on which he wrote to Mr. Whitton from Cuckfield.

There is no record of Shelley having made any other acquaintances at Keswick but Southey and the Calverts. Coleridge unfortunately was not at the lakes during the period of Shelley's visit. He thinks he might have been of some use to the young philosopher (for at that time he had published nothing under his own name which could give even a faint hope of his becoming a poet) had he been at Keswick, but it so happened that he was not, and Southey received him instead. This he considered a misfortune for Shelley. " I *might* have been of use to him, and Southey could not; for I should have sympathized with his poetics, metaphysical reveries, and the very word metaphysics is an abomination to Southey, and Shelley would have felt that I understood him." Another celebrated writer who could not plead the excuse of absence seems to have regretted in after

years that he did not at this period avail himself of
the opportunity of " showing some little attention to
a brother Oxonian and a man of letters." This was
Thomas De Quincey, who was then living at Grasmere,
thirteen miles from Keswick. From the very am-
biguous way in which De Quincey writes, some careless
readers, as well as Lady Shelley and Mr. Rossetti,
have inferred that he became acquainted though
slightly with Shelley. The simple fact, though involved in a cloud of verbiage, is, that he did *not* call
on him. The fanciful description of Shelley, " that
he looked like an elegant and tender flower, whose
head drooped from being surcharged with rain," was
one which De Quincey " had *heard* of him in some
company." It was probably six years later, when an
interest was created in his mind by the *Revolt of
Islam*, he remembered, no doubt with regret at not
having seen him, that the future author of that poem
had been a neighbour of his for four months. We
have, however, from De Quincey the fact, though indirectly, that Shelley did not make the acquaintance
of Wordsworth, then residing at Grasmere, or of John
Wilson, whose *Isle of Palms* was published in the
year of Shelley's visit to the lakes. Though De
Quincey came, I think, somewhat late to the knowledge
of Shelley's writings, his essay conveys at once an
eloquent and a discriminating estimate both of the
genius and character of the poet. The opening
sentence is particularly true, and should always be
borne in mind by those who write or read of Shelley.
" There is no writer named amongst men," says De
Quincey, " of whom, so much as of Percy Bysshe
Shelley, it is difficult for a conscientious critic to
speak with the profound respect, on the one hand due

to his exalted powers, and yet without offence on the other, to feelings the most sacred which too memorably he outraged" (*Works*, vol. v. p. 1). The essay, however, is full of mistakes, one of which only need be pointed out here. Like Coleridge, De Quincey seems to have thought that he too would have been of more use to Shelley than the Laureate. Speaking of the attractions of Grasmere he says, " Finally, my own library, which being rich in the wickedest of German speculations would naturally have been more to Shelley's taste than the Spanish library of Southey. As Shelley at this time knew as little of German as he did of Spanish, it is difficult to understand how he could have been much interested in these departments of either library. We learn, however, from De Quincey the following interesting fact : — " The Shelleys," he tells us, " had been induced by one of their new friends to take part of a house standing about half a mile on the Penrith road, more I believe, according to that friend's intention, for the sake of bringing them within reach of his own hospitalities than for any beauty in the place." Had this friend been Southey, as Captain Medwin suggests, De Quincey would doubtless have been glad to set off this act of kindness against what Coleridge calls the " harshness" of the Laureate's later manner towards his young neighbour. A more likely person was Mr. Calvert, the " elderly man" whose acquaintance Shelley first made at the Duke of Norfolk's. An unpublished letter, written by Shelley on the 3rd of February, 1812, immediately after his leaving Keswick, confirms this supposition. An extract from that letter will be given in its proper place. In one of the eight un-dated letters to Hogg from Keswick, he says, " The thing is, we are not in, but near Keswick." Attached to this house, but not belonging to their portion of it, was the garden* in which with girlish simplicity and innocence poor Harriet told some of her lady visitors that Percy and herself were let to " run about" when they were tired of sitting within doors. Poor child ! what a race was that for her elsewhere on a certain occasion in the " drear-nighted December" of 1816 !

From the very beginning of Shelley's residence at Keswick, he appears to have been occupied with those questions connected with the state of Ireland which led to the extraordinary and romantic expedition to Dublin in the following February. The quotation from *The Curse of Kehama*, which he adapted to the condition of Ireland, and prefixed as a motto to the poem published to assist in maintaining an Irish patriot in prison, shows that nearly twelve months before his generous enthusiasm had been roused on behalf of that ill-governed and badly treated country.

> " And Famine, at her bidding, wasted wide
> The wretched land, till in the public way,
> Promiscuous where the dead and dying lay,
> Dogs fed on human bones in the open light of day."

Instead of Southey setting his young visitor to sleep, as absurdly narrated by Mr. Hogg, by reading this poem in manuscript, when it had already been published a year, Shelley may possibly have made Southey open *his* eyes in astonishment at finding *The*

---

* In a playful letter to Hartley Coleridge, June 13th, 1807, Southey has the following allusion to the Calverts' garden. " We had one day hotter than had been remarked for fourteen years; the glass was at 85° in the shade; in the sun in Mr. Calvert's garden at 118°."

Curse of Kehama turned already to such vile uses as
to supply a motto for a poem that absolutely expressed
some sympathy for the suffering Irish.   There *was* a
time when Southey himself was not ashamed of sharing
and avowing feelings precisely similar.   Those were
the days when from that very house in Keswick he
apostrophized the shade of Robert Emmett.   Every
one knows the famous and touching entreaty of that
young enthusiast.   " Let no one write my epitaph.
Let my character and my motives repose in obscurity
and peace till other times and other men can do them
justice.   Then shall my character be vindicated, then
may my epitaph be written." Robert Southey thought
it would be hazardous to wait for " other times and
other men," when there was a man then living so
capable, perhaps alone capable, of doing this act of
justice to the memory of his martyred namesake.

Accordingly we have, from the future author of *The
Vision of Judgment,* this mild and modest expostulation
in reference to the last wish and the dying words of his
" young hero."

> " Emmett, no !
> No withering curse hath dried my spirit up,
> That I should now be silent, ... that my soul
> Should from the stirring inspiration shrink,
> Now when it shakes her, and withhold her voice,
> Of that divinest impulse never more
> Worthy, if impious I withheld it now,
> Hardening my heart.   Here, here in this free Isle,
> To which in thy young virtue's erring zeal
> Thou wert so perilous an enemy;
> Here in free England shall an English hand
> Build thy *imperishable monument.*"
>
> *Works,* one vol. ed. p. 140.

Many persons believe that had the spirit of recent legis-
lation influenced the action of government in 1803, " the

often-widowed Erin" would not have had to " mourn the loss" of *one* of " her brave young men" at least. That gentler and wiser spirit commenced in 1829 with the act of Catholic Emancipation, which great measure, though not passed in his lifetime, had no sincerer advocate than Robert Emmett. But what did his panegyrist—he who raised an " imperishable monument" of rather perishable blank verse to his memory—what did he think in 1811 of that question, and of the people who were so deeply interested in its settlement ? Shelley will tell us. In the unpublished letter of the 10th of October, 1811, subsequently referred to, he says :—

" Southey hates the Irish ;* he speaks against Catholic Emancipation. In all these things we differ. Our differences were the subject of a long conversation."

We shall find from another unpublished letter, written immediately after his leaving Keswick three months later, that the " differences" between Shelley and Southey increased every day to such an extent that the youthful admiration of Shelley for the author of *Thalaba* was greatly cooled, if it was not wholly extinguished, while at the same time he admits the possibility of his many private virtues.

---

* Southey appears to have had during his life two contradictory opinions and two opposite states of feeling about everything. In 1801, when in Dublin, he rather liked " the Irish," and gave the people generally some credit even for " genius." In a letter dated Dublin, October 16th, 1801, he says :—" Genius, indeed, immediately appears to characterize them ; a love of saying good things, which 999 Englishmen in 1000 never dream of attempting in the course of their lives."—*Life and Correspondence of Robert Southey*, vol. ii. p. 170.

CHAPTER VII.

THE preparation for the Irish campaign and the exceedingly interesting correspondence with Godwin which Shelley commenced on the 3rd of January, 1812, fill up the whole of that month. The letters to and from Godwin being among the valuable materials confided to Mr. Hogg, he had no opportunity of exercising his very perplexing ingenuity in suppressing, transposing, or otherwise confusing any portion of their contents. The reader is therefore referred to that portion of Mr. Hogg's book with perfect confidence. I shall only make a few extracts in reference to the meditated descent on Dublin to carry Catholic Emancipation and to repeal the Union.

In the second letter to Godwin, January 16th, 1812, he gives the philosopher a list of his writings up to that period; among them is an " Essay on Love," " a little poem," which he says was written after he had become acquainted with the profounder works of his correspondent, seeming thereby to attach to it a greater importance. I have already suggested that this " *Essay* on Love" may have been nothing else than the " Poetical *Essay* on the Existing State of Things" under a new name. He then continues : " In a few days we set off to Dublin. I do not know exactly when, but a letter addressed to Keswick will find me. Our journey has been settled some time. We go principally to forward as much as we (viz.,

Harriet, Eliza, and myself) can the Catholic Emancipation.

" Southey, the poet whose principles were pure and
elevated once, is now the paid champion of every abuse
and absurdity. I have had much conversation with
him. He says, ' you will think as I do when you are
as old.' I do not feel the least disposition to be
Mr. S.'s proselyte."

On January 28th, 1812, he again writes to Godwin :
" Your letter has reached me on the eve of our departure for Dublin. I cannot deny myself the
pleasure of answering it, although we shall probably
have reached Ireland before an answer to this can
arrive. You do us a great and essential service by
the enclosed introduction to Mr. Curran : he is a
man whose public character I have admired and
respected. You offer an additional motive for
hastening our journey. . . . .

" With these sentiments I have been preparing an
address to the Catholics of Ireland, which, however
deficient may be its execution, I can by no means
admit that it contains one sentiment which *can* harm
the cause of liberty and happiness. It consists of
the benevolent and tolerant deductions of philosophy
reduced into the simplest language. I know it can
do no harm ; it cannot excite rebellion, as its main
principle is to trust the success of a cause to the energy
of its truth. It cannot " widen the breach between
the kingdoms," as it attempts to convey to the vulgar
mind sentiments of universal philanthropy ; and whatever impressions it may produce, they can be no other
but those of peace and harmony ; it owns no religion
but benevolence, no cause but virtue, no party but the
world. 1 shall devote myself with unremitting zeal,

as far as an uncertain state of health will permit, towards forwarding the great ends of virtue and happiness in Ireland, regarding as I do the present state of that country's affairs as an opportunity which, if I, being thus disengaged, permit to pass unoccupied, I am unworthy of the character which I have assumed."

It has been stated by Mr. Hogg, who was kept in profound ignorance of all these proceedings, and repeated by others on his unsupported assertions, that it was owing to Shelley's disgust at the failure of the project in Dublin that he left that city abruptly before the expiration of the time he had arranged to stay there. This will be found to be quite incorrect. The subsequent residence in Wales was pre-arranged before he left Keswick, and fixed with the same deliberation as the visit to Dublin itself. "We left Dublin," Shelley says in an unpublished letter from which more will be quoted, " because I had done all that I could do." The following passage in the foregoing letter to Godwin shows that before he went to Dublin Shelley had planned the residence in Wales :—

" I will say no more of Wales at present. We have determined next summer to receive a most dear friend, of whom I shall speak hereafter, in some romantic spot. Perhaps I shall be able to prevail on you and your wife and children to leave the tumult and dust of London for awhile. However that may be, I shall certainly see you in London. I am not yet of age. At that time I have great hopes of being enabled to offer you a house of my own. Philanthropy is confined to no spot. Adieu! Direct your next ' Post Office, Dublin.'

" My wife sends her respects.

"Believe me, in all sincerity of heart, yours truly, sincerely,   "P. B. SHELLEY.

"To Mr. William Godwin, London."

The "dear friend" alluded to by Shelley was Miss Eliza Hitchener of Hurstpierpoint, Brighton, with whom he was carrying on a voluminous correspondence at this time. The antecedents of this lady's history will be found a little further on, as sketched by no less a personage than the Right Hon. Thomas Pelham, Earl of Chichester, joint Postmaster-General with the Earl of Sandwich. This lady received intelligence, two days earlier than Godwin, of the intended visit to Dublin. The letter to her has not been published, but I am permitted to make the following extract from it, which contains some very curious information not hitherto known :—

(*From an unpublished letter of Shelley.*)

"Keswick, January 26th, 1812.

"All is prepared. I have been busily engaged in an address to the Irish people which will be printed as Paine's works were, and posted on the walls of Dublin. *My poems will be printed there.*"

I have italicized the last line for the singular interest of the intention which it announces. Dublin, the chosen city where the first collection of Shelley's poems was to have been published! What poems can he have alluded to? Were we to have *Victor* without *Cazire*, and *Fitz-Victor* without Mr. Hogg? That alone I think would have been a happy consummation. But these were rather insignificant materials to be called his "poems." In this collection, beyond all doubt, we would have had the *Poetical Essay on the*

Existing State of Things and the *Essay on Love,* if they
were not the same.   In every point of view it is to be
regretted that this idea was not carried out.   What a
treasure would not that Dublin edition of Shelley's
early poems be, though printed in the style of the
Address to the Irish People or the *Proposals for an
Association.*   It would have contained *one* poem at
least, which I think the world would not willingly let
die—a poem by Shelley on Robert Emmett!   That
might indeed have been the " imperishable monument"
which Southey, with almost incredible vainglory, had
considered his own to be.

   In a subsequent letter, also unpublished, written after
his alleged disgust with Irish politics, Shelley says :—
" I have written some *verses* on Robert Emmett
which you shall see, and which I will insert in my
book of poems."   I am sorry to say that the correspondence from which we learn this interesting fact
does not contain the poem.   The reference to the
Dublin edition of Paine's works is also curious, particularly if it be true that they were ever posted on
the walls of that city.   Shelley may have alluded only
to his own *Declaration of Rights,* which was printed at
Dublin, expressly to be " posted on the farmers' walls."
I do not remember having seen a Dublin edition of
Paine's works, but I have no doubt they were printed
there, as I have in my own possession a Dublin edition
of *The Life of Thomas Pain,* by Francis Oldys, A.M.,
1791.*   The number of booksellers who took a share

* THE LIFE OF THOMAS PAIN, the author of the *Rights of
Man,* with a Defence of his Writings.   By Francis Oldys, A.M.
of the University of Pensylvania.   DUBLIN : Printed for R. Cross,
P. Byrne, P. Wogan, A. Grueber, J. Moore, J. Jones, T. Heery,
W. M'Kenzie, W. Jones, R. M'Alliston, and H. Watts.   MDCCXCI.

in this publication is in itself a striking proof of the intellectual and commercial activity of Dublin before the Union.

After his letter to the "dear friend" at Hurstpierpoint of the 26th of January, and his more elaborate epistle to Godwin of the 28th, Shelley did not lose much time in setting out on his adventurous expedition. The following letter, which is now published for the first time, details the course of his journey from Keswick to Dublin. It is most curious and interesting in many respects. He must be cold indeed who can read without emotion the sanguine and exulting expectation of this generous young man, going forth like a knight of romance to the championship of a nation. His final estimate of Southey is also very interesting. It has been said that, even after their first interview at Keswick, Shelley could speak of Southey " as a great man." He must have changed this opinion very soon, for in one of the unpublished letters so frequently referred to he says the very reverse. Speaking of Southey, he emphatically declares, "He is *not* the great man I first thought him to be." It was in this latter mood that he penned the following letter :—

(*From an unpublished letter of Shelley.*)

"Whitehaven, February 3rd, 1812.

" My dearest Friend,—

"We are now at Whitehaven—a miserable manufacturing sea-port town. I write to you a short letter to inform you of our safety, and that the wind which will fill the sails of our packet to-night is favourable and fresh. Certainly it is laden with some of your benedictions as with the breath of the disembodied virtues who smile upon our attempt. We set off to-night at twelve o'clock, and arrive at the Isle of Man, whence you will hear from us, to-morrow; then we proceed, when the wind serves, to Dublin. We may be detained some days in the Island; if the weather is fine, we shall not regret it; at all events we shall escape this filthy town and horrible inn. . . .

" We felt regret at leaving Keswick. I passed Southey's house without *one* sting. He is a man who *may* be amiable in his private character, stained and false as is his public one. He may be amiable, but, if he is, my feelings are liars, and I have been so long accustomed to trust to them in these cases, that the opinion of the world is not the likeliest corrector to impeach their credibility. But we left the Calverts [qy. with regret]. I hope some day to show you *Mrs.* Calvert; I shall not forget her, but will preserve her memory as another flower to compose a garland which I intend to present to *you.* Harriet and Eliza in excellent spirits bid you affectionate adieu. Adieu!

" Your

" P. B. SHELLEY."

The phrase " but we left the Calverts," strengthens, if it does not confirm, the suggestion already thrown out, that it was in a part of their house " on the Penrith road," as mentioned by De Quincey, that the Shelleys were living.* The well-known letter of Southey, dated

---

* I had come to this conclusion before I was favoured by Mr. Philip H. Howard of Corby Castle with the following exact particulars :—" The residence of Greta Bank, which in 1811 was the property and home of Mr. Calvert, lies on the Keswick and Penrith road to the north side of the beautiful stream and well-wooded banks of the Greta. It cannot be much more than half a mile from the town of Keswick. The railroad there running parallel to

January 14th, 1812, describing "a man at Keswick, who acted upon him as his own ghost would do," says this man, or ghost, meaning Shelley, had "married a girl of seventeen after being turned out of doors by his father, and here they are both *in lodgings,* living upon 200*l.* a year, which her father allows them." Harriet was not seventeen, neither was Shelley turned out of doors. The "200*l.* a year" from Mr. Westbrook may be admitted, as we find Shelley, exactly one month after the date of this letter—on the 14th of February, 1812—stating to Miss Hitchener that he was then in receipt of "400*l.* per annum," half of which must have come from his father, and half from Mr. Westbrook. The other circumstance was one that Southey could not be misinformed about. The Shelleys were "in lodgings," most probably in the house of one who received them, as De Quincey says, merely for the opportunity it afforded of paying them attention. This was Mr. Calvert, the gentleman who had fascinated Shelley so much at the Duke of Norfolk's. Mr. Philip H. Howard, of Corby Castle, the extract from whose mother's journal had led me to identify the "elderly man" of the dinner party at Greystoke with Mr. Calvert, confirms that conjecture in the following interesting passage from one of his letters :—" It was doubtless Mr. Calvert, of Greta Bank, near Keswick, who captivated the poet's fancy; his thoughts were fresh, 'the dew was on

---

the south side of the river is a good deal nearer to the mansion than the old coach road. Skiddaw forms a bold background to the scenery." It is an interesting fact communicated to Mr. Howard by Mr. Spedding of Mirehouse, Keswick, that there is a lady still living in that neighbourhood who remembers Shelley's appearance at this period. " He was very striking looking."

them.' The Duke and his friends were very fond
of him; he promoted all local improvements, and
was a person of great vigour and originality of
mind."

Shelley left Whitehaven for the Isle of Man at
midnight on the 3rd of February, 1812. He seems
to have stopped a few days in the Island, as he said
he would do, and reached Dublin after a stormy
voyage on the night of the 12th. This is twelve days
earlier than any date previously assigned to his arrival. Mr. Hogg knowing nothing about the matter,
took the first letter that came to his hand referring
to the subject, and boldly assigned that as the date.
" A letter from Dublin of the 24th of February states
that they have just arrived there" (vol. ii. p. 76).
The letter, which was to Godwin, in reality states no
such thing. It mentions the delay of " a few days,"
during which period the first of his pamphlets, which
he encloses, had been printed. Yet this erroneous
date is repeated even by Mr. Rossetti. " Shelley
arrived in Dublin, with Harriet and Eliza, about the
24th of February, 1812." Mr. Rossetti had not before him, and probably had never seen, the first
pamphlet printed by Shelley in Dublin, but Mr.
Hogg professes to describe it in the very page in
which he gives this random guess at a date. That
pamphlet in which Shelley says he was then " a week
in Dublin," is dated " No. 7, Lower Sackville Street,
Feb. 22," that is, two days, and a week at least, according to Mr. Hogg's showing, before Shelley had
actually arrived there. Even the name of his friend
Mr. Hogg could not transcribe correctly from the
title page of the second pamphlet. Quoting it in inverted commas he writes, " By Percy B. Shelly :

Dublin," whereas the name is printed in full correctly, as in the first pamphlet, "Percy Bysshe Shelley." The false spelling of Shelley's name in this instance is also repeated by Mr. Rossetti through that over-confidence in Mr. Hogg's assertions, which seems strange in so acute a writer. Shelley's first letter from Dublin puts an end to all doubt as to the exact date of his arrival. It is very short, and is here printed for the first time :—

(Unpublished letter of Shelley.)

"Dublin, February 13th, 1812.

" My dearest Friend,—

" Last night we arrived safe in this city. It was useless to have written to you before. Now I have only time to tell you of our safety. We were driven by a storm quite to the north of Ireland, and yesterday was the end of our journey thence. Expect to hear soon ; all is well.

" Your affectionate

" P. B. Shelley.

" Direct to me at Mr. Dunne's,
  No. 7, Sackville Street, Dublin."

Remembering the bitterness with which he had parted from Southey at Keswick, it seems a sort of retribution that Shelley should have experienced the same unfavourable weather in crossing the Channel that had attended the visit of the elder poet to Ireland eleven years before. A storm " drove him to th' Hibernian shore," as it had done Southey, and drove both considerably out of their way in the same direction. Southey in a letter to his wife, dated October 14th, 1801, makes the curious mistake of saying

that " the wind had drifted them so far *south* that no
possibility existed of their reaching Dublin that night,"
the fact being that, like Shelley, he had been driven
to the *north* of Dublin. " The captain," says Southey,
" a good man and a good sailor, who never leaves his
deck, and drinks nothing but buttermilk, therefore
readily agreed to land us at Balbriggan, and there we
got ashore at two o'clock. Balbriggan is a fishing
and bathing town fifteen miles from Dublin, but miles
and money differ in Ireland from the English standard,
eleven miles being as long as fourteen English."
Southey must have thought the points of the compass
were differently arranged in Ireland also, when he
placed Balbriggan fifteen miles to the *south* of Dublin.

The fifteen miles which Southey crossed in his way
to the metropolis of Ireland were so bare of trees that
he could only account for it by the supposition that
they had all been cut down for pike-handles. The
tract, however, unlike that between Dan and
Beersheba, was not all barren. " One little town
we passed, once famous,—its name Swords : it has the
ruins of a castle, and a church with a round tower
adjoining the steeple, making an odd group." As he
approached Glasnevin, the home of Addison, Tickell,
and Delany, as well as the occasional visiting place
of Swift, he saw " mountains near Dublin most
beautifully shaped." Even Dublin itself came up to
his expectations. He calls it " a very fine city—a
magnificent city—such public buildings, and the streets
so wide !"

It was in the widest of those wide streets that
Shelley took up his residence in Dublin. Sackville
Street in 1812 did not present precisely the same
appearance which is now so familiar to us, either from

actual knowledge or through photographs. The column to Nelson was only in process of erection, and the fine edifice of the Post-Office had not been commenced ; but the effect of the view was equally good, perhaps even better, than it is at present, as but one majestic avenue seemed to unite the historic circle of the Rotunda, where the Volunteers had often assembled, with that beautiful building in which the patriotic resolutions of Dungannon had been confirmed by the Parliament of Ireland. Both of these structures must have been objects of great interest to Shelley, and we shall find subsequently in what terms he spoke of the then actual condition of the latter. The house in which he lived was very favourably situated ; from the balcony of it, which still remains, and from which, as he tells us himself, he was accustomed to fling copies of his pamphlet to whoever appeared to him to be likely recipients, he could see over the roofs of Trinity College and the Bank of Ireland, some of those " beautifully shaped mountains " which had attracted the attention of Southey. But six houses separated him from the river :

" There was the Liffy rolling downe the lea."

And by his side at that time was one to whom with truth could be applied the lines of Tickell. For surely, notwithstanding all the native beauty that had been mirrored in its wave, never before

" Did Liffy's limpid stream
Reflect a sweeter face."

These allusions may be pardoned in one to whom that street is very dear, who was born in it, who spent the best part of his life close to it, and to whom the

residence of Shelley therein gave an additional and an
enduring charm.*

We have already given the short note which
Shelley addressed to his friend at Hurstpierpoint the
day after his arrival in Dublin. On the following day
he again addressed the same lady in a long and
somewhat extravagant epistle. It has, however, a
many-sided interest, and I am permitted to make
some extracts from it which have not been printed.

(*From an unpublished letter of Shelley.*)
" Dublin, 7, Sackville Street, Feb. 14th, 1812.
" Mr. Dunne's, Woollen Draper.

" . . . . At length, however, you are free from
anxiety for our safety, as *here* we have nothing to
apprehend but Government, which will not, assure
yourself, *dare* to be so barefacedly oppressive as to
attack my *Address* ; it will breathe the spirit of peace,

---

* On the 15th of August, 1835, I saw another famous poet
enter the house No. 7, Lower Sackville Street, which then belonged
to Messrs. Köhler & Co., who had succeeded Mr. Dunne. It was
Thomas Moore. I recognised him in Sackville Street in company
with a well-known vocalist of that day, Mr. Morrisson. They
entered the house on some business, and came out in a few minutes.
They proceeded to the theatre in Hawkins Street, and afterwards
to Trinity College. Moore's morning visit to the theatre is explained by the following entry in his diary :—" The playbill of
to-day and yesterday having announced the entertainments of this
evening to have been selected by me, &c. &c., went to look at the
box-book to see what sort of promise it gave " (*Memoirs*, vol. vii.
p. 102). On that evening I attended the theatre, and had the
pleasure of hearing Moore address the house in acknowledgment of
his enthusiastic reception. He spoke from the third box to the right
facing the stage, in which sat his sister Ellen with some Dublin
friends. The speech, which is very slightly alluded to by Moore,
is given in full by Mr. James Burke, A.B., in his *Memoir of
Thomas Moore* (Dublin, 1852), p. 168.

toleration, and patience. . . . As my name, which will be prefixed to the *Address*, will show that my deeds are not deeds of darkness, nor my counsels things of mystery and fear." " Dread nothing for me; the course of my conduct in Ireland (as shall the entire course of my life) shall be marked by openness and sincerity."

The importance which he attached to the junction of his correspondent, even as a political ally, is shown by the following and some succeeding passages:—

" We will meet you in Wales, and *never part again*. You shall not cross the Channel alone. It will not do. In compliance with Harriet's earnest solicitations, I entreated you instantly to come and join our circle, resign your school, *all*, *everything* for us and the Irish cause. This could not be done. . . . But summer will come. The ocean rolls between us. O thou ocean, whose multitudinous billows ever wash Erin's green isle, on whose shores this venturous arm would plant the flag of liberty, roll on ! and with each wave," &c.

A great many romantic apostrophes to the ocean, to Ireland, and to his correspondent here follow. The same feelings and the same hopes found expression in verse, of which some fragments have been preserved. The following may be given as an example:—

To Ireland.

Bear witness, Erin! when thine injured isle,
Sees summer on its verdant pastures smile,
Its cornfields waving in the winds that sweep
The billowy surface of thy circling deep.
Thou tree whose shadow o'er the Atlantic gave
Peace, wealth, and beauty to its friendly wave,

. . . . its blossoms fade ;
And blighted are the leaves that cast its shade ;
Whilst the cold hand gathers its scanty fruit,
Whose chillness struck a canker to its root.

Dublin, February, 1812.

The personal allusions in the remarkable letter from
which these lines are taken are still more interesting:—

" I ought to count myself a favoured mortal," says
Shelley, " *with such a wife and friend."* . . . .

" Your dear little Americans may come and live
with us. (*Suppose there was a little stranger to play
with them.*) This, however, is a hope which I do not
anticipate but at some distance." . . . .

" 400*l.* per annum will be quite enough for us all.
Our publications would supply the deficiency." . . . .

" Have you heard a new Republic is set up in
Mexico ?"

He then introduces the following lines, which,
though printed in Mr. Rossetti's edition, as are the
preceding (vol. ii. pp. 528, 529), may here be given:—

THE MEXICAN REVOLUTION.

I.

Brothers ! between you and me
 Whirlwinds sweep and billows roar ;
Yet in spirit oft I see
 On thy wild and winding shore
Freedom's bloodless banners wave,—
Feel the pulses of the brave
Unextinguished in the grave,—
 See them drenched in sacred gore,—
Catch the warrior's gasping breath,
Murmuring " Liberty or death !"

II.

Shout aloud ! Let every slave,
 Crouching at corruption's throne,
Start into a man, and brave
 Racks and chains without a groan ;

And the castle's heartless glow,
And the hovel's vice and woe,
Fade like gaudy flowers that blow—
  Weeds that peep, and then are gone;
Whilst from misery's ashes risen,
Love shall burst the captive's prison.

III.

Cotopaxi ! bid the sound
  Through thy sister mountains ring,
Till each valley smile around
  At the blissful welcoming !
And O thou stern Ocean deep,
Thou whose foamy billows sweep
Shores where thousands wake to weep
  Whilst they curse a villain king;
On the winds that fan thy breast
Bear thou news of Freedom's rest !

IV.

Ere the daystar dawn of love,
  Where the flag of war unfurled
Floats with crimson stain above
  The fabric of a ruined world—
Never but to vengeance driven
When the patriot's spirit shriven
Seeks in death its native heaven !
  Then to desolation hurled,
Widowed love may watch thy bier,
Balm thee with its dying tear.

Dublin, 14th February, 1812.

After this impassioned invocation, in which we may
already perceive the advancing power of the poet, he
reverts to the great business of his expedition and to
his forthcoming pamphlet.

" My Address will soon come out ; it will be instantly followed by another with downright proposals
for instituting associations for bettering the condition
of human kind; at all events, we will have a

L

debating society, and see what will come out of
that." . . . .

"Godwin has introduced me to Curran; I took
the letter this morning. He was not at home. I
shall see him soon." . . . .

Before adverting to this introduction, which Curran
was very slow in acknowledging, we must conclude
our extracts from this long and remarkable letter of
the 14th of February, 1812. The following paragraph,
though written in all seriousness, has a quiet though
unconscious touch of humour about it.   He tells his
correspondent that Eliza Westbrook was going to
collect the " useful passages " out of Tom Paine's
works and publish them, and then adds the rather in-
consequential piece of information from which we are
glad to learn that the good Eliza was at the moment
more " usefully " employed.   " She is now making a
red cloak which will be finished before dinner." . . . .
" Harriet sends her love. Eliza longs to see you." . . . .
The postscript is by Harriet.

" MY DEAR FRIEND,—I have not yet answered your
kind letters, but depend upon it I shall very soon ;
they are not lost upon me I assure you. In the mean-
time believe me,

"Your affectionate friend,

" H. S."

At the commencement of this long letter, hitherto
unpublished, from which we have taken the foregoing
interesting extracts, Shelley expressed a confident
expectation that the Government would not interfere
with his Address.   On this subject he was a true
prophet.   In the Record Office I have examined all
the State Papers of the Irish Government referring to

this period, and while many important documents have been discovered referring to the political action of the Catholics in preparing for the great meeting of the 28th of February, which had been publicly announced, there is no reference whatever to the eloquent pamphlets which Shelley had printed, and one of which he had circulated before that day. The Government, as may be seen from the letter of the Duke of Richmond there preserved, seemed disposed at first to prohibit the holding of this meeting. Wiser counsels however prevailed, and the meeting took place. Special agents, as might be expected, were sent by the Government to give a private report of the proceedings, and their *résumé* of what took place is preserved among the State Papers. It is curious that although Shelley spoke at this meeting for more than an hour, and produced the extraordinary effect which will be described farther on by " an Englishman," who was an eye-witness of the scene, one of the Government reporters does not mention him at all, while the other merely describes him as " Mr. Shelly, who stated himself to be a native of England." Shelley himself was not prepared for this indifference on the part of the Government. He expected that the suspension of the Habeas Corpus Act at least would have shown the alarm which his pamphlets had inspired. To this possibility he refers in an unpublished letter from Radnorshire immediately after leaving Ireland. Harriet also alludes to it with some appearance of alarm in a most interesting letter, a copy of which I have discovered in the Record Office, and which will be given subsequently in full. His youthful appearance may have had something to do with this carelessness on the

part of the Government. He admits that it interfered
with the effect of his teaching on the public. " My
youth is much against me here," he says, in an
unpublished letter, which will presently be given
almost entire. " To improve on this *advantage*," he
continues, " the servant gave out I was only fifteen
years of age." The servant here alluded to was Daniel
Hill, the hero of Barnstaple and Tanyrallt, of whom we
shall have much more to say. Whatever may have been
the cause of the inaction of the Irish Government, it is
certainly strange that the· same documents which
excited so much alarm when discovered at Holyhead
and Barnstaple as to lead to a remarkable correspondence with Ministers of State and the highest
functionaries of the Post Office, attracted no official
notice in Dublin, though sent gratuitously to sixty
public-houses, and flung openly from the windows of
the author's lodgings in the chief street of that
capital.

It will be seen from Shelley's letter of the 14th of
February that he had lost no time in presenting himself with Godwin's introduction at the house of the
Right Hon. John Philpot Curran, the Master of the
Rolls. Mr. Curran was then residing in the fine mansion
on the south side of St. Stephen's Green, the same
house which was subsequently occupied by the eminent lawyer and judge Mr. Burton. On Judge
Burton's death, the late Sir Benjamin Guinness, the
restorer of St. Patrick's Cathedral, purchased the
house for his town residence, and erected ˙ shortly
before his own demise the new and imposing front
and portico by which it is now easily recognised. In
1811 Mr. Curran had been residing in Harcourt
Street, and in 1807 in Ely Place, to which the only

letter of Godwin's to him which has been preserved was directed. This letter, the original of which has been kindly presented to me by a friend, and which has not been published, will be found a little further on.*

Considering the friendship which had long existed between Curran and Godwin, it seems rather strange that the Master of the Rolls should have taken no notice whatever, for a considerable time, of the young reformer who had been introduced to him by the author of *St. Leon.* He seems studiously to have kept out of his way, and Shelley did not succeed even in seeing him until some time after the 18th of March—a period of at least five or six weeks. Godwin had some misgivings as to the reception Shelley possibly might meet with; for before the latter had made any complaint of inattention, he wrote to him in the following words :—" How did you manage with Curran? I hope you have seen him. I should not wonder, however, if your pamphlet has frightened him. You should have left my letter with your card the first time you called, and then it was his business to have sought you" (*Letter of March* 4th, 1812. *Hogg's Life of Shelley,* vol. ii. p. 89). But this is precisely what Shelley had done ten days before his pamphlet was printed; and in those ten days it is plain that Curran had not thought it his business to walk over to Sackville Street to seek Shelley. *The Address to the Irish People* was first announced for publication on Tuesday, February 25th, 1812. In *The Dublin Evening Post* of that day is the following advertisement :—

---

* I am indebted to my friend W. J. Fitzpatrick, Esq., J.P., of Kilmacud Manor, Stillorgan, for this very interesting document.

" This day is published, price Fivepence, to be had of all
the Booksellers,

A N A D D R E S S T O T H E I R I S H P E O P L E.
By PERCY B. SHELLEY.

" ADVERTISEMENT.—The lowest possible price is set on this
publication, because it is the intention of the Author to awaken in
the minds of the Irish poor a knowledge of their real state, summarily pointing out the evils of that state, and suggesting rational
means of remedy.—Catholic Emancipation, and a Repeal of the
Union Act (the latter the most successful engine that England
ever wielded over the misery of fallen Ireland) being treated of in
the following Address, as grievances which unanimity and resolution
may remove, and associations conducted with peaceable firmness,
being earnestly recommended as means for embodying that unanimity and firmness which must finally be successful."

The same advertisement appears in *The Dublin
Evening Post* of Saturday, February 29th, which also
contains the outline of Shelley's speech delivered at
the meeting of the day before. It is given for the
last time in *The Evening Post* of March 3rd, 1812. Of
the second pamphlet—*The Proposals*—I have not been
able to discover an advertisement.

The Address to the Irish People seems to have left
the printer's hands on Monday, the 24th of February,
twelve days after Shelley's arrival in Dublin. On that
day he wrote to Godwin as follows :—" A most
tedious journey by sea and land has brought us to
our destination. I have delayed a few days informing
you of it, because I enclose with this a little pamphlet
which I have just printed, and thereby save a double
expense. I have wilfully vulgarized the language of
this pamphlet, in order to reduce the remarks it contains to the ' taste and comprehension of the Irish
peasantry, who have been too long brutalized by vice
and ignorance. I conceive that the benevolent passions
of their breasts are in some degree excited, and indi-

vidual interests in some degree generalized by Catholic
disqualifications and the oppressive influence of the
Union Act, that some degree of indignation has arisen
at the conduct of the Prince Regent, which might
tend to blind insurrections.   A crisis like this ought
not to be permitted to pass unoccupied or unimproved.
I have another pamphlet in the press, earnestly recommending to a different class the institution of a
philanthropic society.   No *unnatural unanimity* can
take place if secessions of the minority on any question are invariably made.   It might segregate into
twenty different societies, each coinciding generically,
though differing specifically.

" We have had a most tedious voyage.   We were
driven by a storm completely to the north of Ireland
in our passage from the Isle of Man.   Harriet, my
wife, and Eliza, my sister-in-law, were very much
fatigued after twenty-eight hours' tossing in a galliot
during a violent gale.   They are now tolerably recovered.   I am exceedingly obliged by your letter of
introduction to Mr. Curran.   His speeches had interested me before I had any idea of coming to Ireland.
It seems that he was the only man who would engage
in behalf of the prisoners during the times of horror
of the Rebellions.   I have called upon him twice, but
have not found him at home."—*Hogg*, vol. ii. pp.
77, 78.

The allusion at the beginning of this letter to " a
tedious journey by sea and *land*," as well as the period
of the sea-voyage itself, " twenty-eight hours," lead us
to the conclusion that Shelley, like Southey, had
landed at some northern sea-port, and had thence
proceeded by coach to Dublin.   In this way he must
have passed through Swords and the scenery described
by Southey.

Godwin was not the first to whom Shelley sent a specimen of his pamphlet. There is in existence a sheet or page of a Dublin newspaper called *The Correspondent*, on which is written by Shelley the following unpublished note :—" I send you the first sheet of my first Address as it comes out. The style of this, you will perceive, is adapted to the lowest comprehension that can read. It will be followed by another in my own natural style, though in the same strain. This one will make about thirty such pages as the enclosed : the other as much. Expect to hear soon. Happiness be with you. My dear friend, yours——"

The first sheet of the pamphlet was enclosed in this page of *The Correspondent*, on which the foregoing was written. It was evidently the wrapper which came from the printer, and is directed on one of the margins " Mr. Percy Shelley." As in the case of the copy of the pamphlet sent to Godwin, both were forwarded as newspapers, and charged by the vigilant post-masters according to their weight as letters. Godwin was the greater sufferer, as the whole of the pamphlet was included in his package. It must be admitted that he bore his misfortune with good humour. The following allusion to the subject in his reply to Shelley is amusing :—

" To descend from great things to small, I can perceive that you are already infected with the air of that country.* Your letter, with its enclosures, cost me

---

* According to Mr. Charles Phillips, Godwin had himself visited Ireland as the guest of Mr. Curran. " Godwin had gone on a visit to the Priory " [Curran's residence near Stillorgan, Co. Dublin], " where he had at once an opportunity of enjoying the society of his friend and of studying the manners of a new people." (*Recollections of Curran*, p. 233.) As Godwin is reported to have

by post 1*l.* 1*s.* 8*d.*; and you say in it that ' you send it in this way to save expense.' The post always charges parcels that exceed a sheet or two by weight, and they should therefore always be forwarded by some other conveyance."—*Hogg*, vol. ii. p. 90.

In Shelley's rejoinder to this letter, of the 8th of March, he endeavours to console the philosopher by the following explanation :—" I had no conception that the packet I sent you would be sent by the post; I thought it would have reached you per coach." —*Hogg*, vol. ii. p. 95.

It appears that there were three victims to this rather expensive mode of anticipating the book-post— Mr. Westbrook, Miss Hitchener, and Mr. Godwin. In the copy of the letter of Harriet preserved in the State Paper Office is the following passage :—

" I sent you two letters in a newspaper, which I hope you received safe from the intrusion of the post-masters. I sent one of the pamphlets to my father in a newspaper, which was opened and charged, but which was very trifling to what you and Godwin paid."—*Copy of Harriet's Letter in the Record Office.*

This letter of Harriet, though not directed, was written to Miss Hitchener under the name of " Portia," and was a part of the seizure made at Holyhead on the 30th of March, 1812, as will be fully described in a subsequent page. Harriet's letter is dated March 18th, but ten days earlier Shelley himself

---

heard one of Curran's great oratorical displays, and to have admired nothing but " the manner " of the orator, the visit must have been paid before 1806, when Curran became Master of the Rolls. The story told by Mr. Phillips is rather apocryphal, but the fact of the visit may be received, although Mr. William Henry Curran makes no mention of it in the Life of his father.

had referred to the mistake of sending the first sheet of the pamphlet as a newspaper, in the following passage of an unpublished letter to Miss Hitchener. Writing on March 10th, he says : " In a day or two I shall make up a parcel to you, which will come *per coach.* It is a terrible mistake that of the last; the blundering honest Irishman we have came without it." Here a scapegoat had been found in the person of Daniel Hill already referred to, and who thus makes his second appearance in Shelleyan story.

Shelley was evidently a little annoyed at the inattention of Curran, though he makes no direct complaint of it to Godwin. In an unpublished letter of the 27th of February, 1812, he says :—

" I have not yet seen Curran. I do not like him for accepting the office of Master of the Rolls."

One would think from Shelley's remark that Curran had accepted the office of Master of the Rolls in the interval between the date of his own calling at his house on the 14th of February and the 27th of the same month, when he wrote as above to Miss Hitchener. But Curran had been Master of the Rolls since 1806. The opinion expressed by Shelley was evidently formed from conversations which he had in Dublin with persons who agreed with Lord Cloncurry in thinking that Curran's acceptance of office was a somewhat lowering of the position which he had held in the estimation of his countrymen.* There can be very little doubt who some of those Dublin friends of Shelley were, as will presently be pointed out.

---

* *Personal Recollections of Valentine, Lord Cloncurry,* pp. 169, 170.

CHAPTER VIII.

THE letter of introduction to Curran which Shelley received from Godwin has not been preserved. Indeed it is remarkable that so few of the letters, either written by Curran or addressed to him, have been published. This renders the following letter the more interesting, and it may perhaps serve as a substitute for that which Shelley presented to Curran from Godwin. It is rendered still more interesting by the unexpected and unintended explanations of some of its allusions which I found in the Record Office. As a letter written by Godwin to Curran, it is in itself a document worth preserving, and may not be considered wholly irrelevant to the subject in hand.

Unpublished Letter of Godwin to Curran.

" The Right Honourable the Master of the Rolls,
Ely Place, Dublin.

Somers Town, London, March 7th, 1807.

" DEAR CURRAN,—When last in England, you made me two promises shall I say? No, neither of them was absolutely a promise, but both very interesting to me. One had the word March, with which it was connected in tenour, and the other the word Spring.

" I am very desirous of seeing you in March, and that not only for the immediate pleasure it would give me, but as connected with your visits of September

and December last, it would be a pledge of the
frequency with which I might hope to see you; I
should then think of you as a neighbour; I should
feel as if forty and not four hundred miles was the
distance that separated us. But alas! this is the 7th
of March. I look in my almanac, and find that
Easter Term (curse on the technical phraseology!)
begins April 15th; I ruminate on human frailty, and
begin to suspect both that you are not Jupiter, and
that you have not sworn by Styx that you will come.

" The other subject I allude to, I am sorry to say,
is of a sordid and mercenary cast, such an one as we
shall not be obliged to think on, if ever we meet
hereafter in Utopia or Elysium. What you said of it
was not a promise; yet as it first occurred in
September, and was reconsidered at Christmas, I have
been compelled to rely upon it with some sanguineness
of hope, and, sordid and mercenary as it is, it is necessary I should own that it is intimately connected with
the existence of myself and my family. My commercial affairs are going on with sufficient prosperity
of promise. The Fables, as you know, have been
printed twice; the Pantheon is much in request; the
little History of England, which at first seemed to be
hardly noticed, I am now obliged instantly to send
again to the press, and the Shakspeare Tales I am
pressé to bring out separately in twenty parts (three
are already finished), in which form I have reason to
think I shall sell ten or twenty thousand copies. Yet
amid all this plentifulness of prospect, I suffer a considerable degree of famine of means. Great disburse-
ments are necessary, and you, who (happy, thrice
happy man!) were never entangled in affairs of com-
merce, can have no idea of the unconscionable credit

which traders in this commercial country demand and must obtain. My books of course are principally sold to the booksellers, by whom they are distributed through the town and the empire ; and they will only settle with the dealer once a year, at Christmas, when their accounts are liquidated by bills at three, six, and nine months after date. My demands against them for last Christmas were comparatively small, being at most solely for the two volumes of Fables, and it is therefore impossible that I should find myself entirely at my ease till Christmas next. I can indeed, and shall make a forced sale of some of my books for an earlier payment, but that can only be to a small limited amount. If I were to exceed that, I should part with them almost for waste paper. I should have laboured, and other men would enter into the fruits of my labour. Thus circumstanced, it cannot be but that I shall have to struggle with great difficulties, and to encounter great anxieties during the present year ; but this I shall meet with the utmost chearfulness,* if ease and competence and peace seem likely to be the final result.

" Having thus, my dear friend, [laid the state of my position] before you, the first thing I have [to hope is that you whom I relied entirely] on would not hold me in suspense, [as I have pay]ments to make on the

---

* " Chearfulness."—This old-fashioned mode of spelling the word was nearly extinct in Godwin's time. It is so written in a letter from John Wilkes, dated Naples, May 25th, 1765. Referring to Churchill, he says—" I have a present from Rome of a sepulchral urn of alabaster, which I am going to inscribe to my friend in his three great characters—a *chearful* companion, a bitter satirist, and a true patriot."—See *Notes and Queries*, 4th S. v. p. 48, January 8th, 1870.

2nd and following days [of June?] to the amount of
300*l.*;* and though I have not, and very probably
cannot find any adequate resources independently of
the hopes you have given me, yet the greatest calamity
that could happen to me would be to be kept to the
last moment in vain expectation.

" I have seen Lord Lauderdale twice somewhat in
the way of a message from Lord Holland.   What will
come of it I am unable to say.

" I have just seen an account in a newspaper of
your having been taken ill in court, Feb. 26th. I hope
by the time this reaches you, you will just have forgotten
the circumstance.

" I am, my dear Curran,

"With the sincerest regard and affection,

" Yours,

" W. Godwin.

" Mrs. Godwin begs me to add a line to say how
truly she joins in remembrance."

Few authors, except those who, to use the language
of Lord Byron as applied to his friend Hobhouse,
aim at " foaming into patriots to subside in Newgate,"
can expect that their works should undergo a critical
examination in the office of a Minister of State. Had
there been a Minister of Instruction, as in France, the
subject of the following paper would come legitimately
under his notice ; but to add to the many labours
of the Secretary for the Home Department, the task

---

* Godwin had commenced writing another figure, I think 400*l.*,
which he changed to 300.   The upright stroke of 4 makes the
figure 3 look like 8, but that appears to be too large a sum to ask
his friend, who was only one year on the Bench, to advance him.

of discovering the hidden and perhaps dangerous meaning that may underlie the impenetrable profundity of this poet or of that proser, might deter the most courageous from assuming the dignity and undertaking the responsibilities of office. The Secretary of State for the Home Department in 1813 was Viscount Sidmouth, whose head in 1820 narrowly escaped the honour of being put into a special bag with Lord Castlereagh's by the Cato Street conspirators. He had another escape of a less tragic kind two years earlier. At the earnest solicitation, as it would seem, of Lady Donegal, he was left out of *The Fudge Family.* Moore at first seemed reluctant to yield the point. Alluding to a lady he had spared, at his friend's request, the satirist proceeds, " She is, however, safe, though it has already cost me the strangling of two or three young epigrams in their cradle. *All,* in fact, shall be safe, except Lord Sidmouth; but that the author of the Circular, the patron of spies and informers, the father of the Green Bag, the eulogist of the Knights of Northampton (?), &c. &c., should not have a touch or two, is out of the nature of things. I only promise that he shall neither be called ' Doctor,' nor ' Old Woman,' which is quite as much as his warmest friends could expect."—*Moore to Lady Donegal,* Jan. 9th, 1818. *Moore's Memoirs,* vol. ii. 131.

The friendly mantle, however, of Lady Donegal protected the noble Viscount, as he does not figure in *The Fudge Family,* or in any of Moore's satirical poems. Shelley was made of sterner stuff. The rather ineffective statesman whom Moore spared and Thistlewood had not the opportunity of decapitating, the author of the *Masque of Anarchy* represented, only in metaphor it must be admitted, as riding " on a crocodile."

> Clothed with the Bible as with light
> And the shadow of the night,
> Like Sidmouth next, Hypocrisy
> On a crocodile came by.
>
> *The Masque of Anarchy*, st. vi.

For figuring so conspicuously in the *Masque of Shadows*, which passed before the mind of the dreaming poet as he " lay asleep in Italy," Lord Sidmouth would probably have forgiven the charge of hypocrisy. It is scarcely necessary to say that any who professed to believe in Christianity must have been a hypocrite in Shelley's estimation. One who knew Lord Sidmouth's private character thus speaks of him : " We were also at that poor dear honest man's, Lord Sidmouth's, for a few days. As to your wicked story of his getting drunk and singing ballads with his royal master, there is not a word of truth in it ; it would be much more like him in his cups to give him a high-flown discourse upon all the cardinal virtues and Christian graces. Seriously, I believe him to be as honest, as frank, and as open a character, as free from all little meannesses as any man in the whole world."—*Miss Godfrey to Moore*, Feb. 1816. *Moore's Memoirs*, vol. ii. 95.

This character of Lord Sidmouth, however, renders it the more remarkable that he took no notice of the following State Paper which endeavours to prove the insidious artifice of Godwin in disseminating his peculiar views under the harmless appearance of children's books. The writer of the paper, whose name is not given, probably calculated on the popular estimate of Lord Sidmouth's religious principles for his taking a special interest in the subject. In this he was mistaken. Whether Lord Sidmouth would have preferred to "drink up Esil, eat a crocodile," or ride one, rather than read Godwin's *Juvenile Library*, cannot be stated with absolute certainty; but that he did not do so is plain from the only endorsement which appears on the back of the following remarkable document, the brief but significant word "nil." The paper is to be found in the Record Office : "Domestic, Geo. III., 1813. January to March. No. 217."

"A FEW PARTICULARS CONCERNING GODWIN'S JUVENILE LIBRARY WHICH OUGHT TO BE MADE GENERALLY KNOWN.

"Godwin's Library was carried on for some time in Hanway Yard, Oxford Street, without any name either at the shop or on the several publications published for it. The business has since been removed to Skinner Street,* Snow Hill, for the last three or four years; for some time also it was called the Juvenile Library; no name appeared.

"At length Mr. J. Godwin† was written on the door-post in very small letters; within a very few months it appeared boldly in large letters over the door; still it is very little known that the proprietor

---

* Curran, in a letter to Leonard MacNally, gives the number "Godwin's, 41, Skinner Street, London."—*Life of Curran*, by his Son, vol. ii. p. 172.

† This could scarcely be intended for John Godwin, an elder brother of William, who was a member of the Inner Temple, and died in 1805 (*Notes and Queries*, 3rd S. i. p. 503). Shelley, writing from Field Place, Dec. 20th, 1810, speaks of a John Godwin then living. "It is not William Godwin who lives in Holborn—it is *John*; no relative to the other" (*Hogg*, i. 144). In the same letter Shelley says he had written to William Godwin. The philosopher replied briefly, and addressed his correspondent as "Reverend."

M

is *Godwin,* the author of *Political Justice.* There appears to be a regular system through all his publications to supersede all other elementary books, and to make his library the resort of preparatory schools, that in time the principles of democracy and Theophilanthropy may take place universally.

" In order to allure schools of a moderate and a lower class, he holds out the temptation of an allowance of threepence in every shilling for such books as are published by him. He publishes books with the name of Edward Baldwin, Esq., which are said to be his own writing.

" One of these, *Baldwin's Mythology,* has been introduced at the *Charter House.* It is an insidious and dangerous publication. The preface is calculated to mislead well-disposed persons, who may perhaps be too indolent or misjudging to read through the whole work ; it professes to exalt the purity and show the superiority of Christianity over the heathen morality taught in the Grecian and Roman mythology, and then through the whole work improperly excites the curiosity of young persons to read the grossest stories on the subject, and artfully hints the wisdom of the morality of the heathen world. The principal works he has published are a Grecian, a Roman, and an English History, all three of the size of Goldsmith's abridgments. In these, every democratic sentiment is printed in italics that they may not fail to present themselves to a child's notice, and as a specimen of some ideas contained in these works the following may be mentioned. In the History of Rome, instead of carrying it down to the destruction of the Empire it leaves off at the reign of Augustus, and in italics remarks that it is useless to write the History of the tyrants who governed for the remaining 400 years, for when it ceased to be a *Republic* it ceased to deserve the name of History.

"The History of England opens with some extraordinary remarks on the subject of the Druids and the subsequent introduction of Christianity into the island. When it arrives at the reign of Elizabeth, instead of noticing the Reformation it says she was tinctured with superstition, though in other respects a woman of abilities ; and the reign of George the Third is only remarkable for two events—America declaring her Independence and the Revolution in France.

"Godwin has also among his list Mylius's *English Dictionary*, which has been inadvertently introduced into *Christ's Hospital*. It is a pocket dictionary, the danger of which consists in giving only *one* meaning to words which have several, and omitting all such words as philosophers of the present day do not like to explain. For example, take the word 'revolution,' the meaning given is, 'things returning to their just state.' By their interpretation the Bible is no longer to be understood *The* Book, but according to it there are various bibles, one for every religious sect, for example, the word ' Koran, the Bible of the Mahometans.'

"The next publication is an abridgment of Horne Tooke's *Diversions of Purley*, by Haylets, simplified, as it is pretended, for young people, to the price of 3s. 6d., and again reduced to a one shilling publication. Next, *Fables Ancient and Modern*, by Baldwin, which are amplified to four pages for each fable.

"By these different publications it is evident there is an intention to have every work published for the

M 2

Juvenile Library that can be required in the early instruction of children, and thus by degrees to give an
opportunity for every principle professed by the
infidels and republicans of these days to be introduced to their notice.

" By such means did Voltaire and his brethren
for twenty years before the Revolution in France
spread infidelity and disloyalty through the remotest
provinces of that country, and we know too well how
they succeeded.

" In the *Times'* newspaper of this date (17 Feb.
1813) the various juvenile books of Mr. Godwin are
advertised with a positive statement at the head of
the advertisement that they are *sanctioned by the
schoolmasters of Christ Hospital and used in that institution."*

There is no signature to this paper. No action
seems to have been taken upon it. To the last passage,
which is underlined, there is a " N.B." in pencil in the
margin. The only endorsement except the date,
"17 Feb. 1813," is, as I have said, the word " nil."

Retracing our steps after this digression about
Godwin, we resume our narrative of Shelley's proceedings in Dublin.

Shelley's *Address to the Irish People* came from the
printer's hand on the 24th of February, 1812. On
that day, as we have seen, he sent an early copy by
post to Godwin. On the following day, the 25th,
the pamphlet was published. The advertisement
which appeared in the *Dublin Evening Post* of that
date has already been given. We may be sure that
one of the earliest copies presented personally by
Shelley was to the Master of the Rolls. " I have not

seen Mr. Curran," says Shelley, in a letter to Godwin of the 8th of March. "I have called repeatedly, left my address and my pamphlet. I *will* see him before I leave Dublin." On the day of publication he sent a copy of the *Address to the Irish People* to Hamilton Rowan, with the following letter:—

"7, Lower Sackville Street, Feb. 25th, 1812.

"Sir,—Although I have not the pleasure of being personally known to you, I consider the motives which actuated me in writing the inclosed sufficiently introductory to authorize me in sending you some copies, and waiving ceremonials in a case where public benefit is concerned. Sir, although an Englishman, I feel for Ireland; and I have left the country in which the chance of birth placed me for the sole purpose of adding my little stock of usefulness to the fund which I hope that Ireland possesses to aid me in the unequal yet sacred combat in which she is engaged. In the course of a few days more I shall print another small pamphlet, which shall be sent to you. I have intentionally vulgarized the language of the enclosed. I have printed 1500 copies, and am now distributing them throughout Dublin.

"Sir, with respect,
    "I am your obedient humble servant,
        "P. B. SHELLEY."

Mr. Middleton, in his work called *Shelley and his Writings*, referring to this subject, says, "Dr. Drummond tells us that 'Shelley selected Ireland as a theatre the widest and fairest for the operations of the determined friends of political and religious freedom' (vol. i. p. 210), and adds in a note, 'See Life of

Hamilton Rowan.'" It is quite evident that this gentleman did not consult the work from which he professes to quote. The observation about selecting Ireland is not Dr. Drummond's but Shelley's, and is to be found in the postscript to his first pamphlet. No one who had Dr. Drummond's book before him could fall into this mistake. He says, " In February, 1812, the celebrated poet Percy Bysshe Shelley paid a visit to Dublin, having, as he informs us, ' selected Ireland as a theatre the widest and fairest for the operations of the determined friends of religious and political freedom' " (p. 388). In this extract, however, Dr. Drummond himself has not transcribed the words quite correctly. Shelley says, " the friend," not " the friends " " of religious and political freedom."

The fact that Hamilton Rowan preserved until the day of his death, which took place on the 1st of November, 1834, when he had reached his eighty-fourth year, both the pamphlet and letter of Shelley, shows that he must have felt some interest both in the subject and in the writer. Could he have foreseen the connexion which was ultimately to take place between the daughter of his old friend Mary Wollstonecraft,* and the young political enthusiast of 1812, we may be sure that in him Shelley would have found a sincere

---

* The fact that Mary Wollstonecraft's mother was an Irishwoman may not have been without interest to Hamilton Rowan. " Her father's name was Edward·John," says Mr. Godwin, " and the name of her mother Elizabeth, of the family of Dixons of Ballyshannon, in the kingdom of Ireland " (*Memoirs of the Author of a Vindication of the Right of Woman*, p. 5). Some interesting particulars of Mary Wollstonecraft's life in France during her connexion with Mr. Gilbert Imlay may be found in *The Autobiography of Hamilton Rowan*, by Dr. Drummond.

and useful friend. Shelley in his letter speaks of
" copies" of his pamphlet, but one only it would appear was sent. This particular copy I have seen. On
the death of Mr. Rowan, after a brief delay, his papers
were placed in the hands of the Rev. Dr. Drummond,
one of the ministers of the Unitarian Meeting-house,
Strand Street, Dublin, and with these the letter and
pamphlet of Shelley. *The Address to the Irish People*
was inscribed on the title-page in Mr. Rowan's handwriting, " Mr. Shelley's pamphlet with a letter." The
letter as above stated was printed in the *Autobiography of Hamilton Rowan*, and the original in this way
got separated from the pamphlet. This was sold a
few years ago, after the death of Dr. Drummond, at
the auction of his library. It was bought by a Dublin
bookseller, who deals almost exclusively in works relating to Ireland,* and was resold by him, as he
informs me, to the late learned Dr. Todd, the Librarian
of Trinity College, Dublin, who purchased it either for
himself or the College library. On the sale of Dr.
Todd's valuable library, however, which commenced
on November 15th, 1869, it was not forthcoming;
neither had it been received at the library of Trinity
College a year later, when I inquired for it.

The two days that followed the writing of the
letter to Hamilton Rowan must have been busy and
exciting ones for Shelley. How he was occupied, and
the extraordinary steps he took to circulate his pamphlet among the people of Dublin, will be best shown
by the following copious extracts from a hitherto un-

---

* Mr. John O'Daly, of 9, Anglesea Street, Dublin, in whose
Bibliotheca Hibernica the *Address to the Irish People*, by Percy
Bysshe Shelley, was advertised at the time referred to.

published letter of Shelley to his philosophical female friend at Hurstpierpoint in Sussex. Long as these extracts are, they form only a portion of the letter. I have selected only those passages that refer to the public objects he had in view—such explanations as seem needful will be given at the end.

From an unpublished letter of Shelley to Miss Hitchener.

" Feb. 27 [1812], 7, Lower Sackville Street.

" I have already sent 400 of my Irish pamphlets into the world, and they have excited a sensation of wonder in Dublin. 1100 yet remain for distribution. Copies have been sent to sixty public-houses. No prosecution is yet attempted. I do not see how it can be. Congratulate me, my friend, for everything proceeds well. I could not expect more rapid success. The persons with whom I have got acquainted approve of my principles . . . . but they differ from the mode of my improving their principles " . . . . [Referring to his wish to have his friend with him in Dublin, he says that it did not arise from any private partiality], " but because you would share with me the high delight of awaking a noble nation from the lethargy of its bondage. Expectation is on the tip-toe. I send a man out every day to distribute copies, with instructions where and how to give them. His account corresponds with the multitudes of people who possess them. I stand at the balcony of our window, and watch till I see a man *who looks likely.* I throw a book to him. On Monday my next book makes its appearance : this is addressed to a different class, recommending and proposing associations. I have in my mind a plan for proselytizing the young men at

Dublin College. Those who are not entirely given up to the grossness of dissipation are perhaps reclaimable." . . . . " Whilst you are with us in Wales I shall attempt to organize one there" [that is, a " philanthropic association"], which will co-operate with the Dublin one. Might I not extend them all over England, and *quietly* revolutionize the country ?" . . . . " My *youth* is much against me here. Strange that truth should not be judged by its inherent excellence, independent of any reference to the utterer. To improve on this *advantage,* the servant gave out I was only fifteen years of age." . . . . " I have not yet seen Curran. I do not like him for accepting the office of Master" [of the Rolls]. " O'Connor, brother to the rebel Arthur, is here." [I have] " written to him. Do not fear what you say in your letters. I am resolved. Good principles are scarce here. The public papers are either Oppositionists or Ministerial. One is as contemptible and narrow as the other. I wish I could change this. I am of course hated by both of those parties. The remnant of united Irishmen whose wrongs make them hate England, I have more hope of. I have met with no determined republicans, but have found some who are democratifiable." . . . . " We shall leave this place at the end of April. I must not be idle in Wales : there you will come to us. Bring the dear little Americans, resign your school, and live with us for ever."

The postscript is by Harriet.

" Percy has given me his letter to fill up, but what I'm to say I really do not know. Oh, yesterday I received a most affectionate letter from dear Mrs. C——" [probably Calvert]. " Now don't you be jealous when I mention her name. She is afraid we shall effect no good here, and thinks our opinions will change of the Irish. We have seen very little of them as yet, but when Percy is more known, I suppose we shall know more at the same time. My pen is very bad, according to custom. I am sure you would laugh were you to see us give the pamphlets. We throw them out of window, and give them to men that we pass in the streets. For myself I am ready to die of laughter when it is done, and Percy looks so grave. Yesterday he put one into a woman's hood of a cloak. She knew nothing of it, and we passed her and could hardly get on, my muscles (?) were so irritated."(?)

There is a second postscript by Shelley.

"I have been necessarily called away whilst Harriet has been scribbling. You may guess how much my time is taken up. Adieu—the post will go. You will soon hear again from your affectionate and unalterable　　　　　　　　　　　　　　" PERCY."

The whole of these curious extracts will be read with interest, particularly perhaps the girlish and simple postscript of Harriet. The eleven hundred copies of the *Address to the Irish People* which remained for distribution seem to have been almost all dispersed by the 18th of March, as we shall find by Harriet's remarkable letter of that date which was stopped at Holyhead, and a copy of which, sent to the Home Secretary, is still preserved in the Record Office, that few then remained in the possession of the author. It is to be noticed that at the moment when Shelley " could not expect more rapid success," he had fixed the time of his intended departure from Ireland. This disposes of the statement so frequently repeated that Shelley abandoned his Irish project in disgust. The man whom Shelley sent out every day to distribute the pamphlets, was in all probability "the servant" who gave out that Shelley was only fifteen years of age. This was Daniel Hill, who accompanied the Shelleys to Barnstaple, who was arrested and imprisoned there, who turned up at a critical moment at Tanyrallt, returned with the Shelleys to Dublin, and eventually went with them to London. The letter of Shelley corroborates the story told in the *North British Review,* for November, 1847, in an article on the *Life and Writings of Shelley.* The paper was written by my lamented friend the late Dr. Anster, the translator of *Faust.** He says :—"Shelley's pamphlet is before us. Medwin it seems searched in vain for a copy. Ours was obtained through an Irish friend of Shelley's, whose acquaintance with the poet originated accidentally. A poor man offered the pamphlet for a few pence—its price stated on the title-page was fivepence. On being asked how he got it, he said a parcel of them were given him by a

---

* In the last letter which I had the pleasure of receiving from the celebrated author of the *History of Spanish Literature,* Mr. Ticknor makes the following allusion to Dr. Anster, under date Boston, Aug. 29th, 1870. " I was touched and pleased to see your extract from Anster's *Faustus,* which I have liked ever since parts of it appeared anonymously in *Blackwood's Magazine.* Indeed I knew the author afterwards in Dublin in 1835, and have a copy of the first part, which I value not a little as his gift. I dare say you knew him. Yours very cordially, GEORGE TICKNOR." This tribute of the great American scholar, written a few months before his death, to the memory of a highly accomplished, able, and amiable man will be read with interest.

young gentleman, who told him to get what he could
for them—at all events to distribute them.   Inquiry
was made at Shelley's lodgings to ascertain the truth
of the vendor's story.   He was not at home; but
when he heard of it he went to return the visit, and
kindly acquaintanceship thus arose.   The Shelleys—
husband and wife—were then Pythagoreans.   Shelley
spoke as a man believing in the metempsychosis—and
they did not eat animal food.   They seem however
to have tolerated it; for on one occasion a fowl was
murdered for our friend's dinner.   Of the first Mrs.
Shelley the recollection of our friend is faint, but it is
of an amiable and unaffected person; very young
and very pleasing, and she and Shelley seemed much
attached."   After describing the *Address to the Irish
People*, Dr. Anster says (speaking of Shelley) : " And
he promises another pamphlet, in which he shall
reveal the plan and structure of the proposed association.   Whether he printed that pamphlet we have not
been able to learn."—*North British Review*, vol. viii.
Nov. 1847.

This last sentence raises considerable doubt as to
the extent of the personal acquaintance said to have
existed between Dr. Anster's friend and Shelley.   A
person who had sought Shelley out in consequence of
the interest excited in him by the first pamphlet could
scarcely have been left in ignorance of the second.
Of the second pamphlet Dr. Anster's informant knew
nothing, probably from its not having been mentioned
by Medwin, who was equally ignorant of its existence.
It was published on Monday the 2nd of March,
1812, about a week before the adoption of the Pythagorean system of diet by Shelley and his wife.   The time
at which they commenced to abstain from animal

food is fixed almost to the day by Harriet herself in an unpublished letter which will subsequently be quoted. In another part of Dr. Anster's very interesting paper on Shelley, he speaks from the recollection of the late Chief Baron Woulfe of Shelley's cold and precise mode of addressing a public meeting. This will be found to have arisen from some imperfect recollection of the circumstance by the estimable judge.

The plan for " proselytizing the young men at Dublin College," or at least such of them as were not " *entirely* given up to the grossness of dissipation," has unfortunately not been revealed. We are left in ignorance also whether it was to patriotism, philanthropy, or the Pythagorean system they were to be converted. Whatever may have been the direction of the intended reformation, there may be some who will think that this project was not the least chimerical of those that occupied the mind and heart of the young poet when in Dublin.

The balcony in front of 7, Lower Sackville Street, from which Shelley and Harriet threw the pamphlets to whoever looked " likely," still remains. It runs across the whole width of the house, so that Percy and Harriet had each a window from which they could bombard the astonished town with " books." We have no doubt that he must have enjoyed this mode of diffusing useful knowledge immensely—quite as much as he did the following year at Lymouth when he substituted for it his oil-skin boats and air-tight bottles. The house then belonging to Mr. Dunne was occupied for many years by Messrs. Köhler and Co., and is now in possession of Messrs. Stark Brothers, printsellers and artists. As long as the

balcony remains it will always be an object of interest
to those who regard with something like affection
even the "local habitation" of an author whom they
love as well as admire.

The "O'Connor, brother to the rebel Arthur," to
whom Shelley wrote, was the celebrated Roger
O'Connor, father of the perhaps still more famous
Fergus O'Connor. The history of Arthur O'Connor,
who became a general in the French service, is too
well known to be dwelt on here. Arthur and Roger
O'Connor were nephews of Viscount Longueville, and
the events of both their lives are full of romance and
mystery.* The most famous event in the life of Roger
was the charge, for which he was tried and acquitted
in 1817, of having, with a band of his retainers, robbed
the Galway mail coach in 1812, the year in which the
letter above alluded to was addressed to him by
Shelley. It is stated that plunder was not the
motive of this daring outrage; but that certain documents of a political nature compromising both Roger
O'Connor and Sir Francis Burdett being known to
be in the mail bags, the attempt to secure them was
made and successfully carried out. The active agents
in the matter were, however, not so fastidious in their
tastes. Five of the gang were subsequently hanged
at Cavan for attempting to pass some of the bank-
notes plundered on this occasion. If there had been
any person of rank the leader or tempter in this outrage, the fidelity of these men is very remarkable.
From my own recollection I know that a popular
though unfounded impression exists in Ireland that
Roger O'Connor had something to do with the affair.
That seems to have arisen from an idea that there
was enough of the daring and romantic in the act as

to make it not uncharacteristic of the man. There is no evidence whatever worth a moment's consideration that would in any way connect Sir Francis Burdett with such a lawless proceeding. In fact, the circumstance of his coming to Ireland in 1817 to stand beside his friend, for whose independence of mind on political matters he had a great regard, when Roger O'Connor was tried for this offence and acquitted, is an evidence not only of his own, but of his friend's innocence in the matter. Those who care to read " a sensational story " on the subject, should get the *sixth* edition of Mr. Fitzpatrick's popular work *Ireland before the Union,* as certain misapprehensions connected with Sir Francis Burdett, previously inserted in the work, are corrected in that edition.

Nothing further in Shelley's letter of the 27th of February, 1812, seems to require explanation.

The following extract is taken from another unpublished letter of Shelley to Miss Hitchener. It is undated, but was probably written some time after the preceding. The intended visit to the printer could have no reference to the second pamphlet, which was by that time probably struck off, as it was published three days later. It was more likely in connexion with *The Declaration of Rights,* a broadside intended for posting on walls, which he printed at Dublin, and which formed part of the seizure at Holyhead on the 30th of March, 1812. The establishment of the very peculiar bank of deposit referred to in the following extract, where the common stock of the three travellers was kept for security, was not a discreditable, and may have been a wise precaution on the part of the much abused Eliza Westbrook :—

(*From an unpublished letter of Shelley.*)

".... Things go on in Ireland as you shall know. I have much food for interest and occupation of mind in the events of each day." .... "Eliza keeps our common stock of money for safety in some nook or corner of her dress, but we are not dependent on her, although she gives it out as we want it." .... "You think too meanly of yourself, too highly of me." .... "I proceed (?) in the next street after I have seen the printer."

It may be mentioned that one of the sheets of *The Correspondent*, a Dublin newspaper, previously referred to as having been sent to Miss Hitchener as a wrapper to some enclosure, is part of the number for "Friday, March 13th, 1812." Both the pamphlets were at that date printed and circulated. The other sheet of *The Correspondent* must have belonged to a different and earlier number of that paper, as Shelley writes in it that he sent therewith the first sheet of *The Address to the Irish People.* The second sheet of *The Correspondent*, on which there is a rude pen-and-ink drawing by Shelley, probably contained the proof sheet of *The Declaration of Rights,* and this fixes the time of its being printed, which was certainly before the 18th of March, on which day it was forwarded to Holyhead with all the copies of the pamphlets then remaining in Shelley's hands.

This may be the fitting time to introduce the first of these remarkable pamphlets, *The Address to the Irish People.* Excepting an occasional correction of some obvious error of the press, it is here printed exactly as in the original. From many of the historical parallels and deductions I entirely differ, as will doubtless most of my readers. .Those who do not may study with advantage the following judicious remarks of Godwin to Shelley himself on the receipt of this very pamphlet :—

" One principle that I believe is wanting to you, and all our too fervent and impetuous reformers, is the thought that almost every institution or form of society is good in its place, and in the period of time to which it belongs. How many beautiful and admirable effects grew out of Popery and the monastic institution, in the period when they were in their genuine health and vigour. To them we owe almost all our logic and our literature."—*Letter to Shelley,* March 4th, 1812.*

---

* The great excuse of Shelley lies in " his want of religious education at home," which his friend Captain Medwin in the words just quoted frankly admits (*Life of Shelley,* vol. ii. p. 357). In that best of schools the feelings of love and reverence which are usually implanted in the minds and hearts of most children seem to have been entirely omitted in the case of the neglected Shelley. To his ill-chosen college friend Mr. Hogg, with whom at the time he was only acquainted six months, he could thus write of the most hallowed circle in the world—that which is drawn around the fireside of one's home. " Certain members of my family," says Shelley, " are no more Christians than Epicurus himself" (*Hogg,* vol. i. p. 377). We may deplore the sad condition of such a childhood, but we cannot admit that the experience which is here so painfully acknowledged prepared the writer to be either a just or competent critic of the effects of religious teaching on the minds of others who happily were subject to far different influences. As for the supposed facts, historical and theological, in Shelley's pamphlet, they are for the most part simply untrue. The unconscious libel on the religion of the people he addressed, which he calls " fair," is, under the circumstances of the case, absolutely amusing.

N

AN ADDRESS

TO THE

IRISH PEOPLE.

BY PERCY BYSSHE SHELLEY.

ADVERTISEMENT.

The lowest possible price is set on this publication, because it is the intention of the Author to awaken in the minds of the Irish poor a knowledge of their real state, summarily pointing out the evils of that state, and suggesting rational means of remedy.—Catholic Emancipation, and a Repeal of the Union Act (the latter, the most successful engine that England ever wielded over the misery of fallen Ireland) being treated of in the following Address, as grievances which unanimity and resolution may remove, and associations conducted with peaceable firmness, being earnestly recommended as means for embodying that unanimity and firmness which must finally be successful.

𝔇ublin:

1812.

Price 5d.

AN ADDRESS

TO THE

IRISH PEOPLE.

———

FELLOW MEN,—

I am not an Irishman, yet I can feel for you. I hope there are none among you who will read this address with prejudice or levity, because it is made by an Englishman; indeed, I believe there are not. The Irish are a brave nation. They have a heart of liberty in their breasts, but they are much mistaken if they fancy that a stranger cannot have as warm a one. Those are my brothers and my countrymen who are unfortunate. I should like to know what there is in a man being an Englishman, a Spaniard, or a Frenchman that makes him worse or better than he really is. He was born in one town, you in another, but that is no reason why he should not feel for you, desire your benefit, or be willing to give you some advice, which may make you more capable of knowing your own interest, or acting so as to secure it. There are many Englishmen who cry down the Irish, and think it answers their ends to revile all that belongs to Ireland: but it is not because these men are Englishmen that they maintain such

opinions, but because they wish to get money, and
titles, and power. They would act in this manner to
whatever country they might belong, until mankind is
much altered for the better, which reform, I hope,
will one day be effected. I address you, then, as my
brothers and my fellow men, for I should wish to see
the Irishman who, if England was persecuted as
Ireland is, who, if France was persecuted as Ireland
is, who, if any set of men that helped to do a public
service, were prevented from enjoying its benefits as
Irishmen are—1 should like to see the man, I say,
who would see these misfortunes, and not attempt to
succour the sufferers when he could, just that I might
tell him that he was no Irishman, but some bastard
mongrel bred up in a court, or some coward fool who
was a democrat to all above him, and an aristocrat to
all below him. I think there are few true Irishmen
who would not be ashamed of such a character, still
fewer who possess it. I know that there are some, not
among you, my friends, but among your enemies, who,
seeing the title of this piece, will take it up with a
sort of hope that it may recommend violent measures,
and thereby disgrace the cause of freedom, that the
warmth of an heart desirous that liberty should be
possessed equally by all, will vent itself in abuse on
the enemies of liberty, bad men who deserve the contempt of the good, and ought not to excite their
indignation to the harm of their cause. But these
men will be disappointed—I know the warm feeling
of an Irishman sometimes carries him beyond the
point of prudence. I do not desire to root out, but
to moderate this honourable warmth. This will dis-
appoint the pioneers of oppression, and they will be
sorry that through this address nothing will occur

which can be twisted into any other meaning but
what is calculated to fill you with that moderation
which they have not, and make you give them that
toleration which they refuse to grant to you. You
profess the Roman Catholic religion which your fathers
professed before you. Whether it is the best religion
or not I will not here inquire : all religions are good
which make men good ; and the way that a person
ought to prove that his method of worshipping God is
best is for himself to be better than all other men.
But we will consider what your religion was in old
times and what it is now : you may say it is not a fair
way for me to proceed as a Protestant, but I am not a
Protestant, nor am I a Catholic, and therefore not
being a follower of either of these religions, I am
better able to judge between them. A Protestant is
my brother, and a Catholic is my brother. I am
happy when I can do either of them a service, and no
pleasure is so great to me than that which I should
feel if my advice could make men of any profession of
faith, wiser, better, and happier.

The Roman Catholics once persecuted the Protestants, the ·Protestants now persecute the Roman
Catholics. Should we think that one is as bad as the
other? No, you are not answerable for the faults of
your fathers any more than the Protestants are good
for the goodness of their fathers. I must judge of
people as I see them ; the Irish Catholics are badly
used. I will not endeavour to hide from them their
wretchedness; they would think that I mocked at them
if I should make the attempt. The Irish Catholics now
demand for themselves and proffer for others unlimited toleration, and the sensible part among them,
which I am willing to think constitutes a very large

portion of their body, know that the gates of Heaven
are open to people of every religion, provided they are
good.   But the Protestants, although they may think
so in their hearts, which certainly, if they think at all,
they must, seem to act as if they thought that God was
better pleased with them than with you ; they trust the
reins of earthly government only to the hands of their
own sect.   In spite of this, I never found one of them
impudent enough to say that a Roman Catholic, or a
Quaker, or a Jew, or a Mahometan, if he was a virtuous
man, and did all the good in his power, would go to
Heaven a bit the slower for not subscribing to the
thirty-nine articles ; and if he should say so, how ridiculous in a foppish courtier not six feet high to direct
the spirit of universal harmony in what manner to
conduct the affairs of the universe !

The Protestants say that there was a time when the
Roman Catholics burnt and murdered people of different sentiments, and that their religious tenets are
now as they were then.   This is all very true.   You
certainly worship God in the same way that you did
when these barbarities took place, but is that any reason
that you should now be barbarous ?   There is as much
reason to suppose it as to suppose that because a man's
great-grandfather, who was a Jew, had been hung for
sheepstealing, that I, by believing the same religion
as he did, must certainly commit the same crime.   Let
us then see what the Roman Catholic religion has been.
No one knows much of the early times of the Christian
religion until about three hundred years after its beginning ; two great Churches, called the Roman and
the Greek Churches, divided the opinions of men.   They
fought for a very long time—a great many words were
wasted, and a great deal of blood shed.

This, as you may suppose, did no good. Each party, however, thought they were doing God a service, and that he would reward them. If they had looked an inch before their noses, they might have found that fighting and killing men, and cursing them and hating them, was the very worst way for getting into favour with a Being who is allowed by all to be best pleased with deeds of love and charity. At last, however, these two religions entirely separated, and the popes reigned like kings and bishops at Rome, in Italy. The Inquisition was set up, and in the course of one year 30,000 people were burnt in Italy and Spain for entertaining different opinions from those of the pope and the priests. There was an instance of shocking barbarity which the Roman Catholic clergy committed in France by order of the Pope. The bigoted monks of that country, in cold blood, in one night massacred 80,000 Protestants; this was done under the authority of the Pope, and there was only one Roman Catholic bishop who had virtue enough to refuse to help. The vices of monks and nuns in their convents were in those times shameful. People thought that they might commit any sin, however monstrous, if they had money enough to prevail upon the priests to absolve them. In truth, at that time the priests shamefully imposed upon the people; they got all the power into their own hands; they persuaded them that a man could not be entrusted with the care of his own soul, and by cunningly obtaining possession of their secrets, they became more powerful than kings, princes, dukes, lords, or ministers. This power made them bad men; for although rational people are very good in their natural state, there are now, and ever have been, very few whose good dispositions despotic power does not destroy. I have now given a fair description of what your religion was; and Irishmen, my brothers will you make your friend appear a liar, when he takes upon himself to say for you that you are not now what the professors of the same faith were in times of yore. Do I speak false when I say that the Inquisition is the object of your hatred? Am I a liar if I assert that an Irishman prizes liberty dearly, that he will preserve that right, and if it be wrong, does not dream that money can give to a priest, or the talking of another man erring like himself, can in the least influence the judgment of the eternal God? I am not a liar if I affirm in your name, that you believe a Protestant equally with yourself to be worthy of the kingdom of Heaven, if he be equally virtuous, that you will treat men as brethren wherever you may find them, and that difference of opinion in religious matters shall not, does not, in the least on your part obstruct the most perfect harmony on every other subject. Ah! no, Irishmen, I am not a liar. I seek your confidence, not that I may betray it, but that I may teach you to be happy and wise and good. If you will not repose any trust in me I shall lament; but I will do everything in my power that is honourable, fair, and open to gain it. Some teach you that others are heretics, that you alone are right; some teach that rectitude consists in religious opinions, without which no morality is good. Some will tell you that you ought to divulge your secrets to one particular set of men. Beware, my friends, how you trust those who speak in this way. They will, I doubt not, attempt to rescue you from your present miserable state, but they will prepare a worse. It will be out of the frying-pan into the fire. Your present oppressors, it is true, will then

oppress you no longer, but you will feel the lash of a
master a thousand times more bloodthirsty and cruel.
Evil designing men will spring up who will prevent
you thinking as you please—will burn you if you do
not think as they do. There are always bad men
who take advantage of hard times. The monks and
the priests of old were very bad men; take care no
such abuse your confidence again. You are not blind
to your present situation; you are villanously treated;
you are badly used. That this slavery shall cease, I
will venture to prophesy. Your enemies dare not to
persecute you longer, the spirit of Ireland is bent, but
it is not broken, and that they very well know. But
I wish your views to embrace a wider scene—I wish
you to think for your children and your children's
children; to take great care (for it all rests with you)
that whilst one tyranny is destroyed, another more
terrible and fierce does not spring up. Take care
then of smooth-faced impostors, who talk indeed of
freedom, but who will cheat you into slavery. Can there
be worse slavery than the depending for the safety of
your soul on the will of another man? Is one man
more favoured than another by God? No, certainly,
they are all favoured according to the good they do, and
not according to the rank and profession they hold.
God values a poor man as much as a priest, and has
given him a soul as much to himself. The worship
that a kind Being must love, is that of a simple affectionate heart, that shows its piety in good works, and
not in ceremonies, or confessions, or burials, or proces-
sions, or wonders. Take care then that you are not
led away. Doubt everything that leads you not to
charity, and think of the word " heretic" as a word
which some selfish knave invented for the ruin and

misery of the world, to answer his own paltry and
narrow ambition. Do not inquire if a man be a heretic,
if he be a Quaker, a Jew, or a Heathen; but if he be a
virtuous man, if he loves liberty and truth, if he wish
the happiness and peace of human kind. If a man be
ever so much a believer and love not these things, he
is a heartless hypocrite, a rascal, and a knave. Despise
and hate him as ye despise a tyrant and a villain.
Oh, Ireland! thou emerald of the ocean, whose sons
are generous and brave, whose daughters are honourable and frank and fair, thou art the isle on whose
green shores I have desired to see the standard of
liberty erected—a flag of fire—a beacon at which the
world shall light the torch of Freedom!

We will now examine the Protestant religion. Its
origin is called the Reformation. It was undertaken
by some bigoted men who showed how little they
understood the spirit of reform by burning each other.
You will observe that these men burnt each other,
indeed they universally betrayed a taste for destroy-
ing, and vied with the chiefs of the Roman Catholic
religion in not only hating their enemies, but those
men who least of all were their enemies, or anybody's
enemies. Now do the Protestants or do they not
hold the same tenets as they did when Calvin burnt
Servetus? They swear that they do. We can have no
better proof. Then with what face can the Protestants
object to Catholic Emancipation on the plea that
Catholics once were barbarous; when their own establishment is liable to the very same objections, on the
very same grounds? I think this is a specimen of barefaced intoleration, which I had hoped would not have
disgraced this age; this age, which is called the age
of reason, of thought diffused, of virtue acknowledged,

and its principles fixed—oh! that it may be so. I have mentioned the Catholic and Protestant religions more to show that any objection to the toleration of the one forcibly applies to the non-permission of the other, or rather to show that there is no reason why both might not be tolerated; why every religion, every form of thinking might not be tolerated. But why do I speak of *toleration?* This word seems to mean that there is some merit in the person who tolerates : he has this merit if it be one, of refraining to do an evil act, but he will share the merit with every other peaceable person who pursues his own business, and does not hinder another of his rights. It is not a merit to tolerate, but it is a crime to be intolerant : it is not a merit in me that I sat quietly at home without murdering any one, but it is a crime if I do so. Besides, no act of a national representation can make anything wrong which was not wrong before; it cannot change virtue and truth, and for a very plain reason : because they are unchangeable. An Act passed in the British Parliament to take away the rights of Catholics to act in that assembly, does not really take them away. It prevents them from doing it by force. This is in such cases the last and only efficacious way. But force is not the test of truth; they will never have recourse to violence who acknowledge no other rule of behaviour but virtue and justice.

The folly of persecuting men for their religion will appear if we examine it. Why do we persecute them? to make them believe as we do. Can anything be more barbarous or foolish. For although we may make them say they believe as we do, they will not in their hearts do any such thing, indeed they cannot; this devilish method can only make them false hypocrites. For what is belief? We cannot believe just what we like, but only what we think to be true; for you cannot alter a man's opinion by beating or burning, but by persuading him that what you think is right, and this can only be done by fair words and reason. It is ridiculous to call a man a heretic because he thinks differently from you; he might as well call you one. In the same sense the word orthodox is used; it signifies "to think rightly," and what can be more vain, presumptuous in any man or any set of men, to put themselves so out of the ordinary course of things as to say—"What we think is right, no other people throughout the world have opinions anything like equal to ours." Anything short of unlimited toleration, and complete charity with all men, on which you will recollect that Jesus Christ principally insisted, is wrong, and for this reason. What makes a man to be a good man? Not his religion, or else there could be no good men in any religion but one, when yet we find that all ages, countries, and opinions have produced them. Virtue and wisdom always so far as they went produced liberty or happiness long before any of the religions now in the world have ever [been?] heard of. The only use of a religion that ever I could see, is to make men wiser or better; so far as it does this it is a good one. Now if people are good, and yet have sentiments differing from you, then all the purposes are answered which any reasonable man could want, and whether he thinks like you or not is of too little consequence to employ means which must be disgusting and hateful to candid minds; nay, they cannot approve of such means. For, as I have before said,

you cannot believe or disbelieve what you like—
perhaps some of you may doubt this, but just try. I
will take a common and familiar instance. Suppose
you have a friend of whom you wish to think well ; he
commits a crime which proves to you that he is a
bad man. It is very painful to you to think ill of
him, and you would still think well of him if you
could. But mark the word, you *cannot* think well of
him, not even to secure your own peace of mind can
you do so. You try, but your attempts are vain. This
shows how little power a man has over his belief, or
rather, that he cannot believe what he does not think
true. And what shall we think now ? What fools
and tyrants must not those men be who set up a particular religion, say that this religion alone is right, and
that every one who disbelieves it ought to be deprived
of certain rights which are really his, and which would
be allowed him if he believed. Certainly if you
cannot help disbelief, it is not any fault in you. To take
away a man's rights and privileges, to call him a
heretic, or to think worse of him, when at the same
time you cannot help owning that he has committed
no fault, is the grossest tyranny and intoleration.
From what has been said I think we may be justified
in concluding that people of all religions ought
to have an equal share in the State, that the words
heretic and orthodox were invented by a vain villain,
and have done a great deal of harm in the world, and
that no person is answerable for his belief whose
actions are virtuous and moral, that the religion is
best whose members are the best men, and that no
person can help either his belief or disbelief. Be in
charity with all men. It does not therefore signify
what your religion *was,* or what the Protestant

religion *was*, we must consider them as we find them.
What are they *now?* Yours is not intolerant; indeed,
my friends, I have ventured to pledge myself for you
that it is not. You merely desire to go to Heaven
in your own way, nor will you interrupt fellow
travellers, although the road which you take may not
be that which they take. Believe me that goodness of heart and purity of life are things of more
value in the eye of the Spirit of Goodness, than idle
earthly ceremonies and things which may have anything
but charity for their object. And is it for the first or
the last of these things that you or the Protestants contend? It is for the last. Prejudiced people indeed
are they who grudge to the happiness and comfort of
your souls, things which can do harm to no one. They
are not compelled to shares in these rites. Irishmen!
knowledge is more extended than in the early period
of your religion, people have learned to think, and
the more thought there is in the world, the more
happiness and liberty will there be:—men begin now
to think less of idle ceremonies and more of realities.
From a long night have they risen, and they can
perceive its darkness. I know no men of thought
and learning who do not consider the Catholic
idea of purgatory much nearer the truth than the
Protestant one of eternal damnation. Can you think
that the Mahometans and the Indians, who have done
good deeds in this life, will not be rewarded in the
next? The Protestants believe that they will be eternally damned, at least they swear that they do. I
think they appear in a better light as perjurers
than believers in a falsehood so hurtful and un-
charitable as this. I propose unlimited toleration,
or rather the destruction both of toleration and in-

toleration. The act permits certain people to worship God after such a manner, which, in fact, if not done, would as far as in it lay prevent God from hearing their address. Can we conceive anything more presumptuous, and at the same time more ridiculous, than a set of men granting a licence to God to receive the prayers of certain of his creatures? Oh, Irishmen! I am interested in your cause; and it is not because you are Irishmen or Roman Catholics that I feel with you and feel for you; but because you are men and sufferers. Were Ireland at this moment peopled with Brahmins, this very same Address would have been suggested by the same state of mind. You have suffered not merely for your religion, but some other causes which I am equally desirous of remedying. The Union of England with Ireland has withdrawn the Protestant aristocracy and gentry from their native country, and with these their friends and connections. Their resources are taken from this country, although they are dissipated in another; the very poor people are most infamously oppressed by the weight of burden which the superior ranks lay upon their shoulders. I am no less desirous of the reform of these evils (with many others) than for the Catholic Emancipation.

Perhaps you all agree with me on both these subjects. We now come to the method of doing these things. I agree with the Quakers so far as they disclaim violence, and trust their cause wholly and solely to its own truth. If you are convinced of the truth of your cause, trust wholly to its truth; if you are not convinced, give it up. In no case employ violence; the way to liberty and happiness is never to transgress the rules of virtue and justice. Liberty and happiness are founded upon virtue and justice; if you

o

destroy the one you destroy the other. However ill
others may act, this will be no excuse for you if you
follow their example ; it ought rather to warn you from
pursuing so bad a method. Depend upon it, Irishmen,
your cause shall not be neglected. I will fondly hope
that the schemes for your happiness and liberty, as well
as those for the happiness and liberty of the world,
will not be wholly fruitless. One secure method of
defeating them is violence on the side of the injured
party. If you can descend to use the same weapons
as your enemy, you put yourself on a level with him on
this score : you must be convinced that he is on these
grounds your superior. But appeal to the sacred
principles of virtue and justice, then how is he awed
into nothing ? How does truth show him in his real
colours, and place the cause of toleration and reform
in the clearest light ? I extend my view not only to
you as Irishmen, but to all of every persuasion, of
every country. Be calm, mild, deliberate, patient ;
recollect that you can in no measure more effectually
forward the cause of reform than by employing your
leisure time in reasoning or the cultivation of your
minds. Think and talk and discuss : the only subjects
you ought to propose are those of happiness and
liberty. Be free and be happy, but first be wise and
good. For you are not all wise or good. You are a
great and a brave nation, but you cannot yet be all
wise or good. You may be at some time, and then
Ireland will be an earthly paradise. You know what
is meant by a mob. It is an assembly of people who,
without foresight or thought, collect themselves to
disapprove of by force any measure which they dislike.
An assembly like this can never do anything but
harm ; tumultuous proceedings must retard the period

when thought and coolness will produce freedom and happiness, and that to the very people who make the mob. But if a number of human beings, after thinking of their own interests, meet together for any conversation on them, and employ resistance of the mind, not resistance of the body, these people are going the right way to work. But let no fiery passions carry them beyond this point. Let them consider that in some sense the whole welfare of their countrymen depends on their prudence, and that it becomes them to guard the welfare of others as their own. Associations for purposes of violence are entitled to the strongest disapprobation of the real reformist. Always suspect that some knavish rascal is at the bottom of things of this kind, waiting to profit by the confusion. All secret associations are also bad. Are you men of deep designs, whose deeds love darkness better than light? Dare you not say what you think before any man? Can you not meet in the open face of day in conscious innocence? Oh, Irishmen, ye can! Hidden arms, secret meetings, and designs violently to separate England from Ireland are all very bad. I do not mean to say the very end of them is bad; the object you have in view may be just enough, whilst the way you go about it is wrong—may be calculated to produce an opposite effect. Never do evil that good may come; always think of others as well as yourself, and cautiously look how your conduct may do good or evil, when you yourself shall be mouldering in the grave. Be fair, open, and you will be terrible to your enemies. A friend cannot defend you, much as he may feel for your sufferings, if you have recourse to methods of which virtue and justice disapprove. No cause is in itself so dear to liberty as yours. Much

depends on you; far may your efforts spread either
hope or despair: do not then cover in darkness
wrongs at which the face of day and the tyrants who
bask in its warmth ought to blush. Wherever has
violence succeeded? The French Revolution, although
undertaken with the best intentions, ended ill for the
people, because violence was employed. The cause
which they vindicated was that of truth, but they gave
it the appearance of a lie by using methods which
will suit the purposes of liars as well as their own.
Speak boldly and daringly what you think; an Irishman was never accused of cowardice, do not let it be
thought possible that he is a coward. Let him say
what he thinks; a lie is the basest and meanest
employment of men: leave lies and secrets to courtiers
and lordlings. Be open, sincere, and single-hearted.
Let it be seen that the Irish votaries of Freedom dare
to speak what they think; let them resist oppression,
not by force of arms, but by power of mind and
reliance on truth and justice. Will any be arraigned
for libel—will imprisonment or death be the consequences of this mode of proceeding? Probably not.
But if it were so? Is danger frightful to an Irishman
who speaks for his own liberty and the liberty of his
wife and children? No; he will steadily persevere, and
sooner shall pensioners cease to vote with their benefactors than an Irishman swerve from the path of
duty. But steadily persevere in the system above laid
down, its benefits will speedily be manifested. Persecution may destroy some, but cannot destroy all, or
nearly all; let it do its will. Ye have appealed to
truth and justice, show the goodness of your religion
by persisting in a reliance on these things, which must
be the rules even of the Almighty's conduct. But

before this can be done with any effect, habits of
SOBRIETY, REGULARITY, and THOUGHT must be entered
into, and firmly resolved upon.

My warm-hearted friends who meet together to
talk of the distresses of your countrymen until social
chat induces you to drink rather freely, as ye have
felt passionately, so reason coolly. Nothing hasty can
be lasting; lay up the money with which you usually
purchase drunkenness and ill-health to relieve the pains
of your fellow sufferers. Let your children lisp of
freedom in the cradle—let your deathbed be the
school for fresh exertions—let every street of the city
and field of the country be connected with thoughts
which liberty has made holy. Be warm in your cause,
yet rational and charitable and tolerant—never let
the oppressor grind you into justifying his conduct
by imitating his meanness.

Many circumstances, I will own, may excuse what
is called rebellion, but no circumstances can ever make
it good for your cause, and however honourable to
your feelings, it will reflect no credit on your judg-
ments. It will bind you more closely to the block of
the oppressor, and your children's children, whilst they
talk of your exploits, will feel that you have done
them injury instead of benefit.

A crisis is now arriving which shall decide your
fate. The King of Great Britain has arrived at the
evening of his days. He has objected to your emancipation; he has been inimical to you; but he will in
a certain time be no more. The present Prince of
Wales will then be king. It is said that he has
promised to restore you to freedom: your real and
natural right will, in that case, be no longer kept from
you. I hope he has pledged himself to this act of

justice, because there will then exist some obligation
to bind him to do right. Kings are but too apt to
think little as they should do : they think everything
in the world is made for them ; when the truth is,
that it is only the vices of men that make such people
necessary, and they have no other right of being
kings but in virtue of the good they do.

The benefit of the governed is the origin and
meaning of government. The Prince of Wales has
had every opportunity of knowing how he ought to
act about Ireland and liberty. That great and good
man Charles Fox, who was your friend and the friend
of freedom, was the friend of the Prince of Wales.
He never flattered or disguised his sentiments, but
spoke them *openly* on every occasion, and the Prince
was the better for his instructive conversation. He
saw the truth, and he believed it. Now I know not
what to say; his staff is gone, and he leans upon a
broken reed ; his present advisers are not like Charles
Fox, they do not plan for liberty and safety, not for
the happiness but for the glory of their country ; and
what, Irishmen, is the glory of a country divided from
their happiness ? It is a false light hung out by the
enemies of freedom to lure the unthinking into their
net. Men like these surround the Prince, and whether
or no he has really promised to emancipate you—
whether or no he will consider the promise of a
Prince of Wales binding to a King of England, is yet
a matter of doubt. We cannot at least be quite
certain of it : on this you cannot certainly rely. But
there are men who, wherever they find a tendency to
freedom, go there to increase, support, and regulate
that tendency. These men, who join to a rational
disdain of danger a practice of speaking the truth,

and defending the cause of the oppressed against the oppressor—these men see what is right and will pursue it. On such as these you may safely rely : they love you as they love their brothers; they feel for the unfortunate, and never ask whether a man is an Englishman or an Irishman, a catholic, a heretic, a christian, or a heathen, before their hearts and their purses are opened to feel with their misfortunes and relieve their necessities : such are the men who will stand by you for ever. Depend then not upon the promises of princes, but upon those of virtuous and disinterested men : depend not upon force of arms or violence, but upon the force of the truth of the rights which you have to share equally with others, the benefits and the evils of government.

The crisis to which I allude as the period of your emancipation is not the death of the present King, or any circumstance that has to do with kings, but something that is much more likely to do you good : it is the increase of virtue and wisdom which will lead people to find out that force and oppression are wrong and false; and this opinion, when it once gains ground, will prevent government from severity. It will restore those rights which Government has taken away. Have nothing to do with force or violence, and things will safely and surely make their way to the right point. The Ministers have now in Parliament a very great majority, and the Ministers are against you. They maintain the falsehood that, were you in power, you would prosecute [persecute ?] and burn, on the plea that you once did so. They maintain many other things of the same nature. They command the majority of the House of Commons, or rather the part of that assembly who receive pensions from Government or whose relatives receive them. These men of course are against you, because their employers are. But the sense of the country is not against you; the people of England are not against you—they feel warmly for you —in some respects they feel with you. The sense of the English and of their governors is opposite—there must be an end of this; the goodness of a Government consists in the happiness of the governed. If the governed are wretched and dissatisfied, the government has failed in its end. It wants altering and mending. It will be mended, and a reform of English government will produce good to the Irish—good to all human kind, excepting those whose happiness consists in others' sorrows, and it will be a fit punishment for these to be deprived of their devilish joy. This I consider as an event which is approaching, and which will make the beginning of our hopes for that period which may spread wisdom and virtue so wide as to leave no hole in which folly or villany may hide themselves. I wish you, O Irishmen, to be as careful and thoughtful of your interests as are your real friends. Do not drink, do not play, do not spend any idle time, do not take everything that other people say for granted—there are numbers who will tell you lies to make their own fortunes: you cannot more certainly do good to your own cause than by defeating the intentions of these men. Think, read, and talk; let your own condition and that of your wives and children fill your minds; disclaim all manner of alliance with violence: meet together if you will, but do not meet in a mob. If you think and read and talk with a real wish of benefiting the cause of truth and liberty, it will soon be seen how true a service you are tendering, and how sincere you are in your professions; but mobs and violence must be discarded. The certain degrce of civil and religious liberty which the usage of the English Constitution allows, is such as the worst of men are entitled to, although you have it not; but that liberty which we may one day hope for, wisdom and virtue can alone give you a right to enjoy. This wisdom and this virtue I recommend on every account that you should *instantly begin* to practise. Lose not a day, not an hour, not a moment. Temperance, sobriety, charity, and independence will give you virtue; and reading, talking, thinking, and searching will give you wisdom; when you have those things you may defy the tyrant. It is not going often to chapel, crossing yourselves, or confessing that will make you virtuous; many a rascal has attended regularly at mass, and many a good man has never gone at all. It is not paying priests or believing in what they say that makes a good man, but it is doing good actions or benefiting other people; this is the truc way to be good, and the prayers and confessions and masses of him who does not these things are good for nothing at all. Do your work regularly and quickly : when you have done, think, read, and talk; do not spend your money in idleness and drinking, which so far from doing good to your cause, will do it harm. If you have anything to spare from your wife and children, let it do some good to other people, and put them in a way of getting wisdom and virtue, as the pleasure that will come from these good acts will be much better than the headache that comes from a drinking bout. And never quarrel between each other; be all of one mind as nearly as you can; do these things, and I will promise you liberty and happiness. But if, on the contrary of these things, you neglect to

improve yourselves, continue to use the word heretic,
and demand from others the toleration which you are
unwilling to give, your friends and the friends of
liberty will have reason to lament the death-blow of
their hopes. I expect better things from you : it is
for yourselves that I fear and hope. Many Englishmen are prejudiced against you ; they sit by their own
firesides, and certain rumours artfully spread are
ever on the wing against you. But these people who
think ill of you and of your nation are often the
very men who, if they had better information, would
feel for you most keenly. Wherefore are these reports
spread ? How do they begin ? They originate from the
warmth of the Irish character, which the friends of
the Irish nation have hitherto encouraged rather than
repressed ; this leads them in those moments, when
their wrongs appear so clearly, to commit acts which
justly excite displeasure. They begin therefore from
yourselves, although falsehood and tyranny artfully
magnify and multiply the cause of offence. Give no
offence.

I will for the present dismiss the subject of the
Catholic Emancipation ; a little reflection will convince you that my remarks are just. Be true to yourselves, and your enemies shall not triumph. I fear
nothing, if charity and sobriety mark your proceedings.
Everything is to be dreaded—you yourselves will be
unworthy of even a restoration to your rights, if you
disgrace the cause, which I hope is that of truth and
liberty, by violence ; if you refuse to others the toleration
which you claim for yourselves. But this you will not
do. I rely upon it, Irishmen, that the warmth of your
character will be shown as much in union with Englishmen and what are called heretics, who feel for you

and love you, as in avenging your wrongs, or forwarding their annihilation. It is the heart that glows and
not the cheek. The firmness, sobriety, and consis-
tence of your outward behaviour will not at all show
any hardness of heart, but will prove that you are
determined in your cause, and are going the right
way to work. I will repeat that virtue and wisdom
are necessary to true happiness and liberty. The
Catholic Emancipation, I consider, is certain. I do
not see that anything but violence and intolerance
among yourselves can leave an excuse to your enemies
for continuing your slavery. The other wrongs under
which you labour will probably also soon be done
away. You will be rendered equal to the people of
England in their rights and privileges, and will be in
all respects, so far as concerns the State, as happy.
And now, Irishmen, another and a more wide prospect
opens to my view. I cannot avoid, little as it may
appear to have anything to do with your present situation, to talk to you on the subject. It intimately
concerns the well-being of your children and your
children's children, and will perhaps more than anything prove to you the advantage and necessity of
being thoughtful, sober, and regular ; of avoiding foolish
and idle talk, and thinking of yourselves as of men
who are able to be much wiser and happier than you
now are ; for habits like these will not only conduce
to the successful putting aside your present and immediate grievances, but will contain a seed which in
future times will spring up into the tree of liberty,
and bear the fruit of happiness.

There is no doubt but the world is going wrong, or
rather that it is very capable of being much improved.
What I mean by this improvement is, the inducement

of a more equal and general diffusion of happiness and
liberty. Many people are very rich and many are
very poor. Which do you think are happiest? I can
tell you that neither are happy, so far as their station
is concerned. Nature never intended that there
should be such a thing as a poor man or a rich one.
Being put in an unnatural situation, they can neither
of them be happy, so far as their situation is concerned.
The poor man is born to obey the rich man, though
they both come into the world equally helpless and
equally naked. But the poor man does the rich no
service by obeying him—the rich man does the poor
no good by commanding him. It would be much
better if they could be prevailed upon to live equally
like brothers—they would ultimately both be happier.
But this can be done neither to-day nor to-morrow;
much as such a change is to be desired, it is quite
impossible. Violence and folly in this, as in the other
case, would only put off the period of its event.
Mildness, sobriety, and reason are the effectual methods
of forwarding the ends of liberty and happiness.

Although we may see many things put in train
during our life-time, we cannot hope to see the work
of virtue and reason finished now; we can only lay the
foundation for our posterity. Government is an evil;
it is only the thoughtlessness and vices of men that
make it a necessary evil. When all men are good and
wise, government will of itself decay. So long as men
continue foolish and vicious, so long will government,
even such a Government as that of England, continue
necessary in order to prevent the crimes of bad men.
Society is produced by the wants, government by the
wickedness, and a state of just and happy equality by
the improvement and reason of man. It is in vain to

hope for any liberty and happiness without reason and virtue, for where there is no virtue there will be crime, and where there is crime there must be government. Before the restraints of government are lessened, it is fit that we should lessen the necessity for them. Before government is done away with, we must reform ourselves. It is this work which I would earnestly recommend to you. O Irishmen, REFORM YOURSELVES, and I do not recommend it to you particularly because I think that you most need it, but because I think that your hearts are warm and your feelings high, and you will perceive the necessity of doing it more than those of a colder and more distant nature.

I look with an eye of hope and pleasure on the present state of things, gloomy and incapable of improvement as they may appear to others. It delights me to see that men begin to think and to act for the good of others. Extensively as folly and selfishness have predominated in this age, it gives me hope and pleasure at least to see that many know what is right. Ignorance and vice commonly go together : he that would do good must be wise. A man cannot be truly wise who is not truly virtuous. Prudence and wisdom are very different things. The prudent man is he who carefully consults for his own good : the wise man is he who carefully consults for the good of others.

I look upon Catholic Emancipation and the restoration of the liberties and happiness of Ireland, so far as they are compatible with the English Constitution, as great and important events. I hope to see them soon. But if all ended here, it would give me little pleasure. I should still see thousands miserable and wicked ; things would still be wrong. I regard then the accomplishment of these things as the road to a greater reform, that reform after which virtue and wisdom shall have conquered pain and vice—when no government will be wanted but that of your neighbour's opinion.   I look to these things with hope and pleasure, because I consider that they will certainly happen, and because men will not then be wicked and miserable.   But I do not consider that they will or can immediately happen ; their arrival will be gradual, and it all depends upon yourselves how soon or how late these great changes will happen.   If all of you to-morrow were virtuous and wise, government which to-day is a safeguard, would then become a tyranny. But I cannot expect a rapid change.   Many are obstinate and determined in their vice, whose selfishness makes them think only of their own good, when in fact the best way even to bring that about is to make others happy.   I do not wish to see things changed now, because it cannot be done without violence, and we may assure ourselves that none of us are fit for any change, however good, if we condescend to employ force in a cause which we think right.   Force makes the side that employs it directly wrong, and as much as we may pity we cannot approve the headstrong and intolerant zeal of its adherents.

Can you conceive, O Irishmen ! a happy state of society—conceive men of every way of thinking living together like brothers ?   The descendant of the greatest prince would then be entitled to no more respect than the son of a peasant.   There would be no pomp and no parade ; but that which the rich now keep to themselves would then be distributed among the people.   None would be in magnificence, but the superfluities then taken from the rich would be sufficient when spread abroad to make every one comfortable. No lover would then be false to his mistress, no mistress could desert her lover. No friend would play false ; no rents, no debts, no taxes, no frauds of any kind would disturb the general happiness : good as they would be, wise as they would be, they would be daily getting better and wiser. No beggars would exist, nor any of those wretched women who are now reduced to a state of the most horrible misery and vice by men whose wealth makes them villainous and hardened ; no thieves or murderers, because poverty would never drive men to take away comforts from another when he had enough for himself. Vice and misery, pomp and poverty, power and obedience, would then be banished altogether. It is for such a state as this, Irishmen, that I exhort you to prepare. " A camel shall as soon pass through the eye of a needle, as a rich man enter the kingdom of heaven." This is not to be understood literally. Jesus Christ appears to me only to have meant that riches have generally the effect of hardening and vitiating the heart; so has poverty. I think those people then are very silly, and cannot see one inch beyond their noses, who say that human nature is depraved ; when at the same time wealth and poverty, those two great sources of crime, fall to the lot of a great majority of people ; and when they see that people in moderate circumstances are always most wise and good. People say that poverty is no evil : they have never felt it, or they would not think so ; that wealth is necessary to encourage the arts—but are not the arts very inferior things to virtue and happiness ?— the man would be very dead to all generous feelings who would rather see pretty pictures and statues than a million free and happy men.

It will be said that my design is to make you dissatisfied with your present condition, and that I wish
to raise a Rebellion.   But how stupid and sottish must
those men be who think that violence and uneasiness of
mind have anything to do with forwarding the views of
peace, harmony, and happiness.   They should know
that nothing was so well fitted to produce slavery,
tyranny, and vice as the violence which is attributed
to the friends of liberty, and which the real friends of
liberty are the only persons who disdain.   As to your
being dissatisfied with your present condition, anything
that I may say is certainly not likely to increase that
dissatisfaction.   I have advanced nothing concerning
your situation but its real case ; but what may be proved
to be true.   I defy any one to point out a falsehood
that I have uttered in the course of this Address.   It
is impossible but the blindest among you must see
that everything is not right.   This sight has often
pressed some of the poorest among you to take something from the rich man's store by violence, to relieve
his own necessities. I cannot justify, but I can pity him.
I cannot pity the fruits of the rich man's intempe-
rance.   I suppose some are to be found who will
justify him.   This sight has often brought home to a
day-labourer the truth which I wish to impress upon
you that all is not right.   But I do not merely wish to
convince you that our present state is bad, but that
its alteration for the better depends on your own
exertions and resolutions.

But he has never found out the method of mending
it who does not first mend his own conduct, and then
prevail upon others to refrain from any vicious habits
which they may have contracted, much less does the
poor man suppose that wisdom as well as virtue is

necessary, and that the employing his little time in reading and thinking, is really doing all that he has in his power to do towards the state, when pain and vice shall perish altogether.

I wish to impress upon your minds that without virtue or wisdom there can be no liberty or happiness; and that temperance, sobriety, charity, and independence of soul will give you virtue, as thinking, inquiring, reading, and talking will give you wisdom. Without the first the last is of little use, and without the last the first is a dreadful curse to yourselves and others.

I have told you what I think upon this subject, because I wish to produce in your minds an awe and caution necessary, before the happy state of which I have spoken can be introduced. This cautious awe is very different from the prudential fear which leads you to consider yourself as the first object, as, on the contrary, it is full of that warm and ardent love for others that burns in your hearts, O Irishmen! and from which I have fondly hoped to light a flame that may illumine and invigorate the world.

I have said that the rich command and the poor obey, and that money is only a kind of sign which shows that according to government the rich man has a right to command the poor man, or rather that the poor man being urged by having no money to get bread, is forced to work for the rich man, which amounts to the same thing. I have said that I think all this very wrong, and that I wish the whole business was altered. I have also said that we can expect little amendment in our own time, and that we must be contented to lay the foundation of liberty and happiness by virtue and wisdom. This then shall be my work; let this be yours, Irishmen. Never shall that

P

glory fail, which I am anxious that you shall deserve—
the glory of teaching to a world the first lessons of
virtue and wisdom.

Let poor men still continue to work. I do not wish
to hide from them a knowledge of their relative condition in society, I esteem it next [to] impossible to do
so. Let the work of the labourer, of the artificer—let
the work of every one, however employed, still be
exerted in its accustomed way. The public communication of this truth ought in no manner to impede
the established usages of society, however it is fitted
in the end to do them away. For this reason it ought
not to impede them, because if it did, a violent and unac-
customed and sudden sensation [cessation?] would take
place in all ranks of men, which would bring on violence
and destroy the possibility of the event of that which
in its own nature must be gradual however rapid, and
rational however warm. It is founded on the reform
of private men, and without individual amendment it
is vain and foolish to expect the amendment of a state
or government. I would advise them, therefore, whose
feelings this Address may have succeeded in affecting
(and surely those feelings which charitable and tempe-
rate remarks excite can never be violent and intolerant), if they be, as I hope those whom poverty has
compelled to class themselves in the lower orders of
society, that they will as usual attend to their business
and the discharge of those public or private duties
which custom has ordained. Nothing can be more
rash and thoughtless than to show in ourselves singular
instances of any particular doctrine before the general
mass of the people are so convinced by the reasons of
the doctrine, that it will be no longer singular. That
reasons as well as feelings may help the establishment

of happiness and liberty, on the basis of wisdom and
virtue, be our aim and intention. Let us not be led
into any means which are unworthy of this end, nor, as
so much depends upon yourselves, let us cease carefully
to watch over our conduct, that when we talk of
reform it be not objected to us, that reform ought to
begin at home. In the interval that public or private
duties and necessary labours allow, husband your time
so that you may do to others and yourselves the most
real good. To improve your own minds is to join
these two views; conversation and reading are the
principal and chief methods of awaking the mind to
knowledge and goodness. Reading or thought will
principally bestow the former of these—the benevolent
exercise of the powers of the mind in communicating
useful knowledge will bestow an habit of the latter :
both united will contribute so far as lies in your individual power to that great reform which will be perfect and finished the moment every one is virtuous
and wise. Every folly refuted, every bad habit conquered, every good one confirmed, are so much gained
in this great and excellent cause.

To begin to reform the government is immediately
necessary, however good or bad individuals may be;
it is the more necessary, if they are eminently the
latter, in some degree to palliate or do away [with ?] the
cause, as political institution has even [ever ?] the
greatest influence on the human character, and is that
alone which differences the Turk from the Irishman.

I write now not only with a view for Catholic
Emancipation, but for universal emancipation; and
this emancipation complete and unconditional, that
shall comprehend every individual of whatever nation
or principles, that shall fold in its embrace all that

think and all that feel: the Catholic cause is subordinate, and its success preparatory to this great cause,
which adheres to no sect but society, to no cause but
that of universal happiness, to no party but the people.
I desire Catholic Emancipation, but I desire not to
stop here; and I hope there are few who having
perused the preceding arguments who will not concur
with me in desiring a complete, a lasting, and a happy
amendment. That all steps however good and salutary which may be taken, all reforms consistent with
the English constitution that may be effectuated, can
only be subordinate and preparatory to the great
and lasting one which shall bring about the peace,
the harmony, and the happiness of Ireland, England,
Europe, the World. I offer merely an outline of that
picture which your own hopes may gift with the
colours of reality.

Government will not allow a peaceable and reasonable discussion of its principles by any association of
men who assemble for that express purpose. But
have not human beings a right to assemble to talk
upon what subject they please? Can anything be more
evident than that as government is only of use as it
conduces to the happiness of the governed, those who
are governed have a right to talk on the efficacy of
the safeguard employed for their benefit? Can any topic
be more interesting or useful than on [one?] discussing
how far the means of government is or could be
made in a higher degree effectual to producing the
end? Although I deprecate violence, and the cause
which depends for its influence on force, yet I can by
no means think that assembling together merely to
talk of how things go on—I can by no means think
that societies formed for talking on any subject,

however Government may dislike them, come in any way under the head of force or violence—I think that associations conducted in the spirit of sobriety, regularity, and thought are one of the best and most efficient of those means which I would recommend for the production of happiness, liberty, and virtue.

Are you slaves or are you men? If slaves, then crouch to the rod and lick the feet of your oppressors; glory [in?] your shame: it will become you, if brutes, to act according to your nature. But you are men: a real man is free, so far as circumstances will permit him. Then firmly yet quietly resist. When one cheek is struck, turn the other to the insulting coward. You will be truly brave: you will resist and conquer. The discussion of any subject is a right that you have brought into the world with your heart and tongue. Resign your heart's blood before you part with this inestimable privilege of man. For it is fit that the governed should inquire into the proceedings of government, which is of no use the moment it is conducted on any other principle but that of safety. You have much to think of. Is war necessary to your happiness and safety? The interests of the poor gain nothing from the wealth or extension of a nation's boundaries, they gain nothing from glory, a word that has often served as a cloak to the ambition or avarice of statesmen. The barren victories of Spain, gained in behalf of a bigoted and tyrannical government, are nothing to them. The conquests in India, by which England has gained glory indeed, but a glory which is not more honourable than that of Buonaparte, are nothing to them. The poor purchase this glory and this wealth at the expense of their blood and labour and happiness and virtue.

They die in battle for this infernal cause. Their labour supplies money and food for carrying it into effect; their happiness is destroyed by the oppression they undergo; their virtue is rooted out by the depravity and vice that prevail throughout the army, and which under the present system are perfectly unavoidable. Who does not know that the quartering of a regiment on any town will soon destroy the innocence and happiness of its inhabitants? The advocates for the happiness and liberty of the great mass of the people, who pay for war with their lives and labour, ought never to cease writing and speaking until nations see, as they must feel, the folly of fighting and killing each other in uniform for nothing at all. Ye have much to think of. The state of your representation in the House, which is called the collective representation of the country, demands your attention.

It is horrible that the lower classes must waste their lives and liberty to furnish means for their oppressors to oppress them yet more terribly. It is horrible that the poor must give in taxes what would save them and their families from hunger and cold;—it is still more horrible that they should do this to furnish further means of their own abjectedness and misery. But what words can express the enormity of the abuse that prevents them from choosing representatives with authority to inquire into the manner in which their lives and labour, their happiness and innocence, are expended, and what advantages result from their expenditure which may counterbalance so horrible and monstrous an evil? There is an outcry raised against amendment; it is called innovation and condemned by many unthinking people who have a good fire and plenty to eat and drink. Hard-hearted or thoughtless beings, how many are famishing whilst you deliberate, how many perish to contribute to your pleasures? I hope that there are none such as these native Irishmen, indeed I scarcely believe that there are.

Let the object of your associations (for I conceal not my approval of assemblies conducted with regularity, *peaceableness,* and thought for any purpose) be the amendment of these abuses, it will have for its object universal emancipation, liberty, happiness, and virtue. There is yet another subject, " the Liberty of the Press." The liberty of the Press consists in a right to publish any opinion on any subject which the writer may entertain. The Attorney-General in 1793, on the trial of Mr. Percy, said, " I never will dispute the right of any man fully to discuss topics respecting Government, and honestly to point out what he may consider a proper remedy of grievances." The liberty of the Press is placed as a sentinel to alarm us when any attempt is made on our liberties. It is this sentinel, oh, Irishmen, whom I now awaken! I create to myself a freedom which exists not. There is no liberty of the Press for the subjects of British government.

It is really ridiculous to hear people yet boasting of this inestimable blessing, when they daily see it successfully muzzled and outraged by the lawyers of the Crown, and by virtue of what are called *ex-officio* informations. Blackstone says, that " if a person publishes what is improper, mischievous, or illegal, he must take the consequences of his own temerity." And Lord Chief Baron Comyns defines libel as " a contumely, or reproach, published to the defamation of the Government, of a magistrate, or of a private person." Now I beseech you to consider the words mischievous, improper, illegal, contumely, reproach, or defamation. May they not make that mischievous or improper which they please? Is not law with them as clay in the potter's hand? Do not the words contumely, reproach, or defamation express all degrees and forces of disapprobation? It is impossible to express yourself displeased at certain proceedings of Government, or the individuals who conduct it, without uttering a reproach. We 'cannot honestly point out a proper remedy of grievances with safety, because the very mention of these grievances will be reproachful to the personages who countenance them; and therefore will come under a definition of libel. For the persons who thus directly or indirectly undergo reproach, will say for their own sakes that the exposure of their corruption is mischievous and improper; therefore the utterer of the reproach is a fit subject for three years' imprisonment. Is there anything like the liberty of the Press in restrictions so positive yet pliant as these? The little freedom which we enjoy in this most important point comes from the clemency of our rulers, or their fear lest public opinion, alarmed at the discovery of its enslaved state, should violently assert a right to extension and diffusion. Yet public opinion may not always be so formidable, rulers may not always be so merciful or so timid; at any rate, evils, and great evils, do result from the present system of intellectual slavery, and you have enough to think of if this grievance alone remained in the constitution of society. I will give but one instance of the present state of our Press.

A countryman of yours is now confined in an English gaol. His health, his fortune, his spirits suffer from close confinement. The air which comes through the bars of a prison-grate does not invigorate the frame nor cheer the spirits. But Mr. Finnerty, much as he has lost, yet retains the fair name of truth and honour. He was imprisoned for persisting in the truth. His judge told him on his trial that truth and falsehood were indifferent to the law, and that if he owned the publication, any consideration whether the facts that it related were well or ill-founded, was totally irrelevant. Such is the libel law : such the liberty of the Press—there is enough to think of. The right of withholding your individual assent to war, the right of choosing delegates to represent you in the assembly of the nation, and that of freely opposing intellectual power to any measure of Government of which you may disapprove, are, in addition to the indifference with which the Legislative and the Executive power ought to rule their conduct towards professors of every religion, enough to think of.

I earnestly desire peace and harmony :—peace, that whatever wrongs you may have suffered, benevolence and a spirit of forgiveness should mark your conduct towards those who have persecuted you :—harmony, that among yourselves may be no divisions, that Protestants and Catholics unite in a common interest, and that whatever be the belief and principles of your countryman and fellow sufferer, you desire to benefit his cause at the same time that you vindicate your own. Be strong and unbiassed by selfishness or prejudice — for, Catholics, your religion has not been spotless, crimes in past ages have sullied it with a stain, which let it be your glory to remove. Nor, Protestants, hath your religion always been characterized by the mildness of benevolence which Jesus

Christ recommended. Had it anything to do with the present subject I could account for the spirit of intolerance which marked both religions ; I will, however, only adduce the fact, and earnestly exhort you to root out from your own minds everything which may lead to uncharitableness, and to reflect that yourselves as well as your brethren may be deceived. Nothing on earth is infallible. The priests that pretend to it are wicked and mischievous impostors ; but it is an imposture which every one more or less assumes who encourages prejudice in his breast against those who differ from him in opinion, or who sets up his own religion as the only right and true one, when no one is so blind as to see that every religion is right and true which makes men beneficent and sincere. I therefore earnestly exhort both Protestants and Catholics to act in brotherhood and harmony, never forgetting because the Catholics alone are heinously deprived of religious rights, that the Protestants and a certain rank of people of every persuasion, share with them all else that is terrible, galling, and intolerable in the mass of political grievance.

In no case employ violence or falsehood. I cannot too often or too vividly endeavour to impress upon your minds that these methods will produce nothing but wretchedness and slavery—that they will at the same time rivet the fetters with which ignorance and oppression bind you to abjectness, and deliver you over to a tyranny which shall render you incapable of renewed efforts. Violence will immediately render your cause a bad one. If you believe in a providential God, you must also believe that he is a good one. And it is not likely a merciful God would befriend a bad cause. Insincerity is no less hurtful than violence; those who are in the habit of either, would do well to reform themselves. A lying bravo will never promote the good of his country—he cannot be a good man. The courageous and sincere may at the same time successfully oppose corruption, by uniting their voice with that of others, or individually raise up intellectual opposition to counteract the abuses of Government and society. In order to benefit yourselves and your country to any extent, habits of sobriety, regularity, and thought are previously so necessary, that without these preliminaries all that you have done falls to the ground. You have built on sand; secure a good foundation and you may erect a fabric to stand for ever—the glory and the envy of the world.

I have purposely avoided any lengthened discussion on those grievances to which your hearts are from custom and the immediate interest of the circumstances, probably most alive at present. I have not, however, wholly neglected them. Most of all have I insisted on their instant palliation and ultimate removal; nor have I omitted a consideration of the means which I deem most effectual for the accomplishment of this great end. How far you will consider the former worthy of your adoption, so far shall I deem the latter probable and interesting to the lovers of human kind. And I have opened to your view a new scene—does not your heart bound at the bare possibility of your posterity possessing that liberty and happiness of which during our lives powerful exertions and habitual abstinence may give us a foretaste? Oh! if your hearts do not vibrate at such as this, then ye are dead and cold—ye are not men.

I now come to the application of my principles, the conclusion of my Address; and, O Irishmen, whatever conduct ye may feel yourselves bound to pursue, the path which duty points to lies before me clear and unobscured. Dangers may lurk around it, but they are not the dangers which lie beneath the footsteps of the hypocrite or temporizer.

For I have not presented to you the picture of happiness on which my fancy doats as an uncertain meteor to mislead honourable enthusiasm, or blindfold the judgment which makes virtue useful. I have not proposed crude schemes, which I should be incompetent to mature, or desired to excite in you any virulence against the abuses of political institution; where I have had occasion to point them out, I have recommended moderation whilst yet I have earnestly insisted upon energy and perseverance; I have spoken of peace, yet declared that resistance is laudable; but the intellectual resistance which I recommend, I deem essential to the introduction of the millennium of virtue, whose period every one can, so far as he is concerned, forward by his own proper power. I have not attempted to show that the Catholic claims, or the claims of the people to a full representation in Parliament, or any of these claims to real rights, which I have insisted upon as introductory to the ultimate claim of *all*, to universal happiness, freedom, and equality; I have not attempted, I say, to show that these can be granted consistently with the spirit of the English Constitution;* this is a point which I do not feel myself inclined to discuss, and which I consider foreign to my

---

* The excellence of the Constitution of Great Britain appears to me to be its indefiniteness and versatility, whereby it may be unresistingly accommodated to the progression of wisdom and virtue. Such accommodation I desire; but I wish for the cause before the effect.

subject. But I have shown that these claims have
for their basis truth and justice, which are immutable,
and which in the ruin of governments shall rise like
a phœnix from their ashes.

Is any one inclined to dispute the possibility of
a happy change in society? Do they say that the
nature of man is corrupt, and that he was made for
misery and wickedness? Be it so. Certain as are
opposite conclusions, I will concede the truth of this
for a moment. What are the means which I take for
melioration? Violence, corruption, rapine, crime?
Do I do evil that good may come? I have recommended peace, philanthropy, wisdom. So far as my
arguments influence, they will influence to these; and if
there is any one *now* inclined to say that "private
vices are public benefits," and that peace, philanthropy, and wisdom will, if once they gain ground,
ruin the human race, he may revel in his happy
dreams; though were *I* this man I should envy Satan's
hell. The wisdom and charity of which I speak
are the *only* means which I will countenance for the
redress of your grievances and the grievances of the
world. So far as they operate, I am willing to stand
responsible for their evil effects. I expect to be accused of a desire for renewing in Ireland the scenes of
revolutionary horror which marked the struggles of
France twenty years ago. But it is the renewal of that
unfortunate era which I strongly deprecate, and which
the tendency of this Address is calculated to obviate.
For can burthens be borne for ever, and the slave
crouch and cringe the while? Is misery and vice so
consonant to man's nature that he will hug it to his
heart? But when the wretched one in bondage
beholds the emancipation near, will he not endure his

misery awhile with hope and patience, then spring to his preserver's arms, and start into a man?

It is my intention to observe the effect on your minds, O Irishmen, which this Address, dictated by the fervency of my love and hope, will produce. I have come to this country to spare no pains where expenditure may purchase you real benefit. The present is a crisis which of all others is the most valuable for fixing the fluctuation of public feeling; as far as my poor efforts may have succeeded in fixing it to virtue, Irishmen, so far shall I esteem myself happy. I intend this Address as introductory to another. The organization of a society whose institution shall serve as a bond to its members for the purposes of virtue, happiness, liberty, and wisdom, by the means of intellectual opposition to grievances, would probably be useful. For the formation of such society I avow myself anxious.

Adieu, my friends! May every sun that shines on your green island see the annihilation of an abuse, and the birth of an embryon of melioration! Your own hearts—may they become the shrines of purity and freedom, and never may smoke to the Mammon of unrighteousness ascend from the unpolluted altar of their devotion!

No. 7, Lower Sackville Street, Feb. 22nd.

POSTSCRIPT.

I have now been a week in Dublin, during which time I have endeavoured to make myself more accurately acquainted with the state of the public mind on those great topics of grievances which induced me to select

Ireland as a theatre, the widest and fairest, for the operations of the determined friend of religious and political freedom.

The result of my observations has determined me to propose an association for the purposes of restoring Ireland to the prosperity which she possessed before the Union Act; and the religious freedom which the involuntariness of faith ought to have taught all monopolists of Heaven long, long ago, that every one had a right to possess.

For the purpose of obtaining the emancipation of the Catholics from the penal laws that aggrieve them, and a repeal of the Legislative Union Act, and grounding upon the remission of the church-craft and oppression, which caused these grievances; *a plan of amendment and regeneration in the moral and political state of society, on a comprehensive and systematic philanthropy which shall be sure though slow in its projects; and as it is without the rapidity and danger of revolution, so will it be devoid of the time-servingness of temporizing reform*—which in its deliberate capacity, having investigated the state of the Government of England, shall oppose those parts of it, by intellectual force, which will not bear the touchstone of reason.

For information respecting the principles which I possess, and the nature and spirit of the association which I propose, I refer the reader to a small pamphlet, which I shall publish on the subject in the course of a few days.

I have published the above Address (written in England) in the cheapest possible form, and have taken pains that the remarks which it contains should be intelligible to the most uneducated minds. Men are not slaves and brutes because they are poor; it has been the policy of the thoughtless or wicked of the higher ranks (as a proof of the decay of which policy I am happy to see the rapid success of a comparatively enlightened system of education) to conceal from the poor the truths which I have endeavoured to teach them. In doing so I have but translated my thoughts into another language ; and as language is only useful as it communicates ideas, I shall think my style so far good as it is successful as a means to bring about the end which I desire on any occasion to accomplish.

A Limerick paper, which I suppose professes to support certain *loyal* and *John Bullish* principles of freedom, has in an essay for advocating the liberty of the Press the following clause : " For lawless licence of discussion never did we advocate, nor do we now." What is lawless licence of discussion ? Is it not as indefinite as the words *contumely, reproach, defamation,* that allow at present such latitude to the outrages that are committed on the free expression of individual sentiment ? Can they not see that what is rational will stand by its reason, and what is true stand by its truth, as all that is foolish will fall by its folly, and all that is false be controverted by its own falsehood ? Liberty gains nothing by the reform of politicians of this stamp, any more than it gains from a change of Ministers in London. What at present is contumely and defamation, would at the period of this Limerick amendment be " lawless licence of discussion," and such would be the mighty advantage which this doughty champion of liberty proposes to effect.

I conclude with the words of Lafayette, a name endeared by its peerless bearer to every lover of the human race, " For a nation to love liberty it is sufficient that she knows it, to be free it is sufficient that she wills it."

CHAPTER IX.

THE allusion towards the end of this Address to Peter Finnerty who had been then twelve months a prisoner in the Castle of Lincoln, will arrest the attention of all readers who remember the singular story I have told of the poem which Shelley had published for his benefit a year before. It shows that his interest in him was undiminished, and strengthens the suggestion I have thrown out, that in the volume of poems which Shelley had proposed to publish in Dublin, *The Poetical Essay on the Existing State of Things* would have been included.

The Limerick paper which Shelley sarcastically alludes to as proposing " to support certain *loyal* and *John Bullish* principles of freedom," was *The Limerick Evening Post*, then recently established. The article was reprinted in *The Dublin Freeman's Journal*, Tuesday, February 18th, 1812, where Shelley must have seen it. It is thus introduced :—

" IRISH PRESS.—The following judicious observations we have extracted from a newly established paper in Limerick—namely, *The Limerick Evening Post.*"

Shelley it is evident formed a very different estimate of this article. He considered it lacked spirit. It is plain that at this period he thought it extremely probable that his own pamphlets which were about to appear would have to bear the brunt of a government prosecution. He must therefore have considered it

Q

rather unfortunate that a Liberal paper thus eulogized
by a metropolitan journal of influence should, as it
were, encourage the Executive in limiting the right of
public discussion on political questions.

The opening passages which provoked his comment
may be given as a specimen of the article thus preserved
from oblivion by the quotation of the poet :—

" The prosecutions so perseveringly continued
against the Press of Ireland—against the journals of
the capital, deserving, we think, that title by pre-
eminence, must anxiously interest every reflecting mind
—every feeling heart. So generally allowed and
axiomatically fixed is the grand right of a *Free Press*—
in other words, of free thought and free discussion—
that the greatest enemies of that greatest bulwark of
human privileges never dared to assail it but in disguise
—but under some factious colourable principle ; its
bitterest foes, at least since the days of the Star
Chamber, have uniformly avowed themselves as friends.
For lawless licence of discussion never yet did we
advocate, nor do we now," &c.

Whether the paper made any reply to the observations of Shelley it is now impossible to say : its very
name is almost forgotten in Limerick, although some
files of it of a much later date are still preserved
in the library of the Royal Dublin Society.

The next important movement made by Shelley in
his Dublin crusade took place three days after the
publication of his *Address to the Irish People*. That
pamphlet had appeared on Tuesday, the 25th of
February, 1812, and on the Friday following, the 28th
of the same month, the long announced Aggregate
Meeting of the Catholics of Ireland took place in the

historic little theatre in Fishamble Street. Shelley attended that meeting, and spoke to an important
resolution for the space of an hour. An outline of
that speech, taken from three different reports in contemporary journals, as well as his own remarks upon
it extracted from one of his unpublished letters, will be
given in due course.

To understand the position of affairs at that period,
and to show the absolute impossibility (even had he
been more guarded in the expression of his anti-religious
fanaticism) of being able to establish a new political
association in Dublin when the Government was absolutely discussing the expediency of suppressing this
one solitary meeting, it will be necessary to take a
brief review of the attitude both of the Catholics and
of the Executive. This is founded principally on
original documents preserved among the State Papers
in the Record Office.

The insidious promises held out to the Catholics at the
time of the Union had been abandoned, and a system of
still stricter and more unconstitutional coercion persevered in. The Catholics were rapidly increasing in
number and in wealth. Headed by every man of rank and
by most of the men of talent of their own communion,
and generously assisted by many enlightened Protestants .
of character and position, they were gradually forming
into that compact organization which eventually
triumphed. The powerful mind and the indomitable
energy of O'Connell had already made themselves felt.
The body known as the " Catholic Committee" was
formed, which very soon attracted to itself the notice of
the Government. It had no secrets. Had there been anything to conceal, dishonest and mercenary instruments
were not wanting to betray it. The State Papers un-

fortunately supply abundant proof of this treachery. Mr. Wellesley Pole, writing from Dublin Castle on the 19th of October, 1811, to the Right Hon. Richard Ryder, Secretary of State for the Home Department, in reference to one of the Meetings of the Committee, says, " I send you a report from one of our spies." The report is enclosed, signed " F. W." There is in the Record Office an elaborate paper consisting of twenty-six quarto pages, written closely on both sides, which is in part a complete history of the Catholic Committee for three years. It is called " *Précis* of the Formation and Proceedings of the Catholic Committee in Ireland, 1809, 1810, 1811." Referring to 1810 we have the following allusion to Mr. Peter Finnerty, the object of Shelley's poetical sympathy in 1811 :—

" On the 2nd of November, 1810, an aggregate meeting took place : Mr. Finnerty recommended a Petition to Parliament for the Catholic Emancipation, one for Parliamentary Reform, and one for the Repeal of the Union. The thanks of the meeting were voted to Mr. Finnerty, and it was resolved, *That the Catholic Committee should have the sole management of Catholic affairs.*"

Another entry in the same *Précis* is as follows :— " On the 9th of July (1811) the aggregate meeting assembled at the Private Theatre, Fishamble Street : it was very numerous." Among other resolutions it was resolved, " That the Committee be appointed ; that the Catholic Peers, Baronets, and the survivors of 1793 have the management of Catholic affairs ; that 500*l.* be given to Mr. Hay (the Secretary); 500*l.* to Mr. W. Todd Jones; and that a subscription be made for Mr. Finnerty."

The speech made by Mr. Finnerty at the Catholic

meeting referred to in the first of these extracts, is a memorable one. But for it, Mr. Wellesley Pole informed the Imperial Parliament on the 4th of March 1811, the Convention Act would not have been enforced in Ireland, and the proclamation of the Duke of Richmond would not have been issued. The speech was delivered at an adjourned meeting of the Catholics held at the Repository in St. Stephen's Green, Dublin, on Friday the 2nd of November, 1810. This speech was delivered at the request of the meeting, and produced immense enthusiasm, and, what was more dangerous in the eyes of Mr. Wellesley Pole, unanimity.

Mr. Wellesley Pole subsequently notified to the Secretary of State that a subscription had been opened in Dublin for Mr. Finnerty. The following extract is taken from a letter in the Record Office :—

Ireland, 1811, January to June.   No. 652.

"Young Mr. Curran, son of the Master of the Rolls, has been very active in soliciting from the Catholics subscriptions for Mr. Finnerty, and letters from persons associated in London for promoting that object have been addressed to the Catholics here.

"I have the honour to be,

"&c. &c. &c.

"W. W. POLE.

"The Right Honourable Richard Ryder."

The speech of Mr. Finnerty formed the subject of debate in the House of Commons, March 4th, 1811. The debate is fully reported in the *Examiner*, March 10th. Mr. Finnerty's speech is given at great length in *The Dublin Weekly Messenger*, November 10th, 1810. A copy of the first two volumes of that paper

is preserved in the library of Trinity College, Dublin.
In a tract entitled *Proceedings of the Catholic Committee, as taken from their Accredited Papers,* Dublin,
1811, a report of the speech fills ten pages.

A more formidable personage than Mr. Peter Finnerty was at this time also under the watchful eye of
Mr. Wellesley Pole.*   In a letter dated " Irish Office,
March 11th, 1811," he sends to the Home Secretary,
the Right Hon. Richard Ryder, a lengthy report of
the proceedings at " the Aggregate Meeting of the
Catholics held in Dublin on Friday last, the 8th instant."   Towards the end of it Mr. O'Connell is
alluded to in the following words :—

" It would appear from Mr. O'Connell's speech as
if a repeal of the Legislative Union was now become
as serious an object to the Catholic Managers as
general Emancipation.   He expressed himself thus,
' That the country had been involved in deep calamity
ever since the baneful measure of the Union had been
forced upon distracted Ireland.' " This passage, it may

---

* There is a still earlier allusion to Mr. O'Connell, and to the
demand for a Repeal of the Union, in the State Papers.   It is a
private report of the Aggregate Meeting, September 18th, 1810.
The document is marked " Enclosure No. 2 :"—

" Hutton, a trader (brother to the late Alderman), of the *Presbyterian* Party, moved a petition to the King to insist on the
Repeal of the Union.

" Counsellor O'Connell seconded the motion (he is a *Catholic*).
Motion carried unanimously."   The only names given in this
private report are those of Hutton, MacNally, and O'Connell.
The following observation is added :—" The people who have engaged in this business *will persevere,* and they ought to be attended
to—they ought to be watched."   The benevolent gentleman who
gave this advice seems to have been a certain Mr. " T. Mulock."—
[Ireland, 1810.   August to December.   No. 648.]

be remarked, reads amazingly like that which Shelley
subsequently wrote in the advertisement of his first
pamphlet.   In language stronger than that of Mr.
O'Connell, but yet resembling it, he calls the Union
Act "the most successful engine that England ever
wielded over the misery of fallen Ireland." Mr. Pole,
in the continuation of his letter to Mr. Ryder, thus
refers to one of that useful class whom he had in
more direct but less elegant language called
" spies :"—

   " One ' of the most intelligent and secret agents
employed by the Irish Government states, that in
his judgment their last meeting and debate has most
evidently depressed the Protestant party, who have
opposed the claims of the Catholics, and has increased
their Protestant advocates. Many Protestants were
present, and the Theatre was full in every part. It is
remarkable, however, that there was no crowd at the
door : great pains having been taken, particularly by
the Catholic clergy, to keep the lower orders from
attending in the streets.

   " I have the honour to be, &c. &c.,
                                     " W. W. POLE.
   " Right Honourable Richard Ryder."*

The morning of Friday the 28th of February, 1812,
must have been an exciting one for the three propagan-
dists of philanthropy—Shelley, Harriet, and Eliza Westbrook, as they met together in the drawing-room of
No. 7, Lower Sackville Street, Dublin.   The youthful
Shelley was on that day to present himself before an

   * From State Papers, "Ireland, 1811, January to June.
No. 652."

immense assembly, and to put to the test his power of
addressing or influencing an audience. The ladies we
may be sure had determined to accompany him to the
meeting, and with all her confidence in the ability of
Percy, we can have little doubt that the gentle
Harriet was full of anxiety as to his success. The
presence of ladies at these great gatherings of the
rank and talent of the Irish Catholics was one of
their most attractive features. The following description of a meeting which took place a year before
may serve for that at which Shelley spoke, and we
have no doubt Harriet listened :—

" Fishamble Street Theatre, where the recent Aggregate Meeting of the Roman Catholics was held in
Dublin," says the *Morning Chronicle* of March 14th,
1811, " was brilliantly illuminated, and had a most
interesting effect. The boxes were filled with ladies
full dressed, and the whole is represented as having a
very imposing effect. The presence of their fair country-
women was certainly calculated to prolong the discussion, as the orators were all anxious to display their
eloquence to the greatest advantage."

Fishamble Street Theatre, where Shelley spoke and
Handel played, where the deep tones of O'Connell's
wonderful voice so often roused and controlled the
people ; the scene of so much festivity, the centre of so
many recollections, is now levelled to the ground, but
a slight sketch of its history may not be uninteresting.
The street itself, like that

> " Where London's column, towering to the skies,
> Like a tall bully lifts its head—and lies,"

derives its name from being the place where fish was

exposed for sale to the citizens. In old municipal documents the Dublin Fish-shamble Street is frequently styled " Vicus Piscariorum."* The boats could lie at the river's bank at the foot of the street, which rises in a zigzag direction, like the walls of a fortress, to the top of the slight hill or elevation on which " the Castle still stands." From its vicinity to the Cathedral of the Holy Trinity or Christ Church, to the Courts of Law, and to the Castle, Fishamble Street occupied an important position in the old city. The names of several famous hostelries are connected with it, in which for many years various clubs, musical, masonic, or simply convivial, were in the habit of assembling. The Protestant parish church of St. John still stands midway on the western side of the street, and nearly opposite to it, divided from Fishamble Street by a short and narrow lane, is the Catholic Church of SS. Michael and John, built upon the foundations of the celebrated Smock-alley Theatre.† In the first named Church of St. John, on the 3rd of July, 1746, was baptized a child destined to be for ever memorable in the history of Ireland—Henry Grattan—whose father and grandfather had long been residents in the then flourishing, but now desolate and still decaying Fishamble Street. Five years before the birth of Henry Grattan, the building first called the new Music Hall, but subsequently the Private Theatre, was erected. The building owed its existence to the necessities of a

---

* In a record of the 19th year of Richard II. it is called " Vicus Piscatorius, in parochia Sancti Johannis."

† " The only vestige now existing of Smock-alley Theatre·is a portion of an arched passage on the south-eastern side of this church."—GILBERT's *History of Dublin*, vol. ii. p. 111.

musical club called the "Bull's Head" Society, which
after various migrations from the old tavern from
which it derived its name, finally settled in the new
Music Hall. The "Bull's Head" Society always had
hung upon the outskirts of the Cathedral of Christ
Church, and from time to time decoyed to its reunions
various of the minor dignitaries of that ancient foundation. So ancient indeed, that an inquisition in the
reign of Richard the Second declared that it was
"founded and endowed by divers Irish-men whose
names were unknown, time out of mind, and long
before the Conquest of Ireland." St. Patrick's Cathedral, which may be called the Cathedral founded by
the Anglo-Norman colony in Ireland in a sort of
rivalry to the old Irish Cathedral of the Holy Trinity,
lay also in dangerous proximity to the head-quarters
of the "Bull's Head" Society, and some of its worthy
officers who had "music in their souls" joined their melodious brethren of Christ Church occasionally at their
festive gatherings. A sort of whimsical anathema,
called by him an "exhortation," was hurled at the
heads of these delinquents in 1741 by Dean Swift, the
Dean of St. Patrick's. It reads very like what
Curran the "Prior" of "The Monks of the Screw"
might have issued about forty years later to his rather
lax community. In 1741 "the Dean" requested his
sub-dean and Chapter to punish such vicars as should
appear at the "Club of Fiddlers in Fishamble Street,"
" as songsters, fiddlers, pipers, trumpeters, drummers,
drum-majors, or in any sonal quality, according to the
flagitious aggravation of their respective disobedience,
rebellion, perfidy, and ingratitude." "I also," adds
Swift, "require my sub-dean to proceed to the extremity of expulsion, if the said vicars should be found

ungovernable, impenitent, or self-sufficient, especially
Taberner, Phipps, and Church, who, as I am informed,
have in violation of my sub-dean's and Chapter's
order in December last, at the instance of some
obscure persons unknown, presumed to sing and fiddle
at the Club above mentioned."*

In 1741 the President of the "Club of Fiddlers in
Fishamble Street" was John O'Neil, or Neal, a publisher of music. It was through his exertions the
new Music Hall was erected. This is recorded in a
contemporary poem, from which we may take the four
following lines :—

> " As Amphion built of old the Theban wall,
> So Neal has built a sumptuous Musick Hall :
> The one by pow'rful touches of his lute ;
> The other by the fiddle and the flute. "

But the fiddle and the flute were not to be the only
instruments to resound within the new structure. Six
weeks after it was opened the hand of a great master
was to awaken new harmonies within its walls, perhaps
not thought of by the original projectors. Handel
came to Dublin ; " banished to Ireland," says the
index to the *Dunciad,* " by the English nobility" :—

> " Strong in new arms, lo ! Giant Handel stands,
> Like bold Briareus, with a hundred hands ;
> To stir, to rouse, to shake the soul he comes,
> And Jove's own thunders follow Mars's drums.
> Arrest him, empress, or you sleep no more—
> She heard, and drove him to th' Hibernian shore."

A year later than Handel's visit to Dublin, Pope
paid a graceful compliment to Ireland in his lines to

---

* GILBERT'S *History of Dublin,* vol. i. pp. 69, 70.

Southern.   Alluding to the figure of the harp woven
into the texture of the Irish linen tablecloth hospitably
spread before the aged poet, who was himself a native
of Dublin, he says :—

> " And Ireland, mother of sweet singers,
>   Presents her harp still to his fingers."

The "mother of sweet singers" could not do less
than give Handel a cordial reception.   She had
already presented her harp in some of its most attractive utterances to that "sweet son of song."   The
melodies of Ireland, half a century before Moore
was born, delighted Handel.   He is said to have
declared that he would willingly resign the fame
he had acquired by his most celebrated compositions
for the glory of being the inventor of the air *Aileen
Aroon.**

From 1741, when the genius of Handel threw an unexpected glory over the new Music Hall in Fishamble
Street, until 1812, when the apparition of Shelley
within its walls

> " Bequeathed, like sunset to the skies,
>   The splendour of its prime,"

a period of seventy-one years had elapsed.   The
gradual decay of the street had by this time advanced,
and with it that of the theatre.   This building lay
almost out of view.   It was approached by a wooden
porch or verandah in an angle of the street as you
descend from Werburgh Street and Hoey's Court (the
birthplace of Swift) towards the river.   Many changes

---

* An Account of the Visit of Handel to Dublin; with Incidental
Notices of his Life and Character.   By Horatio Townsend, Esq.,
Barrister-at-Law, p. 64.   Dublin, 1852.

had taken place in the locality. "Hell" itself was proved not to have been eternal. The famous passage or gateway so-called, surmounted by a black figure of the devil carved in oak, had stood nearly opposite the theatre in St. John's Lane. At the time of Shelley's visit, Burns, if he had been living, would have had to seek elsewhere for an illustration of the truth of the story he told in " Death and Doctor Hornbook"—

> " But this that I am gaun to tell,
> Which lately on a night befell,
> Is just as true as the Deil's in Hell
> Or Dublin City."

The " Deil" had disappeared or been metamorphosed into snuffboxes !"*

Fishamble Street Theatre survived for something over half a century after Shelley's visit. In the decaying street there was one flourishing establishment. To that exceptional sign of prosperity it owed its destruction. The growing needs of an enterprising firm adjoining required larger accommodation. The theatre was taken down, and the open show-yard of a thriving iron factory now occupies the space on which it stood.†

The vigilance exercised by the Irish Government in ascertaining through their secret agents the arrangements of the Catholics for the intended meeting of

---

* One of these the author remembers having seen in his boyhood. The box bore on a silver lid the following inscription, which was read with all due awe :—

> " Prime your nose well, and I'd have you be civil,
> For this box it was made of a part of *the Devil !*"

† The site is well defined. It is in the angle of the street, and separates the two establishments of Messrs. Kennan and Sons.

February 28th, 1812, did not relax when the meeting took place. Two persons were sent to Fishamble Street Theatre to furnish special reports of the proceedings. Both reporters were connected with the police—one a chief constable, Mr. Michael Farrell, well known in the local history of the period; the other, a Mr. Manning, who held an inferior position. These reports are preserved among the State Papers in the Record Office. Unfortunately they give us little or no information on the subject of Shelley. In one he is not mentioned at all; in the other he is barely alluded to. Of the two reports, that signed Thos. K. Manning is the longest. In this Shelley's name does not appear. Another young man, afterwards very distinguished, the late Sir Thomas Wyse, the English Ambassador in Greece, made his first appearance in public at the same meeting. He proposed the resolution to which Shelley spoke, and is thus described by Mr. Manning :—

" On this resolution, Mr. Wise, a young boy, delivered a speech of considerable length and replete with much elegant language ; the principal matter it contained of notice was, that he lamented that the Regent should abandon Mr. Fox's principles and join in a shameful coalition, or that he had been so far *womanized*—here he was interrupted by a question of order."

In 1812, Mr. Wyse was twenty-one years of age, having been born in 1791 ; the description " a young boy" could therefore be scarcely applicable to him. Shelley was nineteen years and six months old, but looked so young that his servant could give out with some appearance of truth that he was but fifteen.

The full report of the elaborate speech of Mr. Wyse is now before us, and it contains no language in the slightest degree disrespectful to the Prince Regent, neither was the speaker called to order. In fact, the business of the meeting was to adopt an address to his Royal Highness, and the observations alluded to by the reporter could scarcely have been used by any one who had been selected by the managers to take an important part in its proceedings. Shelley's speech was volunteered. His strong feelings towards the Prince at this time we know from his own letters, and he may easily have strayed into the expression of them. In one of his letters, hitherto unpublished, an extract from which will presently be given, he tells us that some of his observations met with interruption. On the whole we think that Mr. Manning, in copying his notes, transferred the description from Shelley to Mr. Wyse.

The second reporter, Mr. Farrell, the peace officer, mentions Shelley but very slightly. He says :—

" Lord Glentworth said a few words—a Mr. Bennett spoke, also Mr. Shelley, who stated himself to be a native of England."

With these manuscript reports the Lord Lieutenant forwarded to the Home Secretary a copy of *The Dublin Evening Post* of Saturday, the 29th February, 1812, containing a full report of the proceedings at the meeting which took place the day before. It is from this paper that the only version of Shelley's speech hitherto published has been taken. It was originally extracted by the present writer, from whose transcript it was copied into Mr. Middleton's *Shelley and his Writings* (vol. i. p. 212). There are two other versions

of the speech which have not previously been known.
One of these is indeed very short, but as it expressly
mentions the kind manner in which the youthful
speaker was received by the meeting, it is very valuable
as part of the refutation of the calumnious statement
made years after by Mr. Hogg, which has been so
improperly repeated by others who reject Mr. Hogg's
testimony when they dislike it, and adopt it when it
is in accordance with their own prejudices. This brief
report appeared on the morning after the meeting in
The Freeman's Journal of Saturday, Feb. 29th, 1812.
It was repeated in *The Hibernian Journal, or Daily
Chronicle of Liberty*, Dublin, Monday, March 2nd,
1812. And again in a more accessible shape in
Walker's Hibernian Magazine for February, 1812,
p. 83. As it was the earliest report, it may be here
given first :—

*Shelley's Speech at Fishamble Street Theatre, Dublin,
Feb. 28th, 1812.*

From *The Freeman's Journal*, Dublin, Feb. 29th, 1812.

" On the fifth [it should have been the *sixth*]
resolution being proposed, Mr. Shelley, an English
gentleman (very young), the son of a Member of Parliament, rose to address the meeting. He was received
with great kindness, and declared that the greatest
misery this country endured was the Union Law, the
Penal Code, and the state of the representation. He
drew a lively picture of the misery of the country,
which he attributed to the unfortunate Act of Legislative Union."

On the evening of the same day, in the *Dublin
Evening Post* of Saturday, the 29th of February, 1812,

a fuller report of the speech is given. The italics are in the original.

Shelley's Speech.

From *The Dublin Evening Post*, Saturday, 29th Feb. 1812.

"Mr. Shelley requested a hearing. He was an Englishman, and when he reflected on *the crimes committed by his nation on Ireland,* he could not but blush for his countrymen, did he not know that arbitrary power never failed to corrupt the heart of man. (Loud applause for several minutes.)

"He had come to Ireland for the sole purpose of interesting himself in her misfortunes. He was deeply impressed with a sense of the evils which Ireland endured, and he considered them to be truly ascribed to the fatal effects of the legislative union with Great Britain.

"He walked through the streets, and he saw the *fane of liberty converted into a temple of Mammon.* (Loud applause.) He beheld beggary and famine in the country, and he could lay his hand on his heart and say that the cause of such sights was the union with Great Britain. (Hear, hear.) He was resolved to do his utmost to promote a Repeal of the Union. Catholic Emancipation would do a great deal towards the amelioration of the condition of the people, but he was convinced that the Repeal of the Union was of more importance. He considered that the victims whose members were vibrating on gibbets were driven to the commission of the crimes which they expiated by their lives by the effects of the Union."

The third and longest report of Shelley's speech is

R

as follows. It is taken from *The Patriot*, Dublin,
2nd March, 1812:—

" Mr. Shelly then addressed the Chair. He hoped
he should not be accounted a transgressor on the time
of the meeting. He felt inadequate to the task he
had undertaken, but he hoped the feelings which
urged him forward would plead his pardon. He was
an Englishman; when he reflected on the outrages
that his countrymen had committed here for the last
twenty years he confessed that he blushed for them.
He had come to Ireland for the sole purpose of
interesting himself in the misfortunes of this country,
and impressed with a full conviction of the necessity
of Catholic Emancipation, and of the baneful effects
which the union with Great Britain had entailed upon
Ireland. He had walked through the fields of the
country and the streets of the city, and he had in
both seen the miserable effects of that fatal step. · He
had seen that edifice which ought to have been the
fane of their liberties converted to a temple of
Mammon. Many of the crimes which are daily committed he could not avoid attributing to the effect of
that measure, which had thrown numbers of people
out of the employment they had in manufacture, and
induced them to commit acts of the greatest despera-
tion for the support of their existence.   :

" He could not imagine that the religious opinion
of a man should exclude him from the rights of society.
The original founder of our religion taught no such
doctrine. Equality in this respect was general in the
American States, and why not here? Did a change
of place change the nature of man? He would beg
those in power to recollect the French Revolution :

the suddenness, the violence with which it burst forth, and the causes which gave rise to it.

" Both the measures of Emancipation and a Repeal of the Union should meet his decided support, but he hoped many years would not pass over his head when he would make himself conspicuous at least by his zeal for them."*

In these versions of the speech, which are the only ones I have been able to find in the Irish papers of the period, or rather in those of them that are still extant, there is no suggestion that Shelley met with the slightest discourtesy from those he addressed. Indeed, it would be strange if he had. His youth, his enthusiasm, his eloquence, as we will find, delighted the assembly by which, as we are told in *The Freeman's Journal,* " he was received with great kindness." Some slight interruption he *did* meet with at the beginning, but that was, as he tells us himself in the unpublished letter we have referred to, when he spoke of " religion." In this letter, which is dated " 17, Grafton Street, Dublin, March 14, 1812," he says :—

" My speech was misinterpreted. I spoke for more than an hour. The hisses with which they greeted me when I spoke of *religion,* though in terms of respect, were mixed with applause when I avowed my mission. The newspapers have only noted that which did not excite disapprobation."

Without attributing any over-sensitiveness to the

---

* I find that this version of the speech appeared first in *Saunders's News-Letter,* Saturday, February 29th, 1812, the day after the meeting.

meeting, we may well imagine that Shelley's mode of
speaking of religion, " though in terms of respect,"
was not that which would recommend itself very
favourably to an assembly of Irishmen who had not
been " educated" (to use the expression of a modern
statesman) in the higher mysteries of philanthropy.
In his second pamphlet, which was issued four days
after he delivered this speech, there are passages
which, if spoken amid the excitement of a public
meeting, would indeed run some chance of being
" misinterpreted." People could not have time to
decide with accuracy as to what he exactly meant by
" the eyeless monster Bigotry, whose throne has
tottered for two hundred years" (p. 3). Perhaps they
would only have laughed if he had exclaimed as he
has written, " I hear the teeth of the palsied beldame
Superstition chatter, and I see her descending to the
grave! Reason points to the open gates of the
Temple of Religious Freedom, Philanthropy kneels at
the altar of the common God" (p. 3). By the " palsied beldame Superstition" Shelley of course understood the " religion" of the great majority of the
people he addressed, and which he spoke of in such
" terms of respect."

That, however, is not the view which Mr. Hogg,
the poet's biographer, takes of the matter, and here
we shall give that veracious gentleman's statement in
full. We must remind the reader of the mysterious
affair at York, of which something has been said in
the earlier portion of this book. Owing to that event
a total estrangement for a while took place between
Shelley and his college friend. At the time we speak of
(February, 1812) no intercourse whatever had existed
between them for several preceding months, nor was it

renewed for nearly a year afterwards. Shelley had not sent his late friend his Irish pamphlets, he did not write to him on any subject, he gave him no account of his proceedings. At a later period, which Mr. Hogg does not particularize, when his injured friend had generously forgiven him, and let him a little into his confidence once more, he says that Shelley spoke to him " twice, not oftener," he believed, " of his Irish mission." Before this conversation recurred to Mr. Hogg's memory he had made a statement as if on his own authority concerning this very mission. " There was one meeting of philanthropists," says the truthful biographer, " for it was reported in a newspaper, and probably puffed a little, perhaps for a valuable consideration. Whether there were more meetings does not appear. Poor Bysshe made a speech, and proposed his scheme, but it did not succeed." (*Life of Shelley*, vol. ii. p. 108.) It is scarcely necessary to say that there is not one word of truth in all this. There was no " meeting of philanthropists ;" it was never " puffed a little in a newspaper ;" Shelley never made a speech at a meeting of " philanthropists," and never " proposed his scheme." It is no wonder therefore, under these circumstances, that " it did not succeed." After pages of malevolent and ill-concealed contempt for Shelley, and openly avowed hatred of Ireland, Mr. Hogg resumes his narrative. In the passage quoted he had drawn on his imagination for his facts ; he now draws on his memory for his imagination :—

" Twice—not oftener, I believe—he spoke to me of his Irish mission. On one occasion he told me that at a meeting—probably at the meeting of

philanthropists—so much ill-will was shown towards
the Protestants, that thereupon he was provoked to
remark that the Protestants were fellow Christians,
fellow subjects, and as such were entitled to equal
rights, to equal charity, toleration, and the rest. He
was forthwith interrupted by savage yells; a tremendous uproar arose, and he was compelled to be
silent. At the same meeting and afterwards he was
even threatened with personal violence. This un-
reasonable display of Popish and party bigotry went
far to disgust him with his rash enterprise, to open
his eyes, and to convince him that Irish grievances
consisted not in a denial of equal rights—these the
Philanthropic Association did not seek—but the power
and opportunity to tyrannize over and oppress their
Protestant brethren." (Hogg's *Life of Shelley*, vol. ii.
pp. 113, 114.)

Out of the pages of the much maligned Ferdinand
Mendez Pinto—that "liar of the first magnitude,"
who must have been indeed but "the type" of this
cynical biographer—there could not be found within
the same space a greater number of reckless misrepresentations than these, if we must not call them
by a shorter and more emphatic title. That Shelley
ever made them is incredible. They are contradicted
by his own letters at the time, by the facts of the
case, by the evidence already adduced, and by the
important letter of an unimpeachable witness who
happened to be present at the meeting, and whose
unwilling testimony to the cordiality of Shelley's
reception, and the enthusiasm he produced, puts an
end for ever to the monstrous fable of Mr. Hogg.
That fable has unfortunately been adopted by others

Thomas Wyse

From a lithograph by Haverty, A.D. 1829.
Mr Wyse, subsequently the Right Hon. Sir
Thomas Wyse, K.C.B., late British Minister at
Athens, commenced public life at the meeting
in Fishamble Street Theatre, Dublin, Feb. 28th
1812. He seconded the resolution to which
Shelley spoke. See p. 247.

who have publicly impeached the veracity of the authority on which it is founded. It would be easy to point out the injury that is done to society by disseminating statements which a slight examination would prove to be untrue, particularly when such calumnies have no result except in perpetuating and keeping alive national and religious animosities. The subject would however be painful, and perhaps out of place here. It is to be hoped that in future " Shelley Memorials " and " Memoirs " a very different account from that which disfigures those at present in existence will be given of the manner in which the poet was received by those he went to serve.

The Resolution to which Shelley spoke would in itself disprove the story of Mr. Hogg.

"RESOLVED, That the grateful thanks of this Meeting are due, and hereby returned to Lord Glentworth, the Right Hon. Maurice Fitzgerald, and the other DISTINGUISHED PROTESTANTS who have this day honoured us with their presence."

This Resolution, which was passed by acclamation by the assembly, was spoken to by Lord Glentworth, a Protestant nobleman, as well as by the philanthropic Shelley, and was seconded by the distinguished gentleman already referred to, the late Sir Thomas Wyse— then Mr. Wyse—a Catholic. The eloquent speech of Mr. Wyse is given at great length in the Dublin newspaper sent by Shelley to Godwin on the 8th of March, 1812. The concluding passage seems as if it were addressed to the young poet and philanthropist who stood by his side. We print it exactly as it is given in the newspaper.

"On that day of Peace," said Mr. Wyse, "when national animosity is sepulchred beneath the trophies of national harmony, *we shall remember with gratitude the* PROTESTANT *who stood by us in our struggle, and bore our broken standard to the front of the battle,* whilst we prepare the Sacrifice to the Spirit of UN-DISTINGUISHED BROTHERHOOD AND UNIVERSAL EMANCI-PATION."—*The Weekly Messenger,* Saturday, March 7th, 1812.*

---

* This, the maiden speech of the late Sir Thomas Wyse, which fills nearly four columns of *The Weekly Messenger,* March 7th, 1812, is thus introduced by the editor of that journal :—

"MR. WISE, JUNR.

"The report which we now give of the speech delivered by this gentleman, at the late aggregate meeting of the Catholics of Ireland, will be observed by our readers to be the most correct and most accurate as yet presented to the public. It will be found, we hope, that some justice is done to those talents which excited such general applause. That the lover of his country, and the admirer of the growing genius of our Island, will find great satisfaction in the perusal of the following speech, we have no doubt. We trust that every effort which shall hereafter be made by our countrymen will rival the talents which we have already witnessed, and that the eloquence of our young advocate may be a presage of the advantages which the British empire shall hereafter reap from their full and unqualified possession."

CHAPTER X.

THE following important letter, now for the first time given in connexion with the life of Shelley, while it disposes of the calumny so readily believed and so recklessly diffused as to his reception at a public meeting, referred to in the preceding chapter, settles also the interesting question, which has often been raised, of Shelley's probable success as an orator had he devoted himself to the cultivation of eloquence instead of poetry.

Medwin, Trelawny, and Captain Williams the partner of his fate, speak highly of the elevation of Shelley's ordinary conversation, which rose occasionally into an unstudied eloquence. But they never heard him address a public assembly. The only one hitherto recorded—except the anonymous writers subsequently to be mentioned—who had this opportunity, and made some allusion to it, was the late Chief Baron Woulfe. His description leaves the impression that Shelley was a cold, methodical, and ineffective speaker. Chief Baron Woulfe was in bad health when he is reported to have mentioned his recollection of Shelley's manner. Many years had elapsed, and Shelley could have scarcely been recalled to his memory except by an effort. Of far different value is the testimony wrung most reluctantly at the moment from an unwilling witness. That testimony

is contained in the following letter, which was published in the Government organ of the day, *The Dublin
Journal*, a paper originally started by George Faulkner,
the publisher of Swift :—

SHELLEY AS AN ORATOR, DESCRIBED BY
"AN ENGLISHMAN" IN 1812.

"To the Editor of *The Dublin Journal.*

"Saturday, March 7th, 1812.

" Sir,—Our public meetings now-a-days, instead of
exhibiting the deliberations of men of acknowledged
wisdom and experience, resemble mere debating societies, where unfledged candidates for national distinction rant out a few trite and commonplace observations with as much exultation and self-applause as
if they possessed the talents or eloquence of a Saurin
or a Burke. This remark is particularly applicable
to almost the whole of the meetings which have been
assembled within the last twelve months by the
Catholics ; at which young gentlemen of this description have constantly intruded themselves upon the
public notice, and by the unseasonable and injudicious
violence of their language, have not a little prejudiced
the cause they attempted to support. Curiosity and
the expected gratification of hearing a display of
oratory by some of the leading members of the
Catholic body led me on Friday, for the first time, to
the Aggregate Meeting in Fishamble Street. Being
rather late I missed the orations of Mr. Connell [*sic*]
and the leading orators, and only heard a dry mono-
tonous effusion from Counsellor ——, and, to me, a
most disgusting harangue from a stripling, with whom
1 am unacquainted, but who, I am sorry to say, styled

himself my countryman—an Englishman. This young
gentleman, after stating that he had been only a
fortnight in Ireland, expatiated on the miseries which
this country endured in consequence of its connexion with his own, and asserted (from the knowledge, I presume, which his peculiar sagacity enabled
him to acquire in so short a period) that its cities
were depopulated, its fields laid waste, and its inhabitants degraded and enslaved; and all this by its
union with England. If it revolted against my principles, Mr. Editor, to hear such language from one of
my own countrymen, you will readily conceive that my
disgust was infinitely heightened to observe with what
transport the invectives of this renegade Englishman
against his native country were *hailed* by the assembly
he addressed. Joy beamed in every countenance and
rapture glistened in every eye at the aggravated detail:
the delirium of ecstasy got the better of prudential
control; the veil was for a moment withdrawn. I
thought I saw the *purpose*, in spite of the *pretence*,
written in legible characters in each of their faces, and
though emancipation *alone* flowed from the tongue,
separation and ascendancy were rooted in the heart.

"As for the young gentleman alluded to, I congratulate the Catholics of Ireland on the acquisition
of so *patriotic* and *enlightened* an advocate; and
England, I dare say, will spare him without regret.
I must, however, remark that as the love of his
country is one of the strongest principles implanted
in the breast of man by his Maker, and as the affections are more ardent in youth than in maturer years,
that this young gentleman should at so early an
age have overcome the strongest impulses of nature,
seems to me a complete refutation of the hitherto

supposed infallible maxim that *Nemo fuit repente turpissimus.*

" An Englishman."

Thus it will be seen that instead of being "interrupted by savage yells," as Mr. Hogg and Lady Shelley would have us believe, this " stripling," this " renegade Englishman," as he is called by his indignant countryman, " was hailed with delight" by his Irish audience ; " joy beamed in every countenance and rapture glistened in every eye ;" and if there was disposition to " threaten him with personal violence," we may now safely infer from what quarter it would be likely to have come.

The same day, the 7th of March, 1812, on which *The Dublin Journal* published this sarcastic allusion to the speech of "a stripling" it does not condescend to name, is memorable in the life of Shelley as that on which he is first spoken of openly in terms of enthusiastic admiration and praise. With the exception of his appearing among the subscribers to the Poems of Janetta Philipps, and to the Oxford Fund in Sustainment of Peter Finnerty, as previously mentioned, the following is the earliest public allusion to him that can be discovered. It appeared in *The Weekly Messenger*, another Dublin journal, but differing very widely in politics from that which contains the letter of "An Englishman." Shelley seems to have been rather proud of the notice, as he sent it at once to Godwin. Writing to the philosopher on the following day, he says, " You will see the account of ME in the newspapers. I am vain, but not so foolish as not to be rather piqued than gratified at the eulogia of a journal."

The following is this very interesting article, the

first public notice of Shelley. It is printed exactly
as in the original :—

ᚎ

From *The Weekly Messenger*, Dublin, Saturday, March 7th, 1812.

" PIERCE BYSHE SHELLY, ESQ.

" The highly interesting appearance of this young
gentleman at the late Aggregate Meeting of the
Catholics of Ireland, has naturally excited a spirit of
enquiry, as to his objects and views, in coming forward
at *such* a meeting; and the publications which he has
circulated with such uncommon industry, through the
Metropolis, has set curiosity on the wing to ascertain
who he is, from whence he comes, and what his pretensions are to the confidence he solicits, and the character
he assumes. To those who have read the productions
we have alluded to, we need bring forward no evidence
of the cultivation of his mind—the benignity of his
principles—or the peculiar fascination with which he
seems able to recommend them.

" Of this gentleman's family we can say but little,
but we can set down what we have heard from respectable authority. That his father is a member of the
Imperial Parliament, and that this young gentleman,
whom we have seen, is the *immediate* heir of one of
the *first* fortunes in England. Of his principles and
his manners we can say more, because we can collect
from conversation, as well as from reading, that he
seems devoted to the propagation of those divine and
Christian feelings which purify the human heart, give
shelter to the poor, and consolation to the unfortunate.
That he is the *bold* and *intrepid* advocate of those
principles which are calculated to give energy to truth,
and to depose from their guilty eminence the bad and

*A copy of this newspaper is among the Shelley-Whitton
papers collected by Mr. Charles Whitton who lent it to
me. Shelley's speed has been marked*

vicious passions of a corrupt community ;—that a
universality of charity is *his* object, and a perfectibility
of human society *his* end, which cannot be attained by
the *conflicting* dogmas of religious sects, *each* priding
itself on the extinction of the *other*, and *all* existing by
the mutual misfortunes which flow from polemical warfare. The principles of this young gentleman embrace *all* sects and all persuasions. His doctrines,
political and *religious*, may be accommodated to *all ;*
every friend to true Christianity will be his religious
friend, and every enemy to the liberties of Ireland will
be his *political* enemy. The weapons he wields are
those of reason, and the most *social benevolence*. He
deprecates violence in the accomplishment of his views,
and relies upon the mild and merciful spirit of toleration for the completion of all his designs, and the
consummation of all his wishes. To the religious
bigot such a *missionary of truth* is a formidable opponent, by the political monopolist he will be considered
the child of Chimera, the creature of fancy, an imaginary legislator who presumes to make laws without
reflecting upon his *materials*, and despises those considerations which have baffled the hopes of the most
philanthropic and the efforts of the most wise. It is
true, human nature may be too depraved for such a
hand as Mr. Shelly's to form to anything that
is good, or liberal, or beneficent. Let him but take down
one of the rotten pillars by which society is *now*
propped, and substitute the purity of his own principles, and Mr. Shelly shall have done a great and lasting
service to human nature. To this gentleman Ireland
is much indebted, for selecting *her* as the theatre of
his first attempts in this holy work of human regeneration ; the Catholics of Ireland should listen to him with

respect, because they will find that an enlightened
Englishman has interposed between the treason of
their own countrymen and the almost conquered
spirit of their country; that Mr. Shelly has come
to Ireland to demonstrate in his person that there are
hearts in his own country not rendered callous by six
hundred years of injustice; and that the genius of
freedom, which has communicated comfort and content
to the cottage of the Englishman, has found its way
to the humble roof of the Irish peasant, and promises
by its presence to dissipate the sorrows of past ages, to
obliterate the remembrance of persecution, and close
the long and wearisome scene of centuries of human de-
pression. We extract from Mr. Shelly's last production,
which he calls " PROPOSALS FOR AN ASSOCIATION, &c."

A long quotation from this pamphlet follows, which,
as it is printed entire in this book, need not be given.
The writer in *The Weekly Messenger* concludes his
observations with the following important paragraph :—

" We have but one word more to add. Mr. Shelly,
commiserating the sufferings of our distinguished
countryman Mr. Finerty, whose exertions in the
cause of political freedom he much admired, wrote a
very beautiful poem, the profits of which we understand, from *undoubted* authority, Mr. Shelly remitted
to Mr. Finerty; we have heard they amounted to
nearly an hundred pounds. This fact speaks a volume
in favour of our new friend."

Here then is the statement which has led to the
whole of this investigation. It seemed incredible that
a poem thus mentioned to the writer of the foregoing
article, evidently by Shelley himself, should have re-

mained unknown to every one who lived in familiar intimacy with the poet, or who has written about him since his death. The fact of Shelley sending this statement to Godwin without a word of correction confirms its truth. The name of the poem is not given. There was no clue but the fact that the profits of the sale were remitted to Mr. Finnerty. That however, as I have shown, proved sufficient to enable me to identify this "very beautiful poem" with the *Poetical Essay on the Existing State of Things*, published, as it is stated, for the purpose of " assisting to maintain in prison Mr. Peter Finnerty, imprisoned for a libel."

Before alluding to the probable writer of this article in *The Weekly Messenger*, I will here give a letter reflecting upon it, and upon Shelley, who is still not named, which appeared a fortnight later in Faulkner's *Dublin Journal*. The "stripling's" pretensions to be a poet, on the strength of this poem about Finnerty, are sarcastically referred to. The writer now calls himself "a Dissenter" instead of "an Englishman."

" To the Editor of *The Dublin Journal.*

" Saturday, March 21st, 1812.

" Sir,—I question the propriety of contributing to the public introduction of those literary nondescripts and political adventurers who figure occasionally on the Catholic stage. Men there are who, preferring distinction procured by infamy to inglorious obscurity, do not hesitate at the violation of any law, civil or sacred, in order to attain it: swimming at the surface by their own putrescence, these merit not our attention ; silence and contempt are all we owe to the individual whose sole ambition is to become the idol of a mob, and who like Herostratus, could fire a temple the wonder of the world, merely for the sake of transmitting to posterity a name which might otherwise rot.

" Through the medium of your paper, however, the attention of the public has been called to another of the Catholic performers, and a late worthy correspondent has obliged you with some deserved and judicious animadversions upon his début. In a weekly paper, the appearance of this 'very interesting' personage is announced with as much parade as if Dogberry, Verges, and the Watch graced the scene. ' Oh, a stool and a cushion for the sexton.' ' An two men ride of a horse, one must ride behind.' ' The ewe that will not hear her lamb when it baes, will never answer a calf when he bleats.' His panegyrist has described him with the minuteness of an interested biographer; the prospects and the talents of the 'stranger' and his generosity, his amazing generosity to an incarcerated individual [Mr. Peter Finnerty], whose crime was not loyalty, are made the subjects of commendation; and in illustration of the excellence of this modern Apollonius, who travels but for the improvement of the human race, a specimen of his composition is printed and circulated. I do not find that he, like the Cappadocian, has laid claims to miraculous powers, but he is a poet, and his very prose is so full of poetic fire, so vivid, so redundant with words, which, like those often used by a celebrated female novelist, were probably never intended to represent any specific idea—one is tempted to think he must now and then compose under the influence of the moon. Now, sir, though I really can neither ' make occasions,' nor ' improve those that offer,' for perusing the whole of a production which is scarcely to be paralleled in the ravings of Diderot, the rhapsodies of Rousseau, or the

soft sentimental stuff of the Prebend of York, I have
read enough of this specimen to confirm me in the
old-fashioned but honest and conscientious prejudices
which it is evidently the wish of its author to eradicate.
He proposes to 'exterminate the eyeless monster
Bigotry,' and 'make the teeth of the palsied beldame
Superstition chatter.'   This, which is doubtless designed as an allegorical allusion to the Romish Church,
must, if actually accomplished, be its death ; and when
' the teeth of the beldame chatter,' her brats may go beg ;
he proposes to make us all ' kneel at the altar of the
common God,' and to ' hang upon that altar the garland
of devotion,' figures which Deism borrows from the old
Heathen mythology, which are mere poetic smoke, and
resemble most the steams of a perfumer's shop, or the
smock of an Eastern bride smelling of ' myrrh, aloes,
and cassia.'

"In a style less elevated and Heliconian this
modern annihilator of moral and political evil roundly
proposes an association throughout Ireland for the
attainment of ' Catholic Emancipation and the repeal
of the Union Act.'   That the abolition of the aristocracy of the country is a feature in his picture of
Utopian amelioration, though, for reasons obvious, but
lightly touched, and as yet kept in the shade, is evident from the manner and connexion in which he
disapproves ' of other distinctions than those of virtue
and talent'—a disapproval specious indeed, worthy
the head of him who expects a new Jerusalem on
earth, or seeks divine perfection among created beings.
But ignorant, shamefully ignorant, must they be of
human nature, and of the awful events which have
taken place in Europe of late years, who can be gulled
by such a pretext now.   It is ' *Vox et præterea nihil*,'

the very cant of republicans. I would suspect the
cause which recommends itself by such a pretext, as
I would the chastity of a wanton assuming the dress of
a nun—the loyalty of a friar or a presbyter armed with
a pike, or the honesty of a beggar with a casquet of
jewels. 'No distinctions but those of virtue and
talent' was the pretext of Monsieur Egalité, of
Legendre the butcher, of the bloody Roland, and of
that monster in human shape Marat, who proposed,
and was applauded by a banditti of ruffians calling
themselves a National Convention for professing, the
cutting off one hundred and fifty thousand heads as a
sovereign specific for the disorders of France.

  "It is said in a book to whose pages the 'very interesting' Philanthropist seems not to be a stranger,
that 'burning lips and a wicked heart' are 'like a
potsherd covered with silver;' the man I mean has
himself quoted the phrase 'a tree is known by its
fruits,' and if I mistake not, such expressions warrant
the opinion that from certain noisy but worthless
characters nothing but what is noxious can be expected. Men whose private life and known habits
make them the refuse of the political, and the terror
or the stain of the moral world, would make but sorry
reformers of public abuse. I need not whisper 'whence
I steal the waters' when I say, 'Physician, heal thy-
self.' It is usual to commend the Catholic body
for their loyalty; that they are generally loyal is
sometimes acknowledged even by those who, in their
official situations, reprobate the proceedings of the
Catholic Committee. That there are loyal Catholics,
both lay and clerical, is, I believe, probable, but it
would puzzle a conjuror to reconcile with loyalty, as
it is by loyalists understood, some of the Catholic

measures." [Some passages not referring to Shelley are here omitted.] " Leaving this 'interesting stranger' to amuse the admirers of the Catholic Drama by puffing at 'the meteors' of his own creation, ' which play over the loathsome pool' of his own pantomimic invention, I will ask you, sir, what has the Protestant cause, and what has that consummation of political wisdom the British constitution, to fear from a party which has to shelter in the shade of such paltry and unmeaning bombast? The Philanthropist talks bigly of ' blossoms to be matured by the summer sun of improved intellect and progressive virtue,'—but if his root be rotten his blossoms will be dust. . . . From such corrections and such apologists, and from the machinations of all pseudo-philanthropists, may the good Lord deliver us !

"I have the honour to be, Sir,
" Yours, &c.,
" A DISSENTER."*

This letter finally disposes of Mr. Hogg's absurd story, and shows the quarter from which alone Shelley received any actual opposition when in Dublin. The " hint from the police" is equally apocryphal. Shelley's and Harriet's letters prove that he received none.

This may be the most suitable place to reprint the second pamphlet. As a publication it differs in one important particular from the other. It has the printer's name. I have not been able to find an " I. Eton, Winetavern Street," in any of the Dublin Directories. Shelley was greatly interested in the notorious Daniel Isaac Eaton, of London, as proved

---

* Extracted from *Faulkner's Dublin Journal*, Saturday, March 21st, 1812.

by the *Letter to Lord Ellenborough.* He would scarcely have invented his Irish namesake. It is, however, a rather curious coincidence to have not only a Dublin Stockdale, but a Dublin Eaton or Eton. Mr. John Stockdale was the actual printer of *The Press* newspaper, the celebrated organ of the United Irishmen in 1797. The registered printer was Peter Finnerty. On the arrest and imprisonment of the latter, December 23rd, 1797, the name of Arthur O'Connor was substituted as printer, and continued until the suppression of the paper, March 13th, 1798.*

---

* On Tuesday, the 27th of February, 1798, Mr. John Stockdale was brought for the second time to the bar of the Irish House of Lords. On the preceding Saturday he had been before the same tribunal, and declining to answer the question of the Lord Chancellor as to whether *The Press* newspaper was printed at his house, 62, Abbey Street, Dublin, was discharged. On being summoned for the second time, no time was lost in putting superfluous questions. He was directly charged with being the publisher of *The Press;* was sentenced to six months' imprisonment, and to pay a fine of 500*l.* As the editor of *The Press* said, " His accusation, his trial, his conviction, his sentence and its execution were despatched with the rapidity of a cabalistic charm."—*Beauties of The Press.* London: Printed 1800, p. 555.

Dr. Madden tells us that Mr. Stockdale died in Abbey Street, Dublin, January 11th, 1813.—*The United Irishmen, Second Series,* p. 246.

PROPOSALS

FOR AN

ASSOCIATION

OF THOSE

PHILANTHROPISTS,

WHO CONVINCED OF THE INADEQUACY OF THE MORAL AND POLITICAL
STATE OF IRELAND TO PRODUCE BENEFITS WHICH ARE NEVERTHELESS
ATTAINABLE ARE WILLING TO UNITE TO ACCOMPLISH ITS RE-
GENERATION.

BY

PERCY BYSSHE SHELLEY.

Dublin:

PRINTED BY I. ETON, WINETAVERN-STREET.

[1812.]

PROPOSALS

AN ASSOCIATION, &c.

I propose an association which shall have for its immediate objects,
Catholic Emancipation, and the Repeal of the Act of Union between
Great Britain and Ireland; and grounding on the removal of these
grievances, an annihilation or palliation, of whatever moral or po-
litical evil, it may be within the compass of human power to assuage
or eradicate.

MAN cannot make occasions, but he may seize those
that offer. None are more interesting to philanthropy
than those which excite the benevolent passions, that
generalize and expand private into public feelings, and
make the hearts of individuals vibrate not merely for
themselves, their families, and their friends, but for
posterity, *for a people;* till their country becomes the
world, and their family the sensitive creation.

A recollection of the absent, and a taking into consideration the interests of those unconnected with ourselves, is a principal source of that feeling which
generates occasions wherein a love for human kind
may become eminently useful and active. Public
topics of fear and hope, such as sympathize with
general grievance, or hold out hopes of general amendment, are those on which the philanthropist would
dilate with the warmest feeling. Because these are

accustomed to place individuals at a distance from
self; for in proportion as he is absorbed in public
feeling, so will a consideration of his proper benefit be
generalized.   In proportion as he feels with or for a
nation or a world, so will man consider himself less as
that centre to which we are but too prone to believe
that every line of human concern does or ought to
converge.   ·

I should not here make the trite remark, that
selfish motive biasses, brutalizes, and degrades the
human mind, did it not thence follow, that to seize
those occasions wherein the opposite spirit predo-
minates, is a duty which Philanthropy imperiously
exacts of her votaries; that occasions like these are
the proper ones for leading mankind to their own
interest by awakening in their minds a love for the
interest of their fellows.   A plant that grows in every
soil, though too often it is choked by tares before its
lovely blossoms are expanded.   Virtue produces pleasure, it is as the cause to the effect; I feel pleasure
in doing good to my friend, because I love him.   I
do not love him for the sake of that pleasure.

I regard the present state of the public mind in
Ireland to be one of those occasions which the ardent
votary of the religion of Philanthropy dare not leave
unseized.   I perceive that the public interest is excited,
I perceive that individual interest has, in a certain
degree, quitted individual concern to generalize itself
with universal feeling.   Be the Catholic Emancipation
a thing of great or of small misfortune [importance?],
be it a means of adding happiness to four millions of
people, or a reform which will only give honour to a
few of the higher ranks, yet a benevolent and disinterested feeling has gone abroad, and I am willing that

it should never subside. I desire that means should be taken with energy and expedition in this important yet fleeting crisis, to feed the unpolluted flame at which nations and ages may light the torch of Liberty and Virtue!

It is my opinion that the claims of the Catholic inhabitants of Ireland, if gained to-morrow, would in a very small degree aggrandize their liberty and happiness. The disqualifications principally affect the higher orders of the Catholic persuasion, these would principally be benefited by their removal. Power and wealth do not benefit, but injure the cause of virtue and freedom. I am happy, however, at the near approach of this emancipation, because I am inimical to all disqualifications for opinion. It gives me pleasure to see the approach of this enfranchisement, not for the good which it will bring with it, but because it is a sign of benefits approaching, a prophet of good about to come; and therefore do I sympathize with the inhabitants of Ireland in this great cause; a cause which though in its own accomplishment will add not one comfort to the cottager, will snatch not one from the dark dungeon, will root not out one vice, alleviate not one pang, yet it is the foreground of a picture, in the dimness of whose distance I behold the lion lay down with the lamb, and the infant play with the basilisk. For it supposes the extermination of the eyeless monster Bigotry, whose throne has tottered for two hundred years. I hear the teeth of the palsied beldame Superstition chatter, and I see her descending to the grave! Reason points to the open gates of the Temple of Religious Freedom, Philanthropy kneels at the altar of the common God! There, wealth and poverty, rank and abjectness, are names known but as

memorials of past time : meteors which play over the
loathsome pool of vice and misery, to warn the wan-
derer where dangers lie. Does a God rule this illi-
mitable universe? Are you thankful for his benefi-
cence—do you adore his wisdom—do you hang upon
his altar the garland of your devotion? Curse not
your brother, though he hath enwreathed with [it?] his
flowers of a different hue; the purest religion is that
of Charity, its loveliness begins to proselyte the hearts
of men. The tree is to be judged of by its fruit. I
regard the admission of the Catholic claims and the
Repeal of the Union Act as blossoms of that fruit
which the summer sun of improved intellect and progressive virtue is destined to mature.

I will not pass unreflected on the Legislative Union
of Great Britain and Ireland, nor will I speak of it as
a grievance so tolerable or unimportant in its own
nature as that of Catholic disqualification. The latter
affects few, the former affects thousands. The one
disqualifies the rich from power, the other impoverishes
the peasant, adds· beggary to the city, famine to the
country, multiplies abjectedness, whilst misery and
crime play into each other's hands, under its withering
auspices. I esteem, then, the annihilation of this
second grievance to be something more than a mere
sign of coming good. I esteem it to be in itself a
substantial benefit. The aristocracy of Ireland—(for
much as I may disapprove other distinctions than
those of virtue and talent, I consider it useless, hasty,
and violent, not for the present to acquiesce in their
continuance)—the aristocracy of Ireland suck the
veins of its inhabitants and consume the blood in
England. I mean not to deny the unhappy truth
that there is much misery and vice in the world. I

mean to say that Ireland shares largely of both.—
England has made her poor; and the poverty of a
rich nation will make its people very desperate and
wicked.

I look forward then to the redress of both these
grievances, or rather, I perceive the state of the public
mind, that precedes them as the crisis of beneficial
innovation. The latter I consider to be the cause of the
former, as I hope it will be the cause of more compre-
hensively beneficial amendments. It forms that occasion
which should energetically and quickly be occupied.
The voice of the whole human race; their crimes,
their miseries, and their ignorance, invoke us to the
task. For the miseries of the Irish poor, exacerbated
by the union of their country with England, are not
peculiar to themselves. England, the whole civilized
world, with few exceptions, is either sunk in dispro-
portioned abjectness, or raised to unnatural elevation.
The Repeal of the Union Act will place Ireland on a
level, so far as concerns the well-being of its poor, with
her sister nation. Benevolent feeling has gone out
in this country in favour of the happiness of its inhabitants; may this feeling be corroborated, methodized,
and continued! May it never fail! But it will not
be kept alive by each citizen sitting quietly by his own
fireside, and saying that things are going on well, because the rain does not beat on *him*, because *he* has
books and leisure to read them, because *he* has money
and is at liberty to accumulate luxuries to *himself*.
Generous feeling dictates no such sayings. When the
heart recurs to the thousands who have no liberty and
no leisure, it must be rendered callous by long contemplation of wretchedness, if after such recurrence it
can beat with contented evenness. Why do I talk

thus ?   Is there any one who doubts that the present
state of politics and morals is wrong?   They say
show us a safe method of improvement.   There is no
safer than the corroboration and propagation of generous and philanthropic feeling, than the keeping continually alive a love for the human race, than the
putting in train causes which shall have for their consequences virtue and freedom, and because I think that
individuals acting singly, with whatever energy, can
never effect so much as a society; I propose that all
those whose views coincide with those that I have
avowed, who perceive the state of the public mind in
Ireland, who think the present a fit opportunity for
attempting to fix its fluctuations at Philanthropy,
who love all mankind, and are willing actively to
engage in its cause, or passively to endure the perse-
cutions of those who are inimical to its success; I
propose to these to form an association for the purposes, first, of debating on the propriety of whatever
measures may be agitated; and secondly, for carrying,
by united or individual exertion, such measures into
effect when determined on.   That it should be an
association for discussing [diffusing?] knowledge and
virtue throughout the poorer classes of society in Ireland, for co-operating with any enlightened system of
education; for discussing topics calculated to throw
light on any methods of alleviation of moral and political evil, and, as far as lays in its power, actively interesting itself, in whatever occasions may arise for
benefiting mankind.

When I mention Ireland, I do not mean to confine
the influence of the association to this or to any other
country, but for the time being.   Moreover, I would
recommend that this association should attempt to

form others, and to actuate them with a similar spirit, and I am thus indeterminate in my description of the association which I propose, because I conceive that an assembly of men meeting to do all the good that opportunity will permit them to do, must be in its nature as indefinite and varying as the instances of human vice and misery that precede, occasion, and call for its institution.

As political institution and its attendant evils constitute the majority of those grievances which philanthropists desire to remedy, it is probable that existing Governments will frequently become the topic of their discussions, the results of which may little coincide with the opinions which those who profit by the supineness of human belief desire to impress upon the world. It is probable that this freedom may excite the odium of certain well-meaning people, who pin their faith upon their grandmother's apron-string. The minority in number are the majority in intellect and power. The former govern the latter, though it is by the sufferance of the latter that this originally delegated power is exercised. This power is become hereditary, and hath ceased to be necessarily united with intellect.

It is certain, therefore, that any questioning of established principles would excite the abhorrence and opposition of those who derived power and honour (such as it is) from their continuance.

As the association which I recommend would question those principles (however they may be hedged in with antiquity and precedent) which appeared ill adapted for the benefit of human kind, it would probably excite the odium of those in power. It would be obnoxious to the Government, though nothing

would be farther from the views of associated philanthropists than attempting to subvert establishments
forcibly, or even hastily. Aristocracy would oppose
it, whether oppositionists or ministerialists (for philanthropy is of no party), because its ultimate views look
to a subversion of all factitious distinctions, although
from its immediate intentions I fear that aristocracy
can have nothing to dread. The priesthood would
oppose it, because a union of Church and State—contrary to the principles and practice of Jesus, contrary
to that equality which he fruitlessly endeavoured to
teach mankind—is of all institutions that from the
rust of antiquity are called venerable, the least quali-
fied to stand free and cool reasoning, because it least
conduces to the happiness of human kind; yet did
either the minister, the peer, or the bishop know their
true interest, instead of that virulent opposition which
some among them have made to freedom and philanthropy, they would rejoice and co-operate with the
diffusion and corroboration of those principles that
would remove a load of paltry equivocation, paltrier
grandeur, and of wigs that crush into emptiness the
brains below them, from their shoulders, and by per-
mitting them to reassume the degraded and vilified
title of man would preclude the necessity of mystery
and deception, would bestow on them a title more
ennobling, and a dignity which, though it would be
without the gravity of an ape, would possess the ease
and consistency of a man.

For the reasons above alleged, falsely, prejudicedly,
and narrowly will those very persons whose ultimate
benefit is included in the general good, whose promo-
tion is the essence of a philanthropic association, will
they persecute those who have the best intentions
towards them, malevolence towards none.

I do not, therefore, conceal that those who make the favour of Government the sunshine of their moral day, confide in the political creed makers of the hour, are willing to think things that are rusty and decayed venerable, and are uninquiringly satisfied with evils as these are, because they find them established and unquestioned as they do sunlight and air when they come into existence; that they had better not even think of philanthropy.   I conceal not from them that the discountenance which Government will show to such an association as I am desirous to establish will come under their comprehensive definition of danger: that virtue, and any assembly instituted under its auspices, demands a voluntariness on the part of its devoted individuals to sacrifice personal to public benefit; and that it is possible that a party of beings associated for the purposes of disseminating virtuous principles, may, considering the ascendancy which long custom has conferred on opposite motives to action, meet with inconveniences that may amount to personal danger.   These considerations are, however, to the mind of the philanthropist as is a drop to an ocean; they serve by their possible existence as tests whereby to discover the really virtuous man from him who calls himself a patriot for dishonourable and selfish purposes. I propose then, to such as think with me, a Philanthropic Association, in spite of the danger that may attend the attempt.   I do not this beneath the shroud of mystery and darkness.   I propose not an Association of Secrecy.   Let it [be?] open as the beam of day.   Let it rival the sunbeam in its stainless purity, as in the extensiveness of its effulgence.

I disclaim all connexion with insincerity and concealment.   The latter implies the former, as much as

T

the former stands in need of the latter. It is a
very latitudinarian system of morality that permits its
professor to employ bad means for any end whatever.
Weapons which vice *can* use are unfit for the hands of
virtue. Concealment implies falsehood; it is bad, and
can therefore never be serviceable to the cause of
philanthropy.

I propose therefore that the association shall be
established and conducted in the open face of day,
with the utmost possible publicity. It is only vice
that hides itself in holes and corners, whose effrontery
shrinks from scrutiny, whose cowardice lets I *dare not*
wait upon I would, like the poor cat in the adage.
But the eye of virtue, eagle-like,. darts through the
undazzling beam of eternal truth, and from the undiminished fountain of its purity gathers wherewith to
vivify and illuminate a universe.

I have hitherto abstained from inquiring whether
the association which I recommend be or be not consistent with the English Constitution. And here it is
fit, briefly to consider what a constitution is.

Government can have no rights, it is a delegation
for the purpose of securing them to others. Man
becomes a subject of government, not that he may be
in a worse, but that he may be in a better state than
that of unorganized society. The strength of government is the happiness of the governed. All government existing for the happiness of others is just only
so far as it exists by their consent, and useful only
so far as it operates to their well-being. Constitution is to government what government is to law.
Constitution may, in this view of the subject, be
defined to be not merely something constituted for
the benefit of any nation or class of people, but some-

thing constituted by themselves for their own benefit.
The nations of England and Ireland have no constitution, because at no one time did the individuals
that compose them constitute a system for the general
benefit. If a system determined on by a very few, at a
great length of time; if Magna Charta, the Bill of
Rights, and other usages for whose influence the improved state of human knowledge is rather to be
looked to, than any system which courtiers pretend
to exist, and perhaps believe to exist—a system whose
spring of agency they represent as something secret,
undiscoverable, and awful as the law of nature; if
these make a constitution, then England has one.
But if (as I have endeavoured to show they do not) a
constitution is something else, then the speeches of
kings or commissioners, the writings of courtiers, and
the journals of Parliament, which teem with its glory,
are full of political cant, exhibit the skeleton of
national freedom, and are fruitless attempts to hide
evils in whose favour they cannot prove an alibi. As
therefore, in the true sense of the expression, the spot
of earth on which we live is destitute of constituted
government, it is impossible to offend against its
principles, or to be with justice accused of wishing to
subvert what has no real existence. If a man was
accused of setting fire to a house, which house never
existed, and from the nature of things could not have
existed, it is impossible that a jury in their senses
would find him guilty of arson. The English Constitution then could not be offended by the principles of
virtue and freedom. In fact, the manner in which
the Government of England has varied since its earliest
establishment, proves that its present form is the result
of a progressive accommodation to existing principles.

It has been a continual struggle for liberty on the part of the people, and an uninterrupted attempt at tightening the reins of oppression, and encouraging ignorance and imposture by the oligarchy to whom the first William parcelled out the property of the aborigines at the conquest of England by the Normans. I hear much of its being a tree so long growing which to cut down is as bad as cutting down an oak where there are no more. But the best way, on topics similar to these, is to tell the plain truth, without the confusion and ornament of metaphor. I call expressions similar to these political cant, which, like the songs of " Rule Britannia " and " God save the King," are but abstracts of the caterpillar creed of courtiers, cut down to the taste and comprehension of a mob ; the one to disguise to an alehouse politician the evils of that devilish practice of war, and the other to inspire among clubs of all descriptions a certain feeling which some call loyalty and others servility. A Philanthropic Association has nothing to fear from the English Constitution, but it may expect danger from its government. So far, however, from thinking this an argument against its institution, establishment, and augmentation, I am inclined to rest much of the weight of the cause, which my duties call upon me to support, on the very fact that government forcibly interferes when the opposition that is made to its proceedings is profoundly and undeniably nothing but intellectual. A good cause may be shown to be good, violence instantly renders bad what might before have been good. " Weapons that falsehood can use are unfit for the hands of truth "—truth can reason, and falsehood cannot.   ·

A political or religious system may burn and imprison those who investigate its principles; but it is an invariable proof of their falsehood and hollowness. Here there is another reason for the necessity of a Philanthropic Association, and I call upon any fair and rational opponent to controvert the argument which it contains; for there is no one who even calls himself a philanthropist that thinks personal danger or dishonour terrible in any other light than as it affects his usefulness.

Man has a heart to feel, a brain to think, and a tongue to utter. The laws of his moral as of his physical nature are immutable, as is everything of nature; nor can the ephemeral institutions of human society take away those rights, annihilate or strengthen the duties that have for their basis the imperishable relations of his constitution.

Though the Parliament of England were to pass a thousand bills, to inflict upon those who determined to utter their thoughts a thousand penalties, it could not render that criminal which was in its nature innocent before the passing of such bills.

Man has a right to feel, to think, and to speak, nor can any acts of legislature destroy that right. He will feel, he must think, and he *ought* to give utterance to those thoughts and feelings with the readiest sincerity and the strictest candour. A man must have a right to do a thing before he can have a duty; this right must permit before his duty can enjoin him to any act. Any law is bad which attempts to make it criminal to do what the plain dictates within the breast of every man tell him that he ought to do.

The English Government permits a fanatic to assemble any number of persons to teach them the most

extravagant and immoral systems of faith; but a few
men meeting to consider its own principles are marked
with its hatred and pursued by its jealousy.

The religionist who agonizes the death-bed of the
cottager, and by picturing the hell which hearts black
and narrow as his own alone could have invented,
and which exists but in their cores, spreads the un-
charitable doctrines which devote *heretics* to eternal
torments, and represents heaven to be what earth is,
a monopoly in the hands of certain favoured ones
whose merit consists in slavishness, whose success is
the reward of sycophancy. Thus much is permitted,
but a public inquiry that involves any doubt of their
rectitude into the principles of government is not permitted. When Jupiter and a countryman were one
day walking out, conversing familiarly on the affairs
of earth, the countryman listened to Jupiter's assertions on the subject for some time in acquiescence, at
length happening to hint a doubt, Jupiter threatened
him with his thunder. "Ah, ah," says the countryman, "now, Jupiter, I know that you are wrong; you
are always wrong when you appeal to your thunder."
The essence of virtue is disinterestedness. Disinterestedness is the quality which preserves the character
of virtue distinct from that of either innocence or
vice. This, it will be said, is mere assertion. It is
so: but it is an assertion whose truth, I believe, the
hearts of philanthropists are disinclined to deny.
Those who have been convinced by their grandam
of the doctrine of an original hereditary sin, or by
the apostles of a degrading philosophy of the necessary and universal selfishness of man, cannot be philanthropists. Now as an action, or a motive to action,
is only virtuous so far as it is disinterested, or par-

takes (I adopt this mode of expression to suit the
taste of some) of the nature of generalized self-love,
then reward or punishment, attached even by omni-
potence to any action, can in no wise make it either
good or bad.

It is no crime to act in contradiction to an English
judge or an English legislator, but it is a crime to
transgress the dictates of a monitor which feels the
spring of every motive, whose throne is the human
sensorium, whose empire the human conduct. Conscience is a government before which all others sink
into nothingness; it surpasses, and where it can act
supersedes, all other as nature surpasses art, as God
surpasses man.

In the preceding pages, during the course of an
investigation of the possible objections which might be
urged by philanthropy to an association such as I
recommend, as I have rather sought to bring forward
than conceal my principles, it will appear that they
have their origin from the discoveries in the sciences
of politics and morals which preceded and occasioned
the revolutions of America and France. It is with
openness that I confess, nay, with pride I assert, that
they are so. The names of Paine and Lafayette will out-
live the p[o]etic aristocracy of an expatriated Jesuit,*
as the executive of a bigoted policy will die before the
disgust at the sycophancy of their eulogists can subside.

It will be said perhaps that much as principles
such as these may appear marked on the outside with
peace, liberty, and virtue, that their ultimate tendency
is to a Revolution which, like that of France, will end

---

* See *Mémoires de Jucobinisme*, par l'Abbé Baruel.

in bloodshed, vice, and slavery. I must offer therefore my thoughts on that event which so suddenly
and so lamentably extinguished the overstrained hopes
of liberty which it excited. I do not deny that the
Revolution of France was occasioned by the literary
labours of the encyclopædists. When we see two
events together, in certain cases we speak of one as
the cause, the other the effect. We have no other
idea of cause and effect but that which arises from
necessary connexion; it is therefore still doubtful
whether D'Alembert, Boulanger, Condorcet, and other
celebrated characters, were the causes of the overthrow
of the ancient monarchy of France. Thus much is
certain, that they contributed greatly to the extension
and diffusion of knowledge, and that knowledge is
incompatible with slavery. The French nation was
bowed to the dust by ages of uninterrupted despotism.
They were plundered and insulted by a succession of
oligarchies, each more bloodthirsty and unrelenting
than the foregoing. In a state like this her soldiers
learned to fight for Freedom on the plains of America,
whilst at this very conjuncture a ray of science burst
through the clouds of bigotry that obscured the moral
day of Europe. The French were in the lowest state
of human degradation, and when the truth, unaccus-
tomed to their ears, that they were men and equals,
was promulgated, they were the first to vent their
indignation on the monopolizers of earth, because they
were most glaringly defrauded of the immunities of
nature.

Since the French were furthest removed by the so-
phistications of political institution from the genuine
condition of human beings, they must have been most
unfit for that happy state of equal law which proceeds

from consummated civilization, and which demands habits of the strictest virtue before its introduction.

The murders during the period of the French Revolution, and the despotism which has since been established, prove that the doctrines of philanthropy and freedom were but shallowly understood. Nor was it until after that period that their principles became clearly to be explained, and unanswerably to be established.

Voltaire was the flatterer of kings, though in his heart he despised them—so far has he been instrumental in the present slavery of his country. Rousseau gave licence by his writings to passions that only incapacitate and contract the human heart—so far hath he prepared the necks of his fellow-beings for that yoke of galling and dishonourable servitude which at this moment it bears. Helvetius and Condorcet established principles, but if they drew conclusions, their conclusions were unsystematical, and devoid of the luminousness and energy of method. They were little understood in the Revolution. But this age of ours is not stationary. Philosophers have not developed the great principles of the human mind that conclusions from them should be unprofitable and impracticable. We are in a state of continually progressive improvement. One truth that had been discovered can never die, but will prevent the revivification of its apportioned opposite falsehood. By promoting truth and discouraging its opposite, the means of philanthropy are principally to be forwarded. Godwin wrote during the Revolution of France, and certainly his writings were totally devoid of influence with regard to its purposes. Oh! that they had not! In the Revolution of France were engaged men whose

names are inerasable from the records of Liberty.
Their genius penetrated with a glance the gloom and
glare which Church-craft and State-craft had spread
before the imposture and villany of their establishments. They saw the world. Were they men? Yes!
They felt for it !   They risked their lives and happiness for its benefit !   Had there been more of those
men France would not now be a beacon to warn us
of the hazard and horror of Revolutions, but a pattern
of society rapidly advancing to a state of perfection,
and holding out an example for the gradual and
peaceful regeneration of the world.   I consider it to
be one of the effects of a Philanthropic Association to
assist in the production of such men as these, in an
extensive development of those germs of excellence
whose favourite soil is the cultured garden of the
human mind.

Many well-meaning persons may think that the
attainment of the good which I propose as the ultimatum of philanthropic exertion is visionary and
inconsistent with human nature; they would tell me
not to make people happy for fear of overstocking
the world, and to permit those who found dishes
placed before them on the table of partial nature to
enjoy their superfluities in quietness, though millions
of wretches crowded around but to pick a morsel,*
which morsel was still refused to the prayers of
agonizing famine.

I cannot help thinking this an evil, nor help endeavouring, by the safest means that I can devise, to
palliate at present, and in fine to eradicate this evil.
War, vice, and misery are undeniably bad, they embrace

---

* See Malthus on *Population.*

all that we can conceive of temporal and eternal evil. Are we to be told that these are remediless, because the earth would, in case of their remedy, be over-stocked? That the rich are still to glut, that the ambitious are still to plan, that the fools whom these knaves mould, are still to murder their brethren and call it glory, and that the poor are to pay with their blood, their labour, their happiness, and their inno-cence for the crimes and mistakes which the here-ditary monopolists of earth commit? Rare sophism! How will the heartless rich hug thee to their bosoms, and lull their conscience into slumber with the opiate of thy reconciling dogmas!

But when the philosopher and philanthropist con-templates the universe, when he perceives existing evils that admit of amendment, and hears tell of other evils, which, in the course of sixty centuries, may again derange the system of happiness which the amend-ment is calculated to produce, does he submit to pro-long a positive evil, because if that were eradicated, after a millennium of 6000 years (for such space of time would it take to people the earth) another evil would take place.

To how contemptible a degradation of grossest credu-lity will not prejudice lower the human mind! We see in winter that the foliage of the trees is gone, that they present to the view nothing but leafless branches— we see that the loveliness of the flower decays, though the root continues in the earth. What opinion should we form of that man who, when he walked in the freshness of the spring, beheld the fields enamelled with flowers, and the foliage bursting from the buds, should find fault with all this beautiful order, and murmur his contemptible discontents because winter

must come, and the landscape be robbed of its beauty
for a while again? Yet this man is Mr. Malthus.
Do we not see that the laws of nature perpetually act
by disorganization and reproduction, each alternately
becoming cause and effect. The analogies that we can
draw from physical to moral topics are of all others
the most striking.

Does any one yet question the possibility of inducing
radical reform of moral and political evil? Does h ·
object from that impossibility to the association which
I propose, which I frankly confess to be one of the
means whose instrumentality I would employ to attain
this reform. Let them look to the methods which I
use. Let them put my object out of their view and
propose their own, how would they accomplish it?
By diffusing virtue and knowledge, by promoting
human happiness. Palsied be the hand, for ever dumb
be the tongue that would by one expression convey
sentiments differing from these: I will use no bad
means for any end whatever. Know then, ye philanthropists, to whatever profession of faith, or whatever
determination of principles, chance, reason, or education may have conducted you, that the endeavours of
the truly virtuous necessarily converge to one point,
though it be hidden from them what point that is,
they all labour for one end, and that controversies concerning the nature of that end serve only to weaken
the strength which for the interest of virtue should be
consolidated.

The diffusion of true and virtuous principles (for in
the first principles of morality *none* disagree) will produce the best of possible terminations.

I invite to an Association of Philanthropy those of
whatever ultimate expectations, who will employ the

same means that I employ; let their designs differ as
much as they may from mine, I shall rejoice at their
co-operation; because if the ultimatum of my hopes
be founded on the unity of truth, I shall then have
auxiliaries in its cause, and if it be false I shall
rejoice that means are not neglected for forwarding
that which is true.

The accumulation of evil which Ireland has for the
last twenty years sustained, and considering the un-
remittingness of its pressure I may say patiently sustained; the melancholy prospect which the unforeseen
conduct of the Regent of England holds out of its
continuance, demands of every Irishman whose pulses
have not ceased to throb with the life-blood of his
heart, that he should individually consult, and unitedly
determine on some measures for the liberty of his
countrymen. That those measures should be pacific
though resolute, that their movers should be calmly
brave and temperately unbending, though the whole
heart and soul should go with the attempt, is the
opinion which my principles command me to give.

And I am induced to call an association such as
this occasion demands, an Association of Philanthropy, because good men ought never to circum-
scribe their usefulness by any name which denotes
their exclusive devotion to the accomplishment of its
signification.

When I began the preceding remarks I conceived
that on the removal of the restrictions from the
Regent a ministry less inimical than the present to
the interests of liberty would have been appointed. I
am deceived, and the disappointment of the hopes of
freedom on this subject affords an additional argument
towards the necessity of an Association.

I conclude these remarks, which I have indited principally with a view of unveiling my principles, with a proposal for an Association for the purposes of Catholic Emancipation, a repeal of the Union Act, and grounding upon the attainment of these objects a reform of whatever moral or political evil may be within its compass of human power to remedy.

Such as are favourably inclined towards the institution would highly gratify the Proposer if they would personally communicate with him on this important subject, by which means the plan might be matured, errors in the Proposer's original system be detected, and a meeting for the purpose convened with that resolute expedition which the nature of the present crisis demands.

No. 7, Lower Sackville Street.

FINIS.

** The two allusions to the " unforeseen conduct" of the Prince Regent with which in the preceding page Shelley concludes this pamphlet, are identical in spirit with the observations attributed to one of the speakers at the meeting in Fishamble Street Theatre on the 28th of February, 1812, four days before the pamphlet appeared. The report, which I have extracted from the State Papers in the Record Office, has already been given at p. 238. The private Reporter for the Government, referring to a certain resolution, thus writes :—" On this resolution, a young boy delivered a speech of considerable length and replete with much elegant language," &c. At p. 239 I have suggested that in transcribing his notes the Reporter substituted by accident the name of " Mr. Wyse" for " Mr. Shelley." The passages in the pamphlet establish almost conclusively that this surmise is correct.

CHAPTER XI.

FROM some unpublished letters of Shelley and Harriet Shelley, particularly from that most interesting one from Harriet seized at Holyhead, which the present writer discovered in the Record Office, and which hitherto has been unknown, a tolerably complete account can be given of Shelley's remaining stay in Dublin. The letters to Godwin, which may be seen in the second volume of Mr. Hogg's incomplete Life of the poet, are extremely vague, and give no precise details. Both poet and philosopher were merely showing off to each other in profound and abstract essays. Mr. Godwin could scarcely have been the friend of Curran if he was not in favour of that "political justice" to Ireland which he advocated for all mankind. The great point with him in his replies to the young "Philanthropist" was to show that Shelley had no right to deduce the principle, or at least the expediency of "association" from the pages of *Political Justice*. His only allusion to the affairs of Ireland was a comparison of Shelley with Robert Emmett, which I dare say gave intense enjoyment to the poet. Shelley died before the peaceful triumph of the "Catholic Association" proved that he was right and Godwin wrong as to the mode of obtaining political amelioration under the British Constitution. Mr. Godwin himself received the office, which happily

made his latter days comfortable, from a Government
which was mainly floated into power by the Reform
League. The duties of yeoman-usher of the Exche-
quer were not so excessive as to prevent him looking
occasionally into his collection of old letters. It
would be curious to have seen him read the following
passage from one of them addressed to him in 1812
from Dublin, by the young man in whose "letters and
history" "all the females of his family, Mrs. G., and
three daughters" were so much interested (*Hogg*, vol.
ii. p. 100). Shelley, writing from Sackville Street,
Dublin, March 8th, 1812, says, " I am not forgetful or
unheeding of what you said of association. But
Political Justice was first published in 1793; nearly
twenty years have elapsed since the general diffusion
of its doctrines. What has followed? Have men •
ceased to fight? Have vice and misery vanished from
the earth? Have the fireside communications which
it recommends taken place? Out of the many who
have read that inestimable book, how many have been
blinded by prejudice? How many, in short, have taken
it up to gratify an ephemeral vanity, and when the
hour of its novelty had passed, threw it aside, and
yielded with fashion to the arguments of Mr. Malthus ?"—*Hogg*, vol. ii. p. 92.*

---

* In Shelley's second pamphlet, *Proposals for an Association*,
&c , there is, as we have seen, the following brief allusion to Godwin,
which that philosopher must have read with amazement in the copy
presented to himself. Perhaps the whole pamphlet may not have been
sent to Godwin, Shelley confining himself to those parts extracted
in *The Weekly Messenger*, March 7th, 1812, the receipt of which
Godwin acknowledged :—" Godwin wrote during the Revolution of
France, and certainly his writings were totally devoid of influence
with regard to its purposes —Oh ! that they had not !"—*Proposals for an Association*, &c., p. 14.

These unpleasant allusions were too much for the philosopher. So in his next letter he addresses his young catechist in these abrupt terms :—" Shelley, you are preparing a scene of blood," &c. " I wish to my heart you would come immediately to London. I have a friend who has contrived a tube to convey passengers sixty miles an hour. Be youth your tube! I have a thousand things I could say orally, more than I can say in a letter on this important subject. Away! You cannot imagine how much all the females of my family, Mrs. G. and three daughters, are interested in your letters and your history."—*Hogg*, vol. ii. pp. 99, 100.

The most interesting part of Godwin's letter is that which gives a sort of foreshadowing of the atmospheric mode of locomotion and the swiftness of the " Irish Mail," which latter " conveys passengers" without the aid of " a tube" (except the bridge at Bangor) exactly in the time calculated on by Godwin's friend.

Before the 10th of March, 1812, Shelley had removed from 7, Lower Sackville Street, Dublin, to 17, Grafton Street, in the same city. In 1812 the house 17, Grafton Street, was occupied by " Robert Williams, goldsmith and jeweller." It now forms part of the large establishment of Messrs. Brown, Thomas, and Co. Long as the following extracts are, they form but a portion of an exceedingly interesting and hitherto unpublished letter, the joint composition of Shelley and Harriet, which was addressed to their friend at Hurstpierpoint. I shall give the extracts first, and then offer such explanations as may seem necessary :—

Shelley to Miss Hitchener.

" 17, Grafton Street, March 10th, 1812.

" My dear Friend,— . . . . I cannot recount all the
horrible instances of unrestricted and licensed tyranny
that have met my ears : an Irishman has been torn from
his wife and family in Lisbon because he was a patriot,
and compelled to serve as a common soldier in the
Portuguese army by that monster of anti-patriotic in-
humanity, *Beresford,* the idol of the belligerents. You
will soon see a copy of his letter, and soon hear of my
and Sir F. Burdett's exertion in his favour. . . . . We
shall be free; this nation shall awaken. . . . . It is
attended with circumstances singularly characteristic
of cowardice and tyranny. My blood boils to think
of it. A poor boy, whom I found starving in a hiding-
place of unutterable filth and misery, whom I rescued
and was about to teach to read, has been snatched on
a charge of false and villanous effrontery to a magistrate of *Hell,* who gave him the alternative of the
[illegible ; perhaps " treadmill"] or military servitude.
He preferred neither. yet was compelled to be a soldier.
This has come to my knowledge this evening.   I am
resolved to present this business to the very jaws of
Government, snatching if possible the poison from
its fangs. . . . . I am sick of this city, and long to be
with you in peace. The rich grind the poor into abjectedness, and then complain that they are abject.
They grind them to famine, and hang them if they
steal a loaf. . . . . Your new suggestion of our joining you at Hurst is divine. It shall be so. I have
not shown Harriet or E. your letter yet; they are
walking with a Mr. Lawless (a valuable man) whilst I
write this. . . . . In a day or two I shall make up

a parcel to you which will come per coach; it is a terrible mistake that of the last—the blundering honest Irishman we have came without it. Send me the Sussex papers. Insist or make them insert the account of *me*. It may have a good effect on the mind of the people as a preparation. I send you two [probably " papers"] to-night. The association proceeds slowly, and I fear will not be established. . . . . I may succeed, but I fear I shall not in the main object [*i.e.*, of establishing an association.] Dublin is the most difficult of all. In Wales I fear not. In Lewes fear is ridiculous."

Harriet's Postscript.

" Has Percy mentioned to you a very amiable man of the name of Lawless? He is very much attached to the cause, yet not in it. . . . . We have this morning been introduced to his wife. She is a very nice woman, though not equal to him. . . . . What has the Duke of Norfolk been saying of us? Now tell me, as I think I can confute his Lordship. . . . . We have heard from Godwin. Such letters! You must long to read them, I am sure. . . . . But I know you now, and this blessing I should not have had if I had never been to Clapham. So I must be content, and think myself very happy that I did go, though I was not aware of the happiness that would result."

The page is signed " P. B. S."
Except for the date and place, " Keswick, Jan. 7th, 1812," assigned by Mr. Rossetti to the poem entitled *Mother and Son*, which is published by him in his edition of Shelley (vol. ii. p. 526), we should have

attributed the inspiration of that effusion to the incidents recorded in the foregoing letter written from
Dublin, March 10th, 1812. The compulsory enlist-
ment of the Irish patriot in Lisbon and the treatment
of the boy seem to be referred to in the following
lines :—

> " But when the tyrant's bloodhounds forced the child
> For his cursed power unhallowed arms to wield."

It may, however, have been the former incident
alone, which perhaps he heard of at Keswick, that
formed the subject of the poem *Mother and Son*. The
charge against the boy referred to in Shelley's letter
of March 10th, was for stealing a roll, "value one
penny." The "magistrate of hell" may have been
the famous Major Sirr. The allusion to Sir Francis
Burdett is curious. A year later, as is evident from
the interesting papers in the Record Office referring
to Shelley's proceedings at Lymouth, he was in
constant correspondence with that celebrated personage. In fact his letters to Sir Francis Burdett
were so numerous as to attract the notice of the postmaster at Barnstaple, who communicated the circumstance to Mr.—subsequently Sir—Francis Freeling.
These letters, if preserved, would possess a singular
interest. After the lapse of so many years, and the
settlement of most of the questions discussed therein,
no impropriety would be involved in their being made
public. From some inquiries, however, which I have
made, I am inclined to believe that the letters are not
now in existence. The mention of Mr. Lawless is
important. This remarkable man, who is still well
remembered even in England under his popular title
of " Honest Jack," seems to have been the only friend
of any literary or social position (of course excepting

Curran, with whom he dined twice) that Shelley made in Dublin. Lawless was, we have little doubt, the writer of the article in *The Weekly Messenger*,* which appeared on the Saturday preceding the day on which Harriet and Eliza Westbrook were introduced to his wife. Shelley's and Harriet's liking for Mr. and Mrs. Lawless was shared even by the cynical Mr. Hogg, as we find from that eccentric gentleman's account of his own visit to Dublin in 1813. At present we can only refer to Mr. Lawless in connexion with Shelley's first visit. Before doing so it will be more convenient to conclude our explanation of the remaining allusions in Shelley's and Harriet's letter of March 10th. The mistake in sending the pamphlets by post both to Miss Hitchener and Godwin has already been mentioned. The "blundering honest Irishman" was Daniel Hill, who, as we afterwards shall find, suffered six months imprisonment at Barnstaple for distributing some of Shelley's political broadsides there, though he had done precisely the same thing in Dublin without any hindrance.

The two papers sent to Miss Hitchener were probably *The Weekly Messenger* and *The Dublin Journal* of March 7th, 1812. "The account of *me*" which he requests his friend to get inserted in the Sussex papers, was doubtless the same "account of Mr." referred to by Shelley in his letter to Godwin of

---

* The first editor of *The Weekly Messenger* was Frederick William Conway, subsequently the well-known editor and proprietor of *The Dublin Evening Post*. Mr. Lawless was afterwards editor of *The Weekly Messenger*, to which he had been a contributor from the beginning. For a curious statement of Mr. Conway in reference to Shelley's visit to Dublin, see *post*, p. 304.

March 8th—the article headed " Pierce Byshe Shelly, Esq.," which we have already given.

The following letter of Harriet Shelley, which is now printed for the first time, will be read with painful interest. One cannot help regretting that the peaceful future she once pictured to herself was not her fate. The letter may be considered something in the light of a general confession made to one who was singularly ill-suited and incompetent to be her directress :—

Harriet Shelley to Miss Hitchener ; from an unpublished letter.

" 17, Grafton Street, Dublin, March 14th, 1812.

" . . . When I lived with my father I was not likely to gain much knowledge, as our circle of acquaintances was very limited, he not thinking it proper that we should mix much with society. In short, we very seldom visited those places of fashionable amusement which for our age might have been expected : 'twas but seldom I visited my home, school having witnessed the greater part of my life; but do not think from this I was ignorant of what was passing in the great world. Books and newspapers were sufficient to inform me of these. Though then a silent spectator, yet did I look with a fearful eye upon the vices of the great, and thought to myself 'twas better to gain my bread with my needle than be the inhabitant of those great houses where misery and famine howl around. I will tell you my faults, knowing what I have to expect from your friendship. Remember my youth, and if any excuse can be made let that suffice. In London, you know, there are military as everywhere else ; when quite a child I admired these red-coats, and I thought the military the best and most fascinating men in the world, though at the same time I used to declare my determination never to marry one. This was not so much on account of their vices, as from the idea of their being killed. I thought if I married any one it should be a clergyman. Strange idea this, was it not? But being brought up in the Christian religion, 'twas this first gave rise to it. You may conceive with what horror I first heard that Percy was an atheist. At first I did not comprehend the meaning of the word, therefore when it was explained I was truly petrified. I wondered how he could live a moment professing such principles, and solemnly declared that he never should change mine."

The remainder of this autobiographical sketch may be given at another time. I pass on to that portion of it referring to Shelley. The following passage fixes the date at which the poet first began to abstain from the use of animal food. In this, as in everything else, poor Harriet adopted the views of her husband. The change in their mode of living, which on the whole must be considered to have been an unwise one for both, commenced at Dublin on or about the 1st of March, 1812. Harriet, continuing her letter to Miss Hitchener, says :—

" You do not know that we have forsworn meat and adopted the Pythagorean system ; about a fortnight has elapsed since the change, and we do not find ourselves the worse for it. . . . Have you heard anything of the Habeas Corpus Act being suspended? I have been very much alarmed at the intelligence, though I hope it is ill-founded. If it is not, where we shall be is not known, as from Percy's having made himself so busy in the cause of this poor country, he has raised himself many enemies who would take advantage of such a time and instantly exercise their vengeance upon him." . . .

In the same letter Shelley writes :—

" I do not like Lord Fingal or *any* of the Catholic aristocracy. Their intolerance can be equalled by nothing but the hardy wickedness and falsehood of the Prince. My speech was misinterpreted. I spoke for more than an hour. The hisses with which they greeted me when I spoke of *religion,* though in terms of respect, were mixed with applause when I avowed my mission. The newspapers have only noted that which did not excite disapprobation. As to an Association, my hopes daily grow fainter on this subject, as my perception of its necessity strengthens. I shall soon, however, have the command of a newspaper with Mr. Lawless, of whom I shall tell more. This will be a powerful engine of amelioration. Mr. L., though he regards my ultimate hope as visionary, is willing to acquiesce in my views. He is a republican. Adieu. Believe that we are yours. We will live with you at Hurst. What think you of a journey to Italy in the autumn ?"

There is little requiring explanation in this postscript of Shelley. The few hisses which he received at the meeting in Fishamble Street Theatre seemed to have rested on his mind more than the enthusiastic applause which we learn from " An Englishman" he received. Southey mentions an Eastern proverb which declares that the feeling of pain produced by the smallest thorn of the rose far exceeds that of pleasure which its sweetest perfume can bestow. So it was

with the sensitive young orator. As to the " intolc-
rance" of Lord Fingal and the Catholic aristocracy,
we may safely limit it to a disinclination to listen
to Shelley's mode of speaking of "*religion*," even
" though in terms of respect."

The expectation of having a newspaper at his com-
mand in conjunction with Mr. Lawless is very curious.
It was evidently a part of the same project alluded to
in the following letter, written six days later, to Mr.
Medwin senior, which has hitherto been a puzzle to
Shelley's numerous biographers :—

" Dublin, No. 17, Grafton Street,
" March 20th, 1812.

" My dear Sir,—The tumult of business and
travelling has prevented my addressing you before.

" I am now engaged with a literary friend in the
publication of a voluminous History of Ireland, of
which two hundred and fifty pages are already printed,
and for the completion of which I wish to raise two
hundred and fifty pounds. I could obtain undeniable
security for its payment at the expiration of eighteen
months. Can you tell me how I ought to proceed?
The work will produce great profits. As you will see
by the Lewes paper, I am in the midst of overwhelming
engagements. My kindest regards to all your family.
Be assured I shall not forget them or you.

" My dear Sir, yours very truly,
" P. B. Shelley.

" T. C. Medwin, Esq., Horsham, Sussex, England."

The name of this " literary friend" of Shelley has
hitherto baffled inquiry. There can be no doubt that
he was Mr. John Lawless, and that the History of
Ireland alluded to by Shelley, of which two hundred
and fifty pages were printed in 1812, was the *Compen-*

dium of the History of Ireland, published by Mr. Lawless in 1814.*

A sketch of the life of this remarkable man would
be interesting and valuable, but the limits of this publication preclude the possibility of my entering upon it
at present. An account of his death, and an interesting
letter from his son Philip Lawless, Esq., Barrister-at-
law, to the author, with some extracts from the State
Papers, will be found at the end of this volume, Appen-
dix No. 2.

One fact, however, must be mentioned in this
place, not for its possible reference to Mr. Lawless,
though that he was the person alluded ·to by the
writer about to be quoted there can be little doubt,
but for the singular interest it possesses of being the
first instance recorded of Shelley's pecuniary generosity
to his friends—few in number indeed, but making up
by their concentrated avidity for the more diffuse vo-
raciousness of a wider circle. To what extent those
inroads not only on Shelley's purse, but occasionally
on the very furniture of his house, were carried, may
be learned from the curious statement in the second
series of Miss Mitford's *Letters,* recently published.

---

* " *Compendium of the History of Ireland, from the Earliest
Period to the Reign of George I.* By John Lawless, Esq., a
Member of the Catholic Board. Dublin: 1814." The work, though
not published till that year, was well known to be in preparation
shortly after Shelley left Dublin. The following curious allusion
to it will be found in Dr. Brenan's *Milesian Magazine* for July,
1812, p. 87. " Jack Squintum" was the sobriquet of John Lawless
in this scurrilous publication :—

"JACK SQUINTUM'S HISTORY OF IRELAND. The public will
learn, with much attention, that a history of Ireland, from the
Creation to the present hour, is about to be published by that illustrious literator Jack Squintum."

From this suggestive picture of the domestic life of Shelley it will be seen that the airy and pleasant Mr. Harold Skimpole—that self-denying sybarite, content indeed with "claret and Naples biscuits," but pocketing in one sum a thousand pounds of his friend's money as if it were a delicious bit of pleasantry—quite a trifle indeed where two such men of genius were concerned—could carry off the same friend's chairs and tables when the more direct resources of his purse were exhausted. Another well-drawn figure in Miss Mitford's *View of an Interior* is that of the philosophical Mr. Godwin. In 1807, as we have seen, the author of *Political Justice* had some difficulty about his "little bills," and applied to an Irish Judge, the Right Honourable John Philpot Curran, for the modest sum of 300*l.*, which he probably obtained. If St. Leon did not discover the Elixir of Life, he certainly found the *Philosopher's Stone*, and contrived to turn the enthusiasm of his friends into a good deal of solid gold. In 1817, Shelley stood in a nearer relationship to Godwin than he had done in 1812, when he received from his future father-in-law the letter of introduction to Curran. The Philosopher's Stone had by that time lost a little of its virtue, perhaps from over use, so that the author of *Mandeville* had to work on the original of that character by a more potent talisman. After mentioning the clean sweep of Shelley's "chairs and tables and bedsteads !" by Mr. Skimpole, the merciless Miss Mitford thus continues :—" And Mr. Godwin, his papa-in-law, was much worse : he used to threaten to stab himself if his dutiful son-in-law would not accept his bills. Only fancy him down on his knees, flourishing a drawn dagger, and talking tragedy !"—*Miss Mitford's Letters, Second Series.*

Miss Mitford adds to these curious details the pithy remark, " But it was no joke to poor Mr. Shelley." It certainly was not. There was very little comedy on *his* side in the intercourse between himself and his friends. On the whole it was rather tragic. Speaking of one[×]of the earliest chosen and the most boastful of the number, Shelley, in a letter still extant, thus wrote within three months after his marriage with Harriet Westbrook—" He attempted to seduce my wife !" That attempt, it is to be feared, was the beginning of his greatest misfortune, if it had not a more direct bearing on the catastrophe of Harriet's suicide. It is to be hoped that this deliberate intention to " filch" from him his " good name," and what ought to be dearer to him almost than that, was a solitary crime ; but of the rest of Iago's speech one line was certainly applicable to Shelley. Of the " trash" which was seldom allowed to remain long in the purse of the poet, he might well have said, alluding to almost any of his friends :—

" 'Twas mine, 'tis his, and has been slave to thousands."

We have seen that it was in Dublin Shelley received his first recognition as a poet. That was in the interesting article in *The Weekly Messenger* of March 7th, 1812. It is a curious fact that the earliest introduction of Shelley's name to the *English* public did not take place until four years and nine months after this date ! If the reader refers to the article alluded to, p. 253 of the present volume, and compares its warm and generous tone with the frigid and half-apologetic terms in which so late, as December, 1816, Leigh Hunt for the first time mentions the name of Shelley, he will not only be surprised, but perhaps enlightened as to the popular fallacy of Hunt's early knowledge and appreciation of Shelley's genius. Nearly six years after Shelley wrote to him from Oxford—more than five years after Shelley had published a poem in sustainment of a man whose story had been told at such length by Leigh Hunt himself—more than three years after *Queen Mab* had been printed and presumably presented to the editor of *The Examiner*, and more than two years after the author of that poem is represented as visiting the incarcerated editor—" the wit in the dungeon," as Lord Byron in a sudden fit of good humour called him— we find Shelley thus spoken of by Leigh Hunt. It will be seen that Shelley had sent some poetical contributions to *The Examiner*, which the editor had not thought worth preserving. The article is devoted to three " YOUNG POETS." It is curious that as much space is given to the only one of the three that failed to realize the expectations formed of him as to the other two. These were Shelley and Keats. Eleven timid lines are given to Shelley. It will be perceived that Leigh Hunt confesses he had seen no specimen of Shelley's poetry up to December 1st, 1816, except those manuscript contributions offered to *The Examiner*, which speedily found their way to the wastepaper basket. It is thus—

" With bated breath and whispering humbleness"

that Leigh Hunt introduces to the British public the name of Percy Bysshe Shelley :—

" YOUNG POETS.

" The object of the present article is merely to notice three young writers, who appear to us to promise a considerable addition of strength to the new school.

Of the first who came before us, we have, it is true, yet seen only one or two specimens, and these were no sooner sent us than we unfortunately mislaid them ; but we shall procure what he has published, and if the rest answer to what we have seen, we shall have no hesitation in announcing him for a very striking and original thinker. His name is PERCY BYSSHE SHELLEY, and he is the author of a poetical work, entitled *Alastor, or the Spirit of Solitude.*"—*The Examiner, Dec. 1st,* 1816.

It is sad to think that the deplorable suicide of Harriet Shelley must in all probability have occurred a day or two after the appearance of this first public recognition (in England) of her husband. Shelley legalized his connexion with Mary Godwin on the 30th of December, 1816. The article in *The Examiner* appeared on the 1st December. Harriet's suicide took place in the same month. " In December, 1816," says Mr. Peacock, " Harriet drowned herself in the Serpentine river, and to her father's house in Chapel-street his daughter's body was carried" (*Fraser's Magazine,* January, 1860, p. 100). The exact date is not given, but it is almost certain that the catastrophe occurred very early in the month. The commonest decency or humanity, not to speak of legal impediments, including the holding of a coroner's inquest, which doubtless took place, though no report of it has been yet discovered, might be supposed to have necessitated a delay of over three weeks before the formal ceremony of marriage was gone through by Shelley and his second wife. This brings us very near the 1st of December, on which day this perhaps fatal notice of " a very striking and original thinker"—and

actor—was published. " His name is PERCY BYSSHE
SHELLEY," says Leigh Hunt, introducing with rather
faint eulogy his recently discovered friend to the
English public. There was one at least in England
who, unhappily for herself, knew that name too well.
For five years she had borne it. Three years before
this " young poet" was openly spoken of in an English
journal, she had been " the inspiration of his song"
and his sole public. Who can doubt the bitterness of
her recollection if she read (as there can be but little
doubt that she *did* read) the paragraph in *The Examiner?* What a contrast to the pride and joy with
which more than four years earlier she must have
drank in with delighted eyes the far more emphatic
praises of her husband in *The Dublin Weekly Messenger* of 7th March, 1812! She was then the
associate in his plans, the sharer of his dreams and of
his hopes—his " purer mind." Well might Shelley
say, as if alluding to that period, and addressing
her (though the lines are capable of another interpretation)—

> " *That* time is dead for ever, child,
> Drowned, frozen, dead for ever!"

And what was she in December, 1816? As yet we
do not fully know. But the end is given in the line
just quoted, written nearly a year afterwards—

> " *Drowned*, frozen, dead for ever!"

That is the practical answer which we have to those
frenzied questionings which doubtless drove the poor
abandoned " child" to despair. It is no mere fancy
to read in the paragraph of *The Examiner* the death
warrant of Harriet Shelley.

Nearly five years before this period Shelley had

been publicly proclaimed in Dublin not only " a very
striking and original thinker," but A Poet. At about
the same date, and in the same city, it would appear
from the following statement that another fact was
discovered, more interesting to Shelley's personal
friends than to himself. The amiable weakness of
the poet in leaving not only his purse but his credit
to the discretion, or indiscretion, of his associates was
first exhibited in Dublin. The curious fact transpired
about thirty years ago in a correspondence which the
present writer had with the editor of *The Dublin
Evening Post* on the poetical genius of Shelley.
Roused by a slighting allusion to a poet, whom I may
say I had discovered for myself about eleven years
previously, which had appeared in that paper, I wrote
several letters in defence of Shelley, which may be
found in *The Dublin Evening Post*, Nov. 24th, 1842,
Dec. 6th, 1842, and Dec. 8th, 1842. I had made
reference to Shelley's visit to Dublin in 1812, and to
this the editor, after some courteous allusions to the
enthusiasm of my letters, the authorship of which he
was not aware of, thus alludes :—

" As to the rest, we need say nothing. Politics
with Shelley was *a sentiment*, and we honour him for
the clothing it assumed. We knew him a little at
the time mentioned. And we know also that he was
made the pecuniary dupe of a person not less sincere
in his politics, but in money matters less honest."—
The Dublin Evening Post, Thursday Evening, Nov. 17th,
1842.

The editor of *The Dublin Evening Post* in 1842
had been the editor of *The Weekly Messenger* in 1812.
Frederick William Conway and John Lawless had
life-long differences, which commenced about the

latter period, and ended only with the death of Mr. Lawless in 1837. There can be little doubt that Lawless was the writer of the article on Shelley so frequently alluded to. In Shelley's hitherto unpublished letters, from which so many interesting extracts have been taken, there is no mention of Conway, while Lawless is spoken of frequently in terms of affection. Conway, as editor of the paper, must have known something, though perhaps inaccurately, of the efforts made by Shelley, as proved by the letter to Mr. Medwin, to assist Lawless in bringing out his *History of Ireland.* Captain Medwin, with his usual incompleteness and often inaccuracy of detail, does not inform us whether Shelley's instructions to Mr. Medwin, senior, to raise the sum of 250l. for the completion of this work were or were not carried out. From a circumstance in connexion with the affair at Lymouth in the August of the same year, and from the fact that it was to the house of Mr. John Lawless Shelley and Harriet fled, as it were, in March, 1813, after the extraordinary affair at Tanyrallt, there is a strong probability that the money, or some portion of it, was advanced to Mr. Lawless. Knowing what we now know of similar and less excusable transactions—the 1000l. given in a lump to Leigh Hunt—the rather doubtful 500l. to Mr. Madocks for the breakwater at Tremadoc—the 100l. a year to Mr. Peacock—the bills accepted at the dagger's point for Mr. Godwin—the proceeds of carted furniture for Mr. Skimpole, and many other acts of unreflecting and extorted generosity, this contribution to the *History of Ireland* by Mr. Lawless, which Shelley was sure would be repaid " at the expiration of eighteen months," looks in comparison more like a clever speculation, a safe investment of the poet, than

x

a deliberate intention to defraud on the part of the historian. Mr. Lawless died in 1837, and was therefore unable to return the fire of his old antagonist. His explanation of all the circumstances of his acquaintance with Shelley would have been most interesting. There can be no chance of such explanation now. He would probably have demurred to the right of his assailant to sit in judgment on his private intercourse with Mr. Shelley until the censor had explained his own secret correspondence with Lord Sidmouth. In any case Mr. Lawless would have read " with a wild surmise" the following letter, the original of which is to be found in the Record Office :—

STATE PAPERS, " Ireland, 1812. August—December.
No. 657."
" Dublin, November 27th, 1812.

" MY LORD,—I have the honour of enclosing the ' Address' which will be published to-morrow by the Catholic Bishops. I think the Document important, as although your Lordship may have received a Manuscript Copy previously, yet lest *that* should not prove to be the case I have ventured to trouble you with the only copy that has yet left the Printer's possession.

" I shall have the honour of resuming my correspondence to-morrow with Mr. Beckett.

" I have the honour to be, my Lord,
" Your Lordship's most obedient and
" most faithful Servant, •
" F. W. CONWAY."
" Right Hon. Lord Sidmouth."

The document referred to in the foregoing letter is

also preserved in the Record Office. It is a small pamphlet, the title of which is as follows :—

"The Address of the Roman Catholic Prelates, assembled in Dublin on the 18th of November, 1812. To the Clergy and Laity of the Roman Catholic Church in Ireland. Published by Authority. Dublin. Printed and Published by H. Fitzpatrick, Capel Street."

By another memorandum in a separate letter it appears that the opinion of the Attorney General and Solicitor General was taken as to the legality of the publication in question. It was also under the consideration of the Chancellor. The paper containing these facts is not signed. It contains the following observations :—" The course of proceedings with regard to these publications appears to be a matter of much public importance and of some delicacy."

Leaving Mr. Conway to resume his secret correspondence with Lord Sidmouth and Mr. Beckett, we return with a sense of relief to our more immediate subject.

On the 18th of March, 1812, Shelley wrote to Godwin as follows :—

"MY DEAR SIR,—I have said that I acquiesce in your decision, nor has my conduct militated with the assertion. I have withdrawn from circulation the publications in which I erred, and am preparing .to quit Dublin."

Two days after this open recantation we find Shelley negotiating for a loan of two hundred and fifty pounds for the completion of a History of Ireland. That project he kept a profound secret from his vigilant director. The *Declaration of Rights*, a broadside

which Shelley had printed in Dublin for the purpose
of being "posted on the farmers' walls," and which
was the last of his political experiments, he seems not
to have had the courage to send to Godwin. It was,
however, forwarded to his friend at Hurstpierpoint,
and to that circumstance we owe its preservation.

On the 18th of March, 1812, the day on which
Shelley wrote his last letter from Dublin to Godwin,
" a large deal box" had been filled by him with all
the copies of his two pamphlets and *Declaration of
Rights* then remaining in his possession, which was forwarded by the Holyhead packet, with the address—

" Miss Hitchener, Hurstpierpoint, Sussex."

Shelley could only pay the freight to Holyhead; he
expected the box would have been forwarded to Hurst,
when the additional charges would have been paid.
After remaining some days at Holyhead, no one appearing to pass the box, the Surveyor of Customs
opened it, as was his duty, in order to ascertain if it
contained any excisable articles, the ports of England
and Ireland being then watched for this purpose with
greater vigilance than are those of France and England at the present day. The discovery of a case of
Orsini shells, had such instruments been then invented,
could scarcely have created a greater amount of con-
sternation among all the officials of the quiet little
harbour of Holyhead than did the contents of the box.
The discovery was first made by Pierce Thomas, the
Surveyor of Customs. He at once communicated the
fact to William D. Fellowes, who, in the Almanac for
1811 and 1813, under the heading of the General
Post Office, is described as " agent for the Packet
Boats" at Holyhead. This will account for the narrative

of the seizure having been forwarded both to the
Secretary of the Post Office and to the Secretary of
State.   The letters and documents sent to Mr.—afterwards Sir—Francis Freeling remained in his private
possession for many years, and appear to have been
sold after his death.   In 1870 they were advertised in
the catalogue of a London bookseller, and were fortunately bought by the Right Hon. Chichester Fortescue, M.P., President of the Board of Trade, who
in the kindest manner confided them to my hands
for the purpose of transcription and incorporation into
this work.   The letter of Pierce Thomas, the Surveyor
of Customs, was not sent to the head of his own department, but to the Right Hon. Richard Ryder,
Secretary of State.   In this way it has been preserved
in the Record Office, where it rewarded my search in
December, 1870.   I am not aware that any allusion
has ever been made to it or to the exceedingly interesting letter of Harriet Shelley, a copy of which it
contains.   There is with this communication a copy of
the *Declaration of Rights*.   Another copy is also in the
Record Office in connexion with the affair at Barnstaple
in the following year.   The third and only remaining
copy now known to be in existence is in the collection
already alluded to, purchased by the Right Hon.
Chichester Fortescue, M.P., which also contains a copy
of the *Proposals for an Association* (Shelley's second
Irish pamphlet), as well as the autograph letters of
Mr. Fellowes and Lord Chichester.   This collection is
properly inscribed by one of its possessors, certainly
not by Sir Francis Freeling, " Percy Bysshe Shelley,"
" Inflammatory Irish Papers," &c. &c.—a phrase borrowed from the letter of poor Harriet.

Although the letter of Pierce Thomas in the Record

Office is dated a day earlier, it will perhaps be more satisfactory to give the documents forwarded to the Postmaster General, Lord Chichester, as well as his own contribution to the materials which he unconsciously contributed to the biography of Percy Bysshe Shelley. All the letters are given as they were written, no correction of names or spelling being made.

Letter of William D. Fellowes, Esq., Post Office Agent at Holyhead, to Francis Freeling, Esq., Secretary of the General Post Office, London.

" *Most Private.*" " Holyhead, March 31st, 1812.

" MY DEAR SIR,—The Surveyor of the Customs consulted me yesterday on having discovered in the Custom House, a few days since, a Large deal box, directed to ' Miss Hitchener, Hurst per pier, Brighton, Sussex, England,' which had been landed from one of the Packets from Ireland. It contained, besides a great quantity of Pamphlets and printed papers, an *open letter*, of a tendency so dangerous to Government, that I urged him to write without further loss of time, a confidential letter, either to the Secretary of State, or to Mr. Percival, and enclose the letter, and one of each of the Pamphlets and printed Declarations (as they are styled), which he accordingly did by yesterday's Post, to Mr. Percival.

" As the Letter in question, which the Surveyor gave me to read contained a paragraph injurious to the revenue of the P. Office, I think it my duty to make you acquainted with it—it is as follows :—

" ' Percy has sent you a box full of inflammatory * matter, therefore I think I may send this.'

---

* The word is " inflammable" in Mr. Pierce Thomas's transcript of Harriet's letter.

" 'I sent you two *letters in news Papers,* which I hope you received safe from the Intrusion of Post Masters. I sent a Pamphlet to my Father some time since in the same way.'

" '*Disperse the Declarations, Percy says the Farmers are fond of having them stuck on their walls.*'

" Mr. Thomas, the gentleman who gave me this information, having acted by my advice, in order to avoid the delay of reporting to the Custom House, and the possibility of its being considered as a common seizure, of which there are a great many every year— has requested that I would not mention it—and I therefore request you to consider this as confidential. I will send you a Pamphlet in the course of a day or two, but I trust in the mean time this communication may enable the office to detect any future correspondence between the parties under the cover of a news Paper.

" I have the honour to remain,
" Dear Sir,
" Your faithful humble servant,
" WILLIAM D. FELLOWES.
" Francis Freeling, Esq."

" It is a very common custom with the people in Ireland to write in news Papers. I open all that come through my hands, and have charged many from being written in.

" The Person whose letter I have quoted from appears to be English, and to have lately gone to Ireland. I have no doubt but an extensive correspondence will be attempted in the way mentioned. There is no signature to the letter or address."

This letter is endorsed by Sir Francis Freeling in

his well-known autograph, of which there are numerous specimens among the State Papers. " 31 March,
1812, Holyhead, W. D. Fellowes, Esq. *Most Private.*"
" No. 1 " is added in another hand.

The next document in this collection of " Inflammatory Irish Papers " is a short note of Mr. Fellowes,
which explains itself :—

W. D. Fellowes, Esq., to Francis Freeling, Esq.

"April 1st, 1812.

" My DEAR SIR,—I send you the Pamphlet, and
Declaration of Rights, which I mentioned in my letter
of yesterday, and remain yours faithfully,

"WILLIAM D. FELLOWES."

Endorsed by Mr. Freeling :—

"April 1st, 1812, Holyhead, W. D. Fellowes, Esq. (2.)"

These letters of Mr. Fellowes, the copy of Shelley's
second pamphlet and of the *Declaration of Rights,*
were duly forwarded by Mr. Francis Freeling, the
Secretary of the Post Office, to his chief, the Earl of
Chichester, one of the Postmasters General. His
Lordship, though *ex officio* a man of letters, was a
little defective in his orthography, but I have thought
it better to give the letter precisely as it is, than to
attempt any corrections. The opinions formed upon
the social position of Shelley's wife by the magnates
of Sussex are very curious, as is also the sketch of the
antecedents of Miss Hitchener. Altogether the letter
is full of interest.

*The Earl of Chichester, Postmaster General, to Francis
Freeling, Esq., Secretary to the General Post Office.*

"Stanmer, April 5th, 1812.

" DEAR FREELING,—I return the Pamphlet and Declaration, the writer of the first is son of Mr. Shelley, member for the Rape of Bramber, and is by all accounts a most extraordinary man. I hear that he has married a Servant, or some person of very low birth ; he has been in Ireland some time, and I heard of his speaking at the Catholic Convention.

" Miss Hichener, of Hurstperpoint, keeps a school there, and is well spoken of: her Father keeps a Publick House in the neighbourhood, he was originally a smugler,* and changed his name from Yorke to Tichener [Hitchener], before he took the publick House.

"' I shall have a watch upon the Daughter, and discover whether there is any connexion between her and Shelley.

" I shall come to Town on Wednesday.

" As I am to see Mr. Scott to-morrow, I shall keep the Brighton Papers untill I have seen him.

· " Yours most sincerely,

" Chichester.

" I send my Receipt enclosed ; you will be so good as to pay the salary to Messrs. Hoare's."

This letter is endorsed by Mr. Freeling:—" 5th April, 1812. Stanmer. Earl of Chichester. '*Inflammatory Irish Papers addressed to Hurst Perpoint, seized at Holyhead.*'" Mr. Freeling's private address, " Rottingdean," &c., is added.

The Earl of Chichester, by whom the foregoing letter was written, was joint Postmaster General with the Earl of Sandwich. The letter is dated from *Stanmer Park, Sussex.* This will account for Lord Chichester knowing something, though incorrectly, of the private

---

* So written.

affairs of the Shelleys. Why he mistook the place for which Mr. Timothy Shelley was Member of Parliament, was strange. Mr. Shelley, I believe, never sat for any place but Shoreham. William Wilberforce, who had been member for Yorkshire in 1811, was member for Bramber in 1813, having probably been elected for the latter place at the general election of 1812.

"The Brighton Papers" mentioned by Lord Chichester, probably had no reference to Shelley's affair. It should be remembered, however, that in Shelley's unpublished letter to Miss Hitchener (March 10th, 1812), from which I have given a few extracts, he was most anxious that the "Sussex papers" should report his proceedings in Dublin. " Send me the Sussex papers," he says. " Insert, or make them insert the account of *me :*" evidently referring to the account of " Pierce Byshe Shelly, Esq.," which had appeared three days before in *The Weekly Messenger* of March 7th, 1819.

The following letters in the Record Office, which have hitherto been unknown, refer to the same seizure at Holyhead as described in the foregoing papers. They are, I think, of greater interest than those already given.

Documents in the State Paper Office, referring to Shelley, not previously published.

" IRELAND. January to April, 1812. No. 655."

Letter of the Surveyor of Customs at Holyhead to the Secretary of State for the Home Department.

" *Confidential.*"   " Holyhead, March 30th, 1812.

" SIR,—The important contents of the enclosed letter, with a Pamphlet and a Declaration of rights (forming part of the contents of a box detained by me), which I feel it my duty to transmit to you, will, I trust, be a sufficient apology for addressing myself to you in the first instance. Holding as I do an official situation under the Board of Customs, it would perhaps have been more strictly regular to have first, communicated them to my own Board, and if the not having done it should appear to you to be informal, I must trust to your candour in not implicating me for my zealous intentions. Some days since a large deal box, directed to Miss Hitchener, Hurstpierpoint, Brighton, England, was landed from on board one of the Holyhead Packets, and brought to the Custom House, where, as Surveyor and Searcher of the Customs, I opened it, and found the enclosed open letter —the tendency of which at this moment I need not point out; and it still remains in my custody. If it should be your desire to have them transmitted to London, and withheld from the person to whom they are addressed, I should be glad to be honoured with your confidential opinion and commands in what way I ought to forward it, consistent with my public duty as an officer of the Customs, and the respect due to my Board.

> " I have the honour to be,
> " Your very obedient servant,
> " PIERCE THOMAS."

" *Private.*
" The Right Honble. R. Ryder, Secretary."

The communication forwarded by Mr. Pierce Thomas to the Secretary of State was a copy of the " open letter" found in the box containing so much " inflammable matter" in the shape of pamphlets and Declarations of Rights. This letter, which was written

by Harriet Shelley, seems to have been considered
by the officials at Holyhead as a far more dangerous
document than the printed *Address to the Irish People,*
and the other papers that accompanied it. This perhaps arose from the fact that the letter was not signed
.by the writer, and that the person to whom it was
written was addressed under the disguise of a classical
name.   By the " Portia" of poor Harriet's letter was
of course meant *Porcia,* the daughter of Cato and the
wife of Brutus.   This famous name was given to Miss
Hitchener by " Percy's little circle" (to borrow a
phrase from one of Shelley's unpublished letters), not
only in compliment to the republicanism of their correspondent at Hurstpierpoint, but to escape a difficulty which arose from Miss Hitchener's Christian
name being the same as Miss Westbrook's—they were
both Elizas.   In Shelley's hitherto unpublished letter
from Whitehaven, Feb. 3rd, 1812, written on his way
to Dublin, from which we have quoted largely in an
earlier portion of this book, he alludes to this inconvenience.   At that time he was urging Miss Hitchener
at any risk to join him in Dublin—"resign your
school, *all, everything* for us and the Irish cause." He
concludes his letter of February 3rd, 1812, in these
words, which I have reserved in order to explain the
circumstance of Harriet addressing Miss Hitchener by
an adopted name.   Shelley says—

" Pray what are you to be called when you come to
us, for Eliza's name is Eliza, and Miss Hitchener is
too long, too broad, and too deep?   Adieu.
                                        " Your
                                    " P. B. Shelley."

To prevent this clashing of Eliza Westbrook and Eliza Hitchener, the heroic name of Porcia was adopted for the latter. Had Shelley known as much of his fair and philosophical friend at Hurstpierpoint as did the Earl of Chichester, perhaps her real name of "Yorke" would not have been found "too long," "too broad," or "too deep" either for friendly intercourse or correspondence. It would, however, have wanted the delicious romance of suggesting a certain resemblance in principle at least between the heroine of Hurst and the wife of Brutus. By that name, though slightly misspelt by the good and gentle Harriet, she was addressed in the following most interesting letter :—

RECORD OFFICE. "Ireland. January to April, 1812. No. 655."

Harriet Shelley to Eliza Hitchener.

"Dublin, March 18th [1812.]

"MY DEAR PORTIA,—As Percy has sent you such a large Box so full of inflammable matter, I think I may be allowed to send a little but not [of] such a nature as his. I sent you two letters in a newspaper, which I hope you received safe from the intrusion of Post masters. I sent one of the Pamphlets to my Father in a newspaper, which was opened and charged, but which was very trifling when compared to what you and Godwin paid.

" I believe I have mentioned a new acquaintance of ours, a Mrs. Nugent, who is sitting in the room now and talking to Percy about Virtue. You see how little I stand upon ceremony. I have seen her but twice before, and I find her a very greeable, sensible woman. She has felt most severely the miseries of her country in which she has been a very active member. She visited all the Prisons in the time of the Rebellion to exhort the people to have courage and hope. She says it was a most dreadful task; but it was her duty, and she would not shrink from the performance of it. This excellent woman, with all her notions of Philanthropy and justice, is obliged to work for her subsistence—to work in a shop which is a furrier's; there she is every day confined to her needle. Is it not a thousand pities that such a woman should be so dependent upon others? She has visited us this evening for about three hours, and is now returned home. The evening is the only time she can get out in the week; but Sunday is her own, and then we are to see her. She told Percy that her country was her only love, when he asked her if she was married. She called herself *Mrs.* I suppose on account of her age, as she looks rather old for a *Miss.* She has never been out of her own country, and has no wish to leave it.

" This is St. Patrick's night,* and the Irish always get very tipsy on such a night as this. The Horse Guards are pacing the streets and will be so all the night, so fearful are they of disturbances, the poor people being very much that way inclined, as Provisions are very scarce in the southern counties. Poor Irish People, how much I feel for them. Do you know, such is their ignorance that when there is a drawing-room held they go from some distance to see the people who keep them starving to get their

---

* This shows that Harriet's letter was written on the 17th of March, and not on the " 18th," as she has dated it. Unless, indeed, the usual St. Patrick's Ball at the Castle of Dublin was for some reason held on the 18th of March instead of the 17th in the year 1812.

luxuries; they will crowd round the state carriages in great glee to see those within who have stripped them of their rights, and who wantonly revel in a profusion of ill-gotten luxury whilst so many of those harmless people are wanting Bread for their wives and children. What a spectacle! People talk of the fiery spirit of these distressed creatures, but that spirit is very much broken and ground down by the oppressors of this poor country. I may with truth say there are more Beggars in this city than any other in the world. They are so poor they have hardly a rag to cover their naked limbs, and such is their passion for drink that when you relieve them one day you see them in the same deplorable situation the next. Poor creatures, they live more on whiskey than anything, for meat is so dear they cannot afford to purchase any. If they had the means I do not know that they would, whiskey being so much cheaper and to their palates so much more desirable. Yet how often do we hear people say that Poverty is no evil. I think if they had experienced it they would soon alter their tone. To my idea it is the worst of all evils, as the miseries that flow from it are certainly very great; the many crimes we hear of daily are the consequences of Poverty, and that, to a very great degree; I think, the Laws are extremely unjust—they condemn a Person to Death for stealing 13 shillings and 4 pence.

" Disperse the Declarations. Percy says the farmers are very fond of having something posted upon their walls.

" Percy has sent you all his Pamphlets with the Declaration of Rights, which you will disperse to advantage. He has not many of his first Address, having taken great pains to circulate them through this city.

"All thoughts of an Association are given up as impracticable. We shall leave this noisy town on the 7th of April, unless the Habeas Corpus Act should be suspended, and then we shall be obliged to leave here *as soon as possible.* Adieu."

Note on the "Declaration of Rights."

On this interesting subject it may be useful to supplement what has been already said by a fact of some importance.

Of the original broadside containing the *Declaration of Rights* there are probably but four copies in existence. Three of these I have seen. Two of them are in the Record Office, one in the papers connected with the seizure at Holyhead in 1812, the other with those describing the affair at Barnstaple in 1813. The papers are marked respectively, "Ireland, January to April, 1812. No. 655." "Domestic. George III. Nos. 239, 240." A third copy, in the possession of the Right Hon. Chichester Fortescue, M.P., also formed a part of the seizure at Holyhead. It was sent to Mr. Freeling, the Secretary of the Post Office, and remained in his hands. Mention is made of a fourth copy in Lowndes' *Bibliographical Manual,* Bohn's ed. p. 2374, as follows:—" *Queen Mab,* by Percy Bysshe Shelley. Privately printed without a title page, with a hand-bill, called *Declaration of Rights,* drawn up by Shelley and distributed in Ireland." What has become of this interesting volume is unknown. It is extremely probable that Clark's and Carlile's editions of *Queen Mab,* 1821, 1822, were printed from this copy. It is a singular fact, not previously known, that during the life-time of Shelley the *Declaration of Rights* was reprinted by the same Carlile, apparently without his knowing who was the writer. It will be found in the fifth number of *The Republican,* London, Friday, Sept. 24th, 1819. R. Carlile, Printer, 55, Fleet Street, London, p. 75. I am indebted to Mr. John Wilson, Great Russell Street, for a copy of this interesting number of *The Republican.*

CHAPTER XII.

IT would appear from an endorsement in the hand-writing of Mr. Wellesley Pole, that the copy of Harriet's letter given in the last chapter, with the communication of Mr. Pierce Thomas, were forwarded from the Home Secretary's office in London to the office of the Secretary for Ireland in Dublin. "Mr. Goulburn" is also written on one of them, he being the joint under-secretary with Mr. Beckett. All the documents, on which no action seems to have been taken, were sent back to London in an envelope, which still retains the seal with the motto " *Tollet virtus.*" The only observation made by Mr. Wellesley Pole is as follows :—

" The enclosed are returned with Mr. Pole's com-pliments.
" Irish Office, April 8th, 1812."

The chief interest of poor Harriet's letter lies in the additional evidence which it gives of her intelli-gence, good nature, and innocence. Other matters, however, are decided by it. The abandonment of the Association seems in no way to have been affected by the remonstrances of Godwin. The project was given up because it was found to be " impracticable." The letters of Godwin did not accelerate the departure of Shelley from Dublin by one day. He left that city at the precise time he had originally arranged to leave

Y

it. The police had nothing to do with his movements. He received no intimation from them that he should "quit the country." The laconic observation of Mr. Wellesley Pole as to the wonderful mare's-nest discovered by Mr. Pierce Thomas at Holyhead, shows the profound indifference of the Irish Government to his proceedings. What became of the large box of pamphlets is uncertain. It was probably forwarded to Miss Hitchener, who doubtless brought it with her when she joined "Percy's little circle," either in Wales or Devonshire a few months later. At Lymouth, in August, 1812, according to the letter of the town clerk of Barnstaple, "Mr. Shelley had with him large chests, which were so heavy that scarcely three men could lift them, which were supposed to contain papers." These "papers" must have been some copies of the *Address to the Irish People*, a larger supply of the *Proposals for an Association*, possibly the whole impression of the *Declaration of Rights*, also of the poem called *The Devil's Walk*, which like the former was printed as a broadside, but on larger paper. Those "large chests," too, may have contained the *Poetical Essay on the Existing State of Things*, the *Verses on Robert Emmett*, and all the other materials for the edition of his poems which Shelley had projected bringing out in Dublin.

As the *Declaration of Rights* was printed in Dublin, and as it formed part of the seizure made at Holyhead, it may appropriately be introduced here as the concluding exploit of Shelley's wonderful expedition to Ireland in 1812. It has been recently printed by Mr. Rossetti* from a transcript made in the Record

* In *The Fortnightly Review* for January, 1871. But see *note* to last chapter, page 320.

Office, not from the Holyhead documents, but from those connected with the Lymouth and Barnstaple affair of August, 1812, which are also preserved among the State Papers. These will be subsequently referred to, and some corrections and additional information supplied. The transcript from which Mr. Rossetti has printed the *Declaration of Rights* was made by a foreigner, which will account for some of the mistakes which have crept into the published version. There is also an attempt here and there to correct the grammar of the original : occasionally a word is omitted, capital letters and italics, not used by Shelley, are introduced capriciously. Altogether the reprint is unsatisfactory : the *Declaration of Rights* is here reproduced faithfully without any wilful deviation from the original. Mr. Rossetti has drawn attention to certain resemblances between Shelley's *Declaration of Rights* and " the two most famous of similar documents in the history of the great French Revolution—the one adopted by the Constituent Assembly in August, 1789, and the other proposed in April, 1793, by Robespierre." For this ingenious parallel, the reader is referred to the pages of the Review in which it appeared. It is, however, probable that Shelley manufactured his *Declaration of Rights* out of materials nearer to his hand. It is a mere condensation or abridgment of what he had already printed at greater length in his second pamphlet, the *Proposals for an Association.* "The opening thunder-clap" of the *Declaration*, as Mr. Rossetti calls it, is given almost in the same words as in the *Proposals.*

"Government has no rights ; it is a delegation from several individuals for the purpose of securing their own," says the *Declaration.*

"Government can have no rights; it is a delegation for the purpose of securing them to others," says the pamphlet.

Most of the other apothegms of the *Declaration of Rights* may be found in the *Proposals for an Association*, the inspiration of both being doubtless the famous historical documents referred to by Mr. Rossetti.

DECLARATION OF RIGHTS.

1.

GOVERNMENT has no rights; it is a delegation from several individuals for the purpose of securing their own. It is therefore just, only so far as it exists by their consent, useful only so far as it operates to their well-being.

2.

If these individuals think that the form of government which they or their forefathers constituted is ill adapted to produce their happiness, they have a right to change it.

3.

Government is devised for the security of Rights. The rights of man are liberty, and an equal participation of the commonage of Nature.

4.

As the benefit of the governed is, or ought to be, the origin of government, no men can have any authority that does not expressly emanate from *their* will.

5.

Though all governments are not so bad as that of Turkey, yet none are so good as they might be. The majority of every country have a right to perfect their government. The minority, should not disturb them; they ought to secede, and form their own system in their own way.

6.

All have a right to an equal share in the benefits and burdens of Government. Any disabilities for opinion imply, by their existence, barefaced tyranny on the side of Government, ignorant slavishness on the side of the governed.

7.

The rights of man, in the present state of society, are only to be secured by some degree of coercion to be exercised on their violator. The sufferer has a right that the degree of coercion employed be as slight as possible.

8.

It may be considered as a plain proof of the hollowness of any proposition if power be used to enforce instead of reason to persuade its admission. Government is never supported by fraud until it cannot be supported by reason.

9.

No man has a right to disturb the public peace by personally resisting the execution of a law, however bad. He ought to acquiesce, using at the same time the utmost powers of his reason to promote its repeal.

10.

A man must have a right to act in a certain manner, before it can be his duty. He may, before he ought.

11.

A man has a right to think as his reason directs; it is a duty he owes to himself to think with freedom, that he may act from conviction.

12.

A man has a right to unrestricted liberty of discussion. Falsehood is a scorpion that will sting itself to death.

13.

· A man has not only a right to express his thoughts, but it is his duty to do so.

14.

No law has a right to discourage the practice of truth. A man ought to speak the truth on every occasion. A duty can never be criminal; what is not criminal cannot be injurious.

15.

Law cannot make what is in its nature virtuous or innocent to be criminal, any more than it can make what is criminal to be innocent. Government cannot make a law; it can only pronounce that which was the law before its organisation; viz., the moral result of the imperishable relations of things.   .

16.

The present generation cannot bind their posterity : the few cannot promise for the many.

17.

No man has a right to do an evil thing that good may come.

18.

Expediency is inadmissible in morals. Politics are only sound when conducted on principles of morality: they are, in fact, the morals of nations.

19.

Man has no right to kill his brother. It is no excuse that he does so in uniform: he only adds the infamy of servitude to the crime of murder.

20.

Man, whatever be his country, has the same rights in one place as another—the rights of universal citizenship.

21.

The government of a country ought to be perfectly indifferent to every opinion. Religious differences, the bloodiest and most rancorous of all, spring from partiality.

22.

A delegation of individuals, for the purpose of securing their rights, can have no undelegated power of restraining the expression of their opinion.

23.

Belief is involuntary; nothing involuntary is meritorious or reprehensible. A man ought not to be considered worse or better for his belief.

24.

A Christian, a Deist, a Turk, and a Jew, have equal rights: they are men and brethren.

25.

If a person's religious ideas correspond not with your own, love him nevertheless. How different would yours have been had the chance of birth placed you in Tartary or India!

26.

Those who believe that Heaven is, what earth has been, a monopoly in the hands of a favoured few, would do well to reconsider their opinion; if they find that it came from their priest or their grandmother, they could not do better than reject it.

27.

No man has a right to be respected for any other possesssions but those of virtue and talents. Titles are tinsel, power a corruptor, glory a bubble, and excessive wealth a libel on its possessor.

28.

No man has a right to monopolise more than he can enjoy; what the rich give to the poor, whilst millions are starving, is not a perfect favour, but an imperfect right.

29.

Every man has a right to a certain degree of leisure and liberty, because it is his duty to attain a certain degree of knowledge. He may before he ought.

30.

Sobriety of body and mind is necessary to those who would be free; because, without sobriety, a high sense of philanthropy cannot actuate the heart, nor cool and determined courage execute its dictates.

31.

The only use of government is to repress the vices of man. If man were to-day sinless, to-morrow he would have a right to demand that government and all its evils should cease.

Man! thou whose rights are here declared, be no longer forgetful of the loftiness of thy destination. Think of thy rights, of those possessions which will give thee virtue and wisdom, by which thou mayest arrive at happiness and freedom. They are declared to thee by one who knows thy dignity, for every hour does his heart swell with honorable pride in the contemplation of what thou mayest attain—by one who is not forgetful of thy degeneracy, for every moment brings home to him the bitter conviction of what thou art.

Awake !—arise !—or be for ever fallen.

Mr. Hogg says, in complete ignorance of what he was writing about, " The Irish dream which commenced so abruptly being brought as abruptly to an end, the youthful dreamer awoke; then suddenly vanished, and reappeared in Wales" (vol. ii. p. 118). We have proved the reverse of all these statements. The Irish dream did not commence " abruptly," it was not brought to an end " abruptly," and if the youthful dreamer awoke, he did not " suddenly" vanish. Every step that Shelley took in his Irish dream had been taken with his eyes open. The time of his coming, the time of his leaving, had all been pre-arranged, while the period devoted to his preparation for the enterprise and its accomplishment exceeded in length the whole time of his then intercourse with Mr.

Hogg. But that gentleman makes one statement which cannot be controverted, Shelley " reappeared in Wales." It was not, however, to Mr. Hogg that he announced his resurrection ; it was to his philosophical friends Miss Hitchener and Mr. Godwin. The following unpublished letter to the former, though undated, appears to have been the first he wrote after leaving Dublin on the 7th of April, 1812 :—

Shelley to Miss Hitchener.

" Nantgwilt, Rhayader, Radnorshire.

". . . . . We left Dublin and arrived at Holyhead after a passage of unusual length. . . . . You have ere this received our box and its contents. I paid the carriage as far as I could, that is, across the Channel, and I am positive that it did not come by the post. The *Declaration of Rights* would be useful in farmhouses. It was by a similar expedient that Franklin promulgated his commercial opinions among the Americans. Your letter enjoined us to leave Dublin ; we received it a short time before we had settled to depart. The Habeas Corpus Act has not been suspended ; nor probably will they do it. We left Dublin because I had done all that I could do. If its effects were beneficial, they were not greatly so. I am dissatisfied with my success, but not with the attempt. Although the expense of our journey was considerable, I ever bear in my mind that ' economy is the best generosity.' . . . . . I have written some *verses* on Robert Emmett, which you shall see, and which I will insert in my book of poems. We are now embosomed in the solitude of mountains, woods, and rivers, silent, solitary, and old, far away from any town, six miles from Rhayader, which is nearest. A ghost haunts this house, which has frequently been seen by the servants. We have several witches in our neighbourhood, and are quite stocked with fairies and hobgoblins of every description. Well, my dearest friend, I have no larger paper, and therefore must say adieu. Recollect that I am still your friend completely and unalterably. Harriet and Eliza send their love; Harriet is now writing to Mrs. Nugent, an excellent woman whom we discovered in Dublin, and of whom she will tell you. Adieu !

" Yours eternally,
" P. B. SHELLEY."

Shelley was not at this time aware of the fate which had befallen his box at Holyhead, and that Harriet's descriptive letter of Mrs. Nugent had been under the inspection of the Secretary of State for the Home Department in England, and the Irish Secretary in Dublin. I have endeavoured to ascertain something about this Mrs. Nugent, but without success. It is pleasant to find that both Shelley and Harriet retained a kindly feeling towards this benevolent woman after they had left Ireland.

The first published letter of Shelley from Nantgwilt is dated April 25th, 1812, eighteen days after he left Dublin. It is to Godwin, and seems to have been written after the preceding. This letter contains a reference to his Dublin experience, which, as faithful chroniclers of this period of his history, we cannot omit :—

" We are no longer in Dublin. Never did I behold in any other spot a contrast so striking as that which grandeur and misery form in that unfortunate country. How forcibly do I feel the remark which you put into the mouth of Fleetwood, that the distress which in the country humanizes the heart by its infrequency, is calculated in a city, by the multiplicity of its demands for relief, to render us callous to the contemplation of wretchedness! Surely the inequality of rank is not felt so oppressively in England! Surely something might be devised for Ireland, even consistent with the present state of politics, to ameliorate its condition! Curran at length called on me. I dined twice at his house. Curran is certainly a man of great abilities, but it appears to me that he under-values his powers when he applies them to what is usually the subject of his conversation. I may not possess sufficient taste to relish humour, or his incessant comicality may weary that which I possess. He does not possess that mould of mind which I have been accustomed to contemplate with the highest feelings of respect and love. In short, though Curran indubitably possesses a strong understanding and a brilliant fancy, I should not have beheld him with the feelings of admiration which his first visit excited had he not been your intimate friend."—*Letter to Godwin, Hogg,* vol. ii. pp. 122, 123.

In the poetic organization of Shelley there was one great want. He had no genuine humour. Anything he has written in this way never raised a laugh, never perhaps produced a smile. In this respect he was unlike some of the great poets whom in their serious moods he rivalled. The greatest poets, with the exception of Dante, were as remarkable for their playful humour as for their sublimity or their pathos. Homer, Chaucer, Shakspeare, Calderon, Goethe, what would they have been without the comic element? What in Byron is likely to last but his humour—the humour of his letters as well as of his poems? Shelley had nothing of this either in his conversation or in his writings. All was pervaded by a dignified but rather grave seriousness. The poor jaded Master of the Rolls, after a day of exhausting judicial drudgery, thought perhaps that at his dinner-table he might bid a momentary adieu to

" Wrangling courts and stubborn law."

There at least he might have hoped to escape for a brief interval

" The tedious forms, the solemn prate,
The pert dispute, the dull debate"—

and all the other horrors conjured up by the graceful Muse of Sir William Blackstone. But that would not suit Shelley. He evidently expected that the expediency of his political pamphlets, and the wisdom of his *Declaration of Rights*, would have been the chief topic of conversation at the table of the Master of the Rolls, and we dare say he looked even a shade graver while Curran cracked his jokes, than on the memorable occasion when he poked a pamphlet into the hood of an old woman's cloak. Godwin, who knew much more of Curran than Shelley did, and who was not himself particularly jocular, thus speaks both of the convivial as well as forensic talents of John Philpot Curran. The following appeared two days after the death of Mr. Curran in *The Morning Chronicle* of the 16th of October, 1817 :—

" Mr. Curran is almost the last of that brilliant phalanx, the contemporaries and fellow-labourers of Mr. Fox, in the cause of general liberty. Lord Erskine in this country, and Mr. Grattan in Ireland, still survive.

" Mr. Curran is one of those characters which the
lover of human nature and its intellectual capacities
delights to contemplate: he rose from nothing ; he
derived no aid from rank and fortune; he ascended
by his own energies to an eminence which throws rank
and fortune into comparative scorn.   Mr. Curran was
the great ornament of his time of the Irish bar, and
in forensic eloquence has certainly never been exceeded
in modern times.   His rhetoric was the pure emana-
tion of his spirit, a warming and a lighting up of the
soul, that poured conviction and astonishment on his
hearers.   It flashed in his eye, and revelled in the
melodious and powerful accents of his voice.   His
thoughts almost always shaped themselves into imagery,
and if his eloquence had any fault, it was that his
images were too frequent; but they were at the same
time so exquisitely beautiful, that he must have been
a rigorous critic that could have determined which of
them to part with.   His wit was not less exuberant
than his imagination, and it was the peculiarity of Mr.
Curran's wit, that even when it took the form of a
play on words, it acquired dignity from the vein of
imagery that accompanied it.   Every jest was a metaphor. But the great charm and power of Mr. Curran's
eloquence lay in its fervour.   It was by this that he
animated his friends and appalled his enemies, and the
admiration which he thus excited was the child and
brother of love. . . . .

" Mr. Curran had his foibles and his faults ; which
of us has not ?   At this awful moment it becomes us
to dwell on his excellences : and as his life has been
illustrious, and will leave a trail of glory behind, this
is the part of him that every man of a pure mind will
choose to contemplate.   We may any of us have his

faults—it is his excellences that we could wish, for the sake of human nature, to excite every man to copy in his proportion to do so."

Had Mr. Godwin lived to read the attempted biography of his illustrious son-in-law, he would scarcely have found in the immaculate biographer Mr. Hogg one of those men of " pure mind " who choose to contemplate the brighter rather than the darker side of an illustrious man's character.

One other passage may be given from Shelley's letter to Godwin, April 25th, 1812. Speaking of the country near Rhayader, he says :—

" The cheapness, beauty, and retirement make this place in every point of view desirable. Nor can I view this scenery—mountains and rocks seeming to form a barrier round this quiet valley, which the tumult of the world may never overleap ; the guileless habits of the Welsh—without associating *your* presence with the idea, that of your wife, your children, and one other friend, to complete the picture which my mind has drawn to itself of felicity. Steal, if possible, my revered friend, one summer from the cold hurry of business, and come to Wales. Adieu !"—*Hogg*, vol. ii. pp. 123, 124.

Careless readers of Mr. Hogg's book might imagine that the " one other friend" referred to in this passage was Mr. Hogg himself. No one who has accompanied us so far can fall into that mistake ; the " one other friend" was Miss Hitchener.

The interest which Shelley took in Miss Hitchener was altogether intellectual and ideal, arising exclusively from the identity of their opinions, and his admiration of the courage with which she avowed and maintained her principles. It was no wonder, however, that a Platonic affection of this kind should be misunderstood. An unpublished letter of Shelley, dated "Nantgwilt, April 29th, 1812," refers to some gossip on the subject which had been circulating at Cuckfield, the authorship of which he attributes to Mrs. Pilford, the wife of his uncle. He was indignant at these misrepresentations, which he communicated to Miss Hitchener in the most undisguised manner, and exclaimed, in the remarkable passage already quoted:—

"I unfaithful to my Harriet! You a female H—g!" [The reader can easily supply the missing letters written fully in the original.] "Common sense should laugh such an idea to scorn, if indignation would wait till it could be looked upon!"

In the same letter he says, as the most convincing proof of the innocence of his motives:—

"My Harriet's attachment to you will *even* exceed mine."

Finally, he entreats his correspondent to disregard such calumnies. The opinions of others should be indifferent to her. If any doubt arose in her mind as to these matters, her course was simple:—

"Ask what would Percy's little circle say to this?"

Mr. Rossetti, epitomizing the supposed facts of Shelley's life at this period, says:—

"Somewhere about the end of March, the Shelleys and Eliza left Dublin. They passed through the Isle of Man; ranged about North and South Wales in search of a residence; paused at, and again left a 'haunted' house at Nant-Gwilt, near Rhayader; flitted through Cwm Elan; and at last, from the 5th of July, settled down for a short while at Lymouth, in North Devonshire."—*Memoir of Shelley*, p. lxii.

A year later, in the *Fortnightly Review*, January, 1871, Mr. Rossetti makes the date of Shelley's departure from Dublin a little earlier. "Towards the middle of March, the Shelleys and Miss Westbrook left Ireland." These misstatements were of course unintentional on the part of Mr. Rossetti, they seemed necessary to him to sustain the reckless assertions of Mr. Hogg as to the "abrupt" termination of Shelley's "Irish dream," and his "sudden" vanishing out of Dublin. Harriet's letter of the 18th March, 1812, in the Record Office, shows that this "sudden" flight took three weeks to prepare for. "We shall leave this noisy town on the 7th of April," says Harriet; and accordingly they left Dublin on that day, and reached Holyhead after a somewhat longer passage than the average. "We left Dublin, and arrived at Holyhead," writes Shelley to Miss Hitchener, "after a passage of unusual length." The absurdity of making Shelley "pass through the Isle of Man," on his way from Dublin to Holyhead, originated with Captain Medwin. Anything more ludicrously untrue than the following story by the gallant captain was never written :—

"His departure from Ireland was occasioned, *as he told me*, by a hint from the police, and he, in haste, took refuge in the Isle of Man—that then *imperium in imperio*—that extra-judicial place where the debtor was safe from his creditors, and the political refugee found an asylum in his obscurity from the myrmidons of the law. He remained, however, at Douglas but a

short time, and on his passage to some port in Wales
had a very narrow escape from his fatal element. He
had embarked in a small trading vessel which had only
three hands on board. *It was the month of November,*
and the weather, boisterous when they left the harbour,
increased to a dreadful gale. The skipper attributed
to Shelley's exertions so much the safety of the vessel,
that he refused on landing to accept his fare."—
Medwin's Life of Shelley, vol. i. pp. 176, 177.

Making every allowance for Captain Medwin having
confounded something which he may have heard relative to the storm which Shelley encountered when going
to Ireland, with the return voyage in April, it is impossible, unless Shelley was guilty of a deliberate untruth, that he could have told Captain Medwin the other
circumstances of this marvellous narrative. He received
no hint from the police; he never "took refuge" in
the Isle of Man, either "in haste" or with deliberation. Travelling from Whitehaven to Dublin in February, he "passed through the Isle of Man," because
it was his direct route. He never crossed the Channel
in the "month of November." The time at which he
actually left Dublin was the balmy season of early
April. "We left Dublin and arrived at Holyhead
after a passage of unusual length," is the simple fact
out of which Captain Medwin has constructed "a
political refugee"—"a small trading vessel with only
three hands on board"—an apocryphal "month of
November"—an imaginary "skipper"—the undaunted
Shelley—and the generous refusal of the "fare."
And yet this absurd story, and these unfounded statements, have been repeated with a sort of parrot-like
iteration by every subsequent writer who has under-

taken to give us an account of Shelley's life, except indeed Mr. Hogg, who generally commits himself to no one's nonsense but his own. They are adopted without the slightest hesitation by Lady Shelley and Mr. Rossetti (not to speak of Mr. Middleton); but what is stranger still, they are given with several other inaccuracies by Mr. Peacock. This gentleman's remarkable papers in *Fraser's Magazine* were written, as he tells us, for the purpose of "Commenting on what has been published by others" about Shelley, and for "correcting errors." In the following passage of his own paper there is an error almost in every word. " They then went to Ireland, *landed at Cork, visited the lakes of Killarney*, and stayed some time in Dublin, where Shelley *became* a warm repealer and emancipator. They *then* went to the Isle of Man."— *Fraser's Magazine*, June, 1858. Shelley never landed at Cork ; he visited the lakes of Killarney a year later from Dublin; he was a repealer and emancipator before he went to Ireland ; and he did not go to the Isle of Man at all at the time referred to. So much for the correction of previous errors by Mr. Peacock.

Shelley, who had spent something less than a fortnight in traversing "the whole of North, and part of South Wales fruitlessly" in search of a house, was "at length in a manner settled" at Nantgwilt, near Rhayader, in Radnorshire, about the 21st of April, 1812. We have had already his own description of this house in the playful letter to Miss Hitchener, which he wrote from Nantgwilt shortly after his arrival there. Mr. Peacock, who visited Wales in 1813, gives the following minute particulars about the place :—

" Nant Gwillt, the Wild Brook, flows into the Elan (a tributary of the Wye), about five miles above Rhayader. Above the confluence, each stream runs in a rocky channel, through a deep narrow valley. In each of these valleys is or was a spacious mansion, named from the respective streams. Cwm Elan House was the seat of Mr. Grove, whom Shelley had visited there before his marriage in 1811. Nant Gwillt House, when Shelley lived in it in 1812, was inhabited by a farmer, who let some of the best rooms in lodgings. At a subsequent period," continues Mr. Peacock, " I stayed a day in Rhayader, for the sake of seeing this spot. It is a scene of singular beauty."—*Fraser's Magazine*, June, 1858, p. 652.

Shelley resided at Nantgwilt for seven weeks. He changed his residence, not through any restlessness of disposition, for it is evident he was reluctant to leave it, but perhaps owing to the doubts of the " farmer" as to the security of his rent. Such is the interpretation I put upon the following passage in a letter to Godwin, dated " Cwm-Rhayader, June 11th, 1812 :—

" We are unexpectedly compelled to quit Nantgwilt. I hope, however, before long time has elapsed to find a home. These accidents are unavoidable to a minor." —*Hogg*, vol. ii. p. 129.

CHAPTER XIII.

AFTER the date of the letter with which the last chapter concludes, the Shelleys could have stopped but a day or two longer in Wales, as we find them settled at Lynton, near Lymouth, seventeen miles from Barnstaple, North Devonshire, at the beginning of July. It would seem that Godwin having heard from Shelley that he was "compelled" to leave Nant-gwilt, had recommended to him the house of a friend of Mrs. Godwin, a Mr. Eton, in the neighbourhood of Lymouth. Shelley, who was at this time expecting the visit not only of his long-looked-for friend and correspondent, Miss Hitchener, but of Godwin and his "estimable family," found Mr. Eton's house too small. He selected another residence which, though less imposing in appearance, had more accom-modation. Writing to Godwin on the 5th of July from Lymouth, after some days had been spent in this fruitless negotiation with Mr. Eton, he says, "We now reside in a small cottage, but the poverty and humbleness of the apartments is compensated for by their number, and we can invite our friends with a consciousness that there is enclosed space wherein they may sleep, which was not to be found at Mr. Eton's. . . . . The climate is so mild that myrtles of an immense size twine up our cottage, and roses blow

in the open air in winter." "Come, thou venerated
and excellent friend," he says in a letter dated two
days later, "and make us happy."—*Hogg*, vol. ii.
pp. 134, 137, 140.

For some reason or another the rejection of Mr.
Eton's house seems to have ruffled the philosopher
more than might be expected from so slight a cause.
He is absolutely sharp and sarcastic in his reply to the
first letter. There is the faintest trace of a sneer in
the phrase, "This would sound well to Mr. Eton from
the eldest son of a gentleman of Sussex, with ample
fortune" (p. 142). The secret of his displeasure may
be found in the following passages of Shelley's letter
of July 5th, 1812:—

"I have a friend; but first I will make you in
some measure acquainted with her. She is a woman
with whom her excellent qualities made me acquainted.
Though deriving her birth from a very humble source,
she contracted, during youth, a very deep and refined
habit of thinking; her mind, naturally inquisitive and
penetrating, overstepped the bounds of prejudice. She
formed for herself an unbeaten path of life.

"By the patronage of a lady whose liberality of
mind is singular, this woman, at the age of twenty,
was enabled to commence the conduct of a school.
She concealed not the uncommon modes of thinking
which she adopted, and publicly instructed youth as a
Deist and a Republican. When I first knew her, she
had not read *Political Justice,* yet her life appeared to
me in a great degree modelled upon its precepts. Such
is the woman who is about to become an inmate of
our family. She will pass through London, and
I shall take the liberty of introducing her to you, one

whom I do not consider unworthy of the advantage."
—*Hogg*, vol. ii. pp. 135, 136.

There was something in this proposed introduction
of the estimable " Deist and Republican" of Hurstpierpoint, who imparted openly to the little girls of
her school the same "useful knowledge" that Mr.
Godwin had been surreptitiously inculcating under the
pseudonym of Edward Baldwin, that evidently displeased the philosopher.   In his next letter he passes
over the allusion to Miss Hitchener in complete silence.
Possibly he could not forgive her for having practised
the principles of *Political Justice* without having read
the book.   The Prophet Joe Smith would probably have
condemned a bigamist who ventured to take a second
wife without having been strengthened, if not in his
faith, at least in his practice, by the Book of Mormon.
In the very letter which contains the suggestion that
Godwin should take the strong-minded Miss Hitchener
under his wing and fly away to Lymouth to make
" Percy and his little circle" happy, Shelley writes :—

" As soon as we recover our financial liberty we
mean to come to London."

There is a slight flavour of Mr. Micawber's euphuistic
eloquence in the expression " financial liberty." It
seemed in Mr. Godwin's estimation a strange way to
" recover" it to fill his cottage at Lymouth with " a
Deist and Republican" from Hurstpierpoint, accompanied doubtless by " the dear little Americans," of
whom we have already heard, and a Sage from Snow
Hill, surrounded by his " estimable family." The
philosopher was too old a bird to be caught by chaff,
and so let the *ci-devant* schoolmistress find her way to

Lymouth alone, as we shall find she was very well able to do. She got the start of Godwin himself, who eventually paid a solitary visit to Lymouth, with what result will be told in due course.

Another member of Shelley's household at Lymouth was Daniel Hill, the Irish servant who had so "improved" the success of his master's political efforts in Dublin, by giving out that the projector of the Philanthropic Association was only fifteen years of age. The distribution of the pamphlets in Dublin had been doubtless a very amusing occupation for Daniel; he found to his cost that it was rather a serious matter to do the same thing in Devonshire.

Between the first week in July when Shelley was settled at Lymouth, and the 19th of August when this man Daniel Hill was arrested in the streets of Barnstaple for circulating the *Declaration of Rights*, Miss Hitchener must have arrived at the poet's cottage, bringing with her the "large deal box" containing the Irish pamphlets and other printed papers of Shelley opened at Holyhead by the surveyor of Customs, but doubtless forwarded to its address on the full charges being paid. She evidently was the person supposed to be a foreigner, who was Shelley's companion among the rocks at Lymouth when he sent his frail navy afloat, freighted with "inflammable" matter so graphically described by the town-clerk of Barnstaple in 1812.

The curious papers in the Record Office, referring to this extraordinary episode in Shelley's life at Lymouth, have been published by Mr. Rossetti in the *Fortnightly Review* for January, 1871, and therefore need not be further referred to here. Mr. Rossetti was not aware that an outline of this very singular

story, derived from local information, was published
some years ago, before the existence of the papers in
the Record Office was known. It is given in the following very interesting work :—

"SKETCHES OF THE LITERARY HISTORY OF
BARNSTAPLE, &c.
By John Roberts Chanter.
Barnstaple: Printed and sold by E. J. Arnold, High-street."
[1866.]

A correspondence with the author of this attractive
volume, Mr. Chanter, as well as with Lionel Bencraft,
Esq., the present town-clerk of Barnstaple, who in the
most obliging manner responded to my inquiries, enables me to correct previous errors, as well as to supply
some additional information of a very interesting kind
relative to other literary ventures of Shelley at this
period. The following extract from Mr. Chanter's
work shows that the *Letter to Lord Ellenborough* was ·
not printed "in London," as Mr. Hogg says, giving
as a quotation from a letter of Shelley a paragraph
which is not to be found in it, but at Barnstaple.
Of Mr. Syle, the printer of this pamphlet, Mr.
Chanter thus speaks :—

"Mr. Syle, whose name appears as the publisher
of the works before mentioned, and who, by the assistance and encouragement he afforded to young authors,
and in helping forward the literary aspirations of that
day, may well be called the 'John Murray' of Barnstaple, was also a cultivator of the muses himself,
having contributed several poems and sketches to the
pages of the periodicals he published, and the newspaper he subsequently edited. He was the principal
bookseller at Barnstaple for a long period of years.

" In connexion with Mr. Syle, I would here introduce an interesting local episode, referring to that
exquisite poet and wild dreamer, ' Percy Bysshe
Shelley.'

" About the year 1812, just after [a year after] his
ill-omened marriage with Harriet Westbrook, Shelley
and his wife took up their residence at Lynton. He was
then notorious for favouring the most wild and absurd
ideas on religious and political freedom, and had been
expelled from Oxford for publishing a pamphlet *On
the Necessity of Atheism*. During this period Shelley
came into Barnstaple, and called at Mr. Syle's printing-office, bringing with him a bundle of MSS., of
which he desired Mr. Syle to have one thousand copies
printed. This was done, Shelley coming in from time
to time to read the copy and correct the press. The
pamphlet was entitled ' A Letter to Lord Ellenborough, Chief Justice of the King's Bench, on the
prosecution of Daniel Isaac Eaton for the publication
of *Paine's Age of Reason*.'

" This Daniel Isaac Eaton was a bookseller ; he was
sentenced to stand in the pillory for one hour, which
sentence was carried into effect. The contents of the
pamphlet were of the most extreme, not to say violent
character ; but the language was, as is the case in all
Shelley's works, forcible and grand, and full of strong
and indignant remarks on the prosecution, or as
Shelley considered it, *persecution* of the mere publisher of a work on a theological subject. I am
enabled by the kindness of Mr. Barry to give a line
as a specimen. The writer is drawing a contrast
between error and truth, and at the close of it
exclaims, ' Error skulks in holes and corners, letting
I dare not wait upon I would, like the poor cat i' th'

adage, but the eagle eye of truth darts through the undazzling sunbeam of the immutable and just, gathering wherewith to vivify and illumine the universe!'* Shelley had about fifty copies as they were printed; but before publication a strange circumstance occurred. A poor labouring man† of the neighbourhood was taken up for posting bills about the town and neighbourhood, headed 'Government has no Rights.' It being seditious, he was tried and sentenced to three months' imprisonment.‡ His defence was, that a gentleman between Lynton and Barnstaple had given him the bills to post, and paid him 2s. 6d. for doing the job. This gentleman was Percy Bysshe Shelley. Mr. Brooke, who has furnished some of these particulars, and who superintended the printing of the pamphlet, has one of these bills, which was printed in London§ and brought down here by

---

* See note on this passage, p. 349.

† This, of course, is a mistake. The papers in the Record Office show that the person arrested was Daniel Hill, the Irish servant of Shelley, the same who had distributed the pamphlets in Dublin, and who had given out that his master was only fifteen years of age.

‡ The sentence was six months' imprisonment or a penalty of 200*l*. The Town Clerk of Barnstaple, writing to Lord Sidmouth, says :—" Daniel Hill has been convicted by the Mayor in ten penalties of 20*l*. each, for publishing and dispersing Printed Papers without the printer's name being on them, under the Act of 39 George III. c. 79, and is now committed to the common Gaol of this Borough for not paying the penalties, and having no goods on which they could be levied."—*State Papers*, Domestic, George III. No. 240.

§ The *Declaration of Rights* was printed in Dublin, as shown by the hitherto unpublished letters of Shelley already given. Shelley was not in London between his leaving Dublin, on the 7th of April, 1812, and his residence of a few days at the St. James's Coffee House in the November of the same year.

Shelley, who had at that time very wild and crude notions as to government and the regeneration of society.

"This circumstance naturally alarmed Mr. Syle, as the pamphlet was quite as seditious in its tone and contents. He at once suppressed and destroyed the remaining sheets, and had several interviews with Shelley to endeavour to get back the ones previously delivered, but unsuccessfully, as they had been mostly distributed.* One copy came into the hands of Mr. Barry, and was given by him a few years since to Leigh Hunt, the friend and biographer of Shelley, though, I believe, neither the circumstances I have narrated nor the pamphlet itself have ever been noticed or included in any biography of the poet or collection of his works; but the incident as stated is strictly correct."—*Literary History of Barnstaple,* pp. 55, 56.

The documents recently discovered in the Record Office confirm substantially the whole of this interesting statement, which Mr. Chanter gave from the recollection of some of his fellow-townsmen of Barnstaple. Some of the mistakes and discrepancies have been pointed out in the notes I have appended to Mr. Chanter's narrative. A few more remain to be mentioned. The copy of the *Letter to Lord Ellenborough,* presented by Mr. Barry to Leigh Hunt, was probably the one from which Lady Shelley has printed the greater portion of it in her *Shelley Memorials.* The "omitted portions," we are informed, "are the pas-

---

* The fifty copies received from Mr. Syle were, as we have seen, sent up to Mr. Hookham, of New Bond Street, on the 18th of August, the day before the arrest of Daniel Hill.

sages which Shelley introduced into the notes to
Queen Mab, and which are printed in the collected
edition of his works." But the striking passage
quoted by Mr. Chanter in his *Literary History of
Barnstaple* cannot be found either in the "greater
part" of the *Letter* published by Lady Shelley, or
"the omitted portions" introduced into the notes to
*Queen Mab.** We have therefore as yet no complete
copy of the *Letter to Lord Ellenborough.* The notes to
Queen Mab are said also to contain the whole of the
tract entitled *The Necessity of Atheism*, but the quotation alleged to be taken from Lord Bacon's treatise
De Augmentis, given in the solitary advertisement of
the tract which I have discovered, is not to be met with
in the notes to *Queen Mab*, neither have I been able to
find it in the treatise itself.

As the Barnstaple papers deserve to be reprinted
whenever a faithful and detailed Life of Shelley shall

---

* It is very singular to find that this passage alleged by Mr.
Chanter to be quoted from the *Letter to Lord Ellenborough*, is
substantially the same as that in Shelley's second Irish pamphlet,
the *Proposals*, which the reader will find at p. 274 of the present
volume. Shelley may possibly have introduced it again, with some
verbal alterations, into the *Letter*, but that is not likely. It will
be recollected, that along with the fifty copies of the *Letter to
Lord Ellenborough*, Shelley had also sent Mr. Hookham the
"two pamphlets" which he had "printed and distributed in
Ireland" (*Shelley Memorials*, p. 38). It may have been that
a copy of the Irish pamphlet, the *Proposals*, was left by Shelley
with the Barnstaple printer as a guide or pattern for the *Letter.*
In this way the passage may have remained in the memory of
Mr. Brooke, the actual printer, or of Mr. Barry, who is mentioned
as the direct authority, and been quoted years after by either of
them as having been contained in the *Letter to Lord Ellenborough*, when in reality it was in the *Proposals for an Association.*

be published, I may be permitted to point out one or two mistakes in Mr. Rossetti's edition of these papers, into which he was led by the occasionally unfaithful transcript used by him. The following is perhaps the most important. Speaking of the *Declaration of Rights,* Mr. Rossetti says, " On the back of the copy in Hill's possession was written ' Samuel Brembridge, of Barn-staple, 19th August, 1812,' being, I presume, the person to whom Shelley intended this copy to be delivered."—*The Fortnightly Review,* January, 1871, pp. 72, 73.

This is in every way a mistake. In the first place, the name is not " Brembridge," but " Bremridge," and secondly, Daniel Hill had many copies of the *Declaration of Rights* in his possession. Evidence was taken on one, and this one endorsed by the magistrate before whom Hill was in the first instance taken, was sent up to London to Lord Sidmouth. Lionel Ben-craft, Esq., the present town-clerk of Barnstaple, informs me that " Samuel Bremridge was clerk to the county justices in 1812." Mr. Chanter has kindly supplemented this information by the following fact : " Samuel Bremridge was junior alderman in 1812, and as such would be also an acting magistrate."

In the letter of Henry Drake, town-clerk (*Fortnightly Review,* p. 79, line 3), " *some* of these small boxes " is printed for " *one* of these small boxes," a mistake which the context itself plainly points out.

The letter of Henry Drake was referred to " Mr. Litchfield " for his advice. Mr. Rossetti suggests that he may have been " the standing counsel em-ployed by the Home Office." The position held by Mr. Litchfield was that of " Solicitor to the Treasury."

Among the papers found on the person of Daniel

Hill when arrested, was a second printed broadside containing a poem called *The Devil's Walk. A Ballad.* It is printed in three columns, and contains 143 lines. Mr. Rossetti, who reproduces it in the *Fortnightly Review* (not without two or three trifling errors of the press); says, "Probably *The Devil's Walk* was written only a short time before Daniel Hill was commissioned to distribute it, in August, 1812; if so, Shelley had now already begun the writing of *Queen Mab.*" Unless Shelley had commenced the writing of *Queen Mab* in Dublin this is incorrect. Miss Hitchener had been living with Shelley at Lymouth for some time when Daniel Hill was arrested, probably from the first week or two of his residence there. Now there is in existence a long unpublished letter addressed to her previously, containing the greater part of *The Devil's Walk, in manuscript.* Speaking of the stanzas he sends, he says, "perhaps they may amuse you." It is plain from Mr. Brooke's silence that *The Devil's Walk* was not printed at Mr. Syle's office in Barnstaple. It was probably printed, as well as written, in Dublin. The poem itself has little merit: composed almost avowedly in imitation of the well-known pieces of Southey and Coleridge, it lacks the humour and the lyrical felicity of its models. There is occasionally a vigorous line. The following stanza is quite in the spirit of the motto from *The Curse of Kehama* prefixed to the *Poetical Essay on the Existing State of Things.* In the first line Mr. Rossetti has omitted " the " from before " death-birds." The allusion seems to be to the same subject as that on which the verses *Mother and Son* were written.

The poet is describing no less a personage than " the first gentleman in Europe :"—

" Fat as the death-birds on Erin's shore,
   That glutted themselves in her dearest gore,
   And flitted round Castlereagh,* '
   When they snatched the Patriot's heart, that *his* grasp
   Had torn from its widow's maniac clasp,
   And fled at the dawn of day."

The prison books now existing at Barnstaple do not
go back so far as 1812, and therefore there is no record
of the time at which Daniel Hill was discharged. The
matter is not of much importance, except that Mr.
Hogg tells us that " the penalty was paid," and that,
" marvellous to relate, Bysshe took the released bill-
sticker into his service" (vol. ii. p. 213). The latter
observation shows how completely ignorant Mr. Hogg
was of this period of his friend's life. It is not likely
that Shelley could have raised 200*l.* to release his servant, when he had to leave Lymouth in debt to his
landlady, who kindly borrowed 3*l.* also for him from
a neighbour. For this debt and this loan, Godwin
tells us that Shelley left with the " good creature, the
woman of the house," " a draft upon the Honourable
Mr. Lawleys [Lawless], brother to Lord Cloncurry."
Unfortunately Lord Cloncurry had no brother. We

---

* Perhaps there was but one point on which Shelley and Lord
Castlereagh ever agreed, and that was in extravagant admiration of
Lady Morgan's *Missionary*, which was published by John Joseph
Stockdale in 1811. Lady Morgan's literary executor in her
Memoirs says that—" His lordship was, perhaps, the greatest
admirer the *Missionary* ever found," vol. i. p. 424. He had a
formidable rival in Shelley, who several times speaks of " Miss
Owenson's Missionary, an Indian Tale." " It is really a divine
thing," he writes in one of his letters. " Luxima, the Indian, is
an angel. What a pity that we cannot incorporate these creations
of fancy; the very thoughts of them thrill the soul! Since I have
read this book I have read no other."—*Hogg*, vol. i. p. 397 ; see
also pp. 392 and 407.

have no doubt that the draft was on Mr. John Lawless, Shelley's "literary friend" in Dublin, not the
brother, but a distant relation of Lord Cloncurry. We
trust that the good Mrs. Hooper at Lymouth was
not kept out of her money until the "enormous profits" which Shelley so sanguinely expected from the
publication of *The History of Ireland* were realized.
We hear no more of Daniel Hill until six months
later—a period which exactly coincides with the term
of his imprisonment—when he turned up at Tanyrallt,
in North Wales, the day preceding the night on which
the celebrated so-called attempted assassination took
place there.

As soon as Shelley could make his arrangements
after this untoward affair about his servant, he left
Lymouth, and crossing the Bristol Channel proceeded
to Wales, where, after moving about a little, he at
length settled near Tremadoc in a handsome lodge
called Tan-yr-allt, built by W. A. Madocks, M.P.
for Boston.* Three weeks after the Shelleys left
Lymouth, poor Godwin paid the long-expected visit.
"The Shelleys were gone!" as he himself exclaims
in a letter addressed to his wife, which will be
found in Lady Shelley's *Memorials*. Mr. Hogg, who
suffered a disappointment precisely similar six months
later in Dublin, describes the philosopher's bewilder-
ment with some humour. But the facts, as stated by

---

* In an interesting portrait of this gentleman in my possession,
painted by J. Ramsay, engraved by C. Turner, he is called " W.
A. Madocks, Esq., Fellow of All Souls College, and M.P. for
Boston." Through the open window there is a pleasing view of
the sea and the little town of Tremadoc. Mr. Madocks is represented pointing to the "plan of the embankment at Tre-Madoc,
&c.," which lies outspread before him.

A A

him, are all invented, as may be seen by reading Godwin's own account of the matter.

Shelley, speaking of his new residence, says :—

" We simple people live here in a cottage extensive and tasty enough for the villa of an Italian prince. The rent, as you may conceive, is large, but it is an object with us that they allow it to remain unpaid till I am of age."

Tanyrallt seems to have been a favourite resting-place for other wandering bards besides Shelley. Rogers passed a night in it the year before. Writing to Moore from Aberystwith, Sept. 19th, 1811, the author of *The Pleasures of Memory* says :—

" I slept a night at Wm. Madocks's. He is a great lord in his little city of Tre-Madoc—has built a church, and a market-place, and a town-hall, and a square, and a street, where the sea roared a year or two ago ; and this week holds an Eysteddfodd, or Meeting of Bards. The comet is very brilliant here, and every evening makes a *brilliant path* across the water." —*Moore's Memoirs*, vol. viii. p. 94.

In 1812 the sea roared again so dreadfully around this creation of Mr. Madocks's taste and public spirit as to threaten it with destruction. Shelley exerted himself in the most praiseworthy manner in endeavouring to raise a fund for the preservation of the breakwater, on the stability of which the existence of new Tremadoc depended. He even went to London, it is said, to use his influence with the Duke of Norfolk and others for the same good object. It is stated that Shelley headed the subscription list with one from himself of 500*l*. This is scarcely credible, unless indeed it was understood that the subscription, like his rent,

was not to be paid till he came of age. We shall find
that in addition to the ordinary expenses of his household and the cost of going up to London with Harriet
and the two Elizas on this and perhaps other business,
he had to pay, " with a heavy heart and an unwilling
hand," the " stipend" of the amiable " Deist and Republican," whom he had disturbed in her self-support-
ing, if not very useful, calling at Hurstpierpoint. It
is surely impossible that Shelley could have allowed
his servant Daniel Hill to remain all this time confined as a criminal in the gaol of Barnstaple, when
perhaps a third of the sum alleged to be so generously
presented to Mr. Madocks would have relieved him.
Daniel Hill had been Shelley's agent, and was vica-
riously suffering for his master's indiscretion. If,
after spending six months in prison, he heard of such
an uncalled-for and, in Shelley's circumstances at the
time, extravagant outlay, one would be disposed to
forgive him if, as has been argued, he got up the so-
called attempted assassination at Tanyrallt, not for the
purpose of doing Shelley any positive harm, but of
frightening him a little—of " paying him out," as it
has been called, for the scrape into which he had been
brought by his philanthropic young master.

In November, 1812, Shelley went up to London to
forward the subscription for the Tremadoc embankment. He had another object, perhaps not less important to him—namely, to get rid of Miss Hitchener.
That lady, with Harriet and Eliza Westbrook, accompanied Shelley on this short visit. They all put up
at the St. James's Coffee House, in St. James's Street.
Mr. Hogg says he visited them there, and witnessed
the departure of Miss Hitchener from this hotel on a
certain Sunday evening. " The chronology of such

an interview," says Mr. Hogg, " need not be exact."
Exact chronology is certainly not the failing of Mr.
Hogg's book; and so we have two events which must
have occurred on the same day and in the same place,
separated in his book by two hundred pages.*   These
are his dining with Bysshe, Harriet, and Eliza Westbrook at " a hotel near St. James's Palace" " during
Shelley's brief visit to London in November, 1812,"
and the departure or dismissal of Miss Hitchener.   I
have made ample notes of all the discrepancies of
his story, but they would take up too much space
here.

   Mr. Hogg tells us, that after the departure of Miss
Hitchener from the hotel, on the evening he dined
with Shelley, Harriet and Eliza Westbrook withdrew
to pack up for their journey next day to Tanyrallt.
He also tells us that the day was Sunday; but from
Shelley's letter of the 7th November to Mr. Williams
(vol. ii. p. 175), we know that it must have been Wednesday, the 11th.   The Shelleys and Eliza Westbrook
returned to Tanyrallt on the 12th.   Thus the " brief
visit" lasted little more than a week, and Miss Hitchener was with them up to the eve of their departure.
And yet we have the following curious statement by
Lady Shelley :—

   " During his visit to London, Shelley made the
personal acquaintance of Godwin, with whom he lived
for a time ; and to the philosopher's daughter Fanny
he addressed the subjoined letter, after having rather
abruptly left their house."—*Shelley Memorials,* p. 43.

---

   * It is amusing to compare the two descriptions.   See *Hogg,*
vol. ii. p. 171, and the same volume, p. 365.

The reader is referred to the letter in the *Memorials* : it is a very singular one. But how could Shelley have " lived with Godwin for a time" during this brief visit? Did he go alone, leaving " Harriet and the ladies " (who must have been Eliza Westbrook and Eliza Hitchener) at the St. James's Coffee House ?*   Or did the whole party migrate together to Skinner Street? The latter supposition is scarcely probable. Another curious matter is, that Lady Shelley calls " Fanny Godwin" " the philosopher's daughter." This she certainly was not, as any one who reads attentively the *Memoirs of the Author of a Vindication of the Rights of Woman* will see. Fanny, or Frances, was the daughter of Mary Wollstonecraft and Gilbert Imlay. She was born at Havre, on the 14th of May, 1794; so that when she wrote to Shelley in 1812, she had just passed her eighteenth year. This mistake about " Fanny Godwin" is now corrected for the first time. The latest and on the whole the most correct biographer of Shelley thus repeats it :—

" The household of Godwin consisted, besides himself, of his second wife, who had been previously married to a Mr. Clairmont; Mary, his daughter by his first wife ; Fanny, his daughter by his second wife ; and Clare and Charles Clairmont, the children of the second wife by her first marriage."—*Rossetti's Memoir of Shelley*, p. lxxviii.

This list is inaccurate in two ways. In addition to the mistake about Fanny, it omits the only child of Godwin by his second marriage, William his son, who died of cholera in 1832, and a memoir of whom has

---

* Letter to Mr. Williams, the agent of Mr. Madocks, St. James's Coffee House, Nov. 7th, 1812. See *Hogg*, vol. ii. p. 175.

been written by his father. This second marriage of Godwin took place in 1801. Were Fanny even his eldest child by that marriage, she could only have been ten years of age in 1812. It is evident that Shelley's letter published in the *Memorials* was not written to a child of that age. This is but a sample of the incredible number of mistakes that disfigure all the published Lives of Shelley, and destroy their authenticity. As to Mr. Hogg, it is doubtful if he has told one single fact truly.

It is a most melancholy thought if we recall the fact that this poor Fanny Imlay or Godwin, like Harriet Shelley, committed suicide by drowning. Less sad, but almost equally singular, is it to remember that her mother, Mary Wollstonecraft, when abandoned, or at least neglected by Imlay, attempted the same fate from Putney Bridge.* When we add to these the catastrophe of Shelley himself, we have a series of coin-

---

* This event occurred in October, 1795. The details, as published by Mr. Godwin, may be here given.

" She resolved to plunge herself in the Thames ; and, not being satisfied with any spot nearer to London, she took a boat, and rowed to Putney. Her first thought had led her to Battersea Bridge, but she found it too public. It was night when she arrived at Putney, and by that time had begun to rain with great violence. The rain suggested to her the idea of walking up and down the bridge, till her clothes were thoroughly drenched and heavy with the wet, which she did for half-an-hour without meeting a human being. She then leaped from the top of the bridge, but still seemed to find a difficulty in sinking, which she endeavoured to counteract by pressing her clothes closely round her. After some time she became insensible. . . . . . After having been for a considerable time insensible, she was recovered by the exertions of those by whom the body was found."—*Memoirs of the Author of a Vindication of the Rights of Woman.* By William Godwin. London, 1798, pp. 132, 133, 134.

cidences that is exceedingly painful, if not awful to reflect on.

But we must draw this investigation to a close, not indeed through any defect of matter, but from want of space. We shall briefly allude to what is called "the Tanyrallt Mystery," and suggest an explanation not previously given.

Three weeks after Shelley's return to Tanyrallt, he thus writes to Mr. Hogg, whose offence at York in the preceding year had by this time been forgiven. "The Brown Demon" was of course Miss Hitchener, who but nine months before Shelley had invited to "give up her school, abandon everything, and live with him for ever."

"Tanyrallt, Dec. 3rd, 1812.

". . . . The Brown Demon, as we call our late tormentor and schoolmistress, must receive her stipend; I pay it with a heavy heart and an unwilling hand; but it must be so. She was deprived by our misjudging haste of a situation where she was going on smoothly; and now she says that her reputation is gone, her health ruined, her peace of mind destroyed by my barbarity. This is not all fact; but certainly she is embarrassed and poor, and we being in some degree the cause, we ought to obviate it. She is an artful, superficial, ugly, hermaphroditical beast of a woman, and my astonishment at my fatuity, inconsistency, and bad taste was never so great as after living four months with her as an inmate. What would Hell be, were such a woman in Heaven?"—*Hogg*, vol. ii. p. 194.

We have here the position in which the parties stood towards each other on the 3rd of December, 1812 : the lady asserting that her reputation was gone,

her health ruined, and her peace of mind destroyed by
the barbarity of the poet, the poet using towards the
lady nearly the most offensive language that could be
applied to a woman. What Shelley said to Mr. Hogg
he may have repeated to others, perhaps to Miss
Hitchener herself. In any case she must have known
the utter loathing felt for her by her late admirer.
We are not told what was the amount of the " stipend,"
or if it was ever paid. She was dismissed, as we have
seen, on the 11th of November. It is plain that
Shelley's letter of the 3rd of December alludes only
to a promise to pay. On the 11th of February three
months stipend would be due. Between the 11th
and 26th there is just sufficient time for repeated
demands, threats, &c., until the crisis came.

That Shelley had received some threats is certain
from Harriet's well-known letter, written from the house
of Mr. John Lawless, 35, Cuffe Street, Dublin.* " On

---

* It has been conjectured by Dr. Madden in his *Life of Lady
Blessington* (second edition, vol. iii. p. 418), that Shelley's selection of this locality arose from his straitened circumstances at the
time.   Mr. Middleton, in his *Shelley and his Writings*, quoting
the passage says, " He took up his abode at No. 35, Cuffe Street,
Stephen's Green, a locality sufficient to show the nature of the
pecuniary circumstances in which Shelley was placed." This is
an entire mistake. Shelley did not go to Cuffe Street because it
was a cheap place of residence, which it scarcely could have been.
He went there because his friend Mr. John Lawless resided there.
We have seen how intimately he had been connected with him
the year before. The *History of Ireland*, the efforts to raise
money for its production, the curious assertion of the editor of
The Dublin Evening Post, and the draft on Mr. Lawless given
by Shelley to his landlady at Lymouth, all show how intimate
that connexion had been. But the reflection on the street itself
is unfounded. In 1813 it was inhabited chiefly by professional
people, barristers, proctors, and attorneys. The house was a private one, and when Mr. Hogg called there in March, 1813, the

Friday night, the 26th of February, we retired to bed between ten and eleven o'clock. We had been in bed about half an hour, when Mr. Shelley heard a noise proceeding from one of the parlours. He immediately went downstairs with two pistols, which he had loaded that night, *expecting to have occasion for them."* The circumstances of the attack are too well known to be repeated here. Mrs. Shelley continues : " We all assembled in the parlour, where we remained for two hours. Mr. S. then advised us to retire, thinking it impossible he would make a second attack. We left Bysshe and one man-servant [Mr. Hogg's version of the letter gives " *our* man-servant "], who had only arrived that day, and who knew nothing of the house, to sit up." Three hours after this, when " Bysshe had sent Daniel to see what hour it was," the second attack was made. The would-be assassin fired at Shelley, the ball passing through his flannel gown. Bysshe fired at his assailant, but the pistol would not go off. " He then aimed a blow at him with an old sword which we found in the house. The assassin attempted to get the sword from him, and just as he was getting it away, Dan rushed into the room, when he made his escape."—*Shelley Memorials,* p. 59.

By some writers the whole of this alleged attack is supposed to be an entire delusion on the part of

---

door was opened by " a man-servant." And yet the most recent biographer of Shelley improves upon his authority by transferring the mistaken description of the street to the house. " After a short stay in an uninviting house, No. 35, Great Cuffe Street, Dublin," &c. (Rossetti's *Memoir,* p. lxvi.). That it was not " an *uninviting* house " in one sense at least, Mr. Hogg had some pleasant reasons for remembering, as the reader will find by referring to the second volume of the *Life of Shelley,* p. 238.

Shelley; but Harriet's letter is too circumstantial to admit of such an explanation. It is said that Eliza Westbrook in after life spoke frequently with terror of the events of this night. Shelley himself it is plain expected an attack, having loaded his pistols that night, "expecting to have occasion for them." A later solution of the difficulty is, that the whole thing was a practical joke on the part of Daniel Hill, who had arrived on that day, probably after the expiration of his imprisonment, at Barnstaple, the whole term of which would have expired on the 18th of February. In this case he must have had a confidant, who ran the risk of being shot by Shelley; or if he escaped that fate, of being detected and prosecuted for the outrage. It is much more probable that the attack was made in ignorance of the addition to the Tany-rallt garrison, occasioned by the unexpected arrival of Daniel Hill, and that it was frustrated by that fortunate circumstance.

The attack then seems to have been a real one. Shelley evidently had reason for believing that he had provoked the enmity of some one. This hostility was not confined to himself. Harriet says in her post-script to Shelley's first letter of two lines to Mr. Hookham—"It is no common robber we dread, but a person who is actuated by revenge, and who threatens my life, and my sister's as well." All this shows that Shelley and Harriet had been anticipating for some time the violence of a person who was meditating revenge against the whole party. This person was one who had some private injury to revenge. The injury was one for which Shelley, Harriet, and Eliza West-brook were equally responsible. The strange threats of their assailant which Harriet so courageously repeats prove this. The enemy was "no common robber," but one who was "actuated by revenge," who threatened her own life and her sister's as well as Shelley's.

Now in Shelleyan history up to this period, as far as it has yet been revealed to us, there was but one person who had any grounds of complaint against Shelley, Harriet Shelley, and Eliza Westbrook. That person was Miss Hitchener. We know the terms in which Shelley spoke of her, and the charges of "barbarity" she brought against Shelley. Mr. Hogg unconsciously unites the three in the indictment which Miss Hitchener had evidently framed in her mind against them. Speaking of the "Brown Demon," he says :—

"At first she possessed some influence over the young couple : but the charming Eliza would not tolerate any influence but her own. She had worked upon Harriet's feelings, and the good Harriet had succeeded in making his former favourite odious to Bysshe."—Vol. ii. p. 366.

Here we have the three persons against whom the mysterious assailant at Tanyrallt declared open war, all united in an actual depreciation and an implied injury against Miss Hitchener. She declared in some way which Shelley could not misunderstand, that by his conduct towards her she had lost her health, her reputation, and her peace of mind. She was promised some compensation, but we have no evidence that it was paid. Even if it were, the sense of injury would have remained. On her expulsion from "Percy's little circle" in London on the 11th of November, 1812, she returned in all likelihood to her father's house. The Earl of Chichester has told us in his letter to Sir Francis Freeling, that Miss Hitchener's father, whose original name was Yorke, had been a smuggler, and was then a publican at Hurstpierpoint. Surely here is material enough for the romance of Tanyrallt, without dragging in poor Daniel Hill and an imaginary confederate of his—a " gaol-bird" from Barnstaple, who had travelled all the way to Tremadoc, and ran the imminent risk of being shot or hanged merely to oblige " Dan." The wrongs of Miss Hitchener we can have little doubt were discussed around the paternal bar at Hurstpierpoint. The " stipend" may not have been paid. Who knows but that it was after an ineffectual demand, by an agent either of the father or the daughter, for the first quarter's instalment, which was due a few days before the memorable 26th of February, and the threats that may have followed the disappointment, that Shelley may have thought it expedient to load his pistols, " expecting to have occasion for them ?" This may not be the solution of the mystery, but it is the most reasonable that has been yet suggested.

This investigation for the present must terminate here. It extends only over the period of a few years, and yet has resulted in the discovery of some new facts of great importance, and the correction of many errors. If it contained nothing but the history of the *Poetical Essay*, the facts and circumstances connected with which have been so curiously discovered and traced by the present writer, it would form no unimportant addition to our previous knowledge of the poet's life. Many notes referring to the subsequent career of Shelley have already been compiled by the author, the result of much investigation not only in England but in Italy.* The publication of these notes is for the present postponed, in the hope that they may include at no distant day a review of the long-promised justification or *apologia* of Shelley for that circumstance which his warmest admirers must, for the present, consider the most unhappy and the least excusable event of his life.

---

* As an example of the careless way in which the Italian portion of Shelley's life has been written, it may be mentioned that the name of the village near Lerici, beside which stands the celebrated house *Casa Magni*, in which Shelley last resided, has never been correctly given in any Life of the poet. From Mrs. Shelley to Mr. Rossetti it has been called "Sant' Arenzo." Its real name, *S. Terenzio*, is given in the following quotation from the *Guida Pittorica del Golfo della Spezia*, which I bought at Spezia (June 15, 1862) in one of two visits which I paid to this interesting house :—

"Presso *S. Terenzio*, sulla punta che chiude il seno di Lerici, s'innalza la fortezza di S. Teresa, che incrocicchia con l'opposta di S. Maria.

"Sulle alture circostanti osservasi la *Merigola*, amena villegiatura del Marchese Olandini. Ombrosi boschetti le fanno romantico serto; sorprendente è il panorama del Golfo che di lassù si presenta allo sguardo. Nel 1822 su quei verdi poggi sedevano due celebri cantori di Albione, vaghi di contemplare la magnificenza del migliore tra i golfi, Byron cioè coll amico Shelley; ma oimè, che quest' ultimo era destinato a perire miseramente tra quelli stessi tratti di mare, che allora in estasi di ammirazione il rapivano."—p. 40. Spezia, 1861.

The allusion to Shelley in the foregoing extract is in itself very interesting.

SUPPLEMENT,

CONTAINING

SHELLEY'S POLITICAL PAMPHLETS

PUBLISHED IN ENGLAND.

In order to render this collection of Shelley's Political Pamphlets complete, it has been thought advisable to include in the present volume the two tracts which he published in 1817 under the name of *The Hermit of Marlow*. The pamphlets have been sometimes confounded with each other, and are nearly as scarce as those which Shelley printed in Ireland.

𝔄 Proposal

FOR PUTTING

REFORM TO THE VOTE

THROUGHOUT THE KINGDOM.

BY THE HERMIT OF MARLOW.

LONDON:

PRINTED FOR C. AND J. OLLIER,
3, WELBECK STREET, CAVENDISH SQUARE;
By C. H. Reynell, 21, Piccadilly.

1817.

B B

A PROPOSAL, &c.

A GREAT question is now agitating in this nation, which no man or party of men is competent to decide; indeed there are no materials of evidence which can afford a foresight of the result. Yet on its issue depends whether we are to be slaves or free men.

It is needless to recapitulate all that has been said about Reform. Every one is agreed that the House of Commons is not a representation of the people. The only theoretical question that remains is, whether the people ought to legislate for themselves, or be governed by laws and impoverished by taxes originating in the edicts of an assembly which represents somewhat less than a thousandth part of the entire community. I think they ought not to be so taxed and governed. An hospital for lunatics is the only theatre where we can conceive so mournful a comedy to be exhibited as this mighty nation now exhibits: a single person bullying and swindling a thousand of his comrades out of all they possessed in the world, and then trampling and spitting upon them, though he were the most contemptible and degraded of mankind, and they had strength in their arms and courage in their hearts. Such a parable realized in political society is a spectacle worthy of the utmost indignation and abhorrence.

The prerogatives of Parliament constitute a sovereignty which is exercised in contempt of the People, and it is in strict consistency with the laws of human nature that it should have been exercised for the People's misery and ruin. Those whom they despise, men instinctively seek to render slavish and wretched, that their scorn may be secure. It is the object of the Reformers to restore the People to a sovereignty thus held in their contempt. It is my object, or I would be silent now.

Servitude is sometimes voluntary. Perhaps the People choose to be enslaved; perhaps it is their will to be degraded and ignorant and famished; perhaps custom is their only God, and they its fanatic worshippers will shiver in frost and waste in famine rather than deny that idol, perhaps the majority of this nation decree that they will not be represented in Parliament, that they will not deprive of power those who have reduced them to the miserable condition in which they now exist. It is *their* will—it is their own concern. If such be their decision, the champions of the rights and the mourners over the errors and calamities of man, must retire to their homes in silence, until accumulated sufferings shall have produced the effect of reason.

The question now at issue is, whether the majority of the adult individuals of the United Kingdom of Great Britain and Ireland desire or no a complete representation in the Legislative Assembly.

I have no doubt that such is their will, and I believe this is the opinion of most persons conversant with the state of the public feeling. But the fact ought to be formally ascertained before we proceed. If the majority of the adult population should solemnly state their desire to be, that the representatives whom they might appoint should constitute the Commons House of Parliament, there is an end to the dispute. Parliament would then be required, not petitioned, to prepare some effectual plan for carrying the general will into effect; and if Parliament should then refuse, the consequences of the contest that might ensue would rest on its presumption and temerity. Parliament would have rebelled against the People then.

If the majority of the adult population shall, when seriously called upon for their opinion, determine on grounds, however erroneous, that the experiment of innovation by Reform in Parliament is an evil of greater magnitude than the consequences of misgovernment to which Parliament has afforded a constitutional sanction, then it becomes us to be silent; and we should be guilty of the great crime which I have conditionally imputed to the House of Commons, if after unequivocal evidence that it was the national will to acquiesce in the existing system we should, by partial assemblies of the multitude, or by any party acts, excite the minority to disturb this decision.

The first step towards Reform is to ascertain this point. For which purpose I think the following plan would be effectual:—

That a Meeting should be appointed to be held at the *Crown and Anchor* Tavern on the —— of ——, to take into consideration the most effectual measures for ascertaining whether or no, a Reform in Parliament is the will of the majority of the individuals of the British Nation.

That the most eloquent and the most virtuous and the most venerable among the Friends of Liberty, should employ their authority and intellect to per-

suade men to lay aside all animosity and even discussion respecting the topics on which they are dis-
united, and by the love which they bear to their
suffering country conjure them to contribute all their
energies to set this great question at rest—whether
the Nation desires a Reform in Parliament or no?

That the friends of Reform, residing in any part of
the country, be earnestly entreated to lend perhaps
their last and the decisive effort to set their hopes and
fears at rest; that those who can should go to London,
and those who cannot, but who yet feel that the aid
of their talents might be beneficial, should address a
letter to the Chairman of the Meeting, explaining
their sentiments: let these letters be read aloud, let
all things be transacted in the face of day. Let Resolutions, of an import similar to those that follow be
proposed.

1. That those who think that it is the duty of the
People of this nation to exact such a Reform in the
Commons House of Parliament, as should make that
House a complete representation of their will, and
that the People have a right to perform this duty,
assemble here for the purpose of collecting evidence
as to how far it is the will of the majority of the
People to acquit themselves of this duty, and to exercise this right.

2. That the population of Great Britain and Ireland
be divided into three hundred distinct portions, each
to contain an equal number of inhabitants, and three
hundred persons be commissioned, each personally to
visit every individual within the district named in his
commission, and to inquire whether or no that individual is willing to sign the declaration contained in
the third Resolution, requesting him to annex to his

signature any explanation or exposure [exposition?] of his sentiments which he might choose to place on record. That the following Declaration be proposed for signature :—

3. That the House of Commons does not represent the will of the People of the British Nation; we the undersigned therefore declare, and publish, and our signatures annexed shall be evidence of our firm and solemn conviction that the liberty, the happiness, and the majesty of the great nation to which it is our boast to belong,· have been brought into danger and suffered to decay through the corrupt and inadequate manner in which Members are chosen to sit in the Commons House of Parliament; we hereby express, before God and our country, a deliberate and unbiassed persuasion, that it is our duty, if we shall be found in the minority in this great question, incessantly to petition; if among the majority, to require and exact that that House should originate such measures of Reform as would render its Members the actual Representatives of the Nation.

4. That this Meeting shall be held day after day, until it determines on the whole detail of the plan for collecting evidence as to the will of the nation on the subject of a Reform in Parliament.

5. That this Meeting disclaims any design, however remote, of lending their sanction to the revolutionary and disorganizing schemes which have been most falsely imputed to the Friends of Reform, and declares that its object is purely constitutional.

6. That a subscription be set on foot to defray the expenses of this Plan.

In the foregoing proposal of Resolutions, to be submitted to a National Meeting of the Friends of

Reform, I have purposely avoided detail. If it shall
prove that I have in any degree afforded a hint to
men who have earned and established their popularity
by personal sacrifices and intellectual eminence such
as I have not the presumption to rival, let it belong
to them to pursue and develope all suggestions relating
to the great cause of liberty which has been nurtured
(I am scarcely conscious of a metaphor) with their
very sweat, and blood, and tears : some have tended
it in dungeons, others have cherished it in famine, all
have been constant to it amidst persecution and
calumny, and in the face of the sanctions of power :—
so accomplish what ye have begun.

I shall mention therefore only one point relating
to the practical part of my Proposal. Considerable
expenses, according to my present conception, would
be necessarily incurred : funds should be created by
subscription to meet these demands. I have an income
of a thousand a year, on which I support my wife and
children in decent comfort, and from which I satisfy
certain large claims of general justice. Should any
plan resembling that which I have proposed be determined on by you, I will give 100*l.*, being a tenth part
of one year's income, towards its object ; and I will
not deem so proudly of myself, as to believe that I
shall stand alone in this respect, when any rational
and consistent scheme for the public benefit shall have
received the sanction of those great and good men
who have devoted themselves for its preservation.

A certain degree of coalition among the sincere
Friends of Reform, in whatever shape, is indispensable
to the success of this proposal. The friends of Universal or of Limited Suffrage, of Annual or Triennial
Parliaments, ought to settle these subjects on which

they diagsree, when it is known whether the Nation desires that measure on which they are all agreed. It is trivial to discuss what species of Reform shall have place, when it yet remains a question whether there will be any Reform or no.

Meanwhile, nothing remains for me but to state explicitly my sentiments on this subject of Reform. The statement is indeed quite foreign to the merits of the Proposal in itself, and I should have suppressed it until called upon to subscribe such a requisition as I have suggested, if the question which it is natural to ask, as to what are the sentiments of the person who originates the scheme, could have received in any other manner a more simple and direct reply. It appears to me that Annual Parliaments ought to be adopted as an immediate measure, as one which strongly tends to preserve the liberty and happiness of the Nation; it would enable men to cultivate those energies on which the performance of the political duties belonging to the citizen of a free state as the rightful guardian of its prosperity essentially depends; it would familiarize men with liberty by disciplining them to an habitual acquaintance with its forms. Political institution* is undoubtedly susceptible of such improvements as no rational person can consider possible, so long as the present degraded condition to which the vital imperfections in the existing system of government has reduced the vast multitude of men, shall subsist. The securest method of arriving at such beneficial innovations, is to proceed gradually and with caution; or in the place of that order and free-

---

* Shelley uses the same phrase in the second Irish pamphlet, the *Proposals*. See p. 271.

dom which the Friends of Reform assert to be violated now, anarchy and despotism will follow. Annual Parliaments have my entire assent. I will not state those general reasonings in their favour which Mr. Cobbett and other writers have already made familiar to the public mind.

With respect to Universal Suffrage, I confess I consider its adoption, in the present unprepared state of public knowledge and feeling, a measure fraught with peril. I think that none but those who register their names as paying a certain small sum in *direct taxes* ought at present to send Members to Parliament. The consequences of the immediate extension of the elective franchise to every male adult, would be to place power in the hands of men who have been rendered brutal and torpid and ferocious by ages of slavery. It is to suppose that the qualities belonging to a demagogue are such as are sufficient to endow a legislator. I allow Major Cartwright's arguments to be unanswerable; abstractedly it is the right of every human being to have a share in the government. But Mr. Paine's arguments are also unanswerable; a pure republic may be shown, by inferences the most obvious and irresistible, to be that system of social order the fittest to produce the happiness and promote the genuine eminence of man. Yet nothing can less consist with reason, or afford smaller hopes of any beneficial issue, than the plan which should abolish the regal and the aristocratical branches of our constitution, before the public mind, through many gradations of improvement, shall have arrived at the maturity which can disregard these symbols of its childhood.

"WE PITY THE PLUMAGE, BUT FORGET
THE DYING BIRD."

AN

ADDRESS to the PEOPLE

ON

The Death of the Princess Charlotte.

BY

𝕿𝖍𝖊 𝕳𝖊𝖗𝖒𝖎𝖙 𝖔𝖋 𝕸𝖆𝖗𝖑𝖔𝖜.

AN ADDRESS, &c.

I. THE Princess Charlotte is dead. She no longer moves, nor thinks, nor feels. She is as inanimate as the clay with which she is about to mingle. It is a dreadful thing to know that she is a putrid corpse, who but a few days since was full of life and hope ; a woman young, innocent, and beautiful, snatched from the bosom of domestic peace, and leaving that single vacancy which none can die and leave not.

II. Thus much the death of the Princess Charlotte has in common with the death of thousands. How many women die in childbed and leave their families of motherless children and their husbands to live on, blighted by the remembrance of that heavy loss ? How many women of active and energetic virtues ; mild, affectionate, and wise, whose life is as a chain of happiness and union, which once being broken, leaves those whom it bound to perish, have died, and have been deplored with bitterness, which is too deep for words ? Some have perished in penury or shame, and their orphan baby has survived, a prey to the scorn and neglect of strangers. Men have watched by the bedside of their expiring wives, and have gone mad when the hideous death-

rattle was heard within the throat, regardless of the
rosy child sleeping in the lap of the unobservant
nurse.   The countenance of the physician had been
read by the stare of this distracted husband, till the
legible despair sunk into his heart.   All this has been
and is.   You walk with a merry heart through the
streets of this great city, and think not that such
are the scenes acting all around you.   You do not
number in your thought the mothers who die in
childbed.   It is the most horrible of ruins :—In
sickness, in old age, in battle, death comes as to his
own home ; but in the season of joy and hope, when
life should succeed to life, and the assembled family
expects one more, the youngest and the best beloved, that the wife, the mother—she for whom
each member of the family was so dear to one
another, should die !—Yet thousands of the poorest
poor, whose misery is aggravated by what cannot
be spoken now, suffer this.   And have they no affections ?   Do not their hearts beat in their bosoms,
and the tears gush from their eyes ?   Are they not
human flesh and blood ?   Yet none weep for them—
none mourn for them—none when their coffins are
carried to the grave (if indeed the parish furnishes
a coffin for all) turn aside and moralize upon the
sadness they have left behind.

III.· The Athenians did well to celebrate, with
public mourning, the death of those who had guided
the republic with their valour and their understanding, or illustrated it with their genius.   Men do well
to mourn for the dead : it proves that we love something beside ourselves ; and he must have a hard
heart who can see his friend depart to rottenness and

dust, and speed him without emotion on his voyage to "that bourne whence no traveller returns." To lament for those who have benefited the State, is a habit of piety yet more favourable to the cultivation of our best affections. When Milton died it had been well that the universal English nation had been clothed in solemn black, and that the muffled bells had tolled from town to town. The French nation should have enjoined a public mourning at the deaths of Rousseau and Voltaire. We cannot truly grieve for every one who dies beyond the circle of those especially dear to us; yet in the extinction of the objects of public love and admiration, and gratitude, there is something, if we enjoy a liberal mind, which has departed from within that circle. It were well done also, that men should mourn for any public calamity which has befallen their country or the world, though it be not death. This helps to maintain that connexion between one man and another, and all men considered as a whole, which is the bond of social life. There should be public mourning when those events take place which make all good men mourn in their hearts,—the rule of foreign or domestic tyrants, the abuse of public faith, the wresting of old and venerable laws to the murder of the innocent, the established insecurity of all those, the flower of the nation, who cherish an unconquerable enthusiasm for public good. Thus, if Horne Tooke and Hardy had been convicted of high treason, it had been good that there had been not only the sorrow and the indignation which would have filled all hearts, but the external symbols of grief. When the French Republic was extinguished, the world ought to have mourned.

IV. But this appeal to the feelings of men should not be made lightly, or in any manner that tends to waste, on inadequate objects, those fertilizing streams of sympathy, which a public mourning should be the occasion of pouring forth. This solemnity should be used only to express a wide and intelligible calamity, and one which is felt to be such by those who feel for their country and for mankind; its character ought to be universal, not particular.

V. The news of the death of the Princess Charlotte, and of the execution of Brandreth, Ludlam, and Turner, arrived nearly at the same time. If beauty, youth, innocence, amiable manners, and the exercise of the domestic virtues could alone justify public sorrow when they are extinguished for ever, this interesting Lady would well deserve that exhibition. She was the last and the best of her race. But there were thousands of others equally distinguished as she, for private excellences, who have been cut off in youth and hope. The accident of her birth neither made her life more virtuous nor her death more worthy of grief. For the public she had done nothing either good or evil; her education had rendered her incapable of either in a large and comprehensive sense. She was born a Princess; and those who are destined to rule mankind are dispensed with acquiring that wisdom and that experience which is necessary even to rule themselves. She was not like Lady Jane Grey, or Queen Elizabeth, a woman of profound and various learning. She had accomplished nothing, and aspired to nothing, and could understand nothing respecting those great political questions

which involve the happiness of those over whom she
was destined to rule. Yet this should not be said in
blame, but in compassion: let us speak no evil of the
dead. Such is the misery, such the impotence of
royalty—Princes are prevented from the cradle from
becoming anything which may deserve that greatest
of all rewards next to a good conscience, public admiration and regret.

VI. The execution of Brandreth, Ludlam, and
Turner is an event of quite a different character
from the death of the Princess Charlotte. These
men were shut up in a horrible dungeon for many
months, with the fear of a hideous death and of
everlasting hell thrust before their eyes; and at last
were brought to the scaffold and hung. They too
had domestic affections, and were remarkable for the
exercise of private virtues. Perhaps their low station
permitted the growth of those affections in a degree
not consistent with a more exalted rank. They had
sons, and brothers, and sisters, and fathers, who loved
them, it should seem, more than the Princess Charlotte could be loved by those whom the regulations of
her rank had held in perpetual estrangement from
her. Her husband was to her as father, mother, and
brethren. Ludlam and Turner were men of mature
years, and the affections were ripened and strengthened within them. What these sufferers felt shall not
be said. But what must have been the long and
various agony of their kindred may be inferred from
Edward Turner, who, when he saw his brother dragged
along upon the hurdle, shrieked horribly and fell in a
fit, and was carried away like a corpse by two men.
How fearful must have been their agony, sitting in

c c

solitude on that day when the tempestuous voice of
horror from the crowd, told them that the head so
dear to them was severed from the body! Yes—
they listened to the maddening shriek which burst
from the multitude: they heard the rush of ten
thousand terror-stricken feet, the groans and the
hootings which told them that the mangled and dis-
torted head was then lifted into the air. The sufferers
were dead. What is death? Who dares to say that
which will come after the grave?* Brandreth was
calm, and evidently believed that the consequences
of our errors were limited by that tremendous barrier.
Ludlam and Turner were full of fears, lest God should
plunge them in everlasting fire. Mr. Pickering, the
clergyman, was evidently anxious that Brandreth
should not by a false confidence lose the single opportunity of reconciling himself with the Ruler of the
future world. None knew what death was, or could
know. Yet these men were presumptuously thrust
into that unfathomable gulf, by other men, who knew
as little and who reckoned not the present or the
future sufferings of their victims. Nothing is more
horrible than that man should for any cause shed the
life of man. For all other calamities there is a remedy
or a consolation. When that Power through which
we live ceases to maintain the life which it has conferred, then is grief and agony, and the burthen which
must be borne: such sorrow improves the heart. But
when man sheds the blood of man, revenge, and hatred,
and a long train of executions, and assassinations, and
proscriptions, is perpetuated to remotest time.

---

* " Your death has eyes in his head—mine is not painted so."
Cymbeline.

VII. Such are the particular, and some of the general considerations depending on the death of these men. But however deplorable, if it were a mere private or customary grief, the public as the public should not mourn. But it is more than this. The events which led to the death of those unfortunate men are a public calamity. I will not impute blame to the jury who pronounced them guilty of high treason, perhaps the law requires that such should be the denomination of their offence. Some restraint ought indeed to be imposed on those thoughtless men who imagine they can find in violence a remedy for violence, even if their oppressors had tempted them to this occasion of their ruin. They are instruments of evil, not so guilty as the hands that wielded them, but fit to inspire caution. But their death, by hanging and beheading, and the circumstances of which it is the characteristic and the consequence, constitute a calamity such as the English nation ought to mourn with an unassuageable grief.

VIII. Kings and their ministers have in every age been distinguished from other men by a thirst for expenditure and bloodshed. There existed in this country, until the American war, a check, sufficiently feeble and pliant indeed, to this desolating propensity. Until America proclaimed itself a Republic, England was perhaps the freest and most glorious nation subsisting on the surface of the earth. It was not what is to the full desirable that a nation should be, but all that it can be, when it does not govern itself. The consequences, however, of that fundamental defect soon became evident. The government which the imperfect constitution of our representative assembly threw into the hands of a few aristocrats, improved the method of anticipating the taxes by loans, invented by the ministers of William III., until an enormous debt had been created. In the war against the Republic of France, this policy was followed up, until now, the *mere interest* of the public debt amounts to more than twice as much as the lavish expenditure of the public treasure, for maintaining the standing army, and the royal family, and the pensioners, and the placemen. The effect of this debt is to produce such an unequal distribution of the means of living, as saps the foundation of social union and civilized life. It creates a double aristocracy, instead of one which was sufficiently burthensome before, and gives twice as many people the liberty of living in luxury and idleness on the produce of the industrious and the poor. And it does not give them this because they are more wise and meritorious than the rest, or because their leisure is spent in schemes of public good, or in those exercises of the intellect and the imagination, whose creations ennoble or adorn a country. They are not like the old aristocracy, men of pride and honour, *sans peur et sans tache*, but petty peddling slaves who have gained a right to the title of public creditors, either by gambling in the funds, or by subserviency to government, or some other villainous trade. They are not the " Corinthian capital of polished society," but the petty and creeping weeds which deface the rich tracery of its sculpture. The effect of this system is, that the day labourer gains no more now by working sixteen hours a day than he gained before by working eight. I put the thing in its simplest and most intelligible shape. The labourer, he that tills the ground and manufactures cloth, is the man who has to provide, out of

what he would bring home to his wife and children,
for the luxuries and comforts of those whose claims
are represented by an annuity of forty-four millions
a year levied upon the English nation. Before, he
supported the army and the pensioners, and the royal
family, and the landholders; and this is a hard necessity to which it was well that he should submit. Many
and various are the mischiefs flowing from oppression,
but this is the representative of them all—namely,
that one man is forced to labour for another in a
degree not only not necessary to the support of the
subsisting distinctions among mankind, but so as by
the excess of the injustice to endanger the very foundations of all that is valuable in social order, and to
provoke that anarchy which is at once the enemy of
freedom, and the child and the chastiser of misrule.
The nation, tottering on the brink of two chasms,
began to be weary of a continuance of such dangers
and degradations, and the miseries which are the consequence of them; the public voice loudly demanded
a free representation of the people. It began to be
felt that no other constituted body of men could meet
the difficulties which impend. Nothing but the nation
itself dares to touch the question as to whether there
is any remedy or no to the annual payment of forty-
four millions a year, beyond the necessary expenses of
State, for ever and for ever. A nobler spirit also
went abroad, and the love of liberty, and patriotism,
and the self-respect attendant on those glorious emo-
tions, revived in the bosoms of men. The government
had a desperate game to play.

IX. In the manufacturing districts of England discontent and disaffection had prevailed for many years;

this was the consequence of that system of double aristocracy produced by the causes before mentioned. The manufacturers, the helots of our luxury, are left by this system famished, without affections, without health, without leisure or opportunity for such instruction as might counteract those habits of turbulence and dissipation, produced by the precariousness and insecurity of poverty. Here was a ready field for any adventurer who should wish for whatever purpose to incite a few ignorant men to acts of illegal outrage. So soon as it was plainly seen that the demands of the people for a free representation must be conceded if some intimidation and prejudice were not conjured up, a conspiracy of the most horrible atrocity was laid in train. It is impossible to know how far the higher members of the government are involved in the guilt of their infernal agents. It is impossible to know how numerous or how active they have been, or by what false hopes they are yet inflaming the untutored multitude to put their necks under the axe and into the halter. But thus much is known, that so soon as the whole nation lifted up its voice for parliamentary reform, spies were sent forth. These were selected from the most worthless and infamous of mankind, and dispersed among the multitude of famished and illiterate labourers. It was their business if they found no discontent to create it. It was their business to find victims, no matter whether right or wrong. It was their business to produce upon the public an impression, that if any attempt to attain national freedom, or to diminish the burthens of debt and taxation under which we groan, were successful, the starving multitude would rush in, and confound all orders and distinctions, and institutions and laws, in common ruin.

The inference with which they were required to arm the ministers was, that despotic power ought to be eternal. To produce this salutary impression, they betrayed some innocent and unsuspecting rustics into a crime whose penalty is a hideous death. A few hungry and ignorant manufacturers, seduced by the splendid promises of these remorseless blood-conspirators, collected together in what is called rebellion against the State. All was prepared, and the eighteen dragoons assembled in readiness, no doubt, conducted their astonished victims to that dungeon which they left only to be mangled by the executioner's hand. The cruel instigators of their ruin retired to enjoy the great revenues which they had earned by a life of villany. The public voice was overpowered by the timid and the selfish, who threw the weight of fear into the scale of public opinion, and Parliament confided anew to the executive government those extraordinary powers which may never be laid down, or which may be laid down in blood, or which the regularly constituted assembly of the nation must wrest out of their hands. Our alternatives are a despotism, a revolution, or reform.

X. On the 7th of November, Brandreth, Turner, and Ludlam ascended the scaffold. We feel for Brandreth the less, because it seems he killed a man. But recollect who instigated him to the proceedings which led to murder. On the word of a dying man, Brandreth tells us, that " Oliver *brought him to this"* —that, " *but for* Oliver *he would not have been there.*" See, too, Ludlam and Turner, with their sons, and brothers, and sisters, how they kneel together in a dreadful agony of prayer. Hell is before

their eyes, and they shudder and feel sick with fear,
lest some unrepented or some wilful sin should seal
their doom in everlasting fire. With that dreadful
penalty before their eyes—with that tremendous sanction for the truth of all he spoke, Turner exclaimed
loudly and distinctly, *while the executioner was putting
the rope round his neck,* " THIS IS ALL OLIVER AND THE
GOVERNMENT." What more he might have said we
know not, because the chaplain prevented any further
observations. Troops of horse, with keen and glitter-
ing swords, hemmed in the multitudes collected to
witness this abominable exhibition. " When the
stroke of the axe was heard, there was a burst of
horror from the crowd.* The instant the head was
exhibited, there was a tremendous shriek set up, and
the multitude ran violently in all directions, as if
under the impulse of sudden frenzy. Those who resumed their stations, groaned and hooted." It is a
national calamity, that we endure men to rule over
us, who sanction for whatever ends a conspiracy which
is to arrive at its purpose through such a frightful
pouring forth of human blood and agony. But when
that purpose is to trample upon our rights and liberties
for ever, to present to us the alternatives of anarchy
and oppression, and triumph when the astonished
nation accepts the latter at their hands, to maintain
a vast standing army, and add year by year to a
public debt, which already, they know, cannot be discharged ; and which, when the delusion that supports
it fails, will produce as much misery and confusion
through all classes of society as it has continued to

---

* These expressions are taken from *The Examiner*, Sunday,
Nov. 9th.—*Author's Note.*

produce of famine and degradation to the undefended
poor; to imprison and calumniate those who may
offend them at will; when this, if not the purpose, is
the effect of that conspiracy, how ought we not to
mourn?

XI. Mourn then people of England. Clothe yourselves in solemn black. Let the bells be tolled. Think
of mortality and change. Shroud yourselves in solitude and the gloom of sacred sorrow. Spare no
symbol of universal grief. Weep—mourn—lament.
Fill the great city—fill the boundless fields, with
lamentation and the echo of groans. A beautiful
Princess is dead:—she who should have been the
Queen of her beloved nation, and whose posterity
should have ruled it for ever. She loved the domestic
affections, and cherished arts which adorn, and valour
which defends. She was amiable and would have become wise, but she was young, and in the flower of
youth the destroyer came. LIBERTY is dead. Slave!
I charge thee disturb not the depth and solemnity of
our grief by any meaner sorrow. If One has died
who was like her that should have ruled over this
land, like Liberty, young, innocent, and lovely, know
that the power through which that one perished was
God, and that it was a private grief. But *man* has
murdered Liberty, and whilst the life was ebbing from
its wound, there descended on the heads and on the
hearts of every human thing, the sympathy of an
universal blast and curse. Fetters heavier than iron
weigh upon us, because they bind our souls. We
move about in a dungeon more pestilential than damp
and narrow walls, because the earth is its floor and
the heavens are its roof. Let us follow the corpse of

British Liberty slowly and reverentially to its tomb : and if some glorious Phantom should appear, and make its throne of broken swords and sceptres and royal crowns trampled in the dust, let us say that the Spirit of Liberty has arisen from its grave and left all that was gross and mortal there, and kneel down and worship it as our Queen.

FINIS.

*** Whence Shelley derived the curious title of this pamphlet, " We pity the plumage, but forget the dying bird," has not previously been pointed out. It is possible that he found it in the first number of *The Reflector*, which appeared in October, 1810, the month of his matriculation at Oxford. *The Reflector* was a quarterly magazine, edited by Leigh Hunt, of which I have two volumes, to December, 1811. The original passage will probably be found in one of Paine's tracts, of which, since I alluded to them at page 134, I have recently seen a Dublin edition.

" It was pertinently said of the pathetic language which Mr. Burke, in his later writings, occasionally held on constitutional topics, that *he pitied the plumage, but neglected the wounded and suffering bird.*"—*The Reflector*, vol. i. p. 17.

APPENDIX.

No. I.

"THE LATE MR. FINNERTY."

From the Morning Chronicle, May 15th, 1822.

IT is with no ordinary regret that we announce the death of Mr. Peter Finnerty, twenty years a Parliamentary reporter on this journal. For some time his health had been on the decline, but always solicitous to perform his duties, it was only within the last month that the violence of his complaint compelled him to withdraw himself from the more active duties of his situation.

"Mr. Finnerty, from the strength of his mind and the warmth of his feelings, has either so acted or suffered in the public events of his country that such a man ought not to be allowed to descend to his grave as a common individual. He was the son of a tradesman in the town of Loughrea, in the county of Galway, who with slender means had reared and educated a numerous family. Mr. Finnerty, the eldest son, was in early age cast upon his fortunes in the metropolis of Ireland; brought up a printer, he, at the awful crisis of 1798, succeeded [preceded] Mr. Arthur O'Connor as the [registered] printer of the most popular and ably conducted paper which ever appeared in that country— *The Press.* Such a situation naturally brought Mr. Finnerty into perilous contact with the irritated and coercive Government of that day. It was no ordinary predicament in which so young a man, being then scarcely of age, was placed. Under the process of the laws as then administered in Ireland, he was visited with all the penalties of a vindictive prosecution, and the property of the establishment was ultimately demolished by military force. On his trial he had the honour of being defended by Mr. Curran, an advocate whose powers rose with the demands of his country for their exertion, and who seemed to have been destined to the great but dangerous distinction of displaying talents in defence of virtue commensurate to the wrongs which had called them forth. In that court he charged the Government of that day with a vindictive warfare against the only printer who dared to whisper the liberties of Ireland. Mr. Finnerty was sentenced to a punishment more ignominious to the law than to the criminal, but had the honour of being attended by Lord Edward Fitzgerald and many other public characters. The sentence was executed also under the bayonets of a large military force, but could not repress that burst of popular sympathy which attended the first address that he ever made to his suffering countrymen. He passed those dreadful years of '98 and '99 in the prison of Newgate, Dublin, when too frequently the guest of the breakfast-table, as he himself has often described, was hurried forth to sudden execution. Such was the persecution with which he had to contend in consequence of the subversion of his establishment, that he remained for months unemployed before he could obtain a passport for England! Arrived in London, he entered into an engagement on the press, and commenced Parliamentary reporter. The faithful and able manner in which he discharged the important duties of such a trust is well known to all who have had any connexion with the press of the metropolis. Having professionally attended the court-martial which was held at Portsmouth, he became acquainted with Sir Home Popham, and an intimacy commenced which terminated only by his death.* When the expedition to Walcheren took place, Mr. Finnerty, at the

---

* A copy of *The Trial of Sir Home Popham*, probably edited by Peter Finnerty, is in the London Institution, Finsbury Circus. A Memoir of Sir Home Riggs Popham is given in *Public Characters of* 1806. London, 1806, p. 399.

request of Sir Home, sailed with Captain Bartholomew from Woolwich for the avowed purpose of writing the history of that expedition. An order had, however, been circulated through the squadron in the Downs to send Mr. Finnerty on shore if found on board this fleet. This order was ineffectual, as Mr. Finnerty, unaware of its existence, had arrived at Walcheren, and on being made acquainted with it, immediately waited upon the naval commander-in-chief. He was received with great kindness, and after a delay of some weeks, he returned to England in a frigate. Under the irritation of feelings naturally excited by such a strange exercise of authority, he addressed, through this paper, a letter to a noble member of the Administration who held a conspicuous place in the recent and melancholy history of Ireland. That noble person immediately commenced a prosecution against the publisher of this journal. Mr. Finnerty, who had been frequently warned by the late Mr. Perry as to the consequences which would result from the publication of the letter, with the frankness and decision of character which belonged to him, immediately requested that the manuscript should be given up, that the prosecution might affect only the real author. He allowed judgment to go by default; but on being brought up for judgment, he defended the libel on the ground of the provocations which he had received, as well as the truth of his allegations, which he was then prepared with affidavits to sustain. He was sentenced to a long term of imprisonment, that was so rigorously carried into effect, that his constitution received a shock from which it never recovered. While in prison, by an appeal to Parliament he procured an inquiry,* the

---

* It may perhaps be interesting to mention, that the whole report on this very curious inquiry, with the original affidavits of the parties concerned, is preserved in the Record Office. (Domestic, George III., January to March, 1811. No. 226.) The original petition to the Prince Regent, signed in the remarkable autograph of Peter Finnerty, is in the collection of papers, No. 227. Domestic, Geo. III., April to May, 1811. See also p. 93 of this volume.

result of which not only led to a mitigation of his own sufferings, but to the general amelioration of the prison dis-
cipline. On his liberation, he resumed his duties with
this paper. His mind, naturally strong and original, was
invigorated by an experience of the world that enabled
him, with no common acuteness, to perceive both the substance and form of truth, and detect the sophistries of the
most specious imposition. He had a natural eloquence of
a vivid and masculine character, and his colloquial powers
were peculiar and fascinating. But his leading characteristic was an instinctive hatred of oppression whatever
shape it assumed, or by whatever influence it was attempted
to be enforced. We will mention one instance. In the
recent State Trials Mr. Finnerty was the individual who
first discovered that the infamous Thomas Reynolds, personally unknown to his brother-jurors, was actually a
member of the grand jury of the metropolitan court of
England. No sooner was the fact ascertained, and pending the trials in Westminster Hall, than he communicated
the circumstance to a member of the House of Commons,
who in consequence made a disclosure, the electric effect
of which upon the House was only equalled by the indignation that it excited throughout the country.

"From the original information of his mind, his unbending devotedness to the interests of his country, and
hatred of its oppressors, he had drawn upon himself much
political hostility; but for that he was highly compensated
by having the good fortune to enjoy the proud distinction
of being known to Mr. Fox, Mr. Whitbread, and Sir
Samuel Romilly, and of having as his personal and intimate friends Mr. Curran, Mr. Sheridan, and Mr. Grattan,
as well as some of the most eminent public men now
living. Having made this plain and simple statement, we
have only to add that while the memory of Mr. Finnerty
is identified with the history of his country, it will long be
cherished by those associates, who having had the best
opportunity of knowing his good qualities, have the most
reason to deplore him."

The respect thus entertained for Mr. Finnerty by those

who best knew him, seems to have been shared even by
Lord Castlereagh himself. *The Examiner*, August 26th,
1822, p. 533, in an article on the unhappy suicide of that
nobleman has the following passage :—

" *The Tyne Mercury* says, 'The late Mr. Finnerty, who
was for many years at known declared and active enmity
with the Marquis of Londonderry, has often mentioned to
us that his lordship was accustomed to *bow to him* as he
passed him.' "

Mr. Finnerty died on the 11th of May, 1822, at Westminster. In the affidavits prefixed to the report of his
trial in 1811, he is described as Peter Finnerty, of Clement's
Inn, in the county of Middlesex, gentleman. His age at
the time of his death is stated by some writers to have been
fifty-six years ; but this must be a mistake. In his letter to
The Morning Chronicle, published in that journal Tuesday,
January 23rd, 1810, which was the alleged libel for which
he suffered his second imprisonment, he has the following
passage referring to the period subsequent to the expiration
of his sentence at the end of 1799, when he sought for a
passport to go into England, and was refused :—

" What will the public think of Castlereagh's feelings,
when I state that at the period of which I am writing I
was not twenty-one years of age ?"

At the time of his death therefore, in 1822, Mr. Finnerty was only forty-three years old.

Twelve years before Percy Bysshe Shelley conferred
upon Peter Finnerty the honour of publishing a poem for
his benefit, the following lines appeared in the 43rd No.
of *The Press*, January 6th, 1798. With this early tribute
to his worth, we may take our leave of a man who is likely
to obtain a new lease of fame from the singular connexion
with Shelley, which it has been the good fortune of the
present writer to discover, and his anxious effort to explain
to the best of his ability in this book :—

"Lines Addressed to Mr. Finerty.

"Array'd in virtue, and in freedom's cause,
What honest breast but pays to thee applause !
Who thee beholds, amid a dungeon's gloom,
For years incarcerated (awful doom !)
Who, but in sorrow, heaves the pitying sigh !
Victim to sickness, or—perhaps to die !
Then nor lament, nor wail a patriot's fate,
You—far superior to the empty great !
A grateful race shall homage pay to thee,
Thou firm, undaunted friend of Liberty ;
Tho' juries triumph, judges judgment give,
In honour's records thou shalt ever live.

January 6th, 1798."   *Extracts from The Press*,
                                               Philadelphia, 1802, p. 281.

No. II.

MR. JOHN LAWLESS.

The following correspondence between the Earl of Moira
and the Right Honourable Richard Ryder, Secretary of
State for the Home Department, is extracted from the
Collection of State Papers in the Record Office, labelled
"Domestic, George III. 1811. No. 231." The original letters are endorsed by Mr. Ryder, " 27th October,
1811. Lord Moira and Mr. Lawless."

The Earl of Moira to the Right Honourable Richard Ryder.
                                    " Donington, Oct. 27th, 1811.

"My dear Sir,—A Mr. Lawless, brother to an officer
of high rank in Bonaparte's army, left Ireland secretly last
year and went to Paris; about a month ago he returned
privately to Dublin, and took care to be as little seen as
possible. He has just now quitted Ireland in the same
mysterious way, and as he took that route, very probably is
still in London. My informant did not obtain the knowledge of this in due time. I am not at liberty to disclose
from whom I have the communication, but you may depend

upon its accuracy. Lawless's object is probably to get to Heligoland, that having been his former track to the Continent. The arresting him would not be likely to lead to any discovery. But if you could make him out, there would be a chance of getting at his business by fixing a spy upon him. He is a shallow, incautious man, therefore any clever person pretending to go to Heligoland to sell guineas, might worm himself into Lawless's confidence, and find out to whom in Ireland he has been the bearer of messages or letters. Great secrecy must be observed or it might be traced how I got the information, and the source is one which it is important to preserve.

    " I have the honour, my dear'Sir,
       " To remain your very obedient
          and humble servant,
                " MOIRA.

"The Right Hon. R. Ryder, &c."

The Right Honourable Richard Ryder to the Earl of Moira.

" Private.   " Whitehall, Oct. 31st, 1811.

" MY DEAR LORD,—I am much obliged to your Lordship for your communication upon the subject of Mr. Lawless. I have since taken all the steps in my power to ascertain when such a person embarks for Heligoland, if he should take that route, with a view to any ulterior measures that may be thought advisable; but no circumstances being mentioned by your informant from which either the time of his arrival here, or the part of the town where he may be, or the places he may be supposed to frequent, or his person can be described, or even the fact known whether he is in London or not can be learnt, I much doubt, after the inquiries I have made, whether there are any [means] except the chances of accident to take advantage of his information." [The remainder of the letter is taken up with the case of a certain " William Richmond," and concludes],

              " I am, &c. &c.,
                  " RICHARD RYDER.

"The Earl of Moira, &c."

D D

Should Mr. John Lawless have been the person alluded to by the Earl of Moira, the description certainly is not flattering. It is one, however, that might easily be drawn from the hostile allusions to Mr. Lawless in the satirical publications of the day. These attacks commenced with the Right Honourable John Wilson Croker, in his *Familiar Epistles*, and culminated in the scurrility of Dr. Brenan, in *The Milesian*, and Watty Cox, in the *Irish Magazine*. A certain. airiness, not to say flightiness, of manner was always very unfairly seized on by Mr. Lawless's enemies as a point of attack. An instance of this occurred so late as 1821, on the occasion of George IV.'s visit to Ireland. " It appears," says a journal of the period, "by a letter from Mr. John Lawless, of *The Irishman*, published in a contemporary print, that that gentleman did not leap into the sea to shake hands with his Majesty, as stated in one of the papers—

> "Jack Lawless says it was not he
> Clung to the Royal Boat,
> *Yet surely wonder should not be*
> That things so *light* should float."

There is, however, a slight difficulty in identifying with absolute certainty the "Mr. Lawless" of Lord Moira's letter with John Lawless. This arises from the fact that the latter had *two* relatives who were "officers in Bonaparte's army." One was his uncle and one his brother. In the *Memoirs of Miles Byrne, Chef de Bataillon in the service of France, Officer of the Legion of Honour, Knight of St. Louis, &c.*, Paris, 1836, we have a good account of both. Of the two, his uncle attained the higher rank. At the battle of Lowenberg, in Silesia, on the 19th of August, 1813, Colonel Lawless commanded the Irish Regiment. "On the 21st of August, the second day after," says Miles Byrne, " Colonel Lawless, at the passage of the Bober, at the town of Lowenberg, and in the presence of Napoleon, had his leg shot off by a cannon ball " (tom. iii. p. 36). Colonel Lawless was subsequently made General, and died on the 25th of December, 1824.

The phrase " an officer of high rank in the army of

Bonaparte," would of course apply especially to Colonel Lawless ; but I do not find any allusion to a brother of his residing in Dublin at the period mentioned. The officer referred to by Lord Moira must, I think, have been Luke Lawless, the brother of John Lawless. He too held a commission in the French service, but of inferior rank to his uncle. Colonel Miles Byrne devotes several pages to him in his *Memoirs*. He was a Lieutenant and subsequently Captain on the Staff of the Duke of Feltre. After the downfall of Napoleon, in 1815, the Irish Regiment was disbanded, and Captain Lawless with other officers emigrated to America. He resumed his profession as an advocate, greatly distinguished himself at the American bar, and was eventually raised to the rank of Judge at Saint Louis.—See *Memoirs of Miles Byrne*, t. iii. pp. 97, 98.

As there is nothing further on this affair of " Mr. Lawless" in the State Papers, Lord Moira perhaps soon discovered that his informant's zeal had outrun his discretion in the officious communication he had made to him. Mr. John Lawless, if he was the person alluded to, had probably gone to London on private business, and returned shortly after, as we find him in Dublin at the end of February, 1812, the associate of Shelley. The reply of the Right Honourable Richard Ryder to Lord Moira's letter is studiously polite, but unmistakably satirical. " Poor Lord Moira," says Moore in one of his letters, when he began to perceive that his noble patron* was

---

* Lord Moira seems to have played the amiable part of patron-general to young poets and romance writers, before he accepted the more substantial position of Governor-General of India. In 1804 we find " Monk" Lewis dedicating to him *The Bravo of Venice*—a singular offering to a statesman. A copy of this curious book, presented "with Mr. Lewis' compliments" to one of his friends is in my possession. It seems to have been the model on which Shelley constructed his not more absurd Romances of *Zastrozzi* and *St. Irvyne*. Monk Lewis seems to have been as fond of the letter *Z* as Shelley himself. We have *Parozzi*, *Struzza*, and *Baluzzo*—names that may well pair with the *Zastrozzi* and *Verezzi* of his imitator.

about to proceed to " India's coral strand" without him—
" poor Lord Moira! his good qualities have been the ruin
of him!

" Que les vertus sont dangereuses
Dans un homme *sans jugement.*"
Letter to Miss Godfrey, Nov. 6th, 1812.
Moore's Memoirs, vol. i. page 312.

Whether the Right Honourable Richard Ryder considered
the suggestion that a spy should be placed on the movements of a man whose only crime seemed to have been his
want of caution (a strange defect in a supposed confidential agent of Napoleon), was a sample of those " good
qualities" that " ruined " Lord Moira, or not, it is impossible to say ; but he certainly must have seen in the letter
of his lordship, which supplied not the slightest fact that
could be acted on, a remarkable proof of his want of
"judgment."

I have been favoured with the following interesting
letter from Philip Lawless, Esq., Barister-at-law, the only
surviving son of Shelley's "literary friend" in Dublin.

"February 16th, 1870.

" I have to apologize to you for not sooner acknowledging
yours of the 11th inst., and thanking you for your kind expressions about my father. I would be happy to give you
any particulars bearing on the subject of your inquiries, but
unfortunately anything of the kind in my possession are
not worth mentioning. I have a perfect recollection of
my father describing the agreeable society which he enjoyed
with the poet P. B. Shelley, chiefly, I think, at the house
of our great countryman, John Philpot Curran. I think he
said it was about the time you mention, 1812 or 1813. My
father unfortunately seldom ever kept papers or documents.
You are perhaps aware that he was prevented by Lord
Clare going to the bar, and this clouded and surrounded
with difficulties his after life. I ought to mention that I
also recollect my father stating that Shelley lived or lodged
in the same street as himself, Cuffe Street, or in its immediate neighbourhood. The first edition of *The History*

of Ireland must have come out in 1812 or 1813.* I have a copy of the second edition published in 1815. In 1819 he commenced the publication of *The Irishman* in Belfast, and continued it there for about eight years, when he removed to Dublin, and resumed the publication of it. I am sorry I cannot give you some more assistance as to my father's acquaintance with the poet. I have often thought of putting together in a memoir shape whatever materials I could collect, with the hope of doing some justice to my father's memory, and of showing the important and prominent part taken by him, but I have always been deterred by the meagreness of the information in my hands. Again begging you to excuse my delay in writing,

"I am, &c. &c.,
"PHILIP LAWLESS.

"D. F. M. C., Esq."

DESCRIPTION OF JOHN LAWLESS.

" Jack Lawless had many distinguished qualifications as a public speaker. His voice was deep, round, and mellow, and was diversified by a great variety of rich and harmonious intonations. His action was exceedingly graceful and appropriate; he had a good figure, which by a purposed swell and dilation of the shoulders, and an elaborate exactness, he turned to good account, and by dint of an easy fluency, of good diction, a solemn visage, an aquiline nose of no vulgar dimensions, eyes glaring underneath a shaggy brow with a certain fierceness of emotion, a quiz-zing-glass, which was gracefully dangled in any pause of thought or suspension of utterance, and above all by a certain attitude of dignity which he assumed in the crisis of eloquence, accompanied with a flinging back of his coat, which rounded his periods beautifully, ' Honest Jack ' soon became one of the most popular and efficient speakers at the Catholic Board."—*Life and Times of Daniel O'Connell, with Sketches of some of his Contemporaries,* by C. M. O'Keefe. Dublin, 1864, vol. ii. p. 23.

---

* *The History of Ireland* was not published until 1814, as previously stated.

DEATH OF MR. LAWLESS.

From *The Morning Chronicle*, Thursday, August 10th, 1837.

" This gentleman, who for many years has occupied so large a space in the public view, as connected with the politics of Ireland, has terminated his earthly career. He was taken ill on Saturday last, and died on Tuesday, at twenty minutes past twelve, at his lodgings in Cecil Street. Mr. Lawless was at all times a most energetic and uncompromising advocate of his principles, which were decidedly of a liberal character."

The following account of the death of Mr. Lawless is quoted in *The Times* of the same date, from a " Ministerial paper." It is erroneous in two particulars. Mr. Lawless was never called to the bar, and did not receive, he probably would not have accepted, " a small appointment in Ireland." The article in the " Ministerial paper " is as follows:—

" DEATH OF MR. LAWLESS.

" We regret to announce the death of this gentleman, familiarly known in Ireland as ' Honest Jack Lawless.' This event took place yesterday afternoon, at his lodgings in Cecil Street, Strand. Mr. Lawless was early in life a law student, but the Irish Lord Chancellor (Clare) prevented his call on account of his political principles. Later in life, however, he was called in times of less trouble and more freedom. He was one of the leading agitators of the Irish associations, and also connected with the Liberal press, both in Dublin and Belfast. Mr. Lawless had in his declining years, shortly since, obtained some small appointment in Ireland. His eloquence was sometimes declamatory, but ever sincere, and in all the actions of his life John Lawless deserved well of his countrymen."

The following passage is taken from an article on the death of Mr. Lawless in *The Morning Herald* of the same period. As Mr. Lawless had never been called to the bar, the story of the prominent high " legal " appointment is probably unfounded.

" It is strongly rumoured that the ' sickening pangs of

hope deferred,' which Mr. Lawless was doomed to experience had a considerable effect in hastening his end. A
few days prior to his decease intelligence was communicated to Mr. Lawless by an illustrious individual that a
high legal appointment would shortly be conferred on
him, and by many his rather sudden decease is attributed
to the excess of joy caused by this announcement."

FUNERAL OF JOHN LAWLESS.

From *The Morning Chronicle*, Friday, August 18th, 1837.

" The mortal remains of ' Honest Jack ' were yesterday
deposited in the vault attached to the Catholic chapel in
Moorfields. Several friends of the deceased wished to offer
the Irish patriot the tribute of a public funeral ; but the
absence of almost all his political confrères from town induced those more immediately interested to adopt a different
course. Our readers are aware that Mr. Lawless died on
Tuesday, the 8th inst., at his apartments in Cecil Street ;
but those who were invited to follow him to the grave
met at the residence of Henry Williams, Esq., 14, Lincoln's Inn Fields, whence they proceeded to Cecil Street
in three mourning coaches. The hearse being in readiness,
the procession moved slowly along the Strand.

" The first coach contained Philip Lawless, the eldest
son of the deceased, Captain Lawless (his brother), Henry
Williams, Esq., and Dr. Best ; in the second were Sheridan
Knowles, Mr. J. O. Cumming Hill, Mr. Witham, and Mr.
Ireland ; while the third was occupied by Captain Roberts,
R.N., Dr. Alley, Mr. Roberts, and Mr. Shee. The funeral
rites were solemnized by the Hon. and Rev. Mr. Spencer,
brother of Earl Spencer, and the Rev. Mr. Hall. The
ceremony was highly affecting, every individual present
having for years been ' linked in bonds of closest amity '
with the departed.

" Strangulated hernia was the proximate cause of poor
Lawless's death, and the disease, though ultimately acute,
had been (if we may be pardoned the expression) consti-
tutionally chronic for some time. When Dr. Lawrence,
his medical attendant, suggested the absolute necessity of

submitting to an operation, the patient inquired ' whether it was an affair of life or death ?' Dr. Lawrence answered, 'That it might become so if prompt measures were not adopted.' 'Then proceed, sir,' said Lawless; 'delays are dangerous, and I'm quite ready. I did hope that I might have had time to write to my wife and the boys; but go on, sir—I am prepared.'

"After the operation had been performed, the sufferer rallied for a short time, and said, 'That Lawrence is a wonderful fellow; I am a *better man* by a thousand pounds.' His 'ruling passion strong in death' was powerfully developed. He raised himself from his pillow, and with his wonted animation reprobated the conduct of the Middlesex electors towards Hume, at the same time expressing his firm conviction that 'The Boys of Kilkenny' would do their duty. A friend who sat by his bedside delicately hinted that other subjects ought to engross his attention, and inquired whether the reading of a prayer would be agreeable. Lawless thanked the gentleman, and while in this communion with his God he expired.

"No groan, no sigh to speak his soul's release."

It would be curious, considering the connexion which existed between Shelley and John Lawless in 1812 and 1813, if the Captain Roberts, R.N., who attended the funeral of Lawless in 1837, was the same Captain Roberts, R.N., who from the top of the lighthouse at Leghorn, on the fatal 8th of July, 1822, watched with his eyeglass the homeward track of Shelley's vessel until it disappeared in the sudden storm which overwhelmed it.

THE END.

www.ingramcontent.com/pod-product-compliance
Lightning Source LLC
Chambersburg PA
CBHW030953110726

47900CB00004B/1253